STORM BOUND

STORM BOUND

DANI HARPER

Published by Montlake Romance, Seattle

www.apub.com

Amazon, the Amazon logo, and Montlake Romance are trademarks of Amazon.com, Inc., or its affiliates.

ISBN-13: 9781477818237
ISBN-10: 1477818235

Cover design by Kerrie Roberston

Library of Congress Control Number: 2013917819

Printed in the United States of America

For Ron, the man who owns my heart
—and takes such good care of it.

There is no spectre half so terrible
As shadows of old wrongs.

—Frederick Tennyson

ONE

⌒⫶⫶⌒

Black Mountains, Wales
A.D. 1124

Heavy muscles bulged as the tall man strained repeatedly against the fine silver chains that bound him, wrist and ankle, to the high stone wall of the courtyard.

"Such an ungrateful mortal you are, Aidan ap Llanfor," she chided. "Is it not an honor to be a guest of the Tylwyth Teg?"

He lunged at her, but though she stood within an arm's length of him, she neither recoiled nor shrank. Aidan's chains had been forged with faery magic, and as such they would not break, not even for the largest *bwgan*, much less a human. The man's iron-gray eyes, however—were they daggers, she would be pierced, she thought, and her sapphire blood would be poisoned and pooling around her delicate silk slippers.

For the briefest of moments, she felt something, and she thrilled to it, eager for more. But Aidan immediately bridled his anger, reining it back like a blood-crazed warhorse. It was as if he could sense her craving for emotion—any emotion—and refused to give it to her.

"I have not sought to visit your land," he gritted out between his teeth. "Nor have I trespassed upon it. I have given thee no cause to bring me here against my will."

"Are you so certain of that? I seem to remember a bold and comely child playing on the faery mound beyond the village. Such a dear little wooden sword he had, hacking at bushes and slicing at trees like they were dreadful monsters."

The tiniest jolt of surprise flickered briefly behind the man's glare. Celynnen derived great satisfaction from his reaction, although in truth it also puzzled her. How was it that mortals remembered so little when their lives were so short? Years had passed for him, but for her? It was scarcely a day ago that Aidan ap Llanfor had traded his wooden sword for the business of adults, mere hours since he'd apprenticed to the village blacksmith, moments since he'd inherited the forge and took over the business. She had observed it all, fascinated, in the way that a cat is fascinated by a bird.

"I could have spirited you away that first time," she continued, "simply for setting foot on fae territory. But it was much more fun to watch you. You played often at the mound, though you saw me not. I was witness to not one but *many* trespasses, Aidan ap Llanfor. You've lived your life thus far in your tiny mortal world only because I permitted it."

"A child is not held accountable for things he knows not of."

"Human rules," she sniffed. "Why do you waste so much time making them when you have such fleeting lives? You're like the mayflies that dance above the water for less than a day. The Tylwyth Teg are ancient beyond your ability to grasp, and our laws are ancient too—made once, to stand for all time. And by those laws, you are mine to do with as I like."

"Release me, Faery," he said in a dangerous tone.

"Think you to make demands?" She laughed and shook back her hair, well aware of her unearthly beauty and its near-hypnotic effects on most mortals. The man would perceive a tall woman of flawless perfection, a goddess in his eyes—especially since her skin

2

glowed with living light. Her luminous white hair flowed to her hips like a frozen waterfall, tumbling over her vivid red gown. To a human, her dazzling eyes were every color at once and none of them. "Know to whom you speak," she declared. "I am Celynnen of the House of Thorn of the Tylwyth Teg, and my blood is pure."

"You are a *tywysoges*, then, a princess of the Fair Ones."

She shook her head. "*The* princess, human. My great-aunt is the queen, and she is childless. Therefore, I alone am heir to the throne of the Nine Realms."

He gave her the slightest of nods, a scant acknowledgment of her station, and not one mote of reverence more.

Others had died for less, and Celynnen could have killed him herself if she'd been so inclined. Still, for the sake of the entertainment he afforded her, she could forgive him much—for a time. She had often watched him at his forge, hammering hot metals into clever shapes, particularly that most fearful of all elements, iron. Years of striking sparks amidst the glow of flames had not bent his tall frame; they only had added strength. Even when he was clad in his dull brown tunic and scarred leather apron, his face streaked with soot and sweat as he labored over his latest project, she had had to admit that the comely child had grown into a very attractive man. Her people often took human lovers, and she had begun to consider the delicious possibilities.

This morning, however, Aidan had not gone to his forge as usual. He had not donned his rough blacksmith's clothing either. Instead, he had bathed at length and dressed in what passed for finery among these common mortals. His blue woolen tunic was open at the neck to reveal a pale linen shirt beneath. His dark rectangular cloak was newly made and clasped with a large heavy brooch that she had not seen before. It was round, a Celtic cross set with five large garnets. It was a gift that a woman would give, and only a human woman could have done so.

Annwyl.

The raven-haired Annwyl of the village of Aberhonddu was the woman whom Aidan ap Llanfor planned to marry. Today. And that's when Celynnen made her decision to spirit him away to the kingdom far below the Black Mountains.

"Release me, Your Grace," he said.

The significance of the royal title was not lost on her. It was hardly filled with admiration and awe, but it *was* devoid of sarcasm. This was not a man who would beg, ever—but she had just won a major concession from him. *What else can I win?* The thought of such a challenge excited her. She would enjoy playing games with Aidan ap Llanfor just as much as lying with him, perhaps even more. "Nay, I believe I will keep you."

"Do not do this, Your Eminence. For the sake of my bride whom I will wed this day, for the sake of the promises I have made to her and her family. Make me not an oath breaker, for ye yourselves do despise such."

It was an eloquent argument. Once given, the word of any of the Tylwyth Teg was unbreakable. In fact, humans who did not keep their promises to each other often suffered justice at the hands of the Fae. Celynnen brushed her fingers over the brilliant scarlet of her dress and traced the birds and flowers embroidered there in silver thread and seed pearls. "A man of his word *is* a rare commodity, so it seems fitting that such be rewarded. You may put your mind at ease on that point. No oath will be broken."

From her flowing sleeve, she drew a black gem the size and shape of a robin's egg. Not a pearl or a crystal or even an opal, yet it resembled all three. Tiny flashes of blue, green, and purple sparked in its dark depths, and some fae craftsman had dared to carve it with intricate spirals and ancient symbols. Celynnen cupped it in her hand, where the stone gleamed and pulsed like a live thing. Bringing it close to her lips, she whispered a few words in the ancient language, then blew gently over it. A wisp of pale green light, like a luminous spirit, spiraled from the stone and floated towards Aidan.

He drew back as far as the chains would allow, suspicious but unable to avoid the approaching wraith. "What are you doing?" he demanded of Celynnen, and jerked as the eerie radiance touched him. Instantly his entire body was enveloped in a glowing green caul.

"I have simply granted you what you wanted." The emerald light flared outward until it filled the broad expanse of the courtyard, illuminating every petal of each exotic flower in the labyrinthine gardens and every detail of the fine carving and crafted stone that surrounded them. The radiance brightened still, until it was the blinding white of a star's heart. Just as it seemed that the walls must surely melt, the brilliant light abruptly vanished as if it had never been.

Celynnen's iridescent eyes didn't even blink, of course. She was unaffected by the magic she had called, as were the fae flowers in the gardens. Aidan, however, was dazed and reeling, as if struck by a giant's fist. *Good*, she thought. Perhaps he would remember her little display of power and be more cooperative in the future. She tucked the stone back into the hidden pocket in her sleeve as she glided towards the high arched doorway. "I must make an appearance at Court for a time," she called over her shoulder.

"Wait!" he shouted, regaining his alertness far more quickly than she'd expected. "Release me! My wedding—Annwyl will be waiting for me!" He rattled the charmed silver chains that bound him until they pealed like ropes of silver bells.

Celynnen turned and arched a delicate eyebrow. "You did not wish to be an oath breaker, and so you will not be. Your intended is *not* waiting for you. There is no wedding party, and indeed, no betrothal. Therefore, you are quite free of all mortal obligations."

He stilled, and horror crept across his bold features. "What have you done?" he breathed through gritted teeth, bracing as though some part of him already knew.

"I merely revised the tiny history of your boring little village. Annwyl will not mourn you."

"What have you done to her?" Aidan roared, straining so mightily against his bonds that for a brief instant Celynnen thought they might actually give way. Instead, blood ran down his wrists and spattered both floor and walls. A flying droplet struck her hand and she backed out of range, blotting the spot away hastily with her sleeve as it began to burn her skin. Human blood got its curious red color from the iron it contained—and iron was deadly poison to all fae creatures, including the Tylwyth Teg.

The precious fabric failed to cleanse the spot well enough, however. Her hand *hurt*, and pain was not something she was acquainted with. She snapped at him. "You foolish mortal. Did you think I was going to *let you go*? You were concerned for your honor, and I have graciously protected it. Even more merciful, your treasured Annwyl will suffer no broken heart over you. Indeed, her heart will not grieve for anyone, not even her dear mother."

"Her mother died of a fever just over a year ago," he said carefully. "She mourns the loss deeply."

The apprehension in his voice was utterly delicious. "Nay," she whispered, as if confiding a secret. "Dear Annwyl took ill and died at the very same time. She never knew of her mother's death and, much more important, she never met *you*."

The impact of her words was immensely gratifying to her. Celynnen thought of a mighty stag pierced by a silver arrow, stunned and confused, unable to comprehend what had just happened to it.

Aidan struggled to speak. "You killed her."

"Of course I killed her. How else could I secure your precious honor?" she retorted. "Annwyl is gone, her family does not know who you are, and in fact, your own family does not recall that they ever had a son. In short, Aidan ap Llanfor, you have ceased to exist outside of this kingdom. You. Are. Mine."

The shock fell away from him like a curtain suddenly dropped, and Celynnen found herself looking into the face of pure wrath. It was utterly fascinating. The harsh fury in Aidan's gray eyes burned hotter than any iron he had ever drawn from his forge, so hot it seemed it might set her ablaze where she stood. Regrettably, however, the potential for entertainment would have to wait. She had a real burn to attend to, and she swept from the room to find a healer before the tiny mark upon her hand became an abhorrent scar. Halfway down the vast hallway, the last thing she heard from Aidan was a full-fledged snarl: *"By Gofannon, god of the fire that transforms, I will spill your damnable blue blood with weapons forged by my own hand! I swear I will have your life for my Annwyl's!"*

Laughter, cold and crystalline, burst from Celynnen's perfect lips. "My poor, dear human, you will have to remember her first."

TWO

Walla Walla, Washington
Twenty-First Century

I'm sorry, but I can't sell you a spell to *make* somebody love you. I know that you see it in storybooks all the time, but it's unethical." It was the last in a long line of calls to return, and Brooke Halloran's fingers were getting cramped from holding the smartphone. From holding it *together* actually—she needed a new one badly, but it hadn't been in the budget, since she'd set up shop in an old diner. Her business, Handcastings, had grown profitable as an online company, and she'd sold a great deal of pagan, Wiccan, and New Age supplies from her website over the past few years. As a business administration graduate, she would have advised herself against risking investment in a physical location in such an uncertain economy.

As a dedicated witch, however, she needed to make herself more available to those who needed her help. Sure, she'd done plenty of phone consultations, and she still did. But a more personal connection generally led to more effective magic, and she knew she needed a place to consult with clients face-to-face. Brooke had tried meeting with people in their homes, but it was time consuming to make house calls, and she much preferred to have more control over the environment and its energies.

She looked at several locations in Spokane, the city she had grown up in, but nothing had the right *feel*. Finally, some of her friends who had moved to Walla Walla persuaded her to try that city. It was older than Spokane, and the brick buildings and old houses possessed an inviting charm. It wasn't long before she found exactly what she had been hoping for.

The two-story red brick building was a Renaissance Revival style from 1900. Despite the historical appeal of its tall windows and ornate white detailing—or perhaps because of them—it had remained empty for the past several years. It was just off a busy part of the downtown core, nestled in a row of similar buildings, but Brooke had felt both potential and positive energy in *this* one. Plus it had a fairly new furnace and a solid foundation, and it required no major repairs other than a fresh application of sealant on the flat roof. With the real estate market in a tailspin, she'd managed to coax the desperate seller into holding the mortgage for her without any more magic than the contents of her savings account as a down payment. A little cleaning (okay, a helluva *lot* of cleaning), plus some paint and fresh upholstery in a black, turquoise, and silver palette for strength, serenity, and intuition, and *ta-da*, she had a shop of her very own. The financial responsibility of that still scared the bejeebers out of her some days, degree or no degree.

"No, no love potions either." Brooke listened patiently to the caller's negative reaction and refused to be goaded into saying something childish. She couldn't help mouthing it silently though: *I am too a real witch!* And a real witch would seek to bring wisdom to the situation. Somehow she had to instruct instead of argue, right?

Brooke glanced around her shop for inspiration.

The open shelves on the wall behind the main counter had once held stacks of stoneware dishes. Now the plates and mugs had been replaced with big square jars of herbs and ingredients for potions. *Mental note: stock one of those with instructive things to say to potential customers.*

A soft undercurrent of honey scented the air thanks to a display of beeswax candles by the old chrome cash register, but it brought no particular wisdom. The shiny black countertop boasted glass inserts, and beneath them Brooke displayed some of the more costly items she sold. She scanned the illuminated array of large crystals but gleaned no help for her current situation. The arrangement of magical tools—athames, bolines, and even an exquisite silver sword—held no ideas either.

She switched hands and used her stiff fingers to try to comb her chin-length black hair away from her face as she scanned the booths that lined the east wall. They had high partitions between them, making them perfect for clients to enjoy herbal teas, examine books, or have reasonably private consultations. The roomy corner booth on the far end was Brooke's favorite, though—that was where she did her tarot readings for customers. The round table was large enough to accommodate a complete Celtic Cross spread.

Right now, though, that booth held her best friend in the whole world.

"Well, sure, spells like that exist of course." She tried to explain the appropriate uses of magic to her prospective client as she walked to the back of the room. "But I don't do that, no. I believe in doing no harm, and forcing someone into love is . . . well . . . it's . . . it's . . ."

"It's not fair to the other person," whispered George Santiago-Callahan without even looking up. He was engaged in doing what he did most: sketching on a large pad, as his black and blue spiked mohawk bobbed along to whatever tune was being pumped through his earbuds. Brooke was forever losing her own buds, but G's wires were securely threaded through the silver tunnel plugs that pierced his earlobes. He listened to music more or less continuously, yet he always seemed able to hear her. Like now, thank the goddess.

"It's not fair to the other person," she repeated into the phone. "You can't build a lasting relationship on that; you have to respect their choices and their feelings." She paced as she tried to direct her caller to a different solution. "It works better to be open to a love that's right for you rather than having a specific person in mind. I strongly recommend a general spell of attraction, and leave the rest up to the Universe. I—"

The phone's screen abruptly went blank. "Damn. Guess that's not what he wanted to hear."

George glanced up and shook his head. "*Obstinado* is what my mother would say."

She sure would. How many times had Brooke heard his mom say that about George? "That always sounds so much more descriptive than just plain *stubborn*," Brooke said, sliding into the booth across from her friend and resting her chin in one hand with a sigh. "And it's true. No matter what I tell them, some people just want what they want."

"Most of them aren't even happy for long after they get it."

"That's true too, sadly." *You just can't help everybody.* Knowing that didn't keep her from wanting to, though. Brooke put an elastic band around the phone to hold the cover on and tried to put it away with some measure of care into her pocket. Instead, it shot from her hands like a wet bar of soap and crashed onto the black-and-white tiled floor. "Oh, for crap's sake!"

"I got it." George was already in motion, scooping up the debris with one of his long-fingered hands. She could only shake her head in wonder as her cell phone was reassembled before her eyes—and in record time. The elastic had broken, but he conscripted another from his spiked leather pencil case and handed the finished product back to her.

"Thanks, G. What would I do without you?" Rather than take chances, she stood up and held open the right front pocket of her jeans and let him drop the phone in it.

He snorted. "Well, you'd have to buy a lot more phones. And you'd definitely never be able to set your own DVR."

True enough. Heck, she'd be lucky to figure out how to use the TV remote. Brooke privately thought that despite her friend's lack of interest in magic, his ease with technology was downright wizardlike. Of course, George would make an outstanding purveyor of spells, too—he was so graceful, so grounded, in all that he did, everything he touched. *I'll never be that coordinated, that at ease in my own skin.* But then, her friend practiced daily to be just that coordinated, that agile and balanced. George wasn't only an artist; he had also practiced for years to be a welterweight fighter in mixed martial arts, and he had made a local name for himself. He'd tried to teach her a few moves, and she showed a great deal of aptitude—but she was repelled by the idea of actually hurting somebody. She supposed it wasn't all that surprising considering that the Gift was devoted to healing and helping, not to beating the daylights out of an opponent, even if that opponent was willing.

"So I guess I have a topic for tomorrow's blog, huh? 'Why You Shouldn't Mess With Free Will.'"

Now in its fifth year, *Handcastings: Magic for a Modern World* boasted a following of well over a thousand regular subscribers, and the statistics showed there were even more casual readers visiting the site. Through her blog, Brooke was able to exchange tips and spells with other witches, be a source of ingredients and tools, and connect with potential clients. Overall, she emphasized the ethics of the craft and its overarching purpose to help and to heal.

"Free will? You could post that one every week. Too bad Mr. I-Want-What-I-Want won't recognize the hint. Hey, were you still looking for a guest post for Monster Monday?" He stood the sketch pad on the counter to show her his work. "I was thinking about doing a write-up on hellhounds. Been drawing up some big toothy ones for the latest *Devina of Hades* series. See?"

For additional interest, Brooke had added two regular features to her blog: Supernatural Saturday and Monster Monday, where she could write about paranormal phenomena, plus myth and legend. Both had proved popular, helping her to attract a whole new audience. She slid into the booth beside George and studied the heavily muscled beasts snarling on the page. Being rendered in simple pencil didn't detract from their fearsomeness in the least—especially since one of them had a human arm dangling from its jaws. *Nice.* She felt a chill that had nothing to do with the cooling currents of air from the vintage overhead fan. "So what are hellhounds supposed to do—are they watchdogs for the underworld or what?"

"Some are. There're all kinds of myths about them. Vampires are said to employ hellhounds as daytime guardians. A hellhound can be a demon or even the devil in disguise. In *Devina*, her hellhounds are a special breed of dog that help her hunt down killer demons and other nasty creatures." George had found success with the comic series he'd created six years ago, and was now making a comfortable living with its many spin-offs. Brooke was convinced, however, that he'd do it all for free—he loved drawing even more than his martial arts.

"And countries all over the world have old legends of big black dogs that haunt lonely roads," he continued. "They hunt down the guilty, foretell deaths, show up just before terrible storms, or drag lost souls to hell."

"Geez. Why does it have to be a dog? I know I'm more of a cat person, but I like dogs, and all the dogs I know are happy and friendly. I have trouble accepting that *man's best friend* can be evil."

George shrugged. "Hey, I'm just listing off some of the stories. Besides, a hellhound's not evil; it's just doing what it's told, like any dog does, right? And the legends aren't always bad. In some religions, it's a dog that guides your spirit to heaven. In Colima, Mexico, where my uncle lives, people used to get buried with a little clay dog, so it could carry their souls to the right place."

Brooke nodded at that one. Many in her craft believed dogs capable of perceiving both the mortal and the spiritual realm, and even of being able to cross from one to the other.

"Of course, then there's El Guardia—my grandmamma called on him sometimes, and she said he always came to help her."

"Sounds like Zorro. Who the heck is El Guardia?" With a cheesy superhero name like that, it just had to be something George made up to tease her.

"More like a *what*. It's a spectral hound, a ghost dog or something. Sometimes Grandmamma would summon the dog to her circles." George glanced around and lowered his voice as if revealing a secret. "Look, I've never told you this. One night, when I was about seven, I was supposed to be in bed sleeping, but I hid in the big cupboard in *mi abuela*'s spell room to watch her. I saw the dog, Brooke."

She scrutinized her friend's face, but he was on the level. "You're not kidding. You actually *saw it*?"

He nodded, his rigid blue and black mohawk dipping with the movement. "I'm telling you, it was effin' crazy, Brooke. The thing just appeared—walked right out of the damn fire. It was big and black and had wicked-looking teeth, but I remember the glowing eyes the most. Didn't get to see anything else after that, though— I was so scared, I pissed my pajamas and fell out of the cupboard. The dog vanished and *mi abuela* was über-mad at me."

"I'll bet you were grounded for life."

He rolled his eyes at that. "Please. Grandmamma was from a whole different generation. She'd never even *heard* of grounding. I got my butt whacked with a wooden cooking spoon."

"Ouch. But what about the dog, G? Do you know anything else about it?"

"Years later—which is probably how long it took for Grandmamma to finally cool off—she told me that El Guardia protected the integrity of the circle and defended those who were in it. The creature also facilitated difficult castings. She'd call on the dog for help if a spell wouldn't go right, or there was a troublesome situation, or a possibility of danger."

"So he was like a sentinel or something? You never, ever told me that one," chided Brooke.

"I know, I said that, remember? I just—well, you don't tell just anyone you saw a ghost and peed your effin' pants. You're the only one who knows. I didn't tell my mother, and neither did Grandmamma."

"I'd probably wet my pants too, if I saw something like that. El Guardia sounds scary. But the things that he does? I've never heard of calling an animal spirit to fill that role before."

"Not many people call on him because the hound is very strong, but *mi abuela* was—"

"Your grandmother was the most powerful *bruja* in Catemaco. I know, I know. Your mom talks about her all the time, and dammit, I wish I'd met her. Better yet, I wish you'd been more interested in magic and allowed her to train you. Then you could train *me*. There's so much more I need to learn."

"Cut yourself some slack. You've come a long way, to the point where you're able to help a lot of people now. You learn fast and you have *mega* natural ability—your spells almost always work."

She winced at that. "*Almost* is the operative word. You haven't seen the hole in my back wall yet."

"A *hole*? I didn't see one last night when we were watching TV."

"It's only about four inches wide." *Through a solid brick wall.* "It's in the kitchen over the window by the sink and I—um—stuffed the hole with newspaper, sealed it with duct tape, and then hung the clock over it until I can get it fixed." Brooke sighed. "It's my own fault. I was working on a brand new spell last week, and I conjured without buffering the effects, so I got some kind of energy release. I should have known better, but I let myself get too excited about the charm. I'm just glad it blasted through an outside wall instead of shooting into the building next to me."

"It's not like anyone would notice," he laughed. "There's like, what? Three whole businesses on this block? You could shoot a cannon through six of these old buildings and no one would even know." He shoved playfully at her shoulder. "Don't be discouraged, *hermanita*.

"I'm not your *little sister*—I'm six months older than you!" she protested. It was an old argument, and not one she would ever win, the facts notwithstanding. Perhaps it was because he had three older sisters in addition to his twin, Lissy, and no younger siblings. Maybe it was because they'd been best friends ever since the first grade, when he'd bonked her with a storybook, she'd punched him in the nose, and they'd bonded while sitting on the detention bench in the hallway. It might even be because he'd once inserted himself between her and a playground bully—despite the fact that he'd gotten his nine-year-old butt handed to him. Whatever the reason, he had always insisted on treating her like a little sister, his very own *hermanita*. From anyone else, she might have found it patronizing. From G, it was annoying and endearing at the same time. "Anyways, your grandmother really said that about the craft, that it's a matter of practice?"

"Well, technically, no. *Mi abuela* was usually lecturing me on my schoolwork when she said that. You know how much I hated grammar and spelling." George gave a mock shudder. "But the same principle applies. You keep at it and you get better. It's just like art." He waved at the sketch pad in his lap. "So do you want that blog post?"

"Hellhounds sound scary and fascinating, and therefore perfect for Monster Monday. My readers will love to hear about them, and so will I, so yes, please." She leaned over her friend's artwork again. "So have you got more ferocious dog drawings in there?"

George suddenly flipped the sketch pad closed like a clamshell slamming shut. "Nope. Just some rough characters for a brand new series. Not ready for public viewing just yet."

Brooke was surprised, and slightly hurt. "I'm not the *public*! You just confessed you peed your pants to me!"

"I know," he said, grinning at her indignation. "But they say comic books are the purest form of art, and it's definitely bad luck to look upon unfinished art."

She rolled her eyes. "Aren't you always telling me that comics are called graphic novels now? And besides, you made that up. I agree with you totally on the comics-as-art part, but there's no such thing as bad luck."

"Come on, you're a practicing witch and you don't believe in luck?"

"Of course not. People attract their own luck."

"Yeah? What if a meteor fell out of the sky and landed on you?"

"Maybe it's karma. Maybe it's your time. Maybe you secretly wanted it." She rose and straightened her blouse. It was nearly the same shade of turquoise as the walls, a hue that just happened to enhance the blue-green color of her eyes. She didn't feel the need for makeup if she wore turquoise—which was a great reason to choose it a lot.

"*Wanted* it?" George looked shocked. "What the hell kind of thinking is that?"

"If you think about meteors enough, maybe you'll draw one to you."

"Every astronomer on the planet would be squished by now. You're messing with me."

"Yes, I am." She grinned over her shoulder as she sauntered to the front window of the shop. It was time to flip the OPEN sign to CLOSED. One after another, Brooke pulled the blinds down. As always, she imagined the old building was closing its eyelids, ready to nod off after another long day.

Behind the counter, she stubbed her toe on a box with a selection of tarot decks waiting to be priced and displayed, which reminded her of another task undone. Brooke pulled out her phone and punched in the speed dial for her daily tarot reading. It was usually the first thing she did in the morning, but she'd been distracted—on purpose, by her eternally hungry cats, Bouncer, Rory, and Jade. The trio would be expecting a lot of attention as well as dinner when she went upstairs to her apartment. Usually they lounged around the shop while she worked, but Rory had been in a climbing mood. After he'd toppled two separate displays, Brooke had banished the felines for the rest of the day. If she played with them first, was there any chance they would let her work on her taxes in peace?

A moment later, she forgot all about her cats, the shop, and everything else, as she looked down at her phone display where her four-card reading waited for her. *Not again.* It couldn't possibly have done it *again*. She attempted to punch the button that would wipe out the screen, but it was suddenly snatched from her hand. "Geez, G, don't sneak up on me like that!"

"What have we got here?" George teased, and read the cards aloud. "The Moon, the Fool, the Ten of Stars, in the top row . . . and Death lurking down here underneath them? That can't be good."

"It means *change*, not literal death," she said quickly. "And those are pentacles, not stars, as you know perfectly well."

"Change, huh? Must be one helluva *big* change to bring out the Grim Reaper."

"It's symbolism."

"Duh, I get that. Death's the biggest change there is. So the way it's hanging around at the bottom, it looks like you're expecting a big change in whatever the other cards stand for."

Brooke opened her mouth to say something, then closed it again. George had summed it up perfectly. *Nothing like a fresh perspective from someone who doesn't read the cards.* Of course, George had always loved to look through her tarot deck collection for the sake of the artwork—most were extremely beautiful, which was why she had no willpower when a new deck caught her eye. But while she would lovingly make use of the cards, George had zero interest in anything but the pictures. Still, he'd seen what she had not. "That's a pretty astute observation."

"Astute, my ass. It's symbolism, just like you said. So the meaning is kind of universal, isn't it?"

And here she'd spent hours trying to discern a complex meaning from was actually a fairly simple pattern. Nothing like making things harder than they had to be. "I guess I was too busy being spooked from the way it kept showing up over and over again, and—"

"Oh, *really*?" He folded his arms. "Exactly how long has this been going on?"

Damn. She was so used to telling him everything that she'd just blurted it out. *Just as well,* she supposed. It would do her good to tell somebody, and George was her BFF after all. Who else would she have told but him? "This"—she pointed at the screen—"makes nine times in a row that these particular cards have come up."

"Glitch in the program."

"The top cards show up in any order. The Death card is always at the bottom."

"Still a glitch in the program. Try another site."

She gripped the cell phone tightly in both hands and made herself look George in the eye. He had one yellow one and one purple one today. *At least he's not wearing his reptilian contacts.* "I've gotten the same reading on every site I've tried," she whispered. She anticipated his next question: "With every physical deck of cards I've used too. This was my ninth attempt over the past few days."

He whistled at that. "Nine is a powerful number. Three times three."

"You think I don't know that?"

"Okay, two, maybe even three, times could be random, could be coincidence, although the odds are better that you'd win the Powerball jackpot. But *nine*—that's really messed up, Brooke. What kind of message is the Universe trying to send you?"

"I don't know." What she didn't say aloud was how scary it was, even for a witch. Maybe *especially* for a witch. Witches saw meaning in everything, but Brooke couldn't fathom what this strange recurring message was supposed to mean. All that she knew for sure was that there were no coincidences.

"Have you told my mom yet?"

"No. I know I should but . . ." Part of her was a little afraid of what her friend and mentor, Olivia Santiago-Callahan, might say about it. Olivia was a master when it came to tarot. What if the recurring reading was bad news? *Really* bad news? Silly to avoid it, of course, even childish. Besides, it could just as well be good news—although, in her experience, the Universe didn't usually beat people over the head with the positive stuff.

"I want to solve this puzzle myself," she finished at last. Even though she knew full well that flying solo wasn't always the smartest thing to do, she was determined to be independent a little longer. *Or in denial.* Sometimes it looked like the same thing.

George took the phone from her and peered into the touch screen, using his fingers to enlarge each card in turn. "Huh. There's a dog in each of the cards. Does that signify something?"

She frowned and took the phone back from him. The Moon, the Fool, and the Ten of Pentacles all featured a dog somewhere in the picture. In fact, they were the only cards in a tarot deck that did. This time, however, Death had a canine companion as well. She'd seen the somber figure portrayed on a horse, sometimes with ravens or vultures, even cats, but not this. "Dogs and death," she mused aloud. "That's really strange. In the tarot, dogs are always guardians and protectors."

"The big black one beside the Reaper doesn't look very protective. He looks like he could swallow you whole. Great graphic for my hellhounds post."

"It doesn't matter what the dog looks like; the meaning is the same," she insisted. "Dogs can also signify communication— they're often viewed as a bridge between worlds, maybe like your uncle's little clay dogs. Most of the time, though, the appearance of a dog means you're being protected."

"In other words, you're being watched over by the goddamn Hound of the Baskervilles."

She forced a wan smile. "Just what every girl needs."

George put an arm around her shoulders. "I'm sorry. Look, it's gotta be simpler than that. Maybe a dog will *prevent* something bad from happening. Maybe the cards are saying you should adopt a dog for security or something—he could help you watch the shop. You remember Alison, the colorist that works on my comics? She volunteers at the local animal shelter, and they're having a big open house on Saturday. We could go look around, see if you get any vibes."

She shook her head. "You forget that I am already owned by three cats. Bouncer would leave home, Jade would stop talking to me, and Rory would plot my demise if I brought a dog into their house." Brooke turned off the phone and tucked it back into her pocket. "I need to get out my books, do a little research on this. But first I have some spells to do up for people, things to get ready for mailing. Oh, and work on my damn taxes." *Yuck.*

"Want a coffee first? That tarot stuff is pretty intense. So's the taxes."

"Naw, thanks. Gotta save my pennies till the end of the month." She had eleven dollars and some change in her purse, and it had to buy cat food. Her cupboards were devoid of the kind Rory liked best: Little Whiskers, the most expensive brand on the market. Why had she thought he'd forgive her for the bargain box she'd picked up instead? Bouncer and Jade were more understanding about her budget as long as the food was plentiful, but Rory had been expressing his displeasure in no uncertain terms. This morning it had been a 4 a.m. paw smack to her forehead.

"Not taking no for an answer here. I've got *two* spaces on my coffee card that say we can go to Magic Beans for something decadent. And it's only a couple blocks away. Come on, you need some fresh air and a change of scenery before you start unraveling all this juju stuff."

Brooke hesitated. "How decadent are we talking?"

"*Extreme* decadence, *hermanita*. Supersized deluxe."

How could she resist an offer like that? She wasn't sure she *could* unravel the message of the cards, and she was a lot more worried than she dared let on, even to herself.

When the going gets tough, the tough get salted caramel cappuccinos.

THREE

A idan ap Llanfor drowsed in the deep darkness, neither asleep nor awake . . . an hour, a day, a year? Within the Fae realm, time didn't move the same as in the human world, and occasionally it even ran backward. The ethereal kingdom under the Black Mountains was ancient beyond all counting, and yet perpetually young. He had no idea how long he'd been here, only that he had not aged.

At least the body he was *in* had not aged. It wasn't his, any more than this place was his home. And there wasn't a damned thing he could do about it. He'd found that out soon enough. Raging and wild, he'd fought against the fate imposed upon him to no avail. It had been like hurling himself against a stone wall—and flesh and blood, emotion and intellect, could make no impression upon rock that had been solid since the earth was founded. Mere human protests could likewise make no impression on fae ears that had heard those rocks sing when the world was new.

The tywysoges wanted what she wanted. And what she wanted from him was *everything*, both body and soul. Most of all, she wanted him as a willing partner in her bed. The Tylwyth Teg had long been known to seek out human lovers as diversions, but Aidan ap Llanfor had been determined to die before complying with Celynnen's wishes in any way.

23

But it hadn't been that easy.

He was still chained in the courtyard when she came to him one night, dressed in little more than moonlight. Her hair cascaded wildly down her smooth backside like a waterfall of silver, her shapely arms open to reveal her flawless breasts caressed by a transparent fabric that seemed to have tiny stars woven into it. The see-through material wandered its sparkling way between her legs, illuminating the perfection of her vee before winding around her angled hips. Her long legs were naked, her delicate feet bare except for an exquisite silver bracelet around one perfectly turned ankle. Tall and lithe, bold in her nakedness, she was a goddess: Diana the Huntress stalking the earth, with the moon as her consort.

Aidan's chains fell away as she lightly grasped one of his hands. "Come with me." Her voice was a soft, sultry whisper. Her other hand drew a circle around the luscious nipple of her breast, and she licked her lips in such a way that a tiny droplet of sweat ran down his spine in spite of himself. "Let me show you the pleasures of my bed, dearest Aidan. Do mortals not sing songs of the skills of faery lovers?"

Such unearthly beauty coupled with such an alluring offer would have brought a lesser man to his knees. But while Aidan's memories might have been slowly fading under the influence of the faery realm's magic, he refused to forget that this inhuman creature was his captor, the despoiler of his life, the one who had plundered whatever dreams he might have had. He was less than a slave to her; he was a temporary plaything, a toy, and he knew it.

He spat at her, marring the nearly invisible fabric right over the spot where her icy heart likely lay. "I'll not be your pet," he declared, fully aware of the danger to him. Although Celynnen appeared to have no weapon, she was more than capable of killing him with a single word. Aidan stood straight, calmly waiting for the deathblow to fall, his only regret that he was unable to fulfill his vow to bring about her demise as well.

The blow didn't come. He could see the fury in her iridescent eyes, the sharp relief of her features as an unholy anger lit them from within. "You are gravely mistaken, mortal," she said, and her voice was deep with rage. "You will be my *pet* for as long as I will it."

A shard of green lightning suddenly snaked down from a cloudless night sky and wrapped itself around him.

"You will learn to do much more than merely obey me," she declared, as a violent seizure threw him to the ground. Every muscle and tendon, each bone and sinew, suddenly seemed to tear apart from one another and reshape themselves. Convulsing uncontrollably, he would have screamed from the pain had he been able to draw enough breath.

"You will learn to devote yourself to me until you crave my every wish," she intoned.

The bones in his face felt like they'd exploded, reforming into something alien. His spine stretched torturously until his tailbone uncurled and grew, adding fresh agony to his suffering. Skin split and reknit, fingers shortened, toes lengthened. He was able to draw in a great sucking gasp of air just as the torment reached a crescendo—and his scream came out as a long, hideous howl. The sound rose into the night sky like a live thing, as if to plead with the stars themselves for an end to the unbearable. Perhaps they heard him. His body was still ablaze with pain, but compared to what he'd just been through, he could shoulder it. Panting heavily for breath, he lay on his side with his eyes closed.

"You will learn to adore me with every breath you take," she said finally, emphasizing each word. "Until every thought you have is of your undying love for me."

Damn that to hell. Aidan fought to get up then, his eyes opening to a new nightmare. His strong hands and powerful arms, the instruments of his craft, were gone. Instead, long legs stretched out before him, ending in enormous paws. The blackest of fur shrouded his skin, and a long dark muzzle intruded into his field of sight. He glanced about, taking in the thickly muscled torso and haunches, and the strange new appendage of a tail, and as he struggled unsteadily to his feet, Celynnen laughed.

"Did I not say you would be my pet?" She stood boldly in the bright moonlight, her all-but-naked body silvered by it. There was something silver in her hands too, a great wide band crafted of intricate links.

What she held was a collar, as if he were truly and completely a dog. With a lionlike roar, he leapt at her with bared fangs, bent on tearing out her marble-white throat. His fearsome teeth never connected, however. She backhanded him with such power that he struck the stone wall he'd been chained to and left an impression in it, sliding to the ground in a dazed heap. He tried to rally himself for another lunge, but at a word from Celynnen, he was tied with invisible bonds as securely as if he'd been bound with iron chains from his own forge. Even his muzzle was spelled shut, so that all he could do was curl his lip and snarl at her.

Her perfect face was smug with satisfaction as she knelt beside him and placed the heavy collar around his thick neck. There was no clasp. Instead, she ran a finger over the links and recited some sort of spell in a language Aidan had never heard. The collar knit itself together as if it were a live thing, and he winced inwardly as he heard the final snick of the last link.

Still kneeling, she smiled radiantly at him, and suddenly it seemed as if her beauty had intensified somehow. "I think I like you much better like this," she said, and every word was an unwanted caress. The filmy material that had only enhanced her nakedness rather than covered it disappeared, and she leaned down to rub her breasts over his thick fur. "Think of what you might have had, dear Aidan, what bliss you might have known," she purred, and then plunged her fingers into the silvery triangle between her legs. She pleasured herself there in front of him, her head thrown back, her pale nipples erect, and her pelvis rocking to meet her own touch. He closed his eyes against her mockery, sickened by her. Some strange new instinct told him plainly that she was playacting, pretending to be intensely excited when she felt only the barest shadow of it, and somehow that made her all the more repellent.

There was something else. With his new senses, he could smell her—and as he expected, Celynnen's scent was not that of a human woman. Strangely it was not that of a fae either. Instead it was something entirely new—as if he had turned over a rock and could smell the dank, cold earth beneath it. He could suddenly recall all the scents he had breathed in while captive here. *She smelled like none of them . . .*

Eventually, Celynnen tired of her game and left. In the same moment that she vanished, he was freed from whatever magic had held him helpless, and he rose slowly to his feet.

He was no dog.

Massive and powerful, Aidan ap Llanfor was as far from a pet as a dragon was from a house cat. Celynnen had made him one of the most feared creatures in Welsh legend. He was a *grim*, the *gwyllgi* of stories told round the fire, the *barghest* of lore: a monstrous black hound charged with one errand only—to be an omen of death to those unlucky enough to see him.

Within moments he felt the tug and pull of some invisible force. He could sense impending death on the human plane above, and it drew him upwards, impelling him to begin his woeful task.

～

Now—whenever *now* was—Aidan had become much like the Black Mountains themselves. They cared not for the kingdom that lay far beneath them and its flamboyant court. They were blind and deaf to its complex intrigues, spared no thought for its many conspiracies, and ignored its comings and goings in general. Most of all, the mountains *felt* nothing—but that was a state that Aidan had yet to achieve.

He certainly felt very little. No hunger or weariness or physical pain. Heat and cold were the same to him. Memories had been the hardest. At first, they had been traps, whirlpools of unbearable grief and loss, but they had faded all too quickly. Thanks to the magic that both created and ruled this realm, he no longer knew the way to his own past. Except for his name, which he repeated to himself endlessly, when he was in the faery realm he remembered little of what it was like to be human. No matter how hard he'd tried to retain them, the faces of his family, his friends, had gradually dissipated until he could not recall if he had even had any. Gone, all gone.

Sometimes, however, something brushed across his mind like a caress, something that said he'd once had a lover, but what she looked like, how she had felt or sounded, he couldn't say. Even her name was lost to him. He knew only that he had grieved for her, mourned until the very last nuance of her memory vanished from his grasp.

All he had left was a dull throbbing ache in his chest, as if his heart and all its roots had been extracted like a tooth, leaving a gaping void.

It was part of the enchantment of this kingdom that most of the simple joys and struggles that made up mortal life dissolved into nothingness here. He would have forgotten completely that he had ever *had* a life before this one—except his morbid task took him into the human world regularly. There he could not help but recall broken fragments of his previous life, small temporary remembrances, even as he watched mortal joys pass him by.

Mortal sorrow was not so kind. Whichever realm he was in, pain was with him every moment. In the human world above, he remembered some of what caused his anguish. Once he returned to the fae kingdom below, however, all he knew was the pain. And that pain spurred the only other emotions he could still summon. *Wrath. Fury. Rage.*

All the shades of anger were banked like embers and glowed deep down within him, like a volcano biding its time. And with them simmered the desire to turn the cruel injustices he'd suffered back upon the one who had inflicted them. A servant to Celynnen, an orange-eyed crymbil, had once whispered to him that the Tylwyth Teg craved sensation and envied mortals their ability to feel passion and experience emotion. *Celynnen desired to feel?* He remembered her naked performance when he was newly turned, pretending to enjoy her own stroking fingers when, in truth, neither her body nor her heart had been stirred. Aidan wanted to see the cold-blooded female experience for herself the misery that she'd inflicted on him— and yet he knew that was a vain and foolish dream.

How could the heartless be made to feel heartbreak?

What might be possible, however, was to make her afraid. Somehow or other, Aidan would find a way to make her suffer fear. She cared for no one and nothing but herself, so surely she could feel fear for her life? Perhaps she would fear even more for her beauty. A single drop of his mortal blood had been enough to wound her hand. The mark had scarcely been the size of a barley grain, and a healer had erased it as if it had never been. But what would several drops do? A cup? A pint?

Unfortunately, he did not even have that weapon at his disposal. The powerful canine body he inhabited was a fae creation, and when it was in solid form, it bled blue, just like every other living thing in this realm.

Should he ever regain his mortal form, however, he would find a way to make Celynnen afraid, to make her fear him enough to set things aright, frightened enough to return him to the life she had so callously torn from him.

Right before he killed her.

~

Ar y gair, he thought. Speak of the devil.

Aidan's awareness sharpened as the blackness that surrounded him lightened to charcoal and then to gray. It was a false dawn that approached, one that showed up all too often in his view, and as the light grew stronger, so did his ire.

A pulsing white orb appeared, driving away each and every shadow as it expanded to reveal Celynnen.

She stood before him, smiling like an angel, her hands outstretched as if welcoming supplications, as if eager to bestow blessings.

Aidan knew better.

Deliberately ignoring her presence, he rose and stretched, sneezed and yawned, then shook himself all over. He'd much rather lunge and tear out her throat than greet her. Better yet, if he'd been a mortal creature, he'd lift a leg and piss on the hem of her richly embroidered dress. Sadly, outright hostility was ineffective. Ever since a droplet of his blood had spattered the princess's hand, a shield of powerful magic protected her from any action of his, from any physical expression of the roiling anger that churned in his gut at her presence. Words could still penetrate, of course, but he was denied even that. Only human forms could articulate verbal arrows.

He had learned, however, that feigned indifference annoyed the proud fae beings, particularly Celynnen, who was accustomed to being the center of attention. Out of the corner of his eye he witnessed the tiny spark of indignation in hers. Of course, her face remained a saintlike mask, still smiling.

"Dearest Aidan, must we go through the motions yet again? Why do you not rejoice that I have come for you? Surely you will not choose to remain a lapdog when your human form is so pleasing to the eye."

However many times she came to him—and he had long ago lost count—the pretty speech she gave was always the same: "As my consort, Aidan, you know you would want for nothing. Riches if you wish them, exotic foods you've never dreamed of, exquisite clothing, spirited horses. And best of all, I can give you immortality, Aidan. You would live forever, young and handsome, if you would simply take your place by my side."

Perhaps another man would be tempted, but Aidan was unmoved. Celynnen cared not for him, only for the faint and fleeting emotions he might stimulate in her icy heart, the brief and novel sensations he might visit upon her body. Strange that even as he sought the blessed oblivion of no emotion at all, she craved anything that might make her feel—and of course the brief entertainment he might afford her. He had witnessed firsthand that the burden of living nearly forever was often boredom, and the Fair Ones welcomed any distraction. A plaything, a novelty, an insect in a jar—that was all a human would ever be to the Tylwyth Teg. And what the human thought about it mattered not at all to them.

Aidan stifled the deep, low growl that bubbled up from his throat. It would only please her to know she had gained some reaction from him. Instead, he turned his face to the wall. As always, she would leave soon, and he would go about his morbid task. Even now, Aidan could feel the tug of his calling, the scent of approaching death in the mortal world above. It was part and parcel of what Celynnen had made him. No grim could fail to fulfill his dark purpose.

Or escape his dark destiny.

Every monstrous dog wore a heavy chain-mail torc around his neck. The ornate collar was silver, but as a blacksmith skilled in metals, Aidan knew it was no ordinary silver. For one thing, it was pure, and for another, it was inexplicably stronger than the strongest steel he had ever seen. Even in the much-changed mortal world above, no metal was the equal of what he bore around his massive neck. It wasn't the strength of the silver that held him to this place, however. It was faery magic that had forged the torc, magic that held it together, magic that commanded it—and therefore commanded him.

Recently, however, that hadn't seemed sufficient to his jailers. Had he lingered too long in the mortal world, spent too much time watching wistfully as humans went about their lives? Whatever the reason, every link of his collar had been respelled to return to this place without fail, like a magnet that could not be resisted. When Aidan carried out his latest assignment in the mortal world, he quickly discovered that if he did not come back of his own accord by dawn, he would be dragged back through time and space to the stone kennels in the fae kingdom.

"Don't be tiresome, Aidan. Not when I bring you such interesting news."

He kept his face to the wall but slid his gaze sideways to observe her in his peripheral vision. She'd finally dropped that damnable angelic smile, but she'd replaced it with something worse—a practiced pout that matched her petulant tone. A slyness crept into Celynnen's eyes, however, as she realized she'd gained his attention.

"Did you know that one of your fellow grims escaped?" she asked. Aidan bristled at the way she said "your fellow grim," like they were old friends. Grims seldom even saw one another, never mind communicated. All that bound them was their mutual fate at the hands of the fae. And as for escaping—Aidan had almost accepted that it was impossible. Yet if one of the hounds was actually missing . . .

"It's true. A mortal woman broke the enchantment and set him free. The entire court is simply buzzing about it." She imparted the information with a kind of glee, and Aidan understood now why his collar had been magically reinforced. More than likely the collars of all the grims had been spelled so.

"They say Queen Gwenhidw herself intervened to save him and his lover from the Wild Hunt." Celynnen paused for effect, arranging her flowing sleeves to perfection. "Of course, the human woman was some sort of distant fae relation to Her Majesty. No one would bother to save you, of course. You are of no importance to anyone. But I've been thinking that someday it might be very entertaining to see you run."

For a fraction of an instant, Aidan could swear her eyes flashed demon green, the pupils elliptical like a cat's—or a snake's. Her skin appeared as mottled leaves. "Remember *that* the next time you refuse me," she commanded from greenish lips, thin and smooth like leather. He blinked and saw only her angelic face once more as she smiled and disappeared.

Only her laughter lingered in the air, like a glissando of crystal bells.

The great black dog traveled Brecon's High Street openly in the late-afternoon sun. Many humans passed him by, some on foot, most in cars. None of them saw him. Some walked through him, unknowing. He was invisible to all but those whom he was called to, or to the very rare few who had the ability to perceive fae creatures. With his otherworldly form made of finer stuff than the molecules that made up the human world, he had all the powers he needed to accomplish his task. He could will himself as solid as a rock wall, or he could pass through such a wall like a breeze through tall grass.

There wasn't a village in all of Wales that Aidan had not been called to countless times over the centuries. He had been to Brecon often. Much had changed since his time. The village had been called Aberhonddu then, the place where the river Honddu met the greater river Usk. The place where he'd gone to market with his family as a child. And something else too . . . He always felt that there was something else about this place he should remember. *Someone.* But like a word that stubbornly remained on the tip of one's tongue, he could not recall who the person was. He knew only that his heart ached even more each time he tried . . .

In the fae kingdom, the concept of time meant little. The entire human world was focused on time, however. Ten centuries had gone by here, and he had not felt their passing. He could see it, however, progressing in tiny increments, during each and every visit he made to the mortal realm. Still, a few things remained the same from his former life. Brecon was still a market town, and despite the advent of horseless vehicles, many streets and passageways were as narrow as ever. Cars and trucks labored to squeeze through, and more than one had to back all the way out to allow another to pass. The great old castle had once towered over the junction of the rivers, imposed on the site by Norman conquerors before he was born. The walls still stood, but the fortress didn't look so big now that it was surrounded by a modern, white-painted inn. A *hotel* people called it, not an inn. Still, the castle stones were the same ones he had dared his friend, Grigor, to touch when they were small boys. They had both run away laughing as the foreign soldiers shouted at them. The castle had been hated by his people, a symbol of oppression—how strange to feel a kinship with it now!

But it was one of the only things he shared a mote of history with, something that linked him to his own time and place.

Temporarily at least.

As soon as he returned to the kingdom of the Tylwyth Teg, he would once again remember little or nothing of this place, but in these brief moments, he drank in the sights and scents. Perhaps some part of his mind kept things like this, little vignettes stored away like cheeses and wines for some future occasion.

There would be no such future occasions for Maeve Lowri Jones.

He padded silently along Cerrigcochion Lane until he came to a modest home with a once-tidy garden. Despite the spring weather, the grounds were untended, although masses of tulips were blooming red and gold. The tall flowers had pushed their way through a thick blanket of last autumn's leaves. Aidan approached the door, adrift with yellowed newspapers, and listened intently, his head cocked to one side in doglike fashion. His supernatural hearing easily detected labored breathing coming from a second-floor bedroom.

He passed through the door and headed up the stairs. The old woman was in her bed but not asleep. She started when she saw the giant canine, then unexpectedly smiled.

"Ah, 'tis you. I wondered when you would come. It's been harder and harder to get meself up in the mornings lately, and today, well, I found meself just too tired." She studied him with watery blue eyes. "My, aren't you a strapping big fellow? If my little terrier were still alive, he'd be like to bark his head off. Come closer, won't you? Let me get a good look at you."

This had never happened before—most mortals greeted him with fear, loathing, sorrow, or even anger. Instead, Maeve crooked her gnarled fingers on the quilts, and Aidan didn't hesitate. It seemed like the right thing to do, the *human* thing to do, though he was on four legs. He approached the narrow bed and rested his great head next to Maeve, firming his spectral form until he was as solid as any mortal dog. He nuzzled his way beneath her hand so her fingers rested on his broad forehead.

"Aye, there's a good dog. There's a fine fellow. You can keep an old woman company fer a bit before she passes. When I was a girl, me mam spoke of the gwyllgi sometimes when she told me stories of the Fair Ones." Maeve's weak fingers rubbed little circles around the base of his ear. "She'd seen a grim come fer my nainie afore I was born. Afraid of it, she was, but I always liked the idea. Seems fair that you get a little warning when your time comes."

Aidan wished he had the power of speech, but Maeve seemed content to do the talking. Her words were English with a charming Welsh seasoning—few people in this time spoke the language Aidan had been born to—but had she used any other tongue, he would have understood her just as well. As a grim, he'd been exposed to many languages over the centuries and knew them all well.

"You know, we used to leave *yn cynnig*, an offering, on the back porch for the Tylwyth Teg," she said. "We were taught to show respect to the Fair Ones, so they wouldn't be playing tricks on our farm. They love pranks, the Fair Ones do, even cruel ones. Yet quick they were to reward people for generosity and unselfishness. They punished the greedy and the mean spirited. Seems to have kept the balance in the world somehow." Her fingers were barely moving on Aidan's dark head, and her voice became softer. "It's different now, ya know. The older I get, the less balance there seems to be. Some say it's because people stopped believing in the Fair Ones, although I don't know as you have to believe in a thing to make it real. You don't believe in the sun, it still shines, now, don't it?"

He nuzzled her arm to indicate his agreement, and she seemed satisfied.

"Some say the church ran them off, but it would have to admit the Fair Folk existed afore it could do such a thing," she chuckled. "'Sides, the Tylwyth Teg are old, far older than men. Seems they must have a place in the way of things, else they wouldn't be here." Her hand moved to Aidan's neck, grasping weakly in an attempt to ruffle the thick mane of black fur. "Glad I am that you came. Tells me there's still a purpose and a reason behind it all."

Had he believed that once? He licked the old woman's arm like the most faithful of dogs, even as he envied her outlook. She smiled and closed her eyes.

And she was gone.

FOUR

⌒〰⌒

A faint vibration in the links of Aidan's silver collar warned him that he should leave the mortal realm soon, but he ignored it. The magic couldn't drag him away until dawn approached. Instead, he lingered at Maeve Lowri Jones's bedside for a while. He hadn't known Maeve, had never met her before, but it seemed to him that the world was poorer without her. And that his world had been better for a few moments because of her.

Finally, he went downstairs, his great black paws gliding silently over the steps as though he were a ghost. The empty place in Aidan's chest pained him as he approached the front door. Rather than pass through it, he gazed intently at it until it opened wide. A chair slid across the floor and braced itself against the door to hold it in place. All the lights in the house came on at the same time, making the house a beacon in the approaching twilight. Maeve's spirit had gone on, but Aidan was determined that her earthly vessel be found and properly cared for.

He padded down the leaf-littered sidewalk, deep in thought—until a sudden flurry of leaves gathered itself into a whirlwind. The column rose up and up, drawing more and more leaves from the lawn into the swirling vortex. Abruptly, it resolved itself into a dark figure he recognized from the fae realm: Lurien, Lord of the Wild Hunt.

Unlike most of the Fae, Lurien's hair was as black as his riding leathers and hung in hundreds of long, loose braids. Whiplike strands escaped that seemed to have a life of their own. His eyes were dark with secrets and glittered with danger, and a strong jaw seemed to dare the world. No fine features here, no glamor or artifice to make himself appealing. It wasn't necessary. His broad shoulders bore the weight of a power so strong that it buffeted the air surrounding Aidan with its presence alone.

Aidan stood his ground and growled deep, even as his fur rose along his spine. His black lips drew back to reveal fearsome white fangs, and he crouched ready to spring.

"Take your ease, grim," said Lurien. "I have no quarrel with you. I pay honor to Maeve."

Startled, Aidan hid his sharp teeth, though he remained at the ready.

"No doubt that seems strange to you, but she was a fine woman, one of the few mortals left in this land who still believed. Had you entered by the back door, you would have seen the bread and milk she placed outside yesterday night." His voice was contemplative, as if he spoke half to himself. "It was all she had left in the house, the most unselfish of offerings. It cost her dearly to set it upon the step—I feared she wouldn't be able to get back up and provided her an unseen hand. By the stars of the Seven Sisters, she *thanked me*. She could not see me but knew I was there. I have lived a long time, grim, but never have I been thanked by a mortal."

The Lord of the Wild Hunt had shown kindness to an old mortal woman, been surprised by her, and now paid his respects to her as well. Aidan didn't know what to make of such a thing. Celynnen would never have noticed the woman's offering or her need, never mind actually thought to aid her in any way. Celynnen cared only about Celynnen. In fact, if any of the Fair Ones cared about anything other than themselves, he had not seen it.

"What Maeve said to you was quite true, of course. The Tylwyth Teg once kept the balance. Everything changed when King Arthfael was killed—more likely, it was changing before his death and none of us knew it. Queen Gwenhidw holds things together as best as she can, but the Nine Realms beneath this land have splintered like a broken mirror, every faction for itself. There is no unity, and little loyalty left in the kingdom. I wish for a return to the way things were, when the Tylwyth Teg were honorable and just in their dealings."

He couldn't help it. Aidan chuffed at the word *just*.

"You should wish for such too," chided Lurien. "You live a life of servitude, forcibly indentured to Celynnen. Nearly a thousand years have passed since she spirited you away, and she still does not comprehend that you will never give in to her. *You* do not understand that a millennium means nothing to an immortal.

"Therefore you have no hope. I, on the other hand, have some hopes of my own, and I would do us both a favor. I have a proposal."

Traffic cast bright beams of light along the street beyond as Aidan studied Lurien's face. The fae's black gaze was steady—his eyes still promised danger but not necessarily deception. Perhaps it was merely an artful ruse, but what if it was? Aidan had already lost all that he cared about. His family, his siblings, his friends— what few he could remember when he was in the mortal world— all were lost to the dust of time. And none of them had recalled his face or his name. Aidan had left behind no lineage, no legacy— nothing. As Celynnen had declared, he had ceased to exist. The animal sound that emerged from his throat was a cross between anguish and anger. Lurien frowned. "You have been too long without words, and I care not to hear only myself. Speak as a man speaks," he commanded.

The canine flews that covered Aidan's teeth moved strangely, trying to mimic human lips. The voice was not his own—how could it be, coming from a hound's throat? But the forceful words came straight from his heart. "Send me back! *Send me back from whence I came!*" roared Aidan, springing at the tall fae and knocking him to the ground as easily as a large wolf might take down a deer. He planted his massive front paws on either side of Lurien's perfect face and snarled savagely. "*Send me back!*"

The close view of long, sharp teeth failed to make Lurien flinch. "Only Celynnen could do that, as a member of the royal house," he said calmly, as if a monstrous canine weren't a breath away from tearing out his throat. "They alone have the power to affect time. And as I said, she will never let go of you."

An invisible force struck Aidan squarely in the chest like a battering ram, knocking him nose over tail to the far side of the yard and pinning him there. The dark fae rose gracefully from the grass as if he'd only been resting. Not a single midnight hair was out of place, yet he made a show of straightening his leather tunic. No sooner had he done so than the force that had slammed into the great black dog abruptly released him.

Aidan stumbled forward. He braced his front legs, head lowered and teeth bared. The thick fur around his neck had stiffened like a lion's mane with anger, but Lurien only laughed. It was not a merry sound. Something in the tone suggested the tolling of mourning bells, and it played along Aidan's spine like an off-key dirge.

"You will not be the last of Celynnen's acquisitions, and believe me, you are far from the first. And she has never freed any of her pets. Ever," declared the fae. "You have lasted the longest, but do you truly think Celynnen will release you when she tires of you at last? They have all died, one way or another. Usually after the first bedding, in fact."

"How do you know that?" Aidan hissed. "Do you kill them for her?"

Lurien snorted. "Celynnen prefers to do her own killing. She enjoys it, and you'll find she is very inventive at drawing out her entertainment as long as possible."

The remaining tension between Lurien and Aidan was shattered as a half dozen boisterous boys suddenly rocketed along the sidewalk on skateboards, their voices loud and raucous as they passed Maeve's house. It seemed disrespectful to Aidan, even as he knew they could have no idea of her passing. They also had no idea that a monstrous grim and a dark fae observed their antics. Aidan was reminded anew that he was no longer part of the mortal world, and something about that cleared the last of the anger from his head.

He sighed and settled on his muscular haunches. "According to you, if I give in to Celynnen, if I don't give in to Celynnen, the end is the same."

"Exactly. You will die."

His ordeal would be over then, certainly—but where was the justice in that? If he had simply wanted to die, he could have pushed matters to that point a long time ago. What had kept him going all this time was the vow he had made to extract revenge from Celynnen. She deserved to die for what she had inflicted on him. And something else . . . She had committed something truly heinous, he was sure of it, yet exactly what it was eluded him even when he was in the mortal world. "As I said," continued the dark fae. "I have a proposal. You make a fine grim, but when did you last see your human features?"

Aidan had to think hard about that. Memories were so damnably difficult to resurrect. "In the waters of the Usk, leaning over the boat to draw up a fish," he said finally. "I was young." Young enough that he and his friend Grigor had both leaned over the side to practice making faces at their reflections. No one owned mirrors at the time—the church had discouraged them as vanity.

"I saw you when you were first brought to the kingdom beneath the Black Mountains. Know you that your face and mine are similar? Shape and bone and build . . . Truly, we would pass for brothers, one dark, one fair—although I am certainly the more handsome—and therein lies my hope that our beautiful but fickle Celynnen will be willing to transfer her shallow affections to me.

"Of course, that could happen only in the absence of her favorite pet."

"You want me to disappear." Aidan was glad he was sitting down. Surely it was not possible that Lurien wanted the tywysoges. The princess was self-centered, cruel, and incapable of true love or affection. But there was no arguing that she was exquisitely beautiful beyond all dreaming. At least on the surface . . .

"Beauty is a strange master," said Lurien, as though he sensed Aidan's thoughts. "We are possessed by it and strive to possess it in return. But that is my weakness and not yours, apparently. So, the question is, how to make you vanish? Perhaps I could take your place as a hound until the next time Celynnen comes to tempt you—and please her by accepting her offer. I could then appear as you in human form and permit myself to be won over by Celynnen's affections." Lurien grinned wickedly. "It would be a very good game. Eventually, she would discover that the Lord of the Hunt is in her bed and not you, but perhaps she would not be too unhappy about it by then.

"However, someone must take my place and drive the Hunt for a time. That could be you."

"I will have nothing to do with the Wild Hunt," declared Aidan. "I will not ride down the innocent, spirit away those that have done no wrong."

"And that is precisely why a just man like yourself should lead it. You might even be able to do some good with such power behind you."

Aidan shook his head. "Your hunters will not obey me."

"They will follow whoever possesses the light-whip without question. They care not who you are but will ride at your command and obey you until my return. Surely you have heard the gossip over Tyne and Daeria? They seized the whip by magic and drove the Hunt outside of our dominion for murderous purpose, upsetting the balance between realms and causing chaos among innocents. Queen Gwenhidw herself had to set *that* mess to rights."

Indeed, Celynnen and her companions had tittered at length about the incident, seeming to feed on the excitement and the novelty. "I thank you for the generous offer," said Aidan. Lurien appeared friendly—or at least not hostile—but appearances were deliberately deceiving more often than not among the fae. "I will not lead the Hunt."

"I see. You are uncannily resistant to temptation, Aidan ap Llanfor. You do not fall prey to feminine wiles, and you disdain to grasp power when it is presented to you. Perhaps more humans should be like you." Lurien toyed with a silver dagger set with gemstones, then eyed Aidan appraisingly. "I'm rather glad I didn't kill you now. That was my first plan, you know."

It was the one thing that didn't surprise him, and he remained silent until the Lord of the Wild Hunt continued.

"Of course, your outright demise would displease Celynnen greatly. And although you have no reason to believe it, I would also be displeased, since you are guilty of nothing. The old ways prohibit punishing the just, and I happen to agree with them." The fae looked thoughtful. "I trust that Celynnen told you of the grim that escaped? It was lucky for him that he achieved his freedom, but it is also lucky for both of us: we now have a very useful precedent. Should another hound escape, it will seem less strange to the Court."

Faster than Aidan could react, powerful magic seized him, drew him close to the dark fae, and held him in place as effortlessly as though he were a newborn pup, not a massive and muscular fae creature that outweighed Lurien twice over. Aidan roared with fury, and every black hair in his thick pelt bristled as he struggled and fought against the forces that gripped him, seeking to seize the fae in his bone-crushing jaws. Nothing worked.

Lurien seemed unconcerned by Aidan's reaction. All his attention was on the intricate silver torc, identical to every collar that every grim was forced to wear. He ran his long pale hands over the cleverly forged links, but Aidan could not see what the dark fae was doing. He could hear, however, the faintest of murmurings, ancient words that belonged to a time out of mind, words similar to the ones that Celynnen had once used. Something changed, shifted, gave way, and the Hunt master stepped back. The torc remained in place as always, but it *felt* different in a way Aidan could not describe. It was different enough that when the magic released him, Aidan didn't immediately attack the fae lord.

"I believe the spell is undone," declared Lurien. The Lord of the Wild Hunt now stood on the porch of Maeve's house, casually leaning against the wall as though he had been there all along. "If so, the torc no longer has the power to command you."

Aidan shook himself all over and pawed at the collar until the dark fae raised a hand, palm out.

"Leave it on for appearance's sake," he instructed. "Do not attempt to remove it until you make your bid for freedom, lest you attract the attention of others among the Tylwyth Teg—and believe me, *I* want to be the one that hunts you. And should you succeed in escaping, you may want to keep the torc in your possession."

Aidan's canine forehead furrowed deep into a humanlike frown. "So I can remember my captivity? I think I would rather cast it into the nearest fire."

"Fire will not destroy fae silver. And you need not worry that I can use it to track you in the future—if you have a future, that is.

The torc's magics are closed to me now that I myself have unspelled it, and I give you my word on that. However, with the torc, you can find *me*. Permit me the faint hope that someday you may change your mind about leading the Hunt, even temporarily."

The word of a Fair One was solid enough. It was one of the few things in which a human could trust. That much honor remained among the Tylwyth Teg at least. But Lurien's hopes about the Hunt still made no sense at all to Aidan. Why would he want to hand over such power to a human? "Do you tire of your high station, that you are so eager to rid yourself of it?"

"Nay, the Wild Hunt rides the storm." A fragment of something like longing crept into the fae's voice, and his gaze seemed focused on something far away. "There's no feeling like it, and I would not trade it. But I see a time when dividing power will multiply it for the sake of the kingdom. I cannot be everywhere at once."

Aidan had no idea what the dark fae could be talking about, but he decided to leave the topic strictly alone. What the fae kingdom needed or didn't need was no concern of his. If he managed to escape the Tylwyth Teg, he certainly couldn't picture ever needing or wanting to call on any of them, and that included the Lord of the Wild Hunt. He agreed to keep the collar, however—after all, knowing where it was and using it were two different things. "Are you letting me go?"

Lurien shook his head. "I am not *letting* you do anything. I am merely presenting options. As you well know, it's my duty to pursue any prisoner who seeks to flee the kingdom." He vanished and reappeared abruptly at a bus stop a couple houses down the street, seated beside a young woman with a little girl. The woman was unaware of him, but the child kept craning her head about as if she heard something she could not see.

"I am free to pursue an escapee anywhere," continued the fae. "However, the Hunt is bound to the hours of the night. If a prisoner just happened to leave very close to mortal dawn, and if he was clever enough to keep ahead of the Hunt until it was forced to turn back . . . Well, it's easy to see how someone just might—*might*—get clean away."

The little girl turned to her mother then. "Who's getting away?"

Lurien chuckled amiably and was again on the steps of Maeve's house before the sound of his laughter died away. "A most perceptive child, that one. Quite rare these days."

Aidan caught himself before he spoke. It was an ill thing for a child to catch the attention of the fae, something he could attest to personally. Saying anything about it, however, would only bring the little girl more attention. If he left the subject alone, it was possible that the Lord of the Wild Hunt would forget about her. Not all of the Fair Ones spirited mortals away, but he had no way of knowing if Lurien would do so. The Tylwyth Teg never harmed children, of course—in fact, they often protected them, one of the fae's few virtues. But that didn't mean that Lurien would not do as Celynnen had done and bide his time until the charming child became an attractive adult . . .

"Ah, but what if I didn't get away?" asked Aidan, casually moving a few steps to the right and pretending to inspect something on the sidewalk so that Lurien's gaze was on him and away from the little girl. He was relieved when his canine hearing picked up the sound of a bus lumbering its way along, collecting passengers at leisurely intervals throughout the neighborhood. Mentally, he beseeched it to hurry. "There is no question that your hunting skills are legendary—the Court has yet to stop chattering about your last exploit when you captured a giant bwgan alive," he said. "Therefore I allow there is a slight chance that I would not escape you."

"Only slight?" Lurien looked amused. "I think the odds are far better than that."

"Perhaps, perhaps not. Should you overtake me, however, I think it fair that I know what to expect." He kept his eyes on the dark fae until his keen hearing told him that the slow-moving bus had finally done its job and borne the child and her mother away. Luckily, Lurien did not so much as glance in that direction.

"You yourself know that faery law is strict," he said. "I would have no choice but to kill you myself or to return you to Celynnen—and what she would do would likely be far worse. If you knew her better, you would likely beg me to kill you."

The ultimate stakes, then. Aidan knew it was a dangerous enough gamble if Lurien was telling the truth. And if he wasn't? The dark fae seemed sincere, but he could simply be setting Aidan up for an elaborate game to please himself, or much more likely, to please Celynnen. What was it she had said? *It might be very entertaining to see you run.* Still, game or not, it was also the first opportunity for escape—however slim—that had presented itself in nearly a millennium.

At that moment, a police car turned into the laneway, and two officers emerged. Unaware of the powerful fae's presence, they walked right through Lurien as he sat on the steps. Aidan wondered what they would think if they knew.

The Lord of the Wild Hunt vanished and reappeared beside Aidan, and they watched together as more vehicles arrived in a flurry of red and blue and yellow flashing lights. It wasn't long before Maeve's earthly shell was gently removed and taken away. Lurien nodded his approval. "A clever idea you had, grim. A neighbor called the constables because he saw the door was open. He thought there had been a robbery."

Aidan was glad, but already he felt the pull of an invisible string. Another passing life required his unwanted attention. "I have work to do and must take my leave."

"You don't actually." Lurien tapped the side of his own neck and nodded at Aidan's torc. "Unspelled, remember? Because you're attuned to your morbid task, you're simply sensing death at work in the mortal realm. You need not concern yourself further."

Is that so? Aidan realized then that the dark fae not only craved the chase but was anxious for it to begin. He cursed himself for not seeing it sooner. Maybe Lurien really did believe in the things he'd said about justice and honor and the old ways, but when it came right down to it, *he was one of the Fair Ones*—and the game came before all. He was looking forward to hunting an escaped grim, probably even more so since he'd missed out on the last one.

"I think I'll be concerning myself with my work for a while yet," said Aidan carefully. "Free for the first time in a millennium, it would be natural for me to try to run now. But you are prepared for that, and the Hunt would ride me down much too quickly. Not only would I fail to escape, but your pleasure would be cut short before you could truly savor it."

The fae said nothing, and his face showed no expression. Yet Aidan sensed he had struck a chord, and he boldly continued. "You offered me a proposal, Lurien, Lord of the Wild Hunt. Now I will make you one. I propose to *wait*."

Lurien's dark eyes glittered. No doubt he thought he was being mocked, and Aidan knew his canine form could be a pile of ashes at any moment. Finally, the fae spoke, his voice low and dangerous.

"Wait for what, grim?"

Suddenly it was like fishing. How many times as a boy had Aidan bounced a twisted piece of grass on the surface of the water, until the fish could not help but pay attention? "Why, to behave as any worthy prey behaves, and lie low. Waiting, watching, hoping to catch the hunter unawares and seize the right moment to break away. To gain a lead and a chance of true escape, and"—Aidan dropped the last bit like a baited line—"to give a superior hunter the gift of *true sport*."

Was that a glimmer of interest he saw? Aidan had spoken of waiting, but it was nerve-wracking to wait upon the whim of the Fair Ones. Especially the Lord of the Wild Hunt.

"A tempting proposal, but you cannot meet the terms. I will be at the ready."

"I too will be ready." Aidan forced himself to be calm and to meet the dark fae's gaze confidently. It all rested on this, on setting the hook and setting it deeply. Otherwise he was likely dead where he stood. "I will be ready to *surprise you*."

After what seemed like a lifetime, Lurien's brow quirked. "Interesting. I give you credit for originality and accept your proposal, grim."

"I thank you for your mercy." Aidan knew it was the wrong thing to say the moment it left his lips.

The dark fae smiled broadly, but there was no warmth to it. The chill expression resembled Death itself. "The Lord of the Wild Hunt has no mercy. Remember *that*." Without warning, Lurien loomed over him, black eyes flashing green fire. A veritable army of shadows rose behind him, and his voice echoed thunderously inside Aidan's head. *Aidan ap Llanfor, no one has escaped me in ten thousand of your mortal years. Should I overtake you, you will be trampled beneath the hooves of the Hunt until your blood and flesh are pounded into the earth.*

The dark fae vanished and reappeared, seated calmly on Maeve's porch steps. The hellish fire was gone from his eyes, and when he spoke again, it was in a perfectly normal tone of voice. "I too have my masters."

FIVE

⌇

B rooke silently recited the Code, the creed she had committed to memory over a dozen years ago, cultivating the right frame of mind in preparation for working with magic. It was still amazing to her that she even *had* magic to work with. She'd been seventeen before she'd stumbled on the power that lived within her.

It happened during her postgrad weekend, when she was camping out with her girlfriends—Morgan, Sharon, Katie, Tina, and George's twin sister, Lissy. They had set up their tents in the wooded area on Tina's grandparents' farm outside of Spokane Valley. The proms were over, the diplomas gathered, the formal dresses packed away. They had this one last weekend together, a gals' weekend—no guys invited. One last weekend to remember what it was like to be kids together, to swim naked in the pond and stay up all night, and eat junk food, and drink beer, and talk about their current boyfriends or the ones they hoped to meet. They'd done plenty of camping in this very spot whenever the weather allowed . . . This time, however, there'd been an urgency to it, a sense that the adult world was closing in on them. In only a few days, they'd be splitting up to go to summer jobs and colleges, and their little group would never be quite the same again.

It was cold and dark when Brooke got up to pee. The fire had gone out, but she'd huddled hopefully over the fire pit and stretched her hand towards the blackened pile of spent wood. All she had wanted was to feel a little warmth still radiating from it. Instead, a sudden golden blaze erupted skyward from the ashes as if she'd dumped gasoline on them. Instinct helped her leap backwards out of the way, but not before she'd lost one of her eyebrows and, just above it, about a half-inch-wide strip of hair. She feared to think what might have happened if she hadn't fallen asleep with her hair still pulled back in an untidy ponytail . . .

The fire quickly settled down to a low and tidy size, although the flames retained an odd golden color, almost like melting amber. When the girls emerged from their tents in the morning, the fire was still burning brightly, despite the fact that Brooke hadn't added a single stick of wood.

Katie and Sharon pulled out the cast-iron skillets and made a reasonable bacon and egg breakfast, with just enough char on the edges to give it an authentic camping flavor. They'd had no idea it wasn't an ordinary fire they were cooking over. George's sister, Lissy, made some lumpy pancakes. Afterwards, Tina fed the left-overs to her bad-tempered wiener dog, Jake, although Morgan lectured her on why it wasn't good for him. Morgan was sure to be right too—after volunteering at the local animal clinic every summer since forever, she was already taking classes in order to pursue her dream: a degree in veterinary medicine. Brooke picked at her own plate, and in the end, Jake got her food too—but not until Morgan wasn't looking.

Everything was normal, as if nothing had ever happened. Maybe nothing *had* happened, Brooke reasoned. The fire pit got used a lot. Hell, Tina's dad burned trash in it regularly, and last year, Lissy had burned her diary in it (along with photos of her cheating ex-boyfriend and six stuffed animals he had given her over the course of their rocky relationship). Maybe something had been buried, some leftover piece of garbage that had flared into life just as Brooke reached towards the ashes. Maybe it was all just coincidence . . .

She tried to shake it off, joining in the conversation and helping herself to a bowl of Fruity-O's. But it was hard to ignore the cold spot in the pit of her stomach that said *there were no coincidences.*

When the tents were struck and everyone had packed up and was heading for the house to coordinate who was riding with whom, Brooke was left alone to stare at the fire. Having volunteered to put it out, she stood ready to "pour and stir" with a five-gallon bucket of water and a stick. She had no idea what instinct prompted her next move. Brooke stretched her hand in the direction of the campfire and clenched her fingers into a fist. At once, the flames died down and vanished as if they had never been. Shocked, she poked at the pit with the stick, and then finally with her fingers.

The ashes were stone cold.

"Pretty good trick." The voice that had her jumping belonged to her very best friend, George Santiago-Callahan. His hair was platinum blond and flat-topped that day, his fingernails painted black.

"What the hell are you doing here?"

George rolled his eyes. "Duh, I'm here to pick up my sister. Good morning to you too, sunshine. Say, any good ghost stories keep you awake? I could use some ideas for a new comic."

She'd stared at him. "Didn't you just see what happened?"

"Sure I did. It was really cool. So?"

"Did that look normal to you?"

"My grandmamma used to do it all the time. She tried to teach my mom when I was little, but it never worked for her."

"Yeah, but G, *I didn't mean to do it*. It just happened."

Her voice was strained and pitched a little too high, with a fine thread of hysteria bordering it. Later she thought she must have been in some sort of shock. All she remembered was that a few minutes later, George was escorting her up the front steps and into the vibrantly colored kitchen of the Santiago-Callahan home. "Mamá!" he shouted. "Mamá, come quick!" An older woman barely half his height hurried in. She compensated for her stature by piling her naturally curly brunette hair high on top of her head, in the only style Brooke had ever seen her wear. Tendrils were forever escaping, however, and they cascaded wildly down the sides of her face and her neck like springs, giving a tantalizing hint of just how long Olivia Santiago-Callahan's hair really was. Brooke often thought Olivia must have been breathtaking in her youth. Her oval face had few lines even now, and her dark brown eyes—so much like George's— were exotic. Fortunately, her gaze was also ever-friendly, and she loved Brooke just as fiercely as she loved her own children. She beamed at Brooke and swatted George with a dish towel.

"Why do you yell in our house like a street vendor?" she demanded. "And where is your sister?"

"Lissy's coming home with Sharon. This is important, Mamá. Brooke called fire today, just like Grandmamma."

Almost before she had time to blink, Brooke found herself in an overstuffed armchair with a cup of tea and her feet up, while Olivia Santiago-Callahan was telling her how wonderful it was that she'd been blessed with magic. "Although *mi madre* was a very, very powerful *bruja*, and she taught me all that she could, I only inherited a handful of the skills. The full power of the Gift passed me by, and also passed by my children."

"What's a *bruja*?"

"A witch, honey. And it is a good thing, not an evil thing, and not like these silly Halloween witches they tell stories about here.

The *bruja* is to be respected. She is the wise woman, the shaman, the healer of the village."

"I'm not wise. I haven't even gone to college yet."

Olivia patted her hand reassuringly. "You are nervous, but you do not need to fear this, *m'ija*. The Gift itself will teach you much, especially since you have received its full expression."

"What does that mean?"

"It *means* you got the whole enchilada," answered George. "The complete package with all the bells and whistles included."

She looked at them blankly.

"*M'ija*, I cannot call fire. My children cannot call fire. Only those with the fullest manifestation of the Gift, like *mi madre*, can do such a thing," explained Olivia. "That is how I know what you can do. What you will be *able* to do."

"Why didn't *you* get the whole package if your mom was a witch—I mean, a *bruja*? It doesn't seem fair. She must have been disappointed, and you must have been as well. Can't I just give it to you? What about George?"

"That's very sweet, *m'ija*, and rare. Most people would never be willing to let go of the power once they have it. As for George, the Gift rarely goes to men."

"Thanking my lucky stars on that one," he said. "I got *other* things I want to do with my life."

His mother made a face at him. "The Gift can and does go to sons, occasionally, but usually it rests upon the daughters. But although my mother would have liked for me or any of my children to inherit the complete Gift, she knew all too well that it goes to whomever it will, wherever it will. She was the only one in her family to hold it. Many times, it appears in a family with no history of such things."

Boy, is that an understatement . . . Holy crap, her parents gave her a hard enough time over her complete disinterest in the family's church activities. Her younger brothers, Sterling and Lucas, already teased her about being a heathen. Imagine if she tried to explain what just happened to her. *Hey! Mom, Dad, guess what I learned to do today . . .*

"Like mine," she said aloud and took a long drink from her cup, suddenly wishing for something a lot stronger.

"Like yours," nodded Olivia, understanding exactly what she meant. "So it is a good thing that George brought you here, is it not? It is such a shame my mother is no longer alive to help us. But even though I did not inherit very much of the Gift, she fully prepared me to teach it in case one of my grandchildren was born with the power. I can answer your questions about magic."

"That's typical of the *superhero's mentor*—you see it all the time in the comics. *Those who can't do, teach,*" added George. "It's like Giles coaching Buffy—he couldn't go out and kill vampires, but he could coach her on how to do it."

"You are not helping," said George's mother.

"What? I'm translating all this into the highly accessible language of pop culture."

She sighed and turned her attention back to Brooke: "One thing you must know, first and always, is that you do not own the Gift. The Gift belongs to the earth, and it is the earth who permits you to hold this power. It is to be used to help people, to serve others, to do good in the world. That is your calling now, your responsibility, just as it was my mother's."

"Um—I'm not sure this is going to work out. I'm not really the Mother Teresa type."

Olivia only laughed. "Neither was Mother Teresa at first! Besides, you're not going to be a nun, *m'ija*, just a witch. You will still go to college in September, get a job, travel, get married, do whatever it is you want to do with your life."

"She means no vows of poverty or chastity required. Even Spiderman can still have sex," added George, who ducked too late as his mother smacked the back of his head. "Hey, I'm just saying that all superheroes are allowed to have ordinary lives on the side. It's like a rule."

Rules aside, Brooke didn't feel like a superhero in the least. Her parents would be far from reassured in any way by George's argument or his mother's. Even knowing that witches must follow a strict code of ethics (which Olivia insisted was the case) would not soothe her mom's and dad's feelings on the subject. They'd be certain she was going to hell on a greased skateboard, and they would pressure her brothers into starting up an online prayer circle for their wayward sister. *Crap, they might even shop around for an exorcist.*

Fortunately, there was no glaring neon sign on her forehead announcing her strange new state of being. She felt different, but the only physical evidence of the campfire experience was that her left eyebrow grew back white and so did a little lock of hair above it, about the width of a finger. The doctor had reassured her mother that the lack of coloration "sometimes happens with burns" and that Brooke was completely healthy otherwise. To keep her mom from fussing about it, Brooke dyed the hair and penciled over the brow for her remaining months at home. *Out of sight, out of mind.*

As for her magic, she didn't have to make any effort at all to hide it from her folks. Not then. Most people saw what they wanted and expected to see, and what they saw was a daughter aiming for a respectable degree in business administration (not at the university of their choice, mind you, *but that was kids for you*) who currently had a responsible summer job managing the local garden center. And while they also saw a daughter with a decade-old lack of interest in church activity, her parents still viewed that as *just a phase.*

Thankfully, Brooke's brothers had gone off to football camp for the summer, so they weren't there to notice anything at all. It didn't hurt that she was an older sister and affectionately considered "weird." If Lucas and Sterling had spotted anything odd about her, chances were good they wouldn't take it seriously. Chances were even better they'd make a joke about it, or several jokes.

There was no hiding her newly awakened magic from herself, however. Like a hatchling that instinctively seeks to try its wings, Brooke was constantly beset with urges to test the strange new power. She firmly squashed all of them—then learned that she *also* had to be careful with her words and wishes. The garden center had a bargain corner where wilted plants went to die, and she'd always felt sorry for the hopeless things. There were three leafless apple trees, a spruce that was almost completely brown, and a tabletop of various bedding plants that looked like a Saint Bernard had rolled over them. As she watered them just before closing, R.E.M. was playing over the sound system and she found herself singing along to the classic "Shiny Happy People"—only she sang "shiny happy flowers" and "shiny happy trees," making up lyrics with a botanical theme. She was just having fun, glad it was closing time, and looking forward to going out with her friends.

In the morning, Brooke was grateful she was the manager, because it meant she got to the garden center a half hour before anyone else. And she was the first one to see that the bargain corner was crammed with *tall healthy plants*! The spruce was as green and lush as if it had come out of a Pacific rain forest—and it was a foot taller. The apple trees had grown as well, and not only did they have abundant healthy leaves; there were even blossoms and tiny developing fruits on the branches. The tabletop was completely hidden, the mostly dead bedding plants having erupted into a riot of greenery and color. Brooke stood and stared for a long, long minute—then two. Then she sprang into action.

When the staff arrived, she'd already moved all of the magically enhanced plants, incorporating them amongst the regular stock as best as she could, considering the bargain corner residents now looked *better* than the very best she had on hand. *Delivery this morning.* That was all she would dare to say to any staff or customers who noticed them.

By closing time, all of the "new" stock had been sold, and Brooke had reached a decision: it was past time to take Mrs. Santiago-Callahan up on her offer of instruction. It was either live in fear that the magic would leak out and cause something to happen in front of witnesses or learn to control the Gift that had inexplicably chosen her.

The first lesson had been memorizing El Código—the Code. She might not be a card-carrying witch herself, but George's mom certainly knew the lengthy creed by heart, having heard it firsthand from her own mother for many, many years. Olivia shared it patiently, over and over, as her son translated it from the original Spanish and smoothed the words into the nine lines that Brooke committed to memory.

The Code looked simple at first glance, but the more she studied it, the more profound it appeared. Olivia reassured her that it took a lifetime to comprehend El Código. But even if she didn't fully understand all the nuances, Brooke could feel the positive energy each line held, and she recited them before each and every formal spellcasting:

> To hold the Gift is to be both a student and a teacher, ever learning and yet wise.
> To hold the Gift is to be a seeker of truth and a revealer of that which is hidden.
> To hold the Gift is to give without condition and to receive with gratitude.

*To hold the Gift is to give hope to the innocent and to uphold
the cause of the wronged.*

*To hold the Gift is to guard the helpless and to remove power
from the cruel.*

*To hold the Gift is to strengthen the just and to turn greed
upon itself.*

*To hold the Gift is to protect the balance in all things and to
restore harmony.*

*To hold the Gift is to comfort the mind and spirit, and to heal
both heart and body.*

*To hold the Gift is to be a bridge between worlds and to be a
bearer of light.*

Twelve years had passed since she'd first memorized the Code, and tonight, as always, Brooke tried to be one with the words. In the vast second story above Handcastings, she sat on the old hardwood floor with her hands open and resting on her knees as if she were meditating. Her stillness, however, was forced. Restlessness vibrated through her, and she was sorely tempted to jump up and start pacing. She'd already cleaned the entire place within an inch of its life—and then some.

Sighing, she tried to distract herself by studying the immense space around her and allowing herself to feel the satisfaction of what she had created here. Except for the paint and new upholstery, she'd left the downstairs pretty much as it was: a retro fifties diner that turned out to be both charming and practical for her unique business.

Upstairs was a different story—literally. *Talk about a total do-over.* Sure, the space was immense now, made more so by the eighteen-foot ceiling and the large skylight overhead which was situated towards the front of the building. But even the real estate agent hadn't held out much hope for its potential at first. Several walls and half walls had been added over the decades (each one uglier than the last) to divide up the long and narrow space into a warren of rooms without regard to the original design. Fortunately, Brooke hadn't needed magic in order to have vision. She could see not only how the floor had once looked but also what it could be. A lot of weekends had been devoted to demolition, until only the original layout was left.

The north half of the floor had been intended for open storage, spanned and supported by enormous beams in the ceiling and between the floors. The south half had been walled off as office space, but only eight feet up. Above the beautiful oak crown molding, the spacious rooms were wide open to the high ceiling above, where a pair of vintage fans turned lazily under ornate tin tiles. Brooke loved this glorious openness and happily converted the area to living quarters. Her feline roommates, Bouncer, Rory, and Jade, appeared to like the new digs too, but she wasn't fooled. Their favorite part was being able to walk around the tops of the walls like the superior beings they believed themselves to be. Rory (of course it was Rory) even attempted to use Brooke as a trampoline while she was still sound asleep in her bed one morning, leaping from the top of the wall to land squarely on her middle. Her resulting yell had echoed through the second-floor space, and the small black cat had run for his life. Brooke didn't know where he had hidden, but it was hours before he finally reappeared. Thankfully for both of them, he hadn't tried that particular method of ambush again.

If her living quarters were ideal, then the area outside them was absolutely *inspired* for magical purposes. The element of air was present by virtue of the wide-open space alone. The east and west walls were rustic exposed brick, framing all with the element of earth. Two of the tall narrow windows still possessed their original stained-glass borders, as did the enormous skylight over-head. It was not in the exact center of the roof, but rather centered over the open area where she drew her circles. Abundant light flooded the area in the daytime, interspersed with a dappling of colors that radiated both whimsy and pure pleasure. At night, the moon and stars often gleamed through the glass. By drawing the front blinds, Brooke even had complete privacy to work sky clad—it was traditional to work naked whenever possible—while still able to actually see the sky high above. A witch could not have asked for a more ideal setting in which to practice her craft.

Today, however, none of it seemed to be helping Brooke one bit.

Earlier she'd drawn a circle with pure sea salt and dried laven-der blossoms on the aged hardwood floor. Beyond it, east of the sacred circle, her round altar table held flickering amethyst-colored candles with runes inscribed upon them. She'd set the stage, pre-pared herself spiritually, and finally removed her clothing in order not to impede the energy in any way. But the magic simply refused to come at her call no matter how much she entreated it. How on earth was she going to help Rina Carter relax and enjoy her preg-nancy, if she couldn't even conjure a simple spell of peace and well-being? By now, she should be able to do it standing on her head. What was she doing wrong? Obviously, she wasn't focusing hard enough, or maybe . . .

Brooke pinched her wrist and dumped that line of thinking at once, knowing the danger of negative self-messages. Maybe it came with being an oldest child and therefore a perfectionist, but she had a tendency to be her own worst enemy. She still couldn't resist trying the spell again—and again, and again.

She finally was just too tired to continue trying, and her head was starting to hurt. Brooke brushed aside a few inches of the salt and left the circle. Wrapping a turquoise silk kimono around her-self, she plunked down on the thick cushion beside her altar. The low, round table had been used as a kid's play center before she rescued it from a yard sale. Its lines and the oddly shaped legs had intrigued her despite the ghastly yellow and blue stripes that then covered it in thick wrinkled gobs. Few would have guessed that under all those layers of paint was a solid cherrywood antique supported by four lion-footed griffins. Brooke worked on it an inch at a time for *weeks* until the table was beautiful again, and whenever she placed her hand on the smooth waxed surface—even now—she felt centered and grounded.

Many witches preferred to work with oak—and she certainly had lots of it around her in the thick planks of the old hardwood floors—but cherrywood was considered an aid in focusing attention. Goddess knew, she certainly needed all she could get of that. Brooke's wand was cherry as well—another testament that there were no coincidences. She was meant to have the wand, she was meant to have this table, and she was meant to have this incredible space. All of the tools of her craft had come to her in similar fashion.

Why weren't they helping her now?

The only thing she hadn't tried was adding sex to her spells. Arousal created energy, and that natural energy could be used to power magic. Idly, her finger circled her breast through the silk of the kimono as she considered it. Her nipple tightened readily, pressing against the exotic fabric and eliciting an answering quiver from the hidden vee of her legs. A partner definitely wasn't necessary—if she wished, she could bring herself to orgasm, a damn fine one too. But as far as the spell was concerned, the energy produced would be modest at best.

Combining sex with magic was always more successful with a partner, and more powerful with some partners than others. Of course, the very best magical energy was created with a partner to whom she had a strong connection—but Brooke hadn't had one of those in over two years. Lately, she'd second-guessed herself, looking back over her past relationships with men and wondering whether she even knew what a *strong connection* was. And self-service was leaving her dissatisfied on many levels. Most of all, it seemed to underscore her present aloneness, and that just plain annoyed her. Thinking about it was *already* spoiling her carefully nurtured calm.

She smoothed the velvet altar cloth with her fingertips as she thought. Between a clay bowl of pure sea salt and an offering of fresh-cut sunflowers in an earthen vase, rested nine highly polished stones that reflected the candlelight. Once Brooke had completed the spell, she would draw its power into the stones and tie them in a small silk bag containing sprigs of fresh herbs she'd grown herself in her rooftop garden. This is what she typically presented to her customers, and what Rina was waiting for.

If only I can manage to finish the damn thing. Naturally she needed the money too—after all, witches had bills just like everyone else, especially witches who had a mortgage—but she cared about her clients first and wanted Rina to have the beneficial energy as quickly as possible in her condition. Brooke glanced over at a shelf on the wall, where several little bags sat, each with a collection of carefully chosen stones and a label as to who and what it was for. All waiting, all unfinished.

And all apparently because of something weird in her card readings. That was the real problem here, wasn't it? Ever since she'd begun receiving the strange tarot messages, she'd been unable to conjure a damn thing reliably. She'd uttered a few simple words over her coffee to reheat it yesterday, and the cup had shattered in her hand and left her with three cuts to her palm. Luckily—if such a thing could be said to be lucky—it was her left hand. She wasn't sure what effect multiple Band-Aids might have had on her wand hand.

"What the hell am I going to do?" she wondered aloud. Bouncer meowed under the door from the kitchen as if in answer, but he was likely just suggesting that she feed him again.

She'd been too upset to read the tarot again, ever since she revealed her situation to George. But maybe ignoring it had been a mistake. After all, she'd left off at nine, a number of great power, as her friend had been quick to point out. One of two things would happen if she read the cards again—if she got an identical reading, it would be the tenth in a row, and ten was a less potent number. Spookier than ever, of course, but not as powerful from a numerology standpoint. Or she would get a different reading altogether that would break the pattern. Either way, it just might be worth doing . . .

"No," she said aloud and smacked her palm hard on the little tabletop. The sound reverberated from the high ceiling and tall walls as if she'd struck a drum. "If the Universe has gone to all the trouble to bring me this same message again and again, then I need to figure out what it's saying to me."

Easier said than done, however—even though it was just four little cards and not the whole deck. Why couldn't she seem to figure out her own damn reading?

Duh. Because it *was* her own reading. And she was so emotionally tangled up in it that she was practically paralyzed. Maybe what she really needed to do was take herself out of the equation altogether. Pretend that the cards were not for her but for a client.

"Okay, what if a customer drew these cards in an ordinary everyday reading?" she asked herself. Technically, the cards worked much better if the client had a specific question in mind, but a general reading was possible without one.

Brooke took a deep breath, closed her eyes, and tried to picture herself in the corner booth of her shop, talking to someone over a cup of chamomile tea—maybe Mrs. McCardie? *That might work.* At eighty-seven years old, Florence McCardie did two things every Friday morning. She went to the hairdresser's to have her fluffy white hair styled, and then she visited the Handcastings shop for her weekly reading. Riding along in her giant striped handbag was her ancient black and white Chihuahua, Mr. Socks. Although Brooke usually did a complete spread for her client, she had no trouble imagining just four cards on the table in front of them.

"Card number one is the Fool," she would say to Flo—she didn't like to be called *Mrs. McCardie* by her friends, and she considered Brooke a friend. Not wanting to insult her, Brooke would be quick to add that a much more positive name for the card would be the Innocent. "The Fool depicts a traveler at the beginning of a long journey, signifying all sorts of potential and possibilities." Many times, the appearance of the Fool meant a new love, one that was out of the ordinary. Wouldn't *that* win a chuckle from Flo?

Always a very positive card, the Fool still came with a caution. A little white dog in the corner was forever tugging on the traveler's pant leg, pulling him back from a cliff. *Protecting him from himself. See, George? Dogs are a good thing.* Mr. Socks would surely back her up on that.

In her mind, Brooke turned her attention to the next card: the Moon. For a witch, it meant that very powerful magic was involved in some way. But for Flo? "Some people read this card as hidden things needing to rise to the surface, unknown enemies or old hurts that must be dealt with. But for most of us, plain old *fear of change* is usually the real problem."

The third card was the Ten of Pentacles. Technically, George had been right—they really were stars. But each star had a circle around it, and that made it a pentacle, a symbol of life itself. "This is a very, very positive card, Flo. Great gifts are coming your way. It's a card of tremendous transformation, positive and joyful change, but only if you're willing to take an equally large risk."

All could turn out well, though, Brooke thought, because of the dogs that were always pictured on this card. "In the tarot, dogs guard and protect us. Sometimes they enhance communication between people or act as a liaison between one world and another. But mostly, they watch over their people." Brooke still had her eyes closed, but she couldn't help but smile as she imagined Mr. Socks agreeing with her. The old Chihuahua had only three teeth left, but he would no doubt use them if anyone ever messed with his owner.

That left one last card to deal with. "Don't let the Death card scare you, Flo. It only means physical death in bad movie scripts. What it really stands for is *change*." Like George had pointed out, death was the biggest change there was. "Huge changes are coming, changes you can't avoid. They're not to be feared, however, just accepted." Despite its name, Death was not a negative card at all.

There was the dog issue, though. *What the hell is Death doing with a dog?* While the Fool, the Moon, and the Ten of Pentacles were supposed to have dogs in them, she had never seen a deck that depicted a dog as a companion of Death. And now she seemed to be seeing them everywhere. "It can only be a good thing," she said to her imaginary client. "Dogs are our friends." If all four of his legs worked, Mr. Socks would undoubtedly be on the table and licking her face by now, the canine equivalent of a standing ovation.

"So, to sum it all up"—she counted off on her fingers—"major changes are coming, transformational changes. They'll bring good things. They might bring love or wealth, or maybe you're going on an unexpected trip. You need some courage to take a risk and be open to dealing with some past issues once and for all. And as for the presence of so many dogs in the reading, we'll just consider it a lovely bonus."

Brooke opened her eyes and found herself feeling much better. Relieved, even. *See, if I'd just spent the time to sort out the reading instead of getting so stressed out about it . . .*

Ferocious barking outside startled her and she jumped up, wrapping the kimono around her more tightly. Within her darkened living quarters, Brooke could hear Jade growling, low and fierce, like the alley cat she pretended to be, even though she'd never had to live outdoors a day in her pampered life. Not one of the three cats had ever encountered a dog outside of the waiting room of her friend Morgan's animal clinic. *Instinct?* "Misplaced instinct," Brooke muttered aloud as she peered around the window blind. A couple of teens in baggy pants were walking their dogs. Or *shuffling* their dogs—she couldn't figure out how the guys actually managed to walk with their oversized jeans so low. One dog was barking at a bicyclist, although his owner kept trying to tug him along and shush him. Within a few moments, shufflers, dogs, and bicyclist were out of sight and out of her hearing.

"Well, that was pretty damn timely," she said. Did the barking of a dog signify anything? Of course it did. Most people would chalk it up to coincidence. But no witch worth her salt believed in coincidences, according to George's mom, Olivia. *There are no random events in the Universe,* m'ija.

Maybe it was a confirmation that she'd gotten the reading right? She fervently hoped so.

As Brooke tucked the blind back in place, she suddenly remembered the story G had told her, about his grandmother summoning El Guardia (and that *still* sounded like some kind of cheesy superhero name). And now Brooke was not only seeing dogs all over the tarot cards but hearing them outside her shop. A sign? She didn't feel like she needed protection, but George had said that the spectral creature was particularly helpful when spells were difficult. *Boy, that certainly applies.* All of Brooke's carefully constructed conjurings, even the simplest ones, had gone from difficult to downright impossible to perform. It was as if she were being blocked in some way. If El Guardia could facilitate castings, like her friend had said, maybe she needed to call on him for a helping paw.

The big question was, *how?*

Spells were not like recipes. Every witch kept a grimoire, but the spells they recorded inside that book were so personal that they were unlikely to work for anyone else. Whatever George's grandmother had done to call a spirit dog didn't matter. *Intent* was the key to magic, plus whatever would help Brooke focus her intention.

She rose and retrieved a broom from the corner—not her ceremonial besom that brushed away negative energies, but a practical red plastic broom with yellow bristles from the local hardware store. With short efficient strokes, she swept up the salt grains and lavender blossoms that had formed the circle. If she was going to try to summon a spirit dog, it was best to start from scratch. *No pun intended.*

She paused and looked again at the bright flowers on the altar. She had cut them fresh from her rooftop garden at sunset, just as she had done with the herbs. The vivid yellow blossoms were a humble but beautiful offering to the divine that existed in all things and a way of attracting the earth's blessings. *What on earth—literally—do you offer to a spirit dog? How exactly does one attract the goodwill of a supernatural canine?*

The answer popped into her head immediately. *As above, so below.* It was a basic principle of all magic. Maybe Brooke could offer the creature what a physical dog would like. Biscuits, bones, and toys seemed a little silly for such a frightening beast, but it was the symbolism that counted, wasn't it? Besides, maybe she could hedge her bets with some frozen burgers or whatever other meats she could find.

Thank the goddess that Mel's Gas and Grocery is open twenty-four hours a day.

SIX

~⟍⟋~

Time moved forward, folded in on itself and skipped backwards, then wandered off in an indecipherable direction. Aidan had never gotten used to the apparent randomness of the passage of time in the faery realm. A mortal's mind was obviously designed to see time as a simple line with regular intervals. Had there been clocks here, they would have been mad things, wild creations that treated eras and epochs the same as minutes and hours. To the fae, centuries and seconds, past and present, felt exactly the same. To a human being, it was all an indecipherable mess.

If Aidan had not continued the work of a grim, and thereby continued to visit the mortal world regularly, he would not have known how much time had passed before he decided to act on his proposal to the Lord of the Hunt: *forty-two days, eleven hours, nineteen minutes.*

Aidan attended twenty-seven more humans who were marked to depart the mortal realm. None reacted as Maeve Lowri Jones had. In fact, four didn't even see him—although the young blonde waitress serving the last targeted man did. Aidan watched as her face paled, and her hands shook until she'd spilled coffee all over. She ran off on the premise of getting a rag but didn't return. The man, Robert Michael Bell, didn't seem to notice her any more than he'd noticed the big black dog staring at him. Dressed in a suit and tie, Robert's attention was buried in the financial section of the *Telegraph*. Aidan sat on the chair across from him, looming large over the table so his nose could have touched the newspaper. He could read it had he cared to. Still the man failed to notice him at all. A new waitress began mopping up coffee from the table, her cloth passing close enough to brush Aidan's fur if he had been in solid form, but she neither saw nor sensed him.

Tomorrow, thought Aidan. *Tomorrow morning Robert Bell will go to his place of business, and he will never go home again.* Perhaps the man was better off not knowing that. Maybe that was why he couldn't see the grim there to alert him. Maybe only the people who could benefit from a little forewarning saw the great black dog.

Or maybe the whole idea was a relic of the past. *I'm the one who's a relic of the past, in more ways than one . . .* Lurien had unspelled the silver torc around Aidan's neck. Other than being free from its compulsion, Aidan hadn't anticipated any further effects. But memories had started to surface—people, events, and places. And instead of dissipating like the morning dew on the grass upon his return to the faery realm, the memories remained.

Robert Bell picked up a different section of his newspaper and Aidan found himself looking at a small photo of a dark-haired woman with light-colored eyes . . .

And suddenly he recalled the memory he had been missing, the key to his constant unending pain, the real reason for his constantly burning anger and his vow to see Celynnen dead by his own hand.

He remembered Annwyl. The image burst into his brain, vivid and bright, unmarred by the passage of centuries or the machinations of magic: the very first time he'd met his beloved. She had accompanied her father, Deykin the Magistrate, to

Aidan's blacksmith shop from nearby Aberhonddu. It was unusual for a man of such social standing to come to a smithy in person, despite the fact that blacksmiths were generally esteemed members of the community. Aidan had been quick to show the man his very best work. While Deykin appreciated his craftsmanship, Aidan appreciated Annwyl. The name meant "beloved," and truly she was the favorite of her father. It soon became apparent that Deykin was accompanying *her*, not the other way around. Her mother had recently passed after a lingering fever, and Annwyl was overseeing the large household alone. With her practical guidance, Deykin purchased a number of pots and utensils, a pair of kitchen cauldrons, several lengths of chain, and a wide variety of tools and other household items.

Her sea-green eyes had lingered on a clever six-sided needle case. It formed an artful pendant that Aidan had fashioned himself, one of a handful of small pieces he had created in silver. The costly metal was normally beyond his reach, but he had gleaned and hoarded small leftovers from the ornamenting of commissioned swords. He had furbished the needle case with polished amber beads he had painstakingly traded for, all in hopes of winning a high price from a wealthy client one day. But Aidan's mind was changed by Annwyl's single wistful glance. He noticed that she did not bring the pretty item to the attention of her father but focused instead on the task at hand, the refurbishing of a household largely ignored during her mother's slow decline.

Aidan could see that the responsibility weighed heavily on Annwyl's slim shoulders, and that she was determined to carry the burden well. He admired her for that even more than he admired her beauty. And she *was* beautiful. Her hair was as black and glossy as a starling's wing, yet her skin was fair in keeping with those green eyes. She didn't look at Aidan directly, but occasionally he would catch her sidelong gaze and the barest hint of a smile.

When the price was set and their business concluded, Annwyl went outside to look over some gray geese being herded by a small boy. Aidan approached Deykin with the silver needle case in his hand. "Your daughter takes her duties seriously, and she has but recently lost her mother. I would not presume to give her a gift without your permission, but it is my hope to bring a small bit of happiness to her if you will allow it."

Deykin nodded. "Annwyl is the measure of her mother, and we could not have hoped for a more devoted daughter. Of course you may give it to her." He had chuckled then. "Although it is a clever and comely piece, I've a feeling the giver might well please Annwyl more than the gift."

Aidan came to himself with a start. He was still in the restaurant, still seated at Robert Bell's table, although the man himself had long since paid for his expensive meal and left. It was past time for Aidan to go too. No one saw the great black dog glide down the aisle between the tables and booths, then pass through the front door without having to open it.

The quarter moon was high in the human world as Aidan dissolved into dust and allowed the wind to return him to the faery realm. There, the moon was round and full, only just beginning its journey into a sky filled with thousands of stars. Aidan still had no idea how such a thing was possible. Was he looking at the very same moon in a different time, or a strange and different moon in an unknown sky? The kingdom of the Tylwyth Teg was filled with questions unanswerable to mortals. Did the Fair Ones themselves still know the answers?

It didn't matter now. Aidan finally had the answers *he* had needed for centuries, the memory of Annwyl and all that they had shared. The many recollections filled his heart and head to bursting, tumbling over one another as if each was vying for his attention. But there was another memory too, so clear and sharp it cut

him to think of it—*he remembered exactly how he had lost her.*
Grief and rage roiled in his gut as he recalled Celynnen's callous,
unspeakable act.

Annwyl was dead, forever beyond his reach.

He could not remain in this kingdom one moment more. With
the fury that filled him, he would no longer be able to stop himself
from attacking his keepers, and as yet, he had no weapons that
could aid him. Despite his size and power as a grim, he would be
brought down effortlessly, snarling and snapping like a rabid dog,
with a single spoken word of magic. If he was ever to have his
revenge upon Celynnen, his first step must be to escape. According
to the plans he had laid, he headed for the stone kennels, the habit
of a thousand years, but at the last moment he deliberately veered
from the luminous path. Lurien no doubt anticipated that the grim
would attempt his escape from the human world above—gods
knew, it would be easier. Aidan was hoping, however, to lay a false
trail by returning to the enchanted land beneath the Black Mountains of Wales and making his exodus from there.

The timing would be a surprise as well. The Lord of the Wild
Hunt would expect the grim to take his advice and leave near
dawn. He'd even made a point to specify *mortal* dawn, for there
might be several dawns or none in the fae realm between now and
then. There was nothing really wrong with Lurien's counsel—
except that the dark fae would be watching for Aidan to make a
move at that time. There was a slim chance, however, that with
other duties to attend to, Lurien might not be on his guard with
the mortal night still new.

With his back to the kennels, Aidan headed for the royal gardens—another move that would be unexpected. No grim came here,
no dark creature cast a shadow here, whether it was a true member
of the kingdom or not. His great black paws were silent as he padded
by the innumerable flowers of sizes and colors not found in the world

above. Fountains that had been carved from clear crystal glittered in the moonlight, graced by hundreds of sculptures of heart-stopping beauty. One gave him pause, however—it was the only artwork he had ever seen here that included a *human*. Cast in simple bronze, a mortal woman sat beside a faery. Their heads were bent close together and they were laughing over a book. A pair of stocky pug dogs with tightly curled tails—a favored breed of the royal house that was frequently traded for from the mortal world—romped at their feet with a ball. Aidan crept closer. The exquisite face of the faery revealed her to be a young Queen Gwenhidw. He had seen her only a handful of times since he'd been brought here, and always at a distance, but Gwenhidw's face was unforgettable. Even her grandniece, Celynnen, could not match her great-aunt's goddesslike splendor. The mortal woman could only be the queen's beloved friend, the legendary Aylwen. Their friendship had been extraordinary—marked by something that few, if any, humans had ever enjoyed: Aylwen had had the right to come and go from the faery realm *as she pleased*. It seemed to Aidan that granting such freedom only proved that the queen truly had the capacity not only to love but *to love deeply*, a rare thing among the Fair Ones. More so, it was said that Gwenhidw and her husband had also enjoyed the closest of bonds, inseparable in all things—until the king had been betrayed and murdered, and the Nine Realms of the kingdom thrust into disarray.

This simple statuary represented a more innocent time. And although Gwenhidw possessed unearthly beauty, it was the face of her human companion that commanded Aidan's attention. He also had known a more innocent time, and as he stared, he saw not the queen's dearest friend, but his own beloved Annwyl. She had sometimes worn her hair in a similar fashion, long braids circled into a clever crown.

It had been a challenge for Aidan to unwind those fine braids with his big, work-roughened hands—he had had far less trouble undoing the layers of her dress—but it was worth the time and trouble to free her shining black hair. Soft and sweet-smelling, her hair tumbled over her naked shoulders and past her rounded hips. He delighted in parting the thick wavy curtains of her hair to uncover first one pert nipple, then the other. They were as inviting to the taste as dark strawberries, and the soft weight of her breasts in his hands was as heady as the strongest ale.

They had lain together for the first time after their betrothal, reaching for each other eagerly in the warm golden straw of a summer field. His strong fingers made gentle by love, Aidan could still feel the smoothness of her skin, feel Annwyl's curves as he glided a hand over her from shoulder to thigh. Could still feel the air leave his lungs at the first welcome press of her skin to his, feel the racing of his heart as her soft body conformed to his hard, muscled frame. Could still see the inviting cradle of her hips and the glistening vee between her legs just before—

Aidan blinked as though awakening from a dream. Love and loss mingled to create a bitter taste on his tongue. His newly regained memories both delighted his heart and brutally stabbed it to the core, and he would have to be more careful in the future about allowing the past free reign. It was a distraction he could not afford. A glance at the sky—if the fae moon could be trusted—showed that he had lingered much longer than he'd intended.

Other senses told him he had been wrong about Lurien. Perhaps fatally so.

Aidan's canine nostrils picked up the oddly metallic scent of ozone on the breeze at the same time that a faint vibration in the ground made his feet tingle and his gut clench—despite the fact that he didn't exist in a purely physical state, *danger* felt the same to every creature, fae or mortal. Aidan, who was neither hot nor cold, felt a chill along his spine as he turned and saw black clouds roiling on the far horizon of the faery realm. The Wild Hunt had been loosed—*and the hunters had not ridden to the mortal world above.*

If there had ever been a time when the Hunt tore up the emerald sod and trampled the exquisite blooms of the immortal realm, Aidan hadn't heard of it. A prisoner of a thousand years, he had never once witnessed lightning in fae skies, nor heard the thunder of deadly hooves and the baying of faery hounds.

It's me they're looking for. Had an alarm been raised automatically when he didn't return to the kennels after a certain length of time, or had Lurien kept someone watching him all along? The answer no longer mattered. Aidan began to lope through the otherworldly landscape with renewed determination, faster and faster, until he was but a blur. He finally had a chance to leave this place, to find a way to fulfill his vow to bring down Celynnen. But only if he could outrun the Hunt.

The moon still hid behind black storm clouds. He hoped it was a sign that only hours and not days had passed—although night and day followed no mortal clock here. Aidan didn't know what whim caused the sun to rise when the stars were still out, or whose will caused a day to pass in an instant, like a flower that bloomed only for moments before dying. All he knew was that the Hunt was still following him despite his use of every fox's trick he remembered from his mortal life. Constantly changing direction bought him time yet cost him almost as much—it was taking far too long to reach his planned destination. Dissolving into dust and allowing his particles to be spirited along by the breeze was effective—the hounds and the horses couldn't seem to find him very easily in that state—yet it was an agonizingly slow way to travel.

Forever had surely passed before Aidan finally found his way to the Silver Maples. Ten thousand trees strong, the mighty grove had been planted a hundred centuries ago. Their silver and sage leaves fluttered on the great overarching branches like butterflies and massed so thickly that no sun ever reached the ground far below. Scores of dark paths wound through the enormous trees, made by strange fae creatures that could not abide light. Even the soft rays of the moon were too much for the residents of the Maples. But that didn't mean they were weak and helpless. There were no visitors to this place, no travelers passing through. *Only prey.*

Even the Tylwyth Teg, with all their magics, avoided this place as much as possible. And that made it perfect for a fugitive like Aidan. He remained formless, floating slowly over the ground, following first this narrow path and then that one, until the edge of the forest had closed behind him in a solid wall that locked out all the light. Only then did he dare to solidify, his great paws striking the soft earth in a dead run.

A grim could perceive things beyond the physical, a necessity in order to perform his melancholy tasks. Those abilities helped him now. His ghostly, glowing eyes required no light to see varying shades and shadows within the blackness. Some didn't move. Many did. As he ran, he was often aware of eyes watching him pass. A few he could see, and others he could only feel the intensity of their assessing gaze, but all turned away. As a grim, he was big enough that most of the hidden creatures of the Maples wouldn't bother him. Many of those that could consider it would be repelled as soon as they sensed the bright silver of his collar.

If his only goal was to disappear, this was the ideal place to do it. But Aidan had a bigger goal. With an innate sense of direction that didn't need sun or stars to steer by, he headed for the Gray Gate that lay beyond the forest. Older than the trees and ornately carved into a stone hillside, the Gray Gate was like all of the kingdom's gates—it wasn't a door at all but a *way*, connecting far-flung destinations as if they were merely in an adjoining room. Most of the existing ways were much smaller, and they assisted Aidan in his morbid work by allowing him to pass to various places in the mortal realm directly above. But all those deaths over the centuries had taken place in his tiny homeland of Cymru—Wales. The Gray Gate was one of the greater ways, leading to faraway places he'd only heard of.

Like across the Deep Waters.

The darkness that surrounded him slowly began to loosen its black grip. Ahead, he could see the tiny pinpricks of deep gray that revealed themselves as faint gaps in the trees, allowing a scant modicum of the moon's light to penetrate. He could almost see the edge of the forest when a pack of *warths* swarmed out of the under-brush behind him.

The striped creatures were twice as tall as he was, lithe and strong like wolves—if wolves had scales. They yowled and popped their long-toothed jaws in a staccato hunting cry, anxious for a taste of blue blood. As big as a grim was, there wouldn't be more than a bite for each, but the warths didn't care. Like most fae-constructed creatures, Aidan would feel little pain. But he would be very, very dead just the same, and he could not fulfill his vow from beyond the grave.

He ran, a great black shadow amongst shadows, his claws digging into the forest floor, where thousands of seasons of silvery leaves had fallen. It was difficult to get much traction in the soft, slippery mulch, but the warths were equally disadvantaged. They relied on ambush more than the chase—but they weren't giving up. Snapping teeth managed to yank the fur from the end of his tail. A faster warth slashed him from hip to hock with its fangs, and only Aidan's quick dive between the roots of a tree and out the other side interrupted that attack.

He could see the edge of the forest now. The massive trees were smaller here, younger than the giants whose canopies blocked out the sky, and farther apart. The moon's rays struck the ground here, creating pale stepping-stones of dappled light, and Aidan deliberately steered into them. Three warths followed him closely, far too intent on bringing him down to notice their danger. They yelped as the seemingly innocent glow fell upon their scales and burned them badly.

The moon was the enemy of all who made the Silver Maples their home. With howls of disappointment and rage, the warths fell back.

Still running hard, Aidan broke free of the trees and headed for the mountainside beyond. A grim's heart did not beat, but he was laying a trail of blue blood just the same. But then, if the Hunt followed him very far into the forest, they'd guess where he was going anyway.

As he approached, the massive Gate loomed larger than ever, taller than the tallest maple, and far more imposing. The stone was covered with deep-cut carvings of animals and birds, fish and flowers, in a style that borrowed from the ancient and talented Celts, and surpassed them easily. In fact, most of the mountainside surrounding the gate had been similarly carved, with panoramic scenes fading into the distance on either side.

Aidan paused, partly in awe at the scale and scope of the creation, and mostly because he couldn't believe he was actually going to leave his country. He didn't have much left to identify with after a thousand years, but the land—the land was part of him and he was part of it. Wasn't he? One side of him wondered how he could go, but the more sensible side asserted that he had already left long, long ago. He wasn't in Wales—he was *under* it, enslaved to thoughtless masters. When he did walk above, it was in a land much changed from what he knew, and he was doing it on four feet. Not only that, he was forever the silent bearer of the worst of news to anyone who actually saw him. Cut off from the land of the living, removed from his natural form and feelings, isolated from his own kind, and looked down upon by most of the Fair Ones—of what use was it to stay in "his" country?

Especially when the Lord of the Wild Hunt might not expect him to leave it . . .

Aidan snorted. He'd been completely wrong in his estimation of Lurien so far—how mad was it to gamble everything on another guess? Yet, mad or not, traveling to the ends of the earth for the slimmest of chances was far better than lingering in his homeland, where he was certain to be ridden down sooner rather than later. There was no place he could hide and no hope at all here . . .

At least not now, he thought, as the stone gate towered over him.

A grim didn't need to breathe to exist but instead used the action to control his form. Aidan breathed out and out and out, dissipating from solid to shadow. He passed between the great monolithic gate as easily and soundlessly as he had passed through Maeve's front door. And he found himself in a world he had not imagined.

The ocean had many moods, from calm glassy waters that mirrored the many colors of the sky to raging dark waves that foamed like mad horses champing brutal bits. The Gray Gate had deposited him far from the sight of land. Formless, Aidan drifted with the winds just above the water for a while. He didn't want it to be too apparent to any pursuers which direction he was headed—and besides, he didn't know himself where he was going. He could sense his homeland like a fading beacon in the distance, but it was difficult to plot a course from it. For the first time ever he wished he were a sailor and not a blacksmith. The winds from the north and east were sure to be very cold, the ones from the west and south to be warm, but he couldn't feel them, not physically. Nor could he feel the salt spray that occasionally leapt up as if to snatch his scattered particles from the air. It seemed wrong to be so free and yet so detached from the natural world all around him. His human body would have been very uncomfortable, even endangered by the situation, yet Aidan couldn't help but wish he could feel *something*.

And then he did feel something: the faintest pulse of unease, a prickle not on the skin but in the mind. As a fae creation, a grim possessed instincts that humans had never known, powerful primal connections to the earth's many energies—and ripples in those energies. Although Wales was at least a thousand miles behind him, Aidan knew the very instant that the Wild Hunt picked up his trail through the Silver Maples.

What now? In his present formlessness, Aidan couldn't move very quickly. It was difficult to propel a loose association of particles, especially if the prevailing wind was against him. Resuming his shape wasn't an option, however. If he did, he could slice through the air, using it to attain real speed—but the moment he solidified, the Hunt would detect him even through the distance that separated them. Aidan's preternatural senses told him that Lurien's wild band was still tracking him over the cold seas that lapped at Wales on three sides, the Hunt's hounds and horses casting back and forth in the gusts of salt air for his barely discernible trail. Aidan was glad now that he'd thought to allow the winds to take him in many directions at first—too bad it wouldn't slow his pursuers for long.

He spiraled upwards, straining to reach the upper levels of the sky that would permit him to see farther than even his fae abilities would allow. Here, the moon shone like a great frozen pearl. It was from that rarefied atmosphere that Aidan discerned the dark line of thunderheads on the northeastern horizon, blacker than the night sky. Vortices spun off the malignant clouds and stabbed at the surface of the ocean as ghostly waterspouts, illuminated by flashes of ill-colored lightning. The storm was unnatural, of course, created by the powerful and discordant energies of the Hunt.

At first, Aidan sought to rise even higher. He needed a steady wind to bear him away, but he found none that would help him. It seemed the greater the height, the more the winds bore east, and *only* east—if he lingered at this elevation, miles above the waves, his insubstantial self would be carried towards the Wild Hunt and certain death.

There was nothing to do but curse as he allowed himself to glide down to the restless ocean once more and then struggled to bear south and west on his own. Finally, he caught a breeze that would carry him along, but it was weak and his progress was slow. At this rate, Lurien would be able to overtake him with little effort, and mortal dawn was not close enough to aid him. He needed to do the unexpected one last time, *create one more surprise*, or all was lost.

Aidan murmured an ancient prayer he'd once learned from a fisherman. It was not a plea, for the gods who ruled in the depths of the sea had no pity, nor was it a promise, for they could not be bribed. Rather, it was a simple acknowledgment of their power and dominion. They would help him or kill him as they pleased. He passed seamlessly from the turbulent night air into the depths of the restless water itself, a tiny shadow merging with a great pool of darkness.

SEVEN

~⚡~

From his rocky hiding place far below the tossing waves, Aidan watched the Wild Hunt approach, riding upon the salt-sprayed air as if on solid ground. Thunder and lightning exploded overhead from the ugly, roiling clouds of the unnatural storm the Hunt had created. The hounds were ahead, of course, great red-eyed beasts, some white, some black, some mere shadows, and others with foaming jaws. They cast back and forth, ahead and behind, seeking a scent or perhaps the essence of Aidan's soul. The riders had slowed their pace, their impatient mounts stamping their feet and frothing at the mouth as they fought their cruelly barbed bits.

Like most fae creatures, he could do without breathing for very long time, but he felt sorry for any sailors who might be at sea this night. The Hunt would be invisible to them, save for the very rare human who had the gift to perceive it. All they would see is the horrendous storm, and they would wonder both at its fury and at the suddenness with which it had blown up. Would any mortals drown this night because Lurien's host rode outside the usual bounds?

From the depths, Aidan strained to see his enemies. The distance and the surging water distorted and colored his view as if he were looking through thick green glass. He knew what he expected to see, however.

When the Wild Hunt rode upon the land, they conscripted mortal horses from human pastures and stables, as fae horses were rare and few. Mortal men were swept up to ride the captive beasts—the greedy, the unjust, those who lied and cheated, those who stole and murdered, those who plotted and betrayed—however many the Hunt required were ridden down and forced to join. As a point of honor, the Tylwyth Teg would not steal. The horses would always be returned to their owners upon the next mortal morning—but many days might have passed in the faery realm. The hapless beasts would be worn and lathered, exhausted and often bleeding from the gouges of silver spurs. But they would be alive. Unlike the "borrowed" horses, the mortal men would *not* return, and their fate could only be guessed at.

That was how the Wild Hunt ran over the hills and valleys of Wales, and usually, they had no reason to leave Aidan's fair homeland. Besides, what mortal horses could gallop in the air or keep their footing upon a storm-tossed ocean? The handful of Fair Ones who drove the Hunt could compel the beasts to do so, of course, but it would take up a great deal of magic and energy. And as for the mortal men who were usually pressed into service, they could not stay astride the wild-tempered fae horses even if there had been enough of the rare creatures to go around.

Knowing all these things, Aidan had calculated that the hunters who now pursued him over the Deep Waters must be Tylwyth Teg mounted on pure-blooded fae horses—and therefore very few in number.

Instead, a veritable horde passed solemnly overhead at a funereal pace. Here and there, the occasional fiery mount struck sparks from the air as it stamped impatiently, its fae rider wearing glowing leathers and wielding a whip of light that split the air with the deafening energy of lightning and magic combined.

The small company of Fair Ones were driving a vast number of hollow-eyed horses, horses with lank manes and hides that were sunken and shriveled or bloated and split, animals that were merely stretched flesh over bone, and many that had no flesh left at all. They churned the air over the waters far, far above Aidan, with lanky puppetlike limbs that ought not to be able to move at all. The riders were even more horrifying—their faces drawn and eyeless, jaws grinning as they clutched their mounts with bony fingers.

Lurien had called the dead to ride with the Hunt.

As the ghastly procession passed slowly overhead, the storm the Hunt brought with them intensified. All light was blotted out except for the strobing blasts of lightning that struck the waters with explosive force. Had Aidan been mortal, he would have been permanently blinded, even through closed eyelids. As a fae creature, he still had to strain to see past the hammering bolts interspersed with electricity that skittered across the tossing waves in strange bright balls. The few moments between strikes held darkness so complete Aidan felt he was in the very pit of hell, not merely hidden among the rocky spires of the deep ocean floor.

Twin forks of lightning stabbed the surface high above, and a single dark horse cantered from the rear of the eerie procession, parting it like an obsidian knife. Proud of bearing, its black hooves struck sparks from the ozone-laden air, and the crackle of blue static could be seen in the crested mane that fell as a curtain to its knees, and in its high arched tail that alternately flew in the wild air like a banner or draped past its fetlocks. Any resemblance to a mortal mount, however magnificent a specimen, ended there.

The fae horse was Bayard, one of the few stallions left in the realm. Its coat was the ever-changing blue gray of the thunder clouds overhead, and its glowing eyes were the unnerving green of hail-bearing skies. Serrated tusks jutted from its lower jaws, marking it as a flesh eater, and its broad forehead boasted an upswept pair of wicked horns. As frightening as Bayard was, Aidan barely looked at the creature. His eyes were on the dark figure astride the beast's broad back. Bayard's rider used neither saddle nor bridle, and his long hair was wild to the wind. Dark hair, black like his riding leathers . . . Lurien, Lord of the Wild Hunt, was directly above Aidan's hiding place.

Though not in physical form, Aidan found himself instinctively drawing further into the crevices of the rocks. Fronds of kelp waved around him and fish darted to and fro, intent on their business. The strange shapes of large predators loomed out of the darkness from time to time, but they were no threat to a grim. In this moment, nothing on this earth or below it was as threatening as the fae leader high above seeking the black dog's trail along the ocean's surface. Even Lurien's unnatural mount cast about for a scent as if it were a wolf seeking prey. Aidan did not fear pain or death—if they found him, he would go down fighting. But all of his hopes to avenge his Annwyl would be dashed forever.

Strangely, both horse and rider radiated frustration. Had Aidan succeeded in surprising them by secreting himself beneath the waves? In the faery realm, only kelpies, nymphs, and undines frequented water, and only fresh rivers and streams. Was the salt sea the refuge he'd hoped for?

Perhaps the sea gods were in a good mood, or perhaps Gofannon, the god of blacksmiths, had struck a bargain with them. Whatever the reason, no one appeared to discern Aidan's hiding place far below the white-capped waves. If he'd needed to breathe, Aidan might have sighed in relief as the Lord of the Wild Hunt and his terrible horde passed slowly by, circling wider and wider. Suddenly, every head turned and some nameless instinct gripped Aidan's heart. *Dawn approached*—not here in this place, not yet, but far away in his homeland of Cymru. Night was slowly giving way to day in the Black Mountains of Wales.

Above, Lurien cursed in languages not uttered since the dawn of the world itself, and he cracked his light-whip high over his head. The Hunt wheeled as one and galloped at breakneck speed for the faery kingdom. The storm rolled with them, its deafening thunder nearly continuous now and the wild energy splitting the air before them. Aidan waited until they were finally beyond his supernatural sight and hearing, waited until the night sky cleared and the lowering moon returned to light up the green depths before he floated slowly upwards. He collected himself and resumed his form, breaking the surface as a massive black dog . . .

And he was immediately snared by a snaking coil of light. On the other end was Lurien, who sat calmly astride his monstrous mount, holding the whip as easily as a string around a butterfly.

"A good hunt, Aidan ap Llanfor. A very good hunt. The best I've had in time out of mind. I doubted you at first, you know, but you have proved yourself to be very worthy prey indeed." He backed his horse steadily, keeping the whip taut around the grim's throat. "It's truly a shame you did not escape. I was rather hoping you would, and then perhaps we could do this again. In tribute to your effort, however, I will give you a quick death rather than deliver you to Celynnen. She does not deserve you."

Aidan wasn't interested in conversing. He thrashed and snarled and strained against the whip, trying in vain to escape its burning coils. Then, in a fraction of a fae moment, he ceased to pull against his captor and launched his powerful body straight at Lurien. Aidan's action broke the tension in the coils of light, his momentum and size knocked the dark fae from his mount, and his long, sharp teeth seized the hand that held the whip. Lurien roared in pain yet did not let go, but he could do nothing while flailing in the salt water. The Lord of the Wild Hunt was forced to use magic to lift himself from the waves, to stand steady as if on dry land—no small feat with his whip hand trapped clear up to the elbow in the jaws of a giant grim. Muttering curses, the dark fae managed to draw his silver sword with his good hand, and he swung with all his formidable strength.

The faery-forged blade bit deep into the black body, severing it almost in two. Blue fae blood fountained all around as the grim's jaws abruptly released the savaged hand. The Lord of the Wild Hunt swiped the blood from his face with the back of his fine leather sleeve, only to roar again, this time with rage and surprise.

The grim had vanished without a trace—and Lurien had just slain his horse.

Brooke surveyed her preparations. She had used pure white chalk to draw the circle this time, sprinkled with dried dogwood blossoms. Her cherrywood altar was customarily positioned east of her spell circles; now, it stood within the circle, at its very center. (Thankfully, it was round, or she'd be bruising her shins on the corners of the small table.) Cherrywood was said to be ideal for practicing *animal* magic, but so far, her cats had been completely unimpressed—unless you counted Rory sleeping on the table occasionally. Still, it couldn't hurt to try.

Gone were the sunflowers, the amethyst candles, the bowl of salt, and the velvet covering. At Mel's Gas and Grocery, she'd discovered anew that there were no coincidences: the first thing she'd found was a vinyl sheet with dogs on it. The design was on the silly side, but the principle was solid. She was summoning a dog, and she needed anything that would magnify her intent. The canine-decorated vinyl was intended for picnic tables, but she'd reshaped and repurposed it as an altar cloth. George would tease the life out of her if he ever saw it, and even more so if he caught sight of the corny things she'd arranged on top of the cloth—a grouping of rawhide bones, a tidy pile of dog biscuits shaped like fire hydrants, an open can of the most-flavorful-looking dog food on Mel's shelves, and a selection of squeaky toys, all encircled by a bright green leash. Pictures of dogs clipped from magazines were carefully pinned to a trio of large pillar candles on the table. It might have been tempting to laugh at the entire setup—except among the candles, Brooke had placed one of her own treasures, a small stone statue of Hecate. The ancient goddess was poised, with her hand resting on the head of a large, dark hound. Hecate was the mistress of animals and patron of witchcraft and magic—and dogs, above all, were sacred to her.

Once her physical and spiritual preparations were complete, Brooke felt her focus strengthened. She pictured her intent as a narrow beam of brilliant light in her mind and held on to that sensation as she removed her kimono and tucked it neatly out of sight beneath the altar. Naked once more, Brooke paid reverence to the four directions and the five elements. She was one with her purpose, one with the earth, one with the energies that began to swirl around her. Eyes closed, placing one foot carefully in front of the other as if walking a tightrope, she circled the round altar *three times three*. The words that fell from her lips were not from any memorized spell, but instead they came naturally from her heart, from the very core of her being. Entreating El Guardia to aid her in freeing her magic, asking for the great dog's protecting presence as she worked her spells, seeking his help in serving others with the power that had chosen her . . .

There was a vibration beneath her feet. For a split second Brooke thought it was merely a manifestation of power, until the entire building began to shake. Her eyes flew open as she struggled to hold on to her focus and her intention. Her mouth fell open as well when the simple chalk circle began to glow. Without warning, it erupted into a pulsing wall of golden light from oaken floor to high tin ceiling. She looked up to see that the square skylight was neatly enclosed within the circle and that the moon was aligned directly in the middle of the square.

Then, an enormous shadow blotted out the moon just before crashing through that skylight like a dark comet. Brooke got a brief glimpse of black fur, white teeth, and glowing eyes, all framed for a split second in a glittering diamond shower of shattered glass.

There was no time to scream.

The power that preceded the creature knocked her flying from the circle with tremendous force. Brooke struck the wall of her living quarters, slid down it, and knew nothing more.

EIGHT

T he incessant pounding slowly brought Brooke out of the depths of unconsciousness. As she drifted upwards to awareness, she realized that the pounding had a voice, too.

"Goddammit, open this effin' door!" It was George and he sounded absolutely furious—no, it was anger driven by *worry*, she decided.

What did G have to be worried about? Her eyes fluttered open but wouldn't focus. It was bright, too bright. It couldn't be morning, could it? Her hearing seemed to work just fine. The door in question was across the room at the top of the stairs, the door she passed through every night after she locked up the shop below. She didn't lock this particular door—there was no key for it, and she didn't want to replace the beautiful brass hardware—and so she spelled it before she went to bed. The ornate doorknob was rattling, there was another flurry of pounding on the door, and finally there was a huge crash followed by a great deal of swearing. The solid oak held, however, and so did her spell.

"Brooke, I swear to you, I will call the effin' cops. I will call the fire department. I will call *my mother* to come down here *if you do not open up!*"

If George was threatening to bring in the big guns in the form of Olivia Santiago-Callahan, the situation must be dire. Brooke turned her head towards the frantic sounds, feeling her stomach lurch as the door slowly swam into focus. A few words came to mind, as if floating up from an abyss, and she mouthed them silently—

The door unlatched and George came hurtling through the entryway, all windmilling arms and wide eyes as he struggled to remain on his feet. Somehow his amazing balance enabled him to recover. That's when he spotted Brooke and was at her side in a heartbeat. Or maybe it was ten heartbeats, or ten minutes, or ten *whatevers*—her sense of time was totally messed up.

"*Dios mío*, look at you! Who the fuck did this to you?" George ripped off his hoodie, then his T-shirt too, and tucked them over her with surprising gentleness even as he threatened to tear off her attacker's balls with his bare hands.

Belatedly, Brooke realized she was still sky clad—which sounded pretty but still meant "bare-assed naked." "Crap," she managed, her voice dry and raspy.

"Don't try to talk. Who did this to you? Just rest, I'll get you some water. What the *fuck* happened in here?"

She sucked in a full breath, and her brain finally came fully back on line. "You can't ask me questions if you don't want me to talk, G. It was just a spell." She waved him back and tried to move. He protested but nonetheless helped her to a sitting position against the wall of her living quarters. She realized she wasn't even an arm's length from her door—and that Rory had his black paw under it almost to the shoulder, feeling around frantically as he made kittenlike mewls. Poor thing, he was probably worried about her. She reached out and patted his paw with what she hoped was reassurance but yelped as the paw instantly flipped over to hook the side of her hand with needlelike claws. "Ow!" She yanked her hand back. "You little dork, this is no time for playing!"

Growling sounds from somewhere above her meant that Jade was perched, vulturelike, on the top of the apartment wall—looking into the spell room. No, make that staring down at her owner. Brooke could almost feel the force of Jade's *you-haven't-fed-me* gaze boring into her skull. She couldn't guess where Bouncer was. His silence probably meant he was busy trying to solve the problem of how to open the fridge. Any day now she was sure he'd succeed.

"*Just* a spell? A goddamn *spell* did this to you? Did all this?" He waved at the room around them, and suddenly her eyes and brain coordinated to tell her what she was looking at. Her spacious, open workroom with its sweet calming energy was missing. Instead, the sun was pouring through a massive hole in the high ceiling and reflecting off clouds of dust motes that still hung in the air. Broken glass glittered on the floor in all directions, and a pile of twisted debris near the far wall could only be the sad remains of her once-beautiful skylight.

"What the hell were you doing, Brooke? What did you do? It looks like the goddamn apocalypse in here!"

It did indeed, and she pressed her fingertips to her mouth to stifle her gasp. "I needed some help with my magic. It wasn't working, and . . ." And she'd tried to summon El Guardia, an unknown spirit dog, to her circle. The circle that had been obliterated under a seeming ton of wreckage. She looked at the front of the enormous room, and this time she saw that most of the windowpanes were missing, as were the blinds.

"There's glass from hell all over the sidewalk, *chica*. I thought there'd been a fucking explosion." As sensible and steady as her friend usually was, he was all but wringing his hands. It made him look incredibly like his mother, despite the blue mohawk and the reptilian contact lenses. How scary had it been for him to find her in the middle of this disaster?

"You must have had heart failure, G. I'm sorry." She patted his arm and smiled up at him. "I'm glad you came."

"I still don't think you should be sitting up," he declared. "What if something's broken? What if you have internal injuries? What if you're paralyzed?"

"I can't be paralyzed, George. I can move everything—see?" She wiggled fingers and toes. "Really, it's just my head that hurts." Brooke ran her hand through her hair and hissed as she discovered a goose egg the size of, well, *a goose egg.* "Ow."

"I'll get you some ice. Some water. I could call 911—I *should* have called 911 when I first got here, but, *Dios,* all I could think of was finding you and making sure you were okay." He swiped his face on the back of his hoodie sleeve and blew out a breath. "*Fucking hell.* Don't you scare me like that again. And I still think you should get checked over. You look like you've been in a fight and I don't think you won."

"My building sure didn't win," she said as she surveyed the ruins.

"Come on, let me take you to the hospital."

Brooke shook her head—and the damn goose egg made her wish she hadn't. She snatched up George's T-shirt that he'd tucked around her and pulled it over her head (*ow, again*). As she gingerly tugged it down, she happened to look past her friend, across the room. Near the far wall, across a sea of broken glass, the entire wrought-iron framework of the once-beautiful skylight lay not only broken but also twisted and tangled by some unearthly force. A movement beneath a corner of it caught her eye, a strange glittering shape that—Holy crap, it wasn't alive, was it?

"What. The hell. Is *that*?" She pointed past George, who looked over his shoulder and immediately threw his lanky form into full battle posture in front of her.

There was a long, low moan, followed by a string of what could only be curse words, although she didn't recognize the language at all. The heap of debris moved again, and a man—a very large man—managed to draw himself to his knees, heaving up from beneath the heavy iron window frame. His head hung down, and Brooke couldn't see his face for the tangle of dark blond hair that obscured it. What she could see, however, were the hills and valleys in his skin that marked powerful musculature. Bits of glass slid slowly from his back to the floor with a crystalline plink, and she realized he was crisscrossed with a multitude of scratches and cuts.

She realized something else then too. "He's *naked!*"

"Then that's him, isn't it? That's the effin' pervert who did this to you." George drew his phone like a gunfighter pulling a Colt. He'd already punched the 9 and the 1 before Brooke managed to yank hard on his baggy jeans to get his attention. He had to grab his pants to keep them up, and he fumbled to reposition the phone so he could dial one-handed.

"G, stop! Put the phone away."

"Hell no. I'm calling it in, then I'm gonna kill him."

"I said *no!*"

"You're right, I should kill him first—"

"Just stop it, George! I don't want you to do either one."

He paused, finger poised over the final 1. "Are you kidding me, *chica?* A naked guy crashes through your ceiling, and you don't think calling the cops is a good idea? I find you lying here with no clothes on and with bruises and who knows what and *I should put the phone away?* Maybe I should just get naked too and join the goddamn party!"

"He didn't touch me, George. Not. At. All." She emphasized every word as she gripped his arm. "For crying out loud, I haven't even met the guy—hell, I didn't even know he was here! Whatever happened has to have been some kind of a magical accident. He must have gotten caught in my spell somehow."

"Wait a minute. You did this to *him*?" George put the heels of both hands to his forehead, taking a moment to absorb the implications of that. "I hope you have really good insurance, *chica*. We better call *him* an ambulance so he doesn't sue your witchy ass off! What is that, a twenty-foot drop? He should be dead."

"Eighteen. It's eighteen feet," she murmured. And yeah, the stranger should be the one needing an ambulance after a fall like that. Her attention focused on him, seeking, sensing, but the energies she felt were like nothing she'd ever encountered. One thing she was certain of: "He's not dying, and if he's injured, it's not bad. I can feel that much. Just let me go look at him."

George shook his head. "No effin' way. I'm not letting him near you. What kind of weirdo hangs around on the roof with no clothes on? I know witches have this thing about working *sky clad*." He made quotation marks in the air. "But use your head, Brooke. He has to have been spying on you."

"I *am* using my head, thank you." It might be damn sore, but it still worked.

"Really? Because he could have been watching you ever since you moved in here. Seriously, if you won't let me call the police, at least let me call an ambulance for him."

"Gimme a break, G." She snorted. "I know what you're up to. If you dial 911, *everyone* shows up, including the police and the goddamn fire department. My calling is to use my abilities to help people, right? So the Gift will protect me. Just let me do my job, okay? I'll be able to tell if he needs an ambulance, and I will *also* be able to tell if he has evil intent." Actually, she wasn't a hundred percent certain about that last bit, but she sure *hoped* she could tell.

"If it turns out he's some kind of voyeur, I absolutely prom-ise"—she crossed her heart for emphasis—"I will let you beat him into next week, *right after I do*. I swear I'll figure out a spell that'll tie his private parts into a goddamn *knot* so he won't be spying on anyone else ever again."

George narrowed his eyes, deciding whether or not to believe her.

"Besides, if I somehow did this to him, don't you think I need to figure out what the hell happened, what I did wrong?" Brooke continued. "If he leaves now, I'll never know what needs to be fixed, and goddess only knows what might happen the next time I work a spell. I mean, last week I put a hole through a solid brick wall, and now *this*? I don't know about you, G, but that's got me scared. It's like something's wrong with my magic, and that makes it dangerous."

Brooke knew her friend was bursting to argue, but she held his gaze solidly—not a small task when he had those damn lizard contacts in. With their elliptical pupils, it was uncomfortably like trying to stare down a velociraptor, and a stubborn one. Finally, George shrugged an assent, although she could tell he was far from convinced. For one thing, he was muttering under his breath in solid Spanish, a rarity for him. True, he was fluent in Spanish and sprinkled it liberally throughout his everyday English, thanks to his mom's influence, but he'd been born in the same city Brooke had—Spokane, Washington—and his boxer-turned-schoolteacher dad had been more Irish than anything else.

Rarity or not, she didn't have to be fluent in Spanish to know exactly what George was saying: she was crazy, and so was *he* for listening to her. But like the true friend he was, he nodded a reluc-tant agreement and held out his hand to pull her up.

Brooke was far steadier on her feet than she'd expected, although her head throbbed. For once she was glad that G wore his shirts almost as baggy as his pants. His black-on-black skull-patterned T fell to midthigh on her. She tied the sleeves of his red hoodie around her waist for good measure and was about to step forward when George seized her arm in an iron grip.

"*Duh*—glass."

She looked down at her bare toes and rolled her eyes. So much for trying to convince her friend she was fine. "Right. Okay, you stand right here and make sure the guy doesn't go anywhere. I'll get some shoes on." *And don't you dare call the cops*, she added silently. *Not yet, anyway*. Not until she figured out what the hell was going on around here. Brooke slipped into her apartment and was immediately accosted by her three cats. Murmuring an apology for the rush, she ripped the top off a new box of Little Whiskers and dumped the entire thing on the floor to distract them. It bought her enough time to glance around her living quarters and determine that glass hadn't ricocheted in from the catastrophe on the other side of the walls. A loud crash made her wonder if even *more* of the ceiling was coming down out there. The cats didn't even flinch, however, being much too involved with chowing down on the tasty kibble. Thankfully, their focus allowed Brooke to pull on a pair of jeans, get her shoes on the right feet, and get back out the door again without feline help. Most important, their focus kept any of the furry trio from escaping into the mess and hurting themselves.

As she closed the door behind her, she realized George had been right: it *did* look like ground zero of the apocalypse in here. Part of her wondered how she was ever going to get this disaster cleaned up. The other part was worried that if she didn't get some answers about what the hell was happening to her magic, she wouldn't be able to stop it from happening again.

Frowning and shirtless, George looked like a pissed-off marine, but he had been as good as his word and hadn't moved. He was standing with his feet braced and his arms folded, keeping a wary eye on the stranger. Meanwhile, the man in question had gotten one foot underneath him and was resting on one knee. The twisted metal skylight frame lay a few feet from him, as if he'd flung it off himself—that would certainly explain the noise she'd heard. He still wasn't looking in the direction of her or George, however. Instead, he was holding his hands in front of him, studying one, then the other. Flexing his fingers. Checking them for damage?

Nothing looks too damaged from here, Brooke thought. In fact, everything looked pretty damn good—with an emphasis on the *everything* part. He was better built—ahem, his *muscles* were better built—than most of the guys at George's mixed martial arts gym. *Good grief.* She shook off those kinds of thoughts and tried to focus instead on how to help.

If the man *was* injured, she had no traditional first aid supplies other than a handful of sparkly Band-Aids one of her girlfriends had given her as a joke, and a plastic cone that Bouncer had to wear around his head after being neutered. She could fall back on ripping up bedsheets, she supposed, like the characters did in old movies . . . although the hot fuchsia ones on her bed right now would look neither medical nor particularly masculine.

"Are you okay? Do you need help?" she called out, and then took a step in the guy's direction. "I'm really sorry about what happened to you. Maybe we could talk. You know, try to figure it out?"

Her friend was trying to stay in front of her like some kind of human shield, but she kept elbowing him out of the way. "Hey! Hey, you!" George shouted at the stranger, not feeling conciliatory in the least. "What the hell are you doing here?"

The man looked up at last and pushed the shoulder-length tangle of hair out of his face as he did so. Clear gray eyes gazed out from beneath an intelligent brow. A close-trimmed beard accentuated his strong jawline and stronger chin.

"Oh, great," said George. "Hey, the *Fellowship of the Ring* called and they're missing one of their extras."

"Don't be such a drama queen, G."

The stranger was staring at *her* with a mixture of amazement and wonder and a host of other emotions she couldn't even name. And then he slowly smiled, showing even, white teeth.

"*Annwyl? A yw'n chi?*"

George's mouth fell open. "*¡Dios mío!* He really *is* from Middle Earth," he whispered. "What the hell kind of door did you open?"

Brooke shushed him and focused on her unexpected guest. "I'm sorry, I don't understand what you said. You speak English, don't you?" *Please say yes or things are going to get a lot more complicated.* Her spell surely couldn't have snared the man out of some other country—could it? And where the hell was El Guardia, the dog spirit she'd been trying to summon? He was supposed to facilitate difficult spells—not destroy the premises and leave hot naked men in his place.

The man's smile disappeared, replaced by a frown of confusion. He stood up then, still staring at her—and oh, great, *now* she had to work double time to avoid staring at *him*. She was no prude, being comfortable with her own nudity whether she was working with magic or just puttering around the apartment on a hot day. But that didn't mean she was equally at ease with naked *strangers*. Even rugged, well-built, naked strangers of the type that G's sister Lissy would often post on Facebook as *eye candy of the day*.

As for George, he'd had enough of the stranger's lack of clothing and stepped in, literally. He risked his latest pair of Doc Martens by crunching through the debris off to her left and pulling free the circle of dog-printed vinyl that had acted as her altar cloth. He shook the glass from it with an indignant-sounding snap, bundled it up, and tossed it to the stranger. "Hey man, how about covering up your junk in the presence of a lady? What kind of perv are you, anyway? How long you been spying on her from up there?" He nodded in the direction of the yawning hole in the roof that had been the skylight.

The bunched-up vinyl was too light to make the entire twenty-odd feet to its destination, but it didn't matter. It fell to the floor unnoticed, and the stranger walked right over it as he took several steps in Brooke's direction. He was much taller than she'd first thought, and his broad shoulders and arms were heavily muscled in a way she hadn't seen before. Maybe he bench-pressed city buses for a living. Whatever he did, she instinctively knew that his deep-chested physique hadn't come from anything as simple as a gym. Strangely, she didn't feel any fear at all—except for cringing inwardly at the sound of glass crunching beneath his bare feet. He took another step and paused.

"Annwyl," he said again, and then in English: "Is it you? Are you really here?"

Annwyl. It was a *name*. The stranger thought she was someone else. Damned if Brooke didn't feel the teeniest tiniest twinge of disappointment.

Meanwhile, her friend had reached the limits of his strained patience. George placed his body solidly in front of her and squared off against the advancing stranger, though the man was a head taller than he was, and Brooke was trying to hold him back. She might as well not have bothered. The man didn't spare her friend a glance, not when G warned him to stop, and not even when G struck that square chin with what she *knew* were his best punches: an uppercut followed by a blindingly fast left hook. She'd seen him knock opponents out cold with that combo inside the octagon ring. Of course, all of his opponents were in his weight class, and the tall stranger definitely was *not*.

Incredibly, the stranger brushed past her friend as if he wasn't even there. George used his jiu jitsu skills to make a power leap onto the man's back, where he worked to get an arm around the guy's corded neck. Brooke recognized the *hadaka jime* hold from watching G in the ring. More commonly known as the rear naked choke (although nobody was actually supposed to *be* naked!), it would have quickly disabled a normal human being, or forced him to tap out or pass out. But again the stranger proved more like a force of nature. Despite G's carefully honed skills, he was shaken off with apparently little effort. It might have been comical if Brooke hadn't been the obvious target of this unknown male—and she had no idea what he wanted.

She'd always been the type to stand her ground, but in this case, she took a couple steps back.

Memories all but swamped Aidan, as if some inner dam had burst asunder. Perhaps whatever spell had prompted the unexpected return to his human body had also dissolved the thick, impenetrable fog that had settled over his mind in the faery realm. He fully realized who he was—so much more than a name alone—and he knew the family he sprang from and the faces of each and every person who had ever been dear to him.

Dearest of all, however, was the face of his betrothed. Surely, it was deliberate fae malice that had kept him from recalling her, leaving him with only a tantalizing sense that he had once loved someone, that he had been loved in return. In all the damnable centuries, he'd been unable to remember so much as her fair face or her name.

Annwyl. He recalled her name with joy: Annwyl, and it meant "beloved."

Now, Aidan wasn't letting anything get in the way of his reunion with her. Not piles of glass and iron, not his lack of clothing, and certainly not the pugnacious defense launched by this spike-haired barbarian guard. Aidan didn't understand what his beloved was doing here in this place and time—nor was he totally sure what place and time it was—but somehow he and Annwyl were together, and that was all that mattered.

Yet she was backing away from him, and that stopped him in his tracks as nothing else would.

"Surely, you do not fear me, *beloved*?" he said to her. "True it is that I have been gone a long time, but I am no ghost." With the barbarian pacing him every step of the way, daring him to make a wrong move, Aidan approached Annwyl again, much more slowly this time and with his hands up in a peaceful gesture. An arm's length away from her, he stopped, still studying her face with hungry gaze. It was Annwyl, his betrothed, and yet . . . *and yet* . . . He struggled as he searched the memories flooding his mind. His beloved's eyes were the color of sea glass, weren't they? Had they darkened? Could they? Or were his memories still muddled by his time in the faery realm? For there was blue mixed with the green in these lovely eyes.

Slowly, he reached a hand towards her smooth face—only to have it knocked away by the young man who hovered within reach of both of them.

"Don't you touch her, man! Don't you *dare* fucking touch her."

Aidan struggled to disobey his first inclination—which was to silence the interrupter with his fist. But he was Annwyl's companion and admirably trying to protect her, however ineffectively, and so Aidan held himself back. For now.

"George, stop," she said firmly, holding up a hand to the barbarian. "I can feel that it's okay. A little weird, but okay."

Her voice . . . it was the one Aidan wanted to hear above all others, and yet there was something not quite right. Familiar, yes, and yet unique to itself. *Time.* Time was surely the cause of his confusion. So damned much of it had passed.

Her eyes were wary, however, when he traced her left brow with his fingertip. What had happened to make her so suspicious of him, so distrustful, he wondered. And why was one of her fine brows white? Had she been injured? What things had happened in her life while he was gone, while he was a captive all these years? While he wasn't here to protect her . . .

Sense penetrated his brain then: *Why was she as young as ever?* Neither care nor weather nor age had lined her face. Her hair was still glossy like a starling's wing—although above the strangely pale brow was something else new to him, a single delicate lock of snowy white. He wound it gently about his finger and released it, knowing that years had not given her this pale tendril. Its softness encouraged him to reach gently behind her head and slide his hand into her hair. It was full and thick, silky and . . .

Shorn. He'd been expecting it to be bound up at the nape of her neck. Instead the entire length fell barely to her chin. Had she cut off her long beautiful tresses in mourning for him? If that were so, then why were her arms not wound around his neck? Why were her lips not seeking his? Finally, he gave up asking himself questions and allowed simple instinct to take the lead. Instead of withdrawing his hand, he cupped the back of her head in his palm, slid his other arm around the small of her back, and drew her into a long, lingering kiss.

He poured all that he had into it, every yearning moment, every aching emptiness, every longing, every wish, every sigh—all for her. The strange barbarian she had called George was shouting something in the background, but Aidan blocked out the words. All of Aidan's senses, all of his awareness, were *in this moment,* as was everything he had been unable to express for longer than he could call to mind.

Aidan could taste her surprise, her hesitancy. He closed his eyes and softly coaxed her lips to open to him, traced the sensitive corners of her mouth with his tongue, held her close enough to hear her heart beat, and sensed the instant it began to match his. He shared her breath and held it in as if he could keep it there inside him, mingled with his own. He held her gently yet firmly against him, close enough that the scant layer of fabric she wore couldn't hide the press of her nipples against his chest. It was all so right and yet . . .

Not.

Confused, Aidan pulled back to look at her. The wariness had left her beautiful blue-green eyes and been replaced by puzzlement and a kind of wonder, but he could see no sign of recognition in them. None at all.

"Surely, I have not changed so much," he chided, but icy fingers of doubt had already crept into his mind and he cupped her lovely face in his hands. "Have you not missed me, my love, my dear one? Is there no joy in your heart that I have returned?" Anger and panic collided then, and his voice rose accordingly. "Know me, Annwyl. In the name of all that is holy, *you must know me.*"

She didn't try to pull away from him, but instead laid a hand on his cheek. "I'm so sorry that I don't know who you are—but I sure wish I did."

How could this be? His body called out to hers, and her body had answered. She was warm and right in his arms—he knew it, he could feel it—and yet he was a stranger to her?

Meanwhile, her companion had yet to stop speaking, and his tongue was sharp, as if to make up for his lack of success in defeating Aidan. The words finally penetrated his awareness. "I don't know who you're looking for, dude, but you got the wrong woman. *She's not your girl.*"

Conscious thought had nothing to do with what happened next. Aidan simply picked up the young barbarian as though he were nothing more than a sack of flour and hurled him across the room to strike hard against the heavy oak door. Annwyl gasped, but to his credit, George was quick to get to his knees and was working to shake off the blow. She, however, suddenly shoved at Aidan's shoulder. He automatically turned towards her . . .

Just in time to get knocked on his backside with an uppercut to the jaw that was completely out of proportion to her size.

Aidan sat staring up at her, dazed in more ways than one. This had to be a dream or a faery-constructed fantasy. *Had to be.*

"That wasn't about the kiss, mister, in case you're wondering," she said. Her hands rested on her curved hips, and her eyes had darkened to turquoise. "I enjoyed that. But you just crossed the line by putting hands on my friend. I'm not in the business of hitting people, but I will absolutely *spell you* into the middle of next week if you do that again." She called over to the friend in question, who had gotten to his feet. "Are you all right, George?"

"Never better." He coughed and spat as he rolled his shoulder. "Can I kill him now, *chica*?"

"No. Maybe later if you behave."

He snorted. "You always spoil my fun, you know that?" He made his way over the debris and put an arm around her. To Aidan he said: "Look, I told you, man, she's not your girl. She's not the woman you're looking for. So maybe *now* will you get some effin' clothes on and explain what the hell you're doing here? Because I am more than ready to *take you out*."

Aidan was perfectly aware of his nakedness, but surely that would not bother Annwyl overmuch. A betrothal was every bit as binding as a marriage, and they had lain together more than once. For the first time, he dropped his gaze from her face to consider the rest of her. She had always favored a flowing chemise with a green kirtle, but there was no sign of those. Only dark blue leggings like her male companion wore, but narrower, and over them rested a black-on-black tunic that left her arms bare. Stranger still, the finely woven fabric was patterned with life-size shadowy skulls and strange ornate symbols amid a Latin inscription, *Audaces fortuna iuvat.* He had no trouble reading it—*Fortune favors the bold.* It was a warrior's creed, not a saying that many women ascribed to. Certainly far removed from anything his careful and practical Annwyl would ever say—or think.

Common sense returned to him in this uncommon situation, and he realized that his own gentle woman would never, *ever,* wear such masculine garments. Coupled with the slight difference in eye color, and the presence of the snowy brow and matching wisp of white hair above it—not to mention the stunning impact of her small fist on his jaw—there was only one crushing conclusion: however much his body claimed to know her, however much he wanted a miracle, wanted her to really be his betrothed, *this woman was a stranger.*

And that meant Annwyl was dead.

It was right there in his mind, mixed in with all the other memories that had come rushing back to him: the utter horror of what Celynnen had done, the coldness with which she destroyed mortal lives—including the one most dear to him—to suit her own selfish ends.

Aidan stood then, and straightened his shoulders to bear this new pain, even as the disappointment rose thick in his throat, choking him. Fresh grief was in the air he breathed, as tangible as ash.

The strange woman saw it too, as if all of Aidan's thoughts had played out before her like a tragic story. "I don't know who Annwyl is," she said, and his heart was squeezed by an unseen fist. It was not his beloved's voice, not at all. How could he have been so mistaken? "But she is very fortunate," she continued, stroking his pain unawares, sending daggers into his chest with every syllable. "It's obvious that you love her very much."

The strangeness of his surroundings, the way this woman was dressed, the bodyguard with his hair dyed blue like the ancient Picts of Britain—what could it be but some grand game of the Tylwyth Teg, a new and novel form of entertainment? Perhaps he hadn't escaped Lurien after all, perhaps he was still a captive grim . . .

But he wasn't Death's herald anymore—he was human. He'd gained that much at least. It was his *own* body, and it was very mortal indeed. When the slash from the warth had ripped his left leg from hip to knee, he'd bled blue. The transformation from grim to human had sealed the wound, but the thick angry scar hurt like blazes—an unpleasant novelty, since it hadn't caused that kind of pain when he received it.

He was bleeding *red*, however, from other places, from too many nicks and scratches to count. Not only that, he felt like an entire team of draft horses had kicked him, but every bruise and cut seemed a victory of sorts. He was a man again, and just to be able to feel something, anything, was cause to celebrate. No wonder the Fair Ones would stop at nothing to gain sensation and emotion.

Including trying to deceive me with a look-alike of Annwyl.

"Annwyl is dead," he declared, saying it aloud for the first time. The words sounded harsh and absolute in his ears. "I have been deceived. You are not her." Then, not certain if he was trying to convince an unseen fae audience or maybe just himself, he added: "You are *nothing* like her." It came out like an accusation, and an angry one at that.

She paled. "I didn't realize—I'm so very sorry to hear that. But no one was trying to deceive you. Maybe you were just a little confused, you know, from falling through the roof and all that."

He said nothing for a long moment, thinking, considering. This woman sounded sincere, and he wanted to believe her. Yet she might actually *be* one of the Fair Ones; it was a simple matter for a fae to assume a glamor, taking on any image desired, including that of the woman he loved. If that was true, then more was at stake than deception—for him, it could be extremely dangerous. To touch a disguised fae might enact a spell, or perhaps give consent when none was intended. *It is something Celynnen would do* . . . By the gods, he'd actually kissed her—and a large part of him wanted to do it again. He could already be compromised.

The woman tried again. "Look, my name is Brooke Halloran. You're bleeding from the glass and I can see a couple slivers from here," she said. "Will you let me help you? How badly are you injured?"

"Not badly enough," muttered George.

"Your concern is unnecessary," Aidan said. He was still naked but, at the moment, it would have to be her problem, not his. "Tell me where I am and how I got here," he demanded sharply, and with more than a little anger. "And tell me truly who and what you are, *Brooke Halloran*. I do not know you for friend or foe."

"Know *me* for your foe, then, asshole." George stepped between them, putting his face directly in Aidan's line of sight. "You don't talk to her like that, ever." A shaft of sunlight from the ruined roof turned the young barbarian's eyes to sudden bright gold—and it took everything Aidan had not to jump back in surprise.

Brooke Halloran had a demon for a consort.

NINE

⌒⫯⫯⌒

D emons did not willingly associate with the Fair Ones, not
even with the darkest of the fae. The woman currently elbowing the one called George out of the way could not be of the Tylwyth
Teg, then, or of any of the other faery races. She must be mortal,
reasoned Aidan, like himself. It was a relief, and yet she was very
far from ordinary. For one thing, she was now *in front* of the demon.
What creature from the pit would permit that, unless she was in
command of him? He could feel George glaring daggers at him with
those hideous eyes, but Aidan was once again looking into the face
of the woman who had identified herself as Brooke Halloran. And
suddenly he realized something that had been niggling at the edges
of his awareness since the moment he'd kissed her. There was magic
here, a tremendous well of power—and it was coming from *her*.
"You're a *gwddon*," he guessed. "Some would say a *witch*."

She frowned. "Well, that's awfully damn perceptive for a first
meeting," she said, and her demon snorted.

"Have you looked at this place, *chica*?" he whispered to her.
"It doesn't take much *perception* to see that either C-4 or Gandalf
was involved."

Surely, no good could come of acknowledging demons. Aidan
had ignored George since the beginning, and he stuck with that

111

strategy now. The woman was the one in charge here. He must be far too accustomed to living in the faery realm, where magic was as elemental as air, not to have recognized her power sooner. "To what craft do you owe your allegiance, witch? Dark or light? I warn you, do not seek to make me your servant."

"Are you kidding me?" Indignation flashed in her blue-green eyes. "Are you *kidding* me? I take back what I said about being perceptive." She took a step forward and actually poked him in the chest. "If you can tell I'm a witch, you can also tell *there is no evil here*." She punctuated every word with another sharp poke. "My calling is to help and to heal. As to why you're here, I could ask you the same thing. What the hell are you doing in my goddamn house? It's about time you told *me* why I shouldn't have your naked ass dragged off to jail." She folded her arms to mirror his and jutted out her chin.

Even if she hadn't had the power to bring him here, even if she hadn't knocked him down, even if she didn't command a demon, if there was any lingering notion in his mind that this woman might be Annwyl, her demeanor alone would have just dispelled it. His betrothed would never have stood up to him in such a way. She had been raised to be an obedient daughter, devoted to serving her father and her household; she would have been a dutiful and submissive wife. In fact, she would never have given Aidan any cause to be angry in the first place.

And she most certainly would never have used a tavern maid's language.

It was difficult, though, to separate disappointment and grief from anger, and Aidan's anger would not leave him. There had been a time when he had been a reasonable and fair man, a generous and kind man, and most of all, a man in control of himself. Right now, though, his emotions settled uneasily like wary wolves, ready to rend and tear at the slightest provocation. At least his voice, when he found it, was somewhat quieter than it had been to this point. "My senses tell me you intend no harm," he said to Brooke. "But I do not know if they are guiding me aright." It galled him to admit such a weakness, especially to strangers. Yet of what use was it to play games? Games were for the fae. He needed answers, and maybe some basic human honesty was the only way to get them. "Over the years, I have learned never to trust what I see and hear and feel, and even my instincts are suspect." *Did I not just mistake this woman for my betrothed?*

"That is a difficult state to be in, and I do not envy you." Her voice had also softened, but it had lost none of its firmness. "But don't you ever, *ever*, question my motivation again. I may not be perfect at being a witch, but I take the responsibility damn seriously."

No, she was not his beloved, but she *was* human—and he was surprised to find himself hanging on her every word. No spell compelled it, but rather, he was hungry, nay, *starving*, for simple human speech. Not for words that flowed around him and through him, not words intended for others as if he were not present, not words that commanded him or mocked him, but words being directed to *him*. By other mortals. Had he not drunk in every word that Maeve Lowri Jones had said to him? It had been more than comforting; it was an acknowledgment of his existence, his identity, even within a fae-contrived canine body.

Not conversation but *connection*.

Now he was in his own body, and to hear this unusual mortal woman addressing him was like rain on parched earth. Though he knew now she was not Annwyl, the act of being acknowledged was still life affirming. Even if she had cursed him, he would still have been grateful for every damning word.

In fact, perhaps it would be *better* if she shouted curses at him—he wouldn't be so conscious that despite her shorn hair and strange dress, she was pleasing to look upon. Now that he was a man again, he was rapidly becoming aware of things he hadn't noticed in a millennium. Annwyl or no, parts of him were in imminent danger of responding . . .

His *tad*—his father—had been fond of saying *first things first.* Aidan glanced around and spotted the strange cloth that George had thrown at him. It was stiff and shiny on one side, with bright-colored creatures on it, backed with some kind of soft fabric. He girded himself with the awkward material as best as he could, and a great deal of tension left the room at once, including some of his own.

He regarded Brooke, who was still waiting for an answer. Aidan was not afraid of so-called witches—every community depended on those who were skilled with herbs and healing wisdom. Perhaps he could make some peace and win some cooperation if Brooke and her demon knew that he intended no harm to her. "If you do indeed follow the light, then I have naught but praise for you and your kind. A wise woman with skills in your art healed me of a fearful burn when I was but a very young apprentice."

Aidan extended his left arm and turned it to reveal the underside. The skin was faintly shiny from palm to elbow, but it was smooth and unmarked. "I stumbled and fell upon the forge, into the coals. I would not even have had the use of this arm had she not been very skilled and much devoted. She cared for me for days, and as you can see, there is no scar to tell the tale." He didn't bother to add that the blessing had turned into a curse. Had he borne a scar, Celynnen surely would have lost interest in him. *She cannot abide imperfection.*

Brooke studied his arm with grudging approval. "Your healer did a wonderful job, then. Burns are difficult to work with. You say you got this in a forge—what's that? Like a blacksmith shop?"

"I am a smith." If he gave some information, he might gain some in return. "Pledged to Gofannon, the god of all who work metal."

The frown may have lessened somewhat from her fair face, but her demon was as impatient as ever. "Okay, so she's a witch and you're a blacksmith. Heartwarming story, but that still doesn't tell us who the hell you are. Or what made you crash through her window. Were you spying on her? Because I swear I will kill you, man. How do we know you're not some kind of a perv?"

"I have to agree with my friend," said Brooke, before Aidan could continue. "If you're going to spend time in my house *buck naked*, you need to be telling me your name, where you're from, and what the hell you were doing on my roof. Last chance, mister."

On some level, it was satisfying that his lack of clothing had annoyed her. In another time and place he might have teased her on purpose just to see if he could make little cherries of color appear on her cheekbones. Right now, his own patience had thinned out again, and his anger was going to tear through it at any moment. He was out of his element, confused, and strangely glad that someone besides himself was mightily annoyed about it. Plus, he was angry at himself—it *had* to be more than coincidence that Brooke and Annwyl resembled each other so closely, yet he was rapidly losing his battle to be wary.

He shook his head. "Names have power, as you well know," he snapped. "I would have the name of your *cythraul* first, that he can work no mischief on me and mine." At her blank look, he added: "Your demon. Give me his true name."

"But I don't have a—" Understanding dawned, and she looked aghast at the snake-eyed creature beside her. "George! Take out those damn contacts right now!"

Aidan's eyebrows shot up as the two of them argued right in front of him, not as master and servant as he'd assumed, but more like brother and sister. The demon was much louder, but in the end, he finally gave in to her. Still complaining, he turned away and bent his head over his cupped palm. When he turned back, he had brown eyes—*human* brown eyes—and extended his hand so Aidan could see two tiny golden disks in it, as delicate as the scales of a fish. The young man then held up one of them so Aidan could see the light shine through it—and there was the snakelike pupil that had made him appear as a creature from hell.

Well, *damn*. Aidan blew out a breath, feeling more than a little foolish. With all the centuries of watching humanity as an unseen observer, he thought he recognized most fashions, even those of far-off countries as other peoples either visited Wales or adopted it as their home, and including the stranger trends that always seemed to be favored by the young. *Apparently, I have much more to learn.* Besides, he still didn't quite know where he was—outside of Cymru, there was an entire world that was new to him. "It seems I am mistaken," he said to the young man. "Truly, though, you would be a demon in a fight." He rubbed his jaw for emphasis (but truth be told, Brooke's unexpected punch had done more damage).

Somewhat placated, the younger man nodded. "Name's George," he said. "George Santiago-Callahan, from the great state of Washington. Species: *one hundred percent human*. And you have an effin' tough jaw yourself, man." He narrowed his now-brown eyes. "But that doesn't mean we're pals now."

No, it didn't, but at least Aidan was satisfied that he was dealing with creatures of the earthly plane—and there were none of those he feared. He introduced himself. "My name is Aidan ap Llanfor. My shop was near Aberhonddu in the simple country of

Wales and a much simpler time. And where exactly *is* this Wash-ing-tonne I now stand in? And when?"

If he'd thought his introduction would please or at least appease Brooke and George, he was mistaken. They exchanged shocked glances.

"I don't think there's a town called Wales in the States," whispered Brooke.

"I don't think so either, *chica*." George finally cleared his throat and asked Aidan, "Dude, that's not *Wales* as in *Britain*, is it?"

"Aye, it is. I stood upon the soil of my homeland only last night. This last *mortal* night, I mean to say. Time does not move the same in the faery realm."

George's human eyes goggled. "Jesus, every time I think we're getting somewhere, you say something even weirder, man. Fairies? *Really?*" He put an arm around the woman's shoulders. "He's talk-ing about fairies. Let me call the cops now. We've done our best to be patient and make nice, Brooke, but come on, the guy's obviously *trippin'.*"

Brooke silenced him with a look and focused on Aidan. "Wales is a helluva long way from my house, mister. How on earth did you get here?"

"I sought to escape the realm and was pursued by the Wild Hunt. I fought with Lurien, their leader, and I know not which of us might have prevailed. All I remember was that I was suddenly pulled away into a tunnel of stars, then blackness. When I woke up, I was here. And I was human again," he added. "I haven't been inside this body in a thousand years."

"Of course you haven't!" George threw up his hands and walked away, muttering rapidly. He punched an oak window frame and the last of the glass fell from it into the street below.

Brooke sighed in exasperation but didn't take her gaze from Aidan's face. "So is that why this body of yours is in such perfect shape? Because it's in damn excellent condition for being ten centuries old."

The whole story sounded fantastical, even to him. "Perhaps," he said irritably, then added, "Do you like what you see, Brooke Halloran? *Did you like how it felt?*" What the hell was he doing? It wasn't in his nature to be so blatant or so crass. An ale-headed lad seeking to impress a barmaid into smacking him had more manners than he was presently exhibiting. In fact, normally, he would have covered himself *immediately* in the presence of a woman—but nothing was normal at the moment, and it hadn't been for a long, long time.

And so here he stood, annoyed, still half naked, and *daring* Brooke, and he didn't know why—nor did he know precisely what he was daring her to do. Perhaps some childish part of him just wanted some petty retaliation for the fact that she was not his beloved, wanted to kick back against the pain she was causing him just by existing. Every particle of his being had reacted at that first sight of her, thinking she was his Annwyl, and it was a cruel joke that she wasn't. Grief scored his heart with razor claws, and as wrong as he knew it to be, Aidan wished he wasn't the only one hurting.

Apparently, however, Brooke was neither interested in swooning over his physique or slapping him for his rudeness. Her gaze didn't wander in the slightest, and exactly why did he feel as transparent as glass before those discerning blue-green eyes? Were he to lie, she would undoubtedly know it. And he was certain she wouldn't require one bit of magic to detect an untruth.

"Okay, let's recap here, shall we?" She held up her hand and started counting off her fingers. "One, you traveled all the way from Wales to here, which is about five thousand miles or so, within the last twenty-four hours. Two, the *faeries*, as you call them, have been chasing you because you're some sort of escaped prisoner. Three, you don't know how you got here and I'm guessing no airplane was involved. Do you know *where* you are, by the way?"

He shook his head.

"Okay, then. Four, you have no idea where *here* is. And five, your human body has been in storage for centuries and you just now got it back.

"Am I right so far?"

"Aye." It was all true, every bit of it, but he had no way to prove it, and that simply ramped up his frustration to dangerous levels. He found himself wanting to punch something, again and again, until his knuckles bled. Aidan clenched his jaw and his fists, struggling to get his burgeoning anger under control. Especially when Brooke's companion chose that moment to rejoin them. George's hands were in his pockets, and he kicked at the glass as he shuffled through it. The casualness was an act, however. His gaze was sharp and full of purpose. "I think I have the perfect question for you, man. If you haven't been human for a thousand years, then just what the hell *have* you been?"

Demon or not, Aidan wasn't inclined to respond to his question. But it was Brooke's face in front of his own, and he could do nothing but give her the truth. Whether it was for Annwyl's sake or something else, he didn't know, but he gave her the answer.

"The Fair Ones forced me to be a herald of death for the past thousand years. A grim. In Wales, it's called a barghest or a gwyllgi."

Behind them, George snorted. "What kind of a monster is that? Sounds like an elf or a gremlin, or hell, it could be a cute fluffy bunny for God's sake."

"There's nothing *cute* about a grim," said Aidan. "It's a great black—"

"*Dog!*" Brooke's face lost all color and she sank back to lean on the wall, with her hands on her forehead. "Holy crap, George," she said. "The *dogs*. The dogs in the cards, all those readings. That's what the Universe has been trying to tell me. Even the Death card had a . . ." She opened her eyes wide and pointed at Aidan. "That's why Death had a dog! It's *you*. You're his messenger!"

She slowly turned her hand and pointed to herself then, resting her finger between her breasts.

"And I called you here. I thought I was summoning El Guardia, a spirit dog, to my circle and somehow I got *you* instead."

George looked downright shaken. "What have you done, *chica*? What have you *done*? I would never have told you about El Guardia if I thought you'd try to call him up. This is not like dialing a wrong number. You could have been hurt. You could have been *killed*."

Her friend hugged her tight and kissed the top of her head, but Aidan could swear he was drawing as much comfort as he was trying to give. That wasn't surprising. Aidan didn't have the slightest idea what or who the dog spirit was that Brooke had been trying to summon, only that the creature sounded unpleasant—but he *was* surprised to catch himself wishing *he* were the one putting arms around her. And he'd kiss a lot more of her . . .

Damn it all to hell. He would have to be much more careful, more cautious with his emotions. Right now it was no doubt the shock of everything that had happened, the flood of memories and emotions, Brooke's uncanny resemblance to his betrothed, that was addling his brain. He couldn't afford to be so distracted: he had a vow to fulfill.

Now that he'd regained his body, he would learn all that he could and seek to arm himself with knowledge as well as weapons. Perhaps he could persuade this gwddon, this witch, to help him with her magic too. Because he was more determined than ever to return to the faery realm and face Celynnen, even if he had to move heaven and earth to do it.

By Gofannon, he would see fear appear in that cold fae's eyes, right before he avenged his Annwyl.

TEN

⌒ʔ⋔⌒

Brooke was thankful beyond words that Olivia had somehow made sense of her frantic phone call. While the older woman didn't panic in the least (as if strangers fell through skylights every day), she certainly reacted with appropriate haste and brought all that had been asked for, and then some. What Brooke appreciated most, however, was the huge sense of relief she felt when Olivia walked in. Funny how being a grown-up didn't make you any less glad to have a *mom* on the scene. Whether it was your own or someone else's mother, it was like having the cavalry arrive. One way or another, order was darn well going to be restored, at least as much as it could be under the circumstances.

"*Madre de Dios*," said Olivia, dropping her two huge shopping bags in the doorway and crossing herself at the sight of the destroyed room. "There is glass outside all over the sidewalk, but I did not realize—*m'ija*, are you sure you are all right?" She grabbed both of Brooke's hands, and it was a few moments before she was satisfied the young woman was unhurt.

That's when George jerked a thumb in the direction of Aidan, who still wore nothing but the dog-printed tablecloth around his hips. For a split second, Olivia goggled, then crossed herself once more and immediately got down to business. While Brooke and

George had focused on the who and why and how of the situation, George's mother gave her entire attention to the physical reality. Her son was handed a fresh T-shirt, then dispatched to get some tools and to start cleaning up the broken window glass on the pavement in front of the shop. Then she turned to Aidan. Maybe it was that mom thing in action, coupled with the fact that Olivia was a force of nature all out of proportion to her diminutive size, but within seconds she had him sitting down on Brooke's little round altar table, where she could reach him to check him over.

Immediately, she pulled an inch-long chunk of glass out of his shoulder blade with her fingers, then two more from his calf. "He must shower," she pronounced. "And very carefully. There's glass dust and slivers in his hair and embedded in his skin. He certainly can't put clothes on over that, and I need some of this blood washed off so I can see where it's coming from."

"I need no healer," protested Aidan, but that was as far as he got.

"You! Just like every other big strong man in the world, you think you're invincible." Olivia shook her finger at him. That was at his nose level, since he was seated. "But you are not a superhero. There is glass sticking out of your stubborn hide, and you are getting blood all over the place. If you do not care about yourself, fine, but you are not going to make a mess while I am here." She hustled him off to the apartment—and *no way* was Brooke going to dare to complain about that, even if she wasn't sure she liked the idea of the stranger being in her home. In her shower. With warm water running like rain over his . . .

If she hadn't had such a lump on the back of her skull already, she might have smacked herself in the head just to get that image out of her brain. As it was, she was distracted by the absence of her cats as she entered her living quarters. The terrible trio didn't run up to greet Brooke. Nor did they race to check out the stranger Olivia was escorting. Dry cat food was scattered from one corner of the kitchen to the other as if it had been rolled in—one spot looked suspiciously like a *cat angel*—yet the gang had made an admirable dent in the quantity. Easily half the box was gone. She tracked the group to a sunny spot between the window and the couch, where they were sprawled in Little Whiskers–induced comas. Rory was spread-eagled on his back, a bulge in his black-furred belly the only evidence of the feast. She shook her head. Occasionally, a customer would ask if her cats were her *familiars*, and it was always hard for Brooke not to laugh. In the old stories, familiars were alleged to be mystical advisers in animal form, basically a witch's assistants. If only those clients could see the trio now . . . *Assistants, my ass.* More like furry overlords with a taste for expensive food.

Brooke snatched up a turquoise T-shirt out of the clean laundry and changed into it in the pantry—the bathroom was far too close to the bedroom for her to even think of getting dressed there. She hung the skull-festooned T on the coatrack, to return to George. She didn't mind the darkly gothic design, but the shirt had definitely bothered Aidan. In retrospect, she could see that it might have contributed to the whole "evil witch who keeps company with demons" image; and somehow that made her want to wear it again, just to annoy him. *Dark or light, indeed.*

She swept up the remains of the uneaten cat food from the old oak floor in her bright kitchen, grateful for the sense of calm and peaceful energy that still existed in her orderly apartment. A simple spilled box of kibble (even ridiculously *expensive* kibble) couldn't disrupt the chi in her home. The windows were unbroken in this part of the second story, the section of the ceiling high over the apartment was intact, and there wasn't a speck of glass on the floor. What a stark and welcome contrast to the massive chaos in the much larger spell room! Some of that chaos was naturally due to the physical disaster, and it would go away when the mess was dealt with. Much of the chaotic energy, however, was no doubt because of Aidan himself, and that was much harder to figure out. Was it emanating from him, or was he just causing it within her? And had it happened before or after that earthshaking kiss?

All of the above. She had felt attraction of course, despite the bizarre circumstances. She'd also experienced a strange, deep connection that didn't make sense considering she'd never laid eyes on the guy before today. However, there was something more. Not only had he rocked her world with a kiss; Brooke had felt the soundless thrum of power begin to vibrate in her very bones as two magics mixed. Her Gift was one of them. Whatever the other power was, it had belonged to Aidan.

Having given the man in question a lengthy list of instructions about shampoo, conditioner, and other things probably not readily available in medieval Wales, Olivia reappeared. "Are you sure you're all right? George said you tried to summon El Guardia. That's really ambitious, *m'ija*." She made coffee, then sat at the little bistro table in the kitchen as she so often did when she came to visit. This time, though, they weren't talking about décor, or poring over catalogs, or discussing the latest movie. Instead, George's mom questioned Brooke on every step of the spell, every detail and nuance of that night's activities.

Brooke put out cups and condiments as she tried to recall every possible factor leading up to the blast. It wasn't all that hard. "It was all about the intent, Olivia. I thought that was the most important part of every spell. I tried to set the stage to help focus my attention on my goal. All I wanted was for your mother's spirit dog to help me with my magic. How the hell did I grab Aidan out of the Twilight Zone instead?"

"I do not understand it, *m'ija*. I myself have seen El Guardia in my mother's sacred circle more than once, and this is not him.

El Guardia is a *dog*, a big ferocious black dog and always a dog, never a big handsome naked man."

Did Olivia really have to add the *handsome* and *naked* references? The sound of the shower in the next room was not helping, either.

"But I *did* see a dog, Olivia. It was there, just for a moment, before I got slammed out of the circle, but I'm *sure* it was a dog that broke through the skylight. Big, black, with snarling teeth and glowing eyes—everything I'd expected." Brooke stirred more sugar and chocolate creamer into her coffee. After the kind of night she'd had, she figured she deserved it. Her friend was subtly looking out for her nutritional needs, however, and spreading cream cheese on whole-wheat bagels for her.

"I just don't understand where the dog went after he was pulled into my circle. I mean, we know *now* that the dog was really Aidan, but why the big change? Why did my spell restore him to human?"

Olivia sighed. "There is intent, *m'ija*, and there is need. Sometimes the Universe responds to need before intent. I just do not know whose need it was—yours or Aidan's—that prompted such an intervention."

"He said he was in the middle of a fight with the leader of the faery hunt. He didn't know if he would have won."

"Perhaps then he was snatched from a permanent death." Olivia shrugged. "Or perhaps it was the leader's life that needed to be saved. It is impossible to tell. Or maybe Aidan has some important purpose to fulfill, a job to do, that can only be done here."

"But *why* here? And why now? He's not only from Wales, he's from a *past* Wales, one that doesn't even exist anymore." Brooke put her head in her hands. "All I wanted was some help with my magic, and this is what I get!"

"Have you tried any spells since Aidan arrived?"

"Well, I did put a little magic in my punch when I hit Aidan. But other than that, no," said Brooke, and then she couldn't help but laugh. "I don't know why I didn't think of it. I mean, why wouldn't I try out some conjuring just because my house is destroyed and I've been out cold for most of the night?"

Olivia laughed too. "Okay, we'll scratch that question for now. You *have* been a little busy. There will be time enough to experiment with your magic later—but when you do, you may be surprised. I'm sensing that this man has some power of his own. Maybe it's just left over from what happened to him and will fade in time, or maybe he has some latent ability." She waggled her eyebrows then. "Or maybe it's just his good looks that are distracting us both. I'm old and widowed, but I'm very certain, *m'ija*, that I would have forgotten my own name when I saw that handsome face and that powerful body rise from the ruins of your spell room."

"Will you quit that?" Brooke clapped her hands to her head in frustration, and only succeeded in irritating the still-throbbing lump on the back of her skull. But good grief, she *so* did not need the extra help when it came to admiring Aidan's physique. *Rising from the ruins, indeed.* She was still buzzed from his kiss alone and a little desperate to change the subject. "And you should definitely quit that *old* stuff too, Olivia!" she added. "You're hardly middle aged, and you still get whistled at on the street. When you decide to date, I'm sure you'd have one within an hour." A warning look from her friend had Brooke hastily amending that. "*If.* *If* you were to decide to date. But come on, you didn't seem to be drooling a bit when you were ordering Aidan to get his ass into that shower."

"What can I say? First I do what is needed, and *then* I drool," she said simply. "My son calls it *hyperfocused mother mode.*" Olivia made quotation marks in the air.

Brooke snorted her coffee and fumbled for a paper towel. "Omigod, that's true! G nicknamed it that when he and I were in fifth grade, and I confess, we've *both* called it that ever since. It's like your superpower, and now I'm wishing I had it. I definitely get distracted by all kinds of things when I'm doing a reading or in the middle of a spell. *Not this time though,*" she added quickly. "See, that's the thing here, Olivia. *This* time I really felt at one with the energies, like everything was coming together just as it should. I asked for the help I needed—"

"And the Universe dropped a man into your lap. Don't you think that's a sign? Maybe he has something you need." Olivia's smile was more like a pirate's grin.

Brooke knew that look, and there was no way she was going to reveal that she'd already been kissed within an inch of her life by the bold stranger. "You're trying to find me a boyfriend again, aren't you? Maybe I'd rather meet someone who hasn't spent a thousand years as a dog."

"Ah, now you are being picky, *m'ija.*"

"A grim is not a dog," said a deep voice. Aidan stood in the doorway, kilted with a big bath towel. His gray eyes were even more startling with his dark blond hair pulled back from his face. His close-cropped beard still had beads of water in it, but the morning light revealed a decidedly reddish color in it that Brooke hadn't noticed before. The blond hair that dusted his well-developed pecs and curled lightly around his nipples had that same red tint, a hidden highlight that only the sun would reveal. Over his sternum, however, the hair boldened to red gold. Without thinking, Brooke's eyes automatically followed the coppery vee down the center of his taut-muscled belly to where it disappeared into the towel. She snapped her eyes up to his face just in time to realize he knew exactly what she'd just done.

Crap. She could feel the twin spots on her cheekbones heat. "You're bleeding," she said quickly, as if that explained why she was all but drooling over him. Lame, lame, *lame*, but it was the best excuse she could come up with. And he *was* bleeding, from various nicks and cuts on his arms and chest.

Fortunately, Olivia already had it handled. Armed with a pair of tweezers, she broke open a boxful of Band-Aids—thick, sturdy fabric ones, not the little sparkly ones that Brooke had on hand— and had Aidan sit in a kitchen chair so she could work on him. A little pile of glass fragments and plastic wrappers began to grow on the countertop as she plucked and peeled and stuck strips one after another. While she worked, the three cats showed up to check out the stranger in their apartment, first Jade, then Bouncer. Finally, even Rory emerged from his post-pig-out nap to scrutinize the man. The three sat at his feet, staring up at him as if trying to decide what he was. *Or if he could be manipulated into giving them food.*

"Would you like some coffee?" Brooke asked Aidan. She hoped she could manage that much without flubbing it. Although she now kept her gaze strictly above the neck when she spoke to him, *dear goddess*, she couldn't unsee what she had seen. Her traitor fingers kept twitching; first one finger, then another, turned in playful little circles as if they yearned to tousle the hair on that broad muscled chest, and follow where it led . . . *This is what comes of kissing complete strangers. I've definitely lost my mind . . .*

"Aye, I will try a mug. Wales did not yet have coffee when I was—well, when I was a smith there." Even seated, he loomed over the little bistro table. His big hand dwarfed the cup Brooke offered him, and she was grateful she didn't dump it on him. He didn't know she'd already spilled half of it on the counter and had to start over.

Aidan took a sip of the dark liquid and considered. Sipped again, then drank the scalding liquid down without blinking. He helped himself to one of the plain untoasted bagels that had escaped from the bag, biting into it like a doughnut.

That ended her drooling in a hurry. In fact, Brooke's mouth nearly puckered. *A thousand years of not eating and his first food is a dry bagel? Ugh!* She hefted the carafe and refilled his cup—he was *so* going to need to wash down that doughy pastry. "Most people like their bagels sliced and toasted with butter, or cream cheese. Would you like me to fix that for you so you can try it out?" Brooke held out her hand for his bagel.

For a moment, he seemed about to say yes. But a sudden shadow crossed his face, and he shook his head. He drank his coffee and chewed the bread without looking at her again, moving only to take a second bagel. She could sense the anger and hurt that radiated from him, and it didn't take a rocket scientist to figure out he was probably thinking of the departed Annwyl, the woman he'd mistaken Brooke for. His *beloved.* His *dear one.*

What would it be like to have someone think of me *that way?*

"That's the last one," announced Olivia, having applied a final strip to the bottom of Aidan's right foot. "I don't think I've applied that many Band-Aids since George tried to skateboard down the concrete steps of the library when he was twelve. Fortunately, nothing's too deep, so most of these can come off in a couple days. But in the meantime, you won't be staining the clothes I brought for you."

Aidan rose but still made no eye contact with Brooke. "I thank you for your ministrations, Mrs. Santiago-Callahan." Then he said to the older woman in perfect Spanish, "*Discúlpeme mientras tomo la oportunidad de vestirme . . .*"

As he disappeared into the bedroom (with three cats following him), Brooke turned to her friend. "What. The. Hell?"

Olivia shrugged. "He thanked me and now he's going to get dressed. The man speaks Spanish. Very well, in fact. He read the labels on the shampoo and things in my language, then asked me questions about them *en español*. Not only that, he read *and translated* the ingredients in the French hand cream that you order from Canada."

Brooke did the math. "Including his own, that's four languages. Four. That's a lot for the time period he claims he's from, and an awful lot for a blacksmith. Besides that, every one of those languages has evolved and changed over the centuries."

"Oh, so now you second-guess yourself, *m'ija*? You're wondering again if he's telling us the truth about who he is and where he's been all this time?"

"Of course I'm wondering! They don't have language lessons in the faery realm, do they?" She realized she'd just mentioned the place as if it actually existed and pinched the bridge of her nose before her brain exploded. "Maybe George is right after all and he just happened to be watching me from the skylight when the giant dog showed up."

Olivia shook her head. "I don't have a lot of the Gift, but I do have an ear for the truth, and so do you," she chided. "You know he's not lying to us. It's just a lot to take in all at once." She patted Brooke's hand and poured her more coffee. "Tomorrow or the next day, perhaps, we can go to my place and I will get out my scrying bowl. If we work together, you and I, maybe we will find some answers in it. But for now, let's just do what comes next. As Aidan says, he will get dressed. Then we will all move forward together. I brought over a few of Jack's old things that I thought might work," she explained. "They are laid out on the bed for him, so he'd know what went with what."

"That was very kind of you." George's father, Jack, had been a big man with wide shoulders, a boxer in his time before he turned in his gloves for a teaching career at a college in Spokane.

"It's been five years, *m'ija*. It's about time someone got some use from them."

Olivia shrugged as if it were *no big deal,* but Brooke knew better from all the time she'd spent with George and Lissy in the Santiago-Callahan home. Olivia and Jack's relationship had been a love story for the ages. When Jack passed away unexpectedly, Olivia found herself unable to continue living in the house they'd shared for so many years. Instead, she'd picked up stakes and bought herself a place with a half-acre garden in Walla Walla. George had followed her, determined that she shouldn't be alone. Brooke was glad that she, too, had decided to make the city her home. How had she ever managed without Olivia around? She hugged her friend and stand-in mom. "I'm so grateful you came over. Thanks to you, we've got our stranger cleaned up, patched up, and—"

She was about to say *dressed* but the word stuck in her throat as Aidan reappeared in the kitchen doorway. He was dressed all right, but it was hard to tell which affected Brooke more: the fact that she remembered George's gruff yet sweet father in what they had all laughingly called his teacher uniform of a corduroy jacket thrown over a nondescript plaid shirt and jeans, or that the clothes fit Aidan like they had been made for him. He looked *good,* even if he didn't quite have the shirt buttons aligned or the collar right, and the pockets were inside out on everything. The three cats came and lounged on the floor beside him, looking as satisfied as if they'd helped him pick out his wardrobe. Knowing them, however, Brooke figured they'd laid all over the clothing on the bed before he could put in on, so that he now had the obligatory dusting of feline hair that all visitors to her apartment acquired.

At least Brooke felt more comfortable now that Aidan was fully covered, and it appeared that he was also slightly more relaxed. However, she had to work to tune out that annoying little voice in her head that kept telling her that *she should have enjoyed the view while she could . . .* As a result, she didn't dare try to help Aidan out with the finer points of modern American clothing.

Fortunately, Olivia had already jumped in to redirect the buttoning of his shirt, straightening the collar, and instructing him on how to go about tucking in the unruly pockets. "You look very respectable, Aidan. Your last name is Llanfor, isn't it? I've known some Langfords that used to live on my street, but never a Llanfor. I remember that Gladys Langford grew the most beautiful roses in her front yard, and whenever there was a summer wedding . . ."

She sounded cheerful and chatty, but those who were closest to her would recognize that Olivia was just making emergency conversation to cover for a sudden lump in her throat. She probably hadn't looked at those dear clothes in a long time, and to see them on someone as big and strong as her late husband had been— well, it had to be damn hard.

"I am a smith by trade and accustomed to wearing much rougher materials. I am not certain that I am as *respectable* as these fine clothes suggest," said Aidan. He leaned over and surprised Olivia by planting a kiss on her forehead. "Nor as good a man as the one who once wore them. *Diolch i chi*—thank you. My own *mam* would not have been more kind to me."

He then finally looked at Brooke, and his expression held a mix of emotions. The anger and hurt were so very close to the surface still, and the disappointment too. If she had to guess, she'd say he was angry at her that she wasn't his fiancée—and that he also suffered guilt because he knew he had no right to feel the way he did. Small wonder he didn't smile as he spoke to her. This was a good man and one terribly torn. "You, too, have been kind, Brooke Halloran. Your building has been ruined, and yet you have expressed concern for a stranger and prevented your friend, George, from summoning the authorities. You have opened your home to me and called on this woman to help. I . . ." He paused for a moment, as if trying to choose his words. "I have behaved poorly."

It wasn't quite an apology, but it was definitely an admission. Olivia nearly made Brooke laugh by making a face that only she could see—her friend was plainly impressed by any man who could admit he was *wrong*. It was something that her beloved Jack had always had a very hard time with. G still did and probably always would, for that matter. It was a guy thing for sure, and Brooke gave a mini-shrug in reply to Olivia's expression.

To Aidan, she said, "I guess I'd be grouchy too if I'd been dragged through a vortex and slammed through a skylight. George and I really gave you the third degree as well—asked you a lot of questions and generally gave you a hard time when I'm sure you weren't feeling your best. Maybe we should just have a do-over."

That puzzled him. "What is that?"

"It means, we just start over again and pretend that all the dumb stuff didn't happen. We'll act like we just met right now instead of this morning." *Except for the kiss. I don't want to forget about the kiss, even if he thought I was someone else.* She'd never, ever been kissed like that before. Who knew if she'd ever be kissed like that again?

As he appeared to consider her suggestion, she added: "You know, we really should be celebrating the first day of the rest of your life as a human being."

George came in just in time to hear that. "Ha. The first rule of being human is *there is no free lunch*. At least that's what my mother says." He waggled his eyebrows at his mom and she swatted at him but missed. To Aidan, he said: "I've already got the sidewalk cleaned up, so bro, you're gonna help with this floor here." He jerked his head in the direction of the spell room.

Brooke could swear the man looked relieved. But then, work was a universal constant of life, and maybe it was appealing for that reason. He immediately began to take the jacket off, and Olivia jumped up to help him. She showed Aidan how to roll the shirt-sleeves up over his heavily muscled forearms. *Dear goddess,* thought Brooke. *He looks like the sexiest lumberjack I've ever seen.* The fact that she'd never seen a real one notwithstanding, he looked just like she imagined one should. Surely lumberjacks had hands like Aidan—big, strong, calloused, and work roughened. Perfect for gliding over bare skin, leaving a trail of arousal . . .

As the men left the apartment, Olivia glanced back at Brooke. "See? We just do what comes next, *m'ija.*"

"Okay," Brooke said, but she didn't feel reassured. After all, she'd conjured up a death dog from the hitherto-unknown faery realm and turned him into a handsome prince, kissed him long and deep enough that she could *still* feel him, dammit, only to discover his heart belonged to somebody else. Oh, and she'd trashed her mortgaged building in the process.

She wasn't sure she wanted to know *what came next.*

ELEVEN

~⟨⟨∩⟩⟩~

As George shoveled up glass, he swapped his all-out defensive attitude towards Aidan for forty percent friendly mixed with sixty percent of *I-am-so-keeping-an-eye-on-you*. They'd arranged heavy boxes and garbage cans along the wall by the door, trying to separate out the materials from the mountain of debris. No way would the city dump accept this crap unless it was totally recyclable.

Colored-glass squares had once framed the clear skylight in a design original to the old building. The antique glass was thick and distorted things when you looked through it, like some great old marbles he'd found in a basement when he was a little kid. It was amazing how much of the colored stuff there was—the squares hadn't seemed all that big when they were eighteen feet overhead— but he and Aidan set every bit of it aside in sturdy boxes, from the smallest thumb-size shard to pieces that were six or seven inches wide. Brooke knew of a stained-glass artist who would put the vintage material to good use, a friend of their high school class-mate, Morgan Edwards, up in Spokane Valley.

George smiled about that as he worked. Morgan had worked her butt off to achieve her dream of becoming a veterinarian, and had eventually opened her own clinic. In fact, Brooke took her spoiled cats there for their annual checkups and shots. But last year had been special. He and Brooke had gone together to Morgan's wedding, one of those trendy Celtic handfasting affairs. It had been held outdoors at Morgan's farm and more than half the guests came dressed in historical costumes. Bride and groom had their photos taken on the back of the biggest horse George had ever seen up close (though he admitted he hadn't seen many). Lucky for him, the silvery gray monster was docile enough to be allowed to wander freely with its best buddy, Fred—a brindle mastiff that was almost horse-sized itself. George had created some great sketches that weekend, with Fred helping inspire new details for the hellhounds in the *Devina of Hades* comic series.

All in all, the Celtic theme had been pretty cool. There was plenty of good food. And while the ale and mead had been old fashioned, there'd been plenty of it as well, so the décor could have been all pink roses and tuxedos and George would have been okay with it. Personally, though, he'd prefer a Vegas wedding, maybe something with Elvis just because that was kind of classic, but each to his—

George suddenly paused in midscoop, oblivious to the plinking sound of glass shards sliding to the floor from edge of his shovel. Wasn't Morgan's new husband from Wales? His name was Reese or Rhys or something like that. And they and their friends were experts on all kinds of historical stuff, too. *I wonder if that includes relics like Aidan?* George made a mental note to talk to Brooke about it—he would have whipped out his cell right now to ask her, but he'd insisted she go home with his mom for a while. His mom had needed a break, but so did Brooke—*even if she kept saying she didn't.* He was still having trouble wrapping his brain around whatever the hell had happened here, and it had shaken him right down to his Doc Martens that his friend could have been seriously hurt.

Traveling to Morgan's, however, just might fix everything. They could drive up to Spokane Valley and deliver the stained glass in person—but better yet, they could take Mr. I'm-a-Blacksmith-Who-Used-to-Be-a-Dog with them. George would be more than glad to see *that* walking, talking problem handed off to somebody else. Not that Aidan appeared dangerous or dishonest or anything like that. No, George was much more concerned that given Brooke's overdeveloped sense of responsibility, her devotion to the Gift, and her tender and compassionate heart, she'd adopt the stranger as a project. Or worse. *Just what the hell was with that kiss?* Brooke had had relationships before, but he'd never seen her behave quite like that. In fact, he'd never seen anything like it in connection with his best friend, and it had startled him enough that he hadn't physically intervened.

So as best bud and big brother (yeah, yeah, she was six months older), George felt a need to protect her from herself if nothing else.

Physically, though, he had to admit, she'd protected herself from Aidan pretty damn well. He was so effin' proud of her and, *oh, man*, he wished he'd had his cell out so he could video that punch. Her form was perfect—just as George had taught her. And she'd been fast enough that Aidan never saw it coming. So now the guy would think twice or maybe even three times before he touched her again, and that was A-OK with George.

The best part, of course, was that Aidan had no clue that Brooke had "cheated." And George knew only because he had first-hand experience with her secret weapon. She'd tried out that power punch on him one day when they were practicing and sent him flying ass over teakettle. Although he *felt* a blow, her fist had never physically connected with his face—only the explosive force of her magic. Somehow she'd mustered the energy from deep within herself, probably drawing it up from her very toes. And, man, she had *let him have it.* He'd had a headache for a week, and he cheerfully hoped Aidan had one for twice as long.

Meanwhile, he was forced to give Aidan full creds for at least being a hard worker. George had caught sight of him carrying a metal garbage can down the stairs to the alley by himself. The loaded cans were goddamn heavy, and normally *both* men would have had to work together to heft them down the steep steps. Hell, George knew *he* couldn't do it alone even though he worked out two to three hours a day, and sometimes more. Aidan, however, had astonished him by making it look easy. No complaining either. Sure, the dude was bigger than he was—but size alone didn't always determine strength, something he'd often witnessed at the mixed martial arts gym.

Still, truth be told, George's pride was smarting a little that he hadn't been able to take the guy down. Hell, he hadn't been able to *slow* him down. He'd never run into an opponent like that. And could you even call Aidan an *opponent* when he hadn't even participated? The big dude hadn't so much as looked at him. *Magic. It had to be magic of some kind. Maybe something just like Brooke used.* What George wouldn't do for a rematch with Aidan if that supernatural protection ever wore off . . .

Of course, it was hard to stay pissed when Aidan didn't brag or show off in any way. Some of the guys at the gym would have been sure to call attention to themselves, like when they bench-pressed double their own weight or made other big lifts, but Aidan treated his strength like an everyday thing. It was like the guy was used to that kind of a load or something. It made sense that he had to be tough to be a blacksmith, but, *Dios,* this was ridiculous.

It was while Aidan was taking yet another maximum load down to the alley that George spotted something shiny in the rubble that didn't glitter like glass. With his gloved hand, he brushed away some of the debris to reveal the cool gleam of something silver. Some chain from the skylight? He didn't remember it having anything like that—to the best of his memory, the skylight didn't even open. George pulled on it and was surprised at what came out of the rubble. The thick intricate links interlocked like Middle Earth chain mail on steroids, forming a very wide and ornate collar of some sort. At least he figured that's what it must be, although there was no catch, no clasp or fastener of any kind. Not necessary, he supposed—it was more than big enough to fit over the wearer's head. And it was a thing of beauty, that was for sure.

"Kudos to the artist," he murmured, his own inner artist utterly fascinated with the weighty piece. The craftsmanship was flawless, and the links appeared to have no seams at all. In fact, when he squinted, each individual link looked to be etched with beautiful designs and symbols. How the hell had somebody done *that*? The heavy metal shone brightly, but not garishly, as if it had been plated with real silver. Maybe it had—but he couldn't begin to guess what the base metal could be, because no way would anyone make something like this out of *solid* silver, right? He supposed it could be some kind of steampunk design—one of the girls who worked at the gym was really into that stuff. Yet even the links formed patterns, too, designs that swirled and interconnected, neither masculine nor feminine but something unique that borrowed from both and neither.

On second thought, the whole thing seemed more like a replica of some ancient design or a museum piece. In fact, it would have fit right in with Morgan's Celtic-themed wedding, George decided.

He held it in his cupped hands, hefting the weight of it. Despite how heavy it was, the thick links of the collar poured easily from one palm to the other, like a metal waterfall. It made little crystalline sounds, and he was reminded of tiny bells on a long ago Christmas tree. Happy sounds, pleasant sounds. Before he knew it, he had stripped off his T-shirt and put his head through the wide opening of the collar. The metal was cool and smooth against his skin as the heavy links draped sensuously over his collarbones, arranging themselves in a broad dramatic circle over his tanned pecs. It fit perfectly, as if it had been made expressly for him. It *felt* luxurious. Like he was a king, a pharaoh, a warrior prince—better yet, George could see himself entering the ring, commanding the attention and respect of the crowd, and intimidating his opponent before the fight even began. Man, he would look like an effin' *gladiator* with this chain-mail collar. He had to find a mirror, now, right now, and *check this out*. Before he'd taken more than a couple steps towards Brooke's apartment, however, a wave of dizziness hit him hard. His vision tunneled for a moment, as if he'd been hit with a knockout punch.

It only lasted a moment though. The dizziness vanished, his vision cleared, and he could hear Aidan coming up the stairs. Quickly, he pulled his T-shirt over his head, grateful for the over-sized sports logo printed on it—a pair of giant eyes frowned from shoulder to abdomen, hiding any faint bump that the collar might have made, and the red letters on the fabric spelled out a strangely apt message: *Bad Boy*.

Apt because he knew the silver collar could only belong to Aidan. What it meant, what it was for, what it was worth—none of that mattered. George Santiago-Callahan didn't have a dishonest bone in his body and had never stolen a single thing in his entire life—but he wasn't planning on giving the exquisite collar back.

Ever.

∼

"Aidan ap Llanfor was *mine*! Mine to enjoy as I chose. Mine to take to my bed, mine to take his life away or grant it continue. All mine, and *you lost him*!"

Celynnen threw the scrying globe she was holding. It wasn't a surprise that Lurien didn't bother to flinch, even though it missed his head by scarcely a hair's breadth—but it didn't improve her mood. If only he had not removed his helm, then the silver sphere would have dashed itself into satisfying shards against it. As it was, her latest servant, a crymbil with vivid orange eyes, caught the would-be-missile before it could strike the grand arching window over her bed. Bowing, the creature set the orb in its place upon an exquisitely carved shelf.

"Leave us," she snapped, and the crymbil ran from the room, its stubby wings flapping uselessly.

Celynnen circled the Lord of the Wild Hunt as he stood in her palace chambers. Her golden yellow gown and cleverly embroidered shoes were the color of autumn chrysanthemums, her white hair flowing loose with pale glowing blossoms snared in it. She was as a candle flame circling the darkness, the starkest of contrast to Lurien's black leathers, tall boots, and wild black hair. Everything about him was the very opposite of her and completely unlike anyone else in the Court. For one thing, he did not fear her. Any other male among the fae would have stood at rigid attention—had he even been received into her private rooms—but Lurien's stance was casual. "You are entirely too confident," she warned. "You are here only because I wish it, because I would speak privately with you. So far, I do not like the tale you bring me."

"The truth is the truth, my lady."

"So you say. Tell me again how it came to pass that a simple grim eluded the most skilled hunter among our kind."

"With the escape of the previous grim, I tightened all of our precautions. My watcher alerted me that this latest grim had returned from the mortal world as expected and yet failed to arrive at the kennels. It took time to find his trail, even with the hounds, because we could not guess which way he had gone. I traced the grim at last as he left the stone path, tracked him through the royal gardens, and followed his spoor to the Silver Maples, all the way to the Gray Gate. We did not expect him to strike out over the Deep Waters. There, it proved nearly impossible to track him—I'm sure you're aware, princess, that horses and hounds are not aquatic in nature. To make matters more difficult, it seems that the gods of the sea allowed the grim asylum. Not only would they not give him up; they would tell us nothing, and they stirred the waves that we could not find his trail again. We searched until dawn was upon us, and I had no choice but to send the Hunt back to the realm."

She stopped directly in front of him. Like all those of the royal line, she was willowy tall, but she still she had to stand upon her toes to peer into his face—she utterly refused to look up to an inferior. In his eyes she searched not for truth but for the answers she wanted. But while her own eyes were iridescent, as pale and crystalline as her hair, Lurien's were deep black pools. They told her exactly nothing—although a faint quirk of his mouth announced that he was amused by her efforts to read him.

It infuriated her further, even as on some level she knew that was precisely his intent.

"No choice? You had *no choice* but to let a valuable prisoner escape? A servant belonging to the royal family?"

"Your honorable family had nothing to do with this particular prisoner. I doubt they even know of his existence. You alone are the one who captured him and kept him for your own amusement."

She refused to respond to that but began pacing again. Hidden within the long, deep sleeves of her gown, her delicate hands opened and closed, wishing for something else to throw, wanting even more to strike at him with her fists or claw the strong planes of his face with her curving fingernails. Her handsome mortal blacksmith, Aidan ap Llanfor, was gone. She hadn't even finished playing with him yet—the stubborn man had refused to bargain for a return to his comely human body. She had succeeded neither in seducing him nor forcing him into her bed. He couldn't be beyond her grasp, not yet. The game wasn't over.

"You let him go, Lurien! What I am hearing is that you feared the dawn more than you feared *me*." The light outside dimmed as a rare congregation of clouds, heavy with water that made them purple as a bruise, gathered in direct response to her temper. "I doubt that you even tried to recapture him at all!" she accused, and silver needles of rain slashed a slanted path to the ground, piercing the petals of the glowing roses beyond the great arching window.

"I said I sent the Hunt back. I did not say I went with it." To her surprise, Lurien took a step towards her, then another, a dark panther slowly stalking. "And I fear nothing, not even a spoiled tywysoges like yourself."

"You dare much," Celynnen hissed, reminding him that his prey was dangerous. Instead, he moved faster than even fae sight could perceive, and seized her slender upper arms.

"Until now, I have not dared nearly enough."

Outside, the rain fell harder, flattening the jewel-bright grass and beating down the leaves from the trees. There were cries of alarm in the distance as the intricately patterned palace gardens were washed into disarray. Lurien only laughed. "Surely you do not call *that* a storm, Celynnen? Come to *my* bed, and I will undress you by the sheen of lightning and make pleasure pound like thunder in your sapphire blood."

He had nullified her magic somehow. And she could not free herself by struggling. No one had ever laid hands on her before, and certainly no one had ever held her helpless. "I will destroy you for this outrage!" she hissed.

"You can try. But consider this: you have taken countless lovers over the eons—hapless human pets, and Court-climbing fools, and tame Tylwyth Teg nobility. But you have never *been* taken, and you have never lain with one such as I. Are you not curious as to what I can make you feel?"

The tiny silver dagger was heavy in the hem of her sleeve, and her hand was already on its smooth diamond hilt. Another inch or two and she would have impaled him like an insect, although a scratch would suffice, and then laughed as the poison released from the blade paralyzed him. She would have taken her pleasure slowly then, unwrapping him layer by layer as if he were a gift. First the leathers. Then the skin . . .

Would have, except his last sentence completely arrested her attention: *Are you not curious as to what I can make you feel?*

Yessss! screamed something primal within her, aching and anxious for sensation, for emotion, for anything. And there was no more valuable currency in the entire Nine Realms than what the Lord of the Wild Hunt was presently offering her . . .

Something new.

She released her grip on the dagger and allowed it to slide back into its sheath in her sleeve. "We are intrigued," she said, and it pleased her that he did not miss her deliberate use of the royal *we*. "You have our permission, nay, our *command*, to demonstrate the abilities you boast of." Her condescending tone lit fires of annoyance in his gaze, and she met his irritation with her most dazzling smile. If he thought he was going to do the taking, he was gravely mistaken.

Lurien smiled back—and in an eyeblink, they were not only within another chamber but in another place entirely. His strong hands still braceleted her upper arms, but her back was towards him, where she couldn't help but feel the hard press of his proud cock through her heavy gown. Celynnen could also see the full splendor of the vast room he had brought her to. The high ceiling was transparent, formed entirely of enormous quartz crystals.

Although there was nothing but sky above them, the glasslike structures clustered together as if they had grown there, and many stretched down into the room like six-sided stalactites. The towering walls utilized quartz as well, clear polished blocks in a multitude of shapes that fitted perfectly together with narrow slabs of translucent agate. Here and there, smaller gemstones had been inset at random—amethyst, peridot, citrine, and garnet—yet there was nothing feminine about this place. It was organic in the sense that perhaps it had not been built at all, but *grown*, sprouted from some mountainside, or birthed from a volcano's maw, or seeded by some ancient meteor. It was a room meant for the night, one that would reflect and magnify the cold silver light of the moon and its attendant stars as they rode across the dark sky.

The centerpiece was the magnificent bed, six-sided to mimic the quartz crystals high above it, with six carved agate posts. Carelessly tossed upon it was the butter-soft pelt of an enormous golden lion, a creature that had not been seen in the mortal world for thousands of years. The thick luxuriant skin draped the entire bed, promising a treasure trove of sensation. Celynnen was jolted by a tiny coil of excitement deep within her as she thought of how that fur might feel against her naked—

With a single smooth movement, Lurien yanked downwards, tearing the sleeves from her golden-yellow gown at the shoulders and tossing them across the room. Her shock gave her no time to react, and a split second was long enough for him to grasp her wrists and cross them in front of her as he pulled her back against his hard body. "I like my lovers unarmed," he said. "Did you think I would not expect your tricks? Knives and poisons—and let's not forget that pretty black bwgan stone you draw such power from."

At a word from him, the sleeves vanished from sight, and Celynnen gasped. "What have you done? The stone is beyond price! You vulgar oaf, you have ruined my gown and stolen that which is rightfully mine!" She kicked at him, but his tall leather boots resisted her efforts.

"I have stolen nothing, only sent them back to your chambers. You'll find them draped quite tidily over your bedstead." He whispered at the back of her neck, "Perhaps it is *you* I should bend over your bedstead."

"Let me go this instant!" She struggled but he held her all the tighter.

"I cannot. I have yet to fulfill your earlier command, princess. You are here by your own consent, because you wished to know what I can make you feel. Afterwards, you may judge if you wish me to let you go," he breathed. "Or not."

She spat out a dark spell then, a ruthless arrow of magic expressly forbidden under ancient faery law. It should have slain Lurien where he stood—after it had devoured the flesh from his bones. Instead, he laughed as the magic morphed into a harmless shower of diamond sparks that winked out as they came in contact with the stone floor.

"This is *my* territory, Celynnen," he spoke in her ear. His breath was cool and raised tiny shivers over her shoulders and down her spine. "No magic but mine can be worked here." The low rumble of rapidly approaching thunder underscored his words.

Still holding her helpless, he nuzzled aside her waterfall of hair, exposing the nape of her neck to his mouth. His lips were soft for the moment, barely skimming her skin. Slowly, lazily, he tasted her. Such a very small area to be stimulated so, and yet her breasts reacted at once, swelling until her nipples were uncomfortable beneath the exquisite golden bodice that held them.

"This," he whispered, "is what I will do between your thighs." He favored her with long strokes of his tongue, as if he were indeed a panther. And as if she were indeed prey, he bit the back of her neck, a sharp-sweet sensation, and a trickle of moisture ran down the inside of her legs.

As if he knew what he'd unleashed in her, he released her wrists at last. Instead, he slid his hands down her body to clutch her hips tight into the cradle of his where his rampant cock nudged against her like an impatient stallion. "Undo your gown, Celynnen," he murmured, and his voice was deep with want as well. "Free your breasts to the open air, and I will call down the lightning itself to caress you if you so desire."

Her thoughts whirled as she was caught between extremes. She was overwhelmed with sensation, with desire, with need, with want . . . She *felt*. Felt! And craved more. Yet she chafed to be in control, as she was always in control. To command, to be feared and to be obeyed. She was *Celynnen*, blooded princess of the House of Thorn and heir to the throne of the Nine Realms. But it was her own shaking hands doing the obeying, following Lurien's suggestions to the letter, and clawing open the front of her golden gown from neck to midthigh.

He had been right about her lovers. She'd taken more than even she could be bothered to count, and all had quickly bored her. All had been discarded. Her beauty had driven many mad with desire, both human and fae, but none had coaxed this—this *wildness*—out of her. She dropped her dress to the ground and stepped forth as if from a chrysalis, as he stripped off his hunter's clothing. They came together with an unexpected ferocity. It was nothing so simple as an act of sex; it was a feral battle between her and Lurien. Wills, bodies, energies, magics—all wrested with one another and neither she nor Lurien prevailed. Perhaps neither wanted to prevail.

Outside, thunder hammered until it was inside of her too, the vibrations overhead resonating both in the floor and in the bones, pounding in her very blood just as Lurien had promised her. Lightning bolts forked overhead, their violent light broken and scattered by the crystal ceiling until the random flashes became all but continuous. Naked and straining, bodies that had been alternately strobed with bright color and velvet darkness were now luminous with a bluish light of their own.

That had never happened to her before, and as a member of the royal family, she had lived far longer than most. She'd thought it just an old fable, a made-up romantic tale, that faerie lovers might achieve such a state . . .

Celynnen smiled up at Lurien for the first time. It was a real smile, fierce because she was fierce, but neither calculated nor forced. The moment drew out as the living light strengthened, revealing all—each lean muscle on Lurien's tall frame, the gleam of his eyes and flash of teeth, the strong planes of his features. The blue glow lasted long enough for her to see something else too . . .

She screamed out her rage, furious at the sight of that which she abhorred most, and there was a touch of fear in her too. The more her lover tried to calm her, the more she shrieked and slapped at his touch. In fact, she couldn't stop herself from screaming until Lurien drew away from her completely. The glow of their bodies faded as if it had never been. The lightning diminished and ceased, the thunder slunk away like a beaten dog, until silence ruled and they were both left in complete darkness.

TWELVE

⟅⟆

Lurien was in the dark in more ways than one. He could hear Celynnen's sobbing breaths, feel a feral rage radiate from her that bordered on insanity. Even terror and despair swirled amidst the discordant energies she was emanating. Everything he said or did seemed to make things worse, as if she were in a nightmare she could not wake from. Finally, Lurien murmured a spell, and the quartz crystals high above shone with a warm, steady light. Celynnen was on the opposite side of the enormous bed, her back braced against the carved agate post, holding the lion pelt in front of her as if to shield herself.

From *him*.

"Tell me how I have offended. Have I hurt thee in some way?" he asked, not daring to make a move towards her. "How may I comfort you?"

The look she gave him was like nothing he had ever seen in his long, long life. Her gaze was filled with utter loathing, her beautiful lips drawn back in snarling revulsion. "You," she spat out. "You are *marked*." She pointed an accusing finger at him. At his hand.

He surveyed it. His struggle with Aidan ap Llanfor had left him badly wounded. Worse, it had left him without a horse, and it was a hellishly long way back to the faery realm—and a healer—

from the middle of the Deep Waters. When he arrived at last, the healer had been able to restore the full function of his fingers and hand, but the salt water had made the scarring permanent. It mattered little to Lurien—what kind of hunter bore no scars?

"This? This offends you? 'Tis but a battle scar, one I earned from a worthy opponent."

"Marked," she repeated. "You are not perfect, you are *disfigured*. Flawed. Tainted. How dare you touch me with such, such *ugliness*. You are *repugnant*, and beneath me."

It was his turn to stare. "Beneath you? Is that what you truly believe? I am less because my appearance is not *perfect*?" His anger flared, and he summoned more light, adding a unique spectrum to the room that highlighted not only the scars on his hand but also many others on his naked body. "These," he said, pointing to several parallel stripes on his left shoulder. "These are from the poisonous claws of the largest bwgan ever captured alive. And this—" he pivoted to display the back of his right calf, where a ridge of bluish scar tissue ran from the back of his knee to his heel. "This reminds me never to turn my back on a dead warth." Lurien showed her his back, where three small scars punctuated the skin of his broad back. There was a matching one on his collarbone. "These were arrow wounds, received as I fought off an incursion along our borders.

"They are badges of my honor, these scars, every last one of them. Proof of my loyal service to the Nine Realms, to the kingdom."

Evidence too, of his only failure. "And this one, here, nearly took my life." Lurien pointed to his chest, displaying a long thick scar where an iron throwing axe had been lodged in his sternum. Celynnen looked away quickly as if sickened by the sight—and not with any sympathy or sensitivity for what he might have suffered, but only because she found it repellant.

"I was wounded trying to save *your* great-uncle and great-aunt, King Arthfael and Queen Gwenhidw, from their betrayers," he said.

She refused to face him. Instead, she shrugged her beautiful shoulders, the color of exquisite marble, her pale hair tumbling like a waterfall to pool around her hips. "You did *not* save them, so what good is such a hideous blemish? Or you, for that matter?"

What good indeed? "We speak of *your* blood, *your* family. Does that matter not at all to you?"

"The king is dead, and Gwenhidw may as well be, for all the use she is to the Nine Realms." Her voice was harsh. "In fact, had you not interfered, I would be queen at this very moment. All you have done is delay my destiny."

Lurien shook himself free of the past and looked—*truly looked*—at the creature in his bed. He had been obsessed with her beauty for untold centuries, and despite her proud and selfish demeanor, he had believed there was something more within, a pearl inside the cold and prickly shell. True, he had more motive than his attraction to her. If she would accept him as her consort, the combination of her high station and his control of the Hunt might allow them to work together to stabilize the realms. Never had he dreamed that they would come together with a ferocity worthy of a true mating, not just a sexual encounter. It was so much more than he'd hoped for . . .

And now it was so much less.

"It is apparent to me now that your loveliness lies only on the outside," he said. She turned to glare at him, her iridescent eyes stunningly beautiful even when they were filled with hatred and loathing. Celynnen had been named for the eternally green holly tree that bore bright red berries even in the coldest winter. Perhaps it was apt that the leaves of the comely plant were laden with sharp thorns that drew blood from any hand that came near it. He had made a grave error in pursuing her—but it was one he could remedy. "I believe I have fulfilled your initial command to demonstrate my abilities, princess. And it is plain that you have rendered your judgment."

Her expression said more than he cared to know.

"However, as I said before, I alone have power in this place," Lurien continued. "I said you may judge if you wish me to release you. But whether you go or stay is entirely my decision. I could keep you here until you come to appreciate me more . . ."

"You would not dare!" she hissed, and actually bared her teeth. "My presence is required at Court, and my absence noted at once. I would be *missed.*"

"I'm certain that you would, princess. But not by me." Lurien waved a hand, noting that her eyes widened just a split second before she vanished. He imagined many eyes would widen when she appeared in the midst of the glittering, chattering Court . . .

Without her fine clothing.

She would hate him forever (if she didn't already) and attempt revenge from now until time itself sputtered out. That mattered very little now. Better an avowed enemy than a pretended friend— or a lover. Sighing, Lurien sat on the edge of the bed and traced the scar on his chest that had so offended Celynnen. "By the Seven Sisters, I wish it had killed me," he muttered. *If my death would have saved the king.* The night the royal couple was attacked, Lurien had answered the alarm and raced to their chambers with every member of the Hunt at his heels. Too late, all of them everlastingly too late.

The king of the Fair Ones had defended his beloved Gwenhidw against the assassins, all of whom were armed with iron weapons. The queen had had the presence of mind to weave a binding charm to trap the attackers, but all of her skills could not save her Arthfael.

He had died just as Lurien and his huntsmen arrived. The murderers died as well, and horribly. Their capture had triggered a hidden spell—one that they were likely unaware of—that incinerated them from the inside out. Within seconds, there were eight piles of flaked white ash that could not be questioned. Still, the Lord of the Wild Hunt and his followers sought to secure the royal residence and searched every room. Without warning, a ninth assassin erupted from beneath a bench, buried a throwing axe deep into Lurien's chest, and leapt from a window into the clouds high above the rainbow chasm. No body was ever found, though several men loyal to the queen braved the climb into the deep jagged gorge to search for one. Since time began, it had been believed that the jump was simply not survivable, even by a fae, even if that fae had command of all magics. *Not even if that fae had wings.*

It had been obvious that the band of murderers were only tools of a larger conspiracy to drive apart the Nine Realms. As the healers worked on him, Lurien had requested that the assassin's ashes be untouched, left exactly where they had fallen. His hunters might have thought he was raving at the time, but they obeyed him faithfully just the same.

And when Lurien was well enough to sift through the unpleasant contents of the eight surprisingly small mounds, he found several reptilian scales among the ash in every one of them. Not large, perhaps the size of a fingernail, and the colossal heat of the magic-induced fire had fired them into something more resembling obsidian, but they had once been scales nonetheless.

Draigddynion.

The kingdom's Nine Realms were ruled by the Tylwyth Teg, but they were far from the only inhabitants. In fact, they weren't even in the majority. There were as many types of fae creatures as there were leaves on an oak tree—all sprung from the same root when the earth was yet new. And every one unique. The chameleon-like Draigddynion were of the dark fae, living in the same dank, forested regions as the flesh-seeking bwgans. Unlike those monstrous salamanders, the Draigddynion were intelligent, a proud bipedal race whose appearance begat their name: *dragon men*.

But the Draigddynion didn't bother with the politics of the Court. They gave a passing deference to the Crown and little else. In fact, they behaved as many of the faery clans did and kept strictly to themselves. Either the assassins had actually *been* dragon men—or they had carried Draigddynion scales in their pockets. It could be a very clever ruse in case of *fire*.

In all the time since, Lurien had been unable to uncover the source of the intrigue. Perhaps because he had to work alone—he dared not share what he knew, save with the queen, because there was no telling who had been compromised and who had not. And also because the intrigue continued to grow, joined by numerous other plots and schemings. As a result, the kingdom continued to unravel, and he felt powerless to stop it. The Nine Realms might have burst asunder eons ago if Queen Gwenhidw had not been as powerful and as committed as she was.

But even she could not hold it together much longer.

Perhaps it was natural that Lurien's thoughts turned to Aidan ap Llanfor. Now *there* was a just and honorable mortal, one who could put many of the Tylwyth Teg to shame. The Nine Realms could use a leader like that, even if he wasn't fae. He snorted at that and corrected himself: *perhaps* especially *a leader who wasn't fae*. The blacksmith-turned-grim had more than earned his freedom, however, and he deserved to build a life outside of the shadow of the Fair Ones. It was a point of honor that the Lord of the Wild Hunt would never track him further, yet he trusted that Aidan had retained the silver torc as he had promised to do.

Lurien shook his head. Surely, it was the most foolish of all wishes that the man might someday use the symbol of his captivity to reach out to a former captor.

But Lurien hoped nonetheless. After his disastrous tryst with Celynnen, he had nothing else.

∿

Brooke flipped the *off* switch on the monstrous orange Shop-Vac. Despite the ear plugs, her head was ringing from having used the loud machine for the past hour. It had done its job, though. After George and Aidan had removed all the debris they could, the vast open floor had to be vacuumed thoroughly to get rid of the last of the glass splinters and dust. Olivia had worked along behind her with a mop and bucket. Brooke had told her friend that she didn't have to do that, of course, but when had she ever won an argument with Olivia? Together, they surveyed the room.

"It's safe to walk on now. And like *mi madre* taught me, I put some lemon verbena and rosemary in the water. It will help to transform any lingering bad luck into good luck," said the older woman, leaning on her mop. "But I think this place is gonna need a lot more than luck, *m'ija*."

Now, *there* was an understatement. The antique hardwood floors might be clean enough to eat off now, but the oak boards had plenty of brand new scars. Plus, there was a now-permanent ring deeply branded into the wood where Brooke had drawn her salt circle. For once she was glad for her perfectionist nature—she always took great pains to make her spell ring as perfectly round as possible. Little had she suspected it would someday get burned into the floor! The indentation was four inches wide and nearly an inch deep (and thankfully, the old floors were far thicker than that). *I guess I have a template for future circles now.*

That's if she dared to make any. Brooke still hadn't tried to

cast the teeniest, tiniest little spell, not even a simple houseclean-
ing charm. Who knew what might happen? And right now, she
didn't feel like she could handle one more disaster, no matter how
small.

High above the circle, the gaping hole where the skylight used
to be had been covered by a heavy-duty tarp. It was brilliant royal
blue, and Brooke hated it heartily—not because she disliked the
color in and of itself, but because it was dark. George had said it
was waterproof, which was a good thing. Unfortunately it was also
lightproof, and the effect was neither cozy nor pleasant. Brooke
felt like the vast ceiling had been lowered substantially.

At least the guys had stapled *clear* plastic over the missing
front windows. If that light had been blocked off as well, she would
have found it unbearable. A glazier would be here in the next day
or so to replace the glass in the antique wooden frames, but as
George had put it, her once-beautiful skylight was a *whole 'nother
story*. The cost of rebuilding the huge window in the high ceiling
was gasp inducing. G tried to explain how it would be cheaper and
faster to just roof the whole thing over, but that idea had been
horrifying enough to make moisture spring to her eyes. The tears
hadn't fallen, but Olivia had let loose a torrent of Spanish upon her
son that sounded capable of peeling paint from the walls.

If only that had worked. Whatever power had been unleashed
in Brooke's spell circle had not only burned a ring in the floor; it
had stained the walls with various shades of bright sulfurous yellow—and that included the two walls made of brick! They certainly
didn't look charmingly rustic and earthy anymore. Worse, the
bright color changed shade in strange concentric rings, from hot
buttered sunflower near the floor to glowing mustard near the
ceiling, and all of it was crackled as if it had been baked. The half
wall that partitioned off her apartment had suffered similar

damage—but it had effectively shielded all that lay within. *And thank goodness for that—Rory would look terrible in canary yellow.* The outer walls above her apartment didn't begin turning yellow until about ten feet up from the floor.

Olivia linked elbows with her. "When the guy has come and gone to fix the front windows, you and I will do something—perhaps a smudging with sage and sweetgrass—to cleanse this room and rid it of any negative energy that might have crept in."

"Do you know of anything that can get rid of this ghastly color?"

She shook her head slowly, and several tendrils of her long curly hair escaped from the piled tresses on her head. "Only paint, *m'ija*. Lots and lots and *lots* of paint."

Well, that meant it was going to stay the color of fluorescent bananas for a long time. Brooke and George had worked together to paint the entire upstairs right after she'd gutted and renovated it. Not only had it taken forever; she shuddered to think of how many gallons of primer alone they'd used. And now the two brick walls would likely have to be painted as well. Nope, her first priority would be fixing the skylight.

As soon as she finished paying for the front windows.

Brooke sighed—business had better be really, *really* good over the next few months. She'd better double-check her feng shui books—there was something about attracting wealth by putting citrine crystals and lucky cat figurines in the appropriate corners of the shop. But Olivia was right too. "A cleansing is always a good idea," she said to her friend. "But you're not actually feeling any negative energy in here, are you?"

"No." Olivia looked around as if she could physically see it, as she pinned the stray curls of her hair back in place. "Not at all, but there is much more than your own energy here."

"Kind of like *a disturbance in the force* sort of thing, right?" Brooke had been thinking that herself. She'd expected that the positive chi she so carefully nurtured would be restored once the massive mess was cleaned up, but the flow of energy around the room was still *off*, though not in a bad way. It was different—altered and added to in some way. She couldn't blame the outrageous coloration left by the blast—yellow was a very positive color, although it was definitely overstimulating. That left only one possible source. "Do you still think it's coming from Aidan?"

Her friend nodded. "I could feel a powerful energy when I patched him up, as if he had the Gift. It's probably because he's still pretty electrified with *change*. I cannot think of anyone I have ever known who has experienced so much transformation in so short a period of time."

Giant otherworldly dog to regular everyday human. It was a big change, all right. Immediately she thought of the Death card in her multiple tarot readings—but that reading was meant for *her*, wasn't it? "So you think his personal energy is intensified? Because I felt power, a lot of it, when he—well, when I touched him. Before you came." *And please, please, please, don't say George told you that I kissed the guy . . .*

"It may settle down eventually. But as long as his energy is supercharged, you might consider tapping into it for your spell work."

"*Olivia!*"

"I did not mean like *that*, *m'ija*—although a little *amor caliente* might be worth trying too! Were you not complaining that your magic needed a boost?"

"I don't think it needs *that* kind of a boost. And please don't put that picture in my head again, okay?" As if the idea hadn't been there all along . . .

Her mentor laughed. "I'm just saying his energy might balance yours, that's all. And then your magic will be balanced too."

Desperate for distraction, Brooke hefted the big orange Shop-Vac and carried it downstairs, through the center aisle of the Handcastings shop, and out the door into the street. The sidewalk was clean and tidy, and she made a mental note to thank George for his hard work on that—as soon as she found him. His black-on-black pickup truck—Carmelita—was nowhere to be seen.

Olivia came up behind her and set the mop and bucket down beside the vacuum. She checked the texts on her cell phone. "George is just taking the last load to the dump. He says he'll be back in a few minutes."

"I can't believe he's been using own truck for this. I know how he feels about that vehicle. He wouldn't take her within ten miles of a place like that, in case the garbage was contagious or something, never mind drive on a dusty gravel road." Brooke teared up suddenly. "You've both done so much for me today, and I'm so darn lucky to have you. What on earth would I have done with that giant mess by myself?"

"You'd have managed." Olivia patted her on the back. "You're a determined girl and you would have managed. It would just have taken a year or two, that's all."

Brooke laughed and hugged her friend tightly. She had always felt much closer to Olivia than to her own mother, though it used to give her a twinge of guilt every time she thought of it. The guilt had faded over the years as she grew up and realized that she and her folks simply had a difference of personalities. You couldn't pick your relatives, and they couldn't choose you either. Although she often wondered if she'd been left on their doorstep as an infant, Mom and Dad loved her in their own way, and she loved them.

She loved Olivia too. The woman had understood and accepted her son's best friend ever since she first came home with him and Lissy after school in second grade. After that, Brooke had spent every spare moment at the Santiago-Callahan house. Later, she and Olivia grew even closer. Her stand-in mom became her friend and mentor, patiently instructing her in the use of the Gift. But if the Gift had never come to her, Olivia would have loved her just as much. Of that Brooke was certain.

She was certain that her parents still loved her too, even though they weren't currently speaking to her. A couple years after she finished college, she had officially come out of the broom closet. She knew her parents wouldn't like it, and she wasn't surprised when they reacted with bewilderment and anger. She was a little surprised when they sued the school for allegedly influencing her to adopt *unholy practices*. And she was downright shocked when they cut off all contact with her. Except for sending religious brochures (and occasionally preachers or missionaries) to her door, she heard nothing from them.

To hold the Gift is to give without condition, and to receive with gratitude. That went for love too. She would continue to give it. Although to date, all of her letters to her parents were either returned or went unanswered, she wrote to them every couple of months just the same.

"I'm so thankful for you," she said, as she gave Olivia another quick squeeze. "And I can't complain too much about what happened. Nobody got hurt, not even the cats. My apartment is untouched, so I still have a nice place to live, and my shop is okay, so I can carry on with my business without any interruption. Hey, it's only one room that looks like a nuclear testing zone."

"Now there's a positive perspective, *m'ija*. And even if it *is* yellow, the spell room will look much better once the skylight is back in."

Yes it will, thought Brooke. *Except I don't know when that'll be.* The insurance company had been no help at all. The agent needed to know a *cause* for all this damage, a valid explanation for how this room came to be in this condition, before it could be determined whether she had appropriate coverage in her policy. What on earth could she say? Burglars? Vandals? A science experiment gone awry? A meteor? Or there was always the truth—a death dog from the faery realm had accidentally been drawn into her building by a spell. Nope, she was definitely on her own when it came to paying for this mess. And she really didn't want to see her banker again so soon.

As if she'd read Brooke's mind, Olivia gave her one last hug. "Something good will come from all this. You'll see, I promise. Now I am going to wait for my son, drag my old bones home, toss them into my La-Z-Boy, and watch TV until I fall asleep. Maybe I will have George make *my* dinner tonight, eh?"

"You know he'll just dial takeout," giggled Brooke.

"A man has to do what a man has to do. As long as I'm not cooking, I don't care. And you need a break too, *m'ija*. But I think somebody already has that covered for you."

"What's covered?"

"Why, the hole in the roof of course," said Olivia quickly. "The boys put that tarp over the hole where the skylight was. But I don't think you've been up there yet—you really should check out their work, you know, make sure it's waterproof before night falls. Besides, do you even know if your greenhouse or your garden survived the disaster?"

"Oh, *crap*, I haven't checked a thing up there. I hope my plants are okay." What if they'd been damaged when the giant dog came through the skylight? What if they'd been sprayed with glass? Many of the herbs she utilized in her spells and sold in her Handcastings shop were cultivated in her rooftop gardens and greenhouse.

"You will feel much better if you look everything over. Maybe even talk to your plants a little. It's always a very calming thing to do." Olivia sat upon the orange vacuum, playing sudoku on her phone screen. "And I will have George return this monster machine in the morning, so you will not have to worry about it. Now off you go, *m'ija*. Water your plants, and spend some time with your cats, and just *relax*. I will come by to check on you tomorrow."

As advice went, it was pretty appealing. As good-byes went, it was almost a dismissal, albeit a very nice one. Brooke chalked it up to exhaustion—her friend was likely much more tired than she was. Olivia had insisted on helping despite Brooke's protests, so except for a small break hours ago, they'd worked side by side all day. Small wonder her favorite chair was calling her.

Brooke's own body was definitely sending signals that it had had enough and wouldn't mind dropping into a comfy chair for the evening as well. But the plants . . . She really did want to make sure they were all right. The cats would enjoy playing on the roof too. The weather was nice and they'd been locked in the apartment all day during the big cleanup.

Brooke entered her shop and surveyed the steep staircase. Right on cue, her feet started to hurt. *Too bad there isn't an elevator to the roof.*

THIRTEEN

⌒⫯⫯⌒

T here were footsteps on the stairs. Aidan could hear them echoing inside the metal hut that stood in one corner of the rooftop. He stepped back, just past the corner of what Olivia had explained was a *greenhouse*, and watched as the heavy door opened and Brooke and her three cats emerged. She didn't look in his direction at all but headed straight for the tall wooden garden boxes that bordered the waist-high perimeter of the roof on that end of the building. Aidan was accustomed to gardening in the ground, but these clever wooden boxes were deep enough to hold a foot of soil and designed to be easy to reach without bending over. Plus, they had wheels like carts so they could be moved around. He liked the whole idea quite a bit, he decided.

The way to the ill-fated skylight and the rest of the roof was visually blocked by the large greenhouse. Aidan hadn't been able to resist looking inside the glass building earlier. Trellises of every kind lined the walls, overgrown with vines that were heavy laden with all manner of strange fruits. He'd seen them before of course, was well aware that new foods had arrived in Wales from other lands and had been cultivated there over the centuries until they were now as common as clay—but he had never tasted a single one of them. Many were even eaten *raw* now, something that would never have been done in his time.

He had expected more of the wooden carts or some other containers to fill the center of the greenhouse, but the floor space had been left open to accommodate an immense wooden chair, more than long enough to lie down upon. Framed in wood, it was heaped with pillows as if it were a sofa. It seemed an odd thing to find in the middle of a greenhouse—but then, surely no stranger than finding a boxed garden on a rooftop.

More of the garden carts lined up end to end as a fence between the greenhouse and the rest of the roof. These ones had lattice backs that supported all kinds of lush vines and creeping plants. The wall of greenery neatly sectioned off Brooke's charming garden area. And in the very center of it all stood a cluster of big metal drums, painted in bright colors—orange, yellow, pink and purple. They were for gardening as well, holding a soil and straw mix for bigger plants like potatoes that needed more root space than the boxes could provide. The three cats played hide and seek around them and chased insects and one another under the boxes.

The cats were amusing, but it was much more interesting to watch Brooke. She hovered over each of her plants like they were children, watering, untangling leaves, and even talking to them a little—encouraging some, chiding others. Aidan smiled in spite of himself. How many times had he heard his *mam* do the very same in her own garden? It was good to reminisce, he decided, even if it was also bitter to know that he was alone in his recollections. Because of the cold-hearted Celynnen, his *mam* and *tad* didn't even know they had ever had a son. He had finally regained the memories that were rightfully his—but his family and friends had died centuries ago without ever recalling anyone named Aidan ap Llanfor. Maybe that made it even more important that he remember them.

And what of Annwyl? He'd grieved when Celynnen had callously ended her life, grieved and blamed himself, until the enchantment of the faery realm had pulled a curtain over his ability to remember. The curtain was gone now—and so was the buffer between him and his pain. It was a like a live thing, an imp that clung to his clothing, ready to stick an emotional knife between his ribs at any moment. His fingers tightened on the edge of a garden cart, as he struggled to beat back the sudden waves of anger and loss that threatened to swamp his heart. He closed his eyes. He would make good on his oath to kill Celynnen, but what then?

"Are you okay?"

His eyes flew open at the sound of Brooke's voice. "Yes, of course. I am well." *Lies should not be so easy.* He forced his fingers to unclench, wondering if it was possible to leave fingerprints in the wood.

"I'm not buying it."

"Buy what?"

"It's an expression. I mean I don't believe you're completely fine. How could it be anything but a helluva shock to suddenly wake up in a strange place as a man after being a dog for ten centuries?"

"As surprising as it must have been to have a giant dog burst through your ceiling and turn into a man."

She nodded but didn't laugh. "You know what's really surprising, Aidan? Finding you here. You tell me you haven't been spying on me, but now I find you watching me while I'm working. That's kind of creepy. In fact, what are you doing up here at all?" she asked bluntly. "I thought you were with George."

Damn. He should have spoken up and revealed his presence the minute she came up on the roof. "I can see that I am too accustomed to observing as a grim, to being invisible," he said sincerely. "Forgive me for surprising you. I've worked with your friend this day and accompanied him on all of his travels but this last one. There were a few more things to be done up here before nightfall." He nodded over his shoulder at the area behind him, where the skylight had once been.

Brooke eyed him like his mother used to, as if his head was totally transparent, but she must have seen what she needed to because she nodded. "Okay, you're forgiven, but this time only. Got it? Because I'm *this close* to reporting you as some kind of stalker." She pinched her thumb and forefinger together.

"I think I understand." Anxious to change the subject, he waved a hand at her surroundings. "My *mam* would have loved your garden. I recognize many of the plants that she used to grow—the yarrow and buckbean would be for healing, wouldn't they? There are some that are new to me, though." He looked at her hopefully and wasn't disappointed.

"I take it you want the tour, then." She shrugged, picked up her water pitcher, and began to show him the tidy little plant beds, and it wasn't long before she appeared to enjoy herself. Brooke identified each row in turn for him and explained what each herb could be used for. Sage, rue, horehound . . . Aidan was able to recall what ailments they had been used for in his village, which appeared to fascinate her. She hesitated, however, when they came to things like wolfsbane and mugwort, plants that would be grown only for magical purposes. He'd seen them before, many times, but she would have no way of knowing how he would react to them—with acceptance or with condemnation?

In his time, it had been hard to be a gwddon, never knowing whether today's healed patient would deliver you up to the priest tomorrow. The village wise woman was alternately hailed and condemned, according to the whim of the populace or the church (and usually the latter). He'd watched the pattern repeat itself over the centuries. Where such things stood in this time and place, he didn't know, but he didn't like the idea that this woman might be uneasy with him. "As I said before, you have naught to fear from me because you're a witch, Brooke Halloran. In fact, you and I may have some things in common because of it."

"Because you were a grim?"

"Nay, because I am a smith."

She looked at him as if he were teasing her. "What does black-smithing have to do with being a witch?"

"The shaping of iron involves many techniques and measures, most of which are kept absolutely secret and handed down only from master to apprentice." He paused, but it was plain that she didn't understand what he was saying. "Secrets are sometimes mistaken for alchemy and magic, for the devil's work, are they not? Throughout the ages, blacksmiths have sometimes been banned from villages or even burned for their skills, in spite of the good they did and the need for their work. At the very least, smiths have oft been required to ply their trade outside of the town just in case the devil was involved." He nodded at her. "Just like those who practiced the healing arts."

She nodded as she refilled the pitcher. "People often fear what they don't understand."

"Do you fear me?" He was surprised by his own question. Where had that come from?

"No. You're a mystery, which puzzles me. A helluva kisser, which intrigues me. And often rude, which annoys the hell out of me. But I'm not afraid of you."

I'm rude? Before he could protest that, the littlest cat, the young black one called Rory, chose that moment to make a tiger's leap from the top of a chimney to his mistress's shoulder. Rory had misjudged the distance, however, and landed on Brooke's back instead, surprising a yell from her as he scrabbled frantically for purchase. Water soaked the front of her shirt as she released the pitcher she was holding in favor of trying to capture the panicked feline—and from the looks of it, she'd had a lot of practice. Rory's claws were well tangled, however, especially the hind ones, and Aiden had to help extricate them from her shirt (and from her skin as well he feared) while she held the errant cat. Finally, they were free of each other, and she put Rory down with relief. The cat immediately scampered off to play-wrestle with his companions.

"Some of those scratches are deep," Aidan said. "I think you might need some *curitas*."

"*Aha*." She pointed at him. "Those are Band-Aids, right? Olivia said you speak Spanish fluently. And that you might speak some other languages too. Is it true?"

Aidan couldn't say which was more pleasing, the way the fabric matched her widened blue-green eyes or the way the damp cloth clung to her breasts and revealed her nipples. He cleared his throat and coughed, hoping to loosen the invisible fist around his neck that was cutting off his air. "My native tongue is Welsh, but your ears tell you that I can speak in English. It's true that I also know a number of other languages."

"Explain that. How would you learn something like that as a smith?"

He shook his head. "Not as a smith but as a grim. I have walked among humans for centuries. I've had a lot of time to listen and learn. Perhaps being Death's messenger made it both necessary and easier to understand the many languages I encountered."

Understand but never use. He had learned the languages in mute silence, and it was strange to have words all but pouring out of him now. Aidan didn't remember being so inclined to talk before his mortality had been interrupted. He had nothing against conversation, but in his former life, he didn't indulge in it overly much. Perhaps being unable to speak for a thousand years had given him a new appreciation of it—or perhaps this woman was just unusually easy to talk to.

Strange, he couldn't recall having talked with Annwyl very much. He remembered her as quiet, saying little. But then his own parents had seldom conversed. In fact, most couples didn't say much to each other, though there might be great affection between them. From what he had observed, things were very different now—and people themselves seemed different.

And perhaps that included him.

"I guess that makes some sense," Brooke was saying. "I'd like to hear more about it, but, oh man, I have *got* to sit down. It's been a very long day."

Brooke squeezed between the greenhouse and the near-solid wall of garden carts and felt her heart plummet to her shoes. She'd been putting off this moment, delaying the inevitable. Now she stood with her hands numbly at her sides, surveying the damage to the skylight. To the *roof.*

She knew that the iron frame of the twelve-foot window was gone, but she wasn't expecting that the knee-high walls that had supported it were gone as well. No wonder there had been such a mountain of debris in the room below. And of course there was the blue tarp that was presently darkening the interior of the entire second story. Close up, it looked to be the size of Rhode Island, and the way it covered the entire mess reminded her uncomfortably of a crime scene. The tarp was nailed in place with two-by-fours and surrounded by a hastily assembled fence of fluorescent orange mesh to discourage anyone—even the cats—from stepping onto the tenuous blue surface.

What a mess. What would happen if it rained? And how on earth was she going to afford to have this disaster repaired before cold weather came?

Gradually, she emerged from her dismal thoughts and noticed that Aidan was standing close beside her. "It'll be put right. I don't know how, but I give you my word it will be set to rights."

Swallowing hard, Brooke scolded herself. Here she was getting upset over a window, a silly damn *window*, when she should be grateful that she had friends—including this new, though somewhat odd, one—all of whom had been willing to work their asses off to clean up the site and make it safe.

"Thank you," she managed. "Thank you for all the hours you put in to straighten this up and take away all the garbage." Brooke looked Aidan in the eye—possibly a mistake, as once met, those iron-gray eyes were tough to look away from. "It wasn't very fair to you. Here it is, your first day on the planet as a human being again, and instead of celebrating, all you've done is work."

"Seems fair enough, since I'm the one that ruined your roof. Did I not put the hole here? And it's good to work," he said. "I'm a man again, and a man *works*. I like it. I think you'd say it feels *normal*." He chuckled then. "It even feels good to sweat. It reminds me of pounding iron in my shop. Perhaps that seems like a strange thing to miss, but I do." He held out his big hand to her. "You've worked hard today too. Why don't we both sit down?"

She nodded and slid her hand into his—and she could sense power. Magic. Was it left over from being a grim for so long? From spending time in the fae realm? He had asked if she feared him, and here she was alone with him on the rooftop. The answer was still no. It wasn't like he was going to bite her—and she was immediately sorry she'd thought of that, because hey, it sounded kind of *hot*. What she wouldn't give just for a repeat of that killer kiss . . .

Immediately, she felt guilty about her wish. The kiss had not been intended for her at all, but for the fiancée Aidan had lost. Brooke hadn't dared ask any questions yet, but Annwyl must have belonged to his human life before he became a grim. There was no telling how far along he might be in the grieving process, when or if he might be ready to be with someone else. Besides, according to Aidan, Brooke resembled Annwyl—and she wasn't sure she liked that idea.

And she was obviously getting *waaay* ahead of herself. She hadn't known this man for twenty-four hours yet. Aidan could still turn out to be the creepy stalker-pervert who George had initially pegged him as. Should that turn out to be the case, however, she knew plenty of fast spells that would make him damn sorry he'd ever set foot on her property. She supposed she could always just knock him on his ass again too. George had taught her that handy little trick, although it tended to work better with the element of surprise—and the powerful boost of magic she used with it. Right now, though, she was too tired to want to muster that kind of energy (not to mention that Aidan was likely too smart to be caught a second time).

So for now, she would simply trust—trust Aidan and, most of all, trust her Gift—and see where that went. She permitted him to lead her around the big blue scar that was once a hundred-year-old skylight, to what she laughingly called her terrace dining room. It was just a little open-air space with lattice walls on two sides, furnished with a couple of chairs and a table, and in calm weather, a big green umbrella. Sometimes she brought her dinner up here at night and stargazed while she ate. Sometimes she brought her spell books and . . . "Oh!"

The table was set with bright clay dishes on a striped linen cloth. A basket of bread, an assortment of cheeses and meats, and a small pot of butter accompanied a couple of bottles of Tucannon Star Mead. An empty planter with a scrap of plywood across it was being utilized as a serving table and a bright plastic picnic cooler sat there. Rory was already there, standing on his hind legs, trying to discover the contents.

"What's all this?"

"This is why I was on your roof tonight." Aidan looked a little embarrassed. "It is but a gesture, to thank you for your kindness. It was your spell that called me back to my mortal form, and your home has suffered a great deal of damage because of it. I am in your debt and not all can be repaid. I know that *this*"—he waved at the food—"this cannot set anything aright, but good food can sometimes make hard times less burdensome, at least for a short while. And—"

"And?"

"I will try not to be *rude*."

Brooke laughed and slid into a chair. The sun had dipped below the horizon, leaving the city streetlights to keep the coming dark at bay. It was her favorite time of night. Venus, the Evening Star, was hovering low in the colored sky, and a cluster of her scented candles was burning in a glass bowl on the table. Aidan fumbled a little with the cooler lid but eventually extracted two steaming cartons that smelled like heaven surely ought to. "I'm told this is called gumbo," he said. "I asked George to help me find something that was truly American."

It's a wonder he didn't take you to Mickey D's. "It was a good choice," she said, as she spooned rice in her bowl and ladled the fragrant sausage and shrimp over it. She took a bite and closed her eyes to savor the Creole spices intermingled with the famous holy trinity of onion, bell peppers, and celery. "It was a *great* choice."

He nodded in agreement. "I like it too." He flipped open the bread basket and tore a fist-sized chunk off an artisan loaf the color of black coffee, then dunked it in the gumbo. "Better," he mumbled as he chewed. "Much better."

She tore off a considerably smaller piece and spooned butter on it. The bread tasted like a coarse-grain rye and was solid enough to make a meal by itself. Almost solid enough to pound nails with too, but it was flavorful. She could feel her body wake up and pay attention as she chewed—she hadn't realized just how hungry she was. "Better than what?" she suddenly asked.

"Better than the little circles on your table this morning. I fear someone has sold you some very poor flour." He had the grace to look abashed as he realized what he'd said. "Rude?"

"Rude. Lucky for you, I didn't bake the bagels. I bought them at the store." She turned in her chair to look at Mel's Gas and Grocery down the street. The giant gold and red sign lit up just as she pointed her finger at it. "So my feelings aren't too terribly hurt."

Aidan looked relieved. "I may have become far too particular about breads. It comes of being a smith. Most people don't— didn't—have ovens of their own, and a smith must keep a fire going almost all the time. So I built a big brick oven off the back of the forge and people could come and bake their breads in there each day. In return, they'd give me a share of it, or maybe some cheese or a bit of pork if they had some to trade. I came to know who the best cooks were."

"Sounds like *somebody* never had to shop for groceries or make a meal for himself."

"No," he said as he spooned up the last of the gumbo in his bowl. "I didn't. But I would surely travel to market for this if I could." He dished up another helping and ate with a will.

Brooke sampled the cheeses and recognized the brightly colored Talavera pottery plate they were arranged on. "Olivia's dishes?"

He smiled a little. "You have very kind friends, Brooke Halloran."

"And excellent conspirators."

"I simply asked them what I might do for you, to cheer you. You had a very difficult day, and it showed in your face at times."

"It was kind of you to notice, and doubly kind to care enough to do something."

He grinned. "I'm not always rude."

"Okay, I'll give you that," she laughed. "Besides, it's not the usual kind of rudeness as in being impolite or mannerless. Well, maybe about the bagels," she amended. "But it's mostly a case of you being pleasant one moment and extremely abrupt the next. You're *so* angry, all sharp edges sometimes. Perhaps it's grief, and I can understand that. It's natural. But I also feel an absolute fury coming off of you in waves and I don't know why."

As if to illustrate her point, the smile vanished from his face as if it had never existed. His iron-gray eyes looked past her, *through her*, as if seeing something else, and his voice was flat.

"It has nothing to do with you. My ire is all for the Fair Ones, especially the one who took me. It was my wedding day, and a fae princess, Celynnen, stole me away to her realm beneath the Black Mountains. I wouldn't give in to her, wouldn't lie with her, and so she declared I would be her pet until I consented. It was Celynnen that made me into a grim."

He said it so simply, and yet the enormity of what had happened to him rocked Brooke in her chair. She'd read storybooks as a child of course, knew the old tales of faeries kidnapping mortals, but never in a million years would she have imagined it could be true. "On your wedding day? To Annwyl? How horrible for both of you! Did she see what happened to you? Did she know?"

Aiden shook his head. "Celynnen made certain that Annwyl died of a fever a year earlier, when her mother did—and so she never met me, you see. That ice-hearted *gast* then spelled everyone I knew, thinking she was doing me a great favor. I didn't exist in the mortal world anymore, and no one remembered me. Not my friends and family. Not even my own *mam* and *tad*. No one."

Brooke could feel the color drain from her face. "Aidan, she'd have to change time itself to do that. Who has that kind of—well, who has that much power?" *Dark power*, she'd almost said. Messing around with time was acknowledged as one of the darkest arts and highly dangerous. No sane witch would risk trying to manipulate a single hour, never mind a thousand years. "As a member of the royal House of Thorn, Celynnen has exactly that kind of power, and she thinks nothing of using it. It suited her whim, so she could have what she wanted."

"But what she did to you, to all of you, was unspeakably cruel. It was beyond wrong, it was evil."

"Aye, it was all that and more. And I'll not let it stand. Now that I'm human again, I'll be able to face Celynnen as a man and not a dog, and fulfill my vow."

"What vow would that be?" asked Brooke, afraid that she already knew the answer.

"I'll see her blue blood spilled upon the ground, of course—right after I put fear in her icy heart and force her to return me to my life."

FOURTEEN

︿⁀⁀

Whoa. *Wait just a minute.* There were so many things wrong with those goals, on so many levels, she hardly knew where to begin.

"You're going to *kill* somebody?"

"I have sworn to slay Celynnen. You yourself said she was evil."

"Yes, but—"

"Celynnen deserves to die many times over, not only for what she did to Annwyl but also for the countless lives she's either taken or destroyed," declared Aidan, and the anger of a thousand years burned in his hot blue gaze. "Do you not agree that evil must be opposed?"

"True evil must always be opposed, yes. But must it always be killed? I believe in doing no harm."

Aidan shook his head. "You have a gentle heart in you despite that ready fist of yours. But Celynnen is older than you can imagine—and she will live forever and continue to wreak havoc in the human world unless she is stopped once and for all."

She hadn't thought of that. Dear goddess, was it possible that Aidan was right? Were there some cases where some harm must be wrought to prevent greater harm from being done? The daunting question seemed to lodge solidly in her brain, and even now she could feel the beginnings of a headache.

"Okay, I don't know what the answer is. Let's leave that alone for now until I have a chance to think about it, and maybe we'll discuss it later." Brooke knew she would be spending a lot of time meditating over the Code on that particular subject. "But there's something else to be considered, something that might have even greater implications."

His eyebrows went up, and she wished it weren't her job to bring up the issue. Sometimes the responsibilities of her calling made her feel like a goddamn hall monitor. "I can understand that you'd want to return to your world, to the life that was stolen from you, I really can," she said. "I mean, it seems so reasonable to just step back into your old shoes and pick up where you left off. But have you thought about the consequences?"

"There are no consequences. It's my life. I want it back. Simple." Aidan banged his mead bottle down on the table for emphasis.

Oh, good. This was starting to sound like that potential client she'd talked to on the phone recently, the one who *wanted what he wanted,* period. And she so did not feel like getting into an argument now. Maybe she could just excuse herself—it wouldn't be stretching things to say she was tired, right? But a line from the Code came to her mind, strong and clear: *to hold the Gift is to protect the balance, and restore harmony.* And if Aidan pursued his stated course of reinserting himself into the past, balance and harmony might be upset beyond all repair. For many, if not everyone.

She sighed and plunged in. "It might not be that simple. Messing with time is never simple. What did your friends and family do after you disappeared? Do you know?"

Aidan pondered that in silence until she wasn't sure he would answer at all.

"No," he finally said, and his voice was subdued. "I have no idea. I wasn't called to go to Aberhonddu as a grim until almost two centuries of mortal time had passed. Everyone I ever knew there was long dead by then. I believe Celynnen planned it that way. She wanted me to forget everyone but her."

Brooke felt for him so strongly that her eyes stung with tears. He'd been so terribly wronged. But nothing changed the fact that there were things he needed to think about, important things. *Dear goddess, help me say it kindly.* "People don't stay static, Aidan. You were erased from their minds, and that was wrong. But they didn't know and they all had lives to lead. Human beings move on, and so does time. And in this case, ten whole centuries have already unfolded in a certain way, to create a specific pattern."

That fire was in his eyes again. "I'm very well aware of the years."

"I'm sure you are. But look, we all affect each other's lives in hundreds of little ways, every single day. You've been taken out of your life, and everyone you knew went on without you. *Without your influence.* And if you went back to your old life now, it would be like throwing an enormous rock into a pond. The ripples would be felt across the centuries all the way to right here where I'm standing, to this very moment, and beyond."

"History would be set to rights."

She shook her head. "History has already happened. We're talking about a thousand years here, not a two-week vacation. How many families, how many descendants, have been created over ten centuries? That's something like fifty generations! So how many lives will be changed if you go back?" Brooke pointed to the city around them. "Which one of these people will cease to exist if you return to your life, Aidan?"

"None of them. This isn't Wales."

"It's a new world for you, Aidan, a bigger world, and you have to think bigger." She felt like she was poking a wounded bear with a stick, but she had to make him understand. "Many people here in America have Welsh ancestors. Like my friend Morgan. Her grandmother was born in Wales. What if Morgan didn't exist anymore because you went back and changed the past in some small way? Her new husband, Rhys, was born in Wales too. What if he didn't exist anymore, because you chose to alter history?"

Aidan was a man, and a man in pain usually reacted with anger. That sharp-edged fury rushed back like a tsunami, as she fully expected it would. "Celynnen already altered history, damn it all!" he roared. His chair was knocked over as he stood up, ready to take on the entire world. "I can't bring Annwyl back from the dead, but I could still live amongst my family and my friends. I don't want to change the world I came from, *I just want to have been part of it.*"

Cursing in a variety of languages, he kicked his chair out of the way and stalked off. A moment later, she heard the metal door to the stairs slam behind him.

Crap. Brooke considered going after Aidan but thought better of it. Maybe he needed time to think. Maybe he needed time away from her—after all, didn't she look like his fiancée? It couldn't be much fun for him to be constantly reminded of the person he missed the most. Hell, maybe he just needed a break, period. How much rain on his parade could one man take in a single day? She was lucky. Only her roof was ruined. As for Aidan, his entire view of the world had been knocked sideways. Of the two, her problem was a helluva lot easier to fix.

Startled by the slamming door, Bouncer, Jade, and Rory rushed over and pawed at her for reassurance. She sat on the floor and cuddled all three into her lap, taking comfort from them as well. "It's okay, guys, it's just the usual. The client just *wants what he wants.*"

But somehow she had to prevent him from getting it.

∽

It took a lot of walking before Aidan could think clearly again. He traveled miles of sidewalks, barely seeing the city streets, the people and vehicles that traveled them, the shops and businesses that lined them. He had surely managed to be *rude* again to Brooke, but it couldn't be helped. While she knew he was angry, she had no idea just how *much* fury was threatening to break through his control. It was like holding back a volcano, and better for him to leave and leave quickly before she was caught in the explosion. Her pointed questions had lit a powder keg beneath his plans, not to mention ripped fresh wounds in his already-shredded heart. *A thousand damnable years.* He knew better than most that forgetfulness was the first and most powerful side effect for any mortal who spent time in the faery realm. But reality was the real casualty— every last thing that Brooke had said was likely true, and Aidan felt like a complete fool that he hadn't considered one whit of it.

Damn it to hell. He felt cheated through and through, and the bitter pill seemed far too big to swallow.

He walked, until the borrowed shoes he was wearing rubbed blisters into his feet, until the strange clothing chafed his skin in odd places, and until weariness underscored just how human he really was. The sealed wound where the warth had slashed him throbbed as though poison lurked within it. Still he walked, until his pace finally slowed of its own accord and his anger ebbed somewhat from sheer exhaustion.

In that state, reason floated slowly to the surface of Aidan's brain.

He hadn't had enough time, that was all. He was known for being an astute man, and no one who had learned the intricacies of working with metals lacked in intelligence. Eventually, he *would* have asked the same questions that Brooke did, given more hours to think in the mortal world. After all, he had scarcely been a man again for a day and a night.

There was no blame, then, not for him and certainly not for Brooke—she had merely been the messenger, and a courageous one at that. Any and all blame sat squarely on the shoulders of the ice-blooded creature that had stolen Aidan's life and love from him in the first place.

Celynnen.

Just thinking of the cruel fae princess was like applying a bellows to his forge; the flames of wrath immediately hissed and grew hot enough to melt metal. As a grim he'd been able to feel only two things—an aching empty hole where his heart had once lived and complete and utter rage at his captor. Now he felt everything and right now, disappointment was first and foremost.

If even Celynnen could not return him to his life without doing incalculable damage to everything and everyone around him, then somehow he must be man enough to let go of that dream. He would not become like his enemy by insisting on having his own way despite the cost that others would pay. In the meantime, had he not vowed to Gofannon to see Celynnen's blue blood spilled upon the ground by an iron weapon of his own making? He still had a purpose, a goal. And by all that was holy, *he would find a way.* In the meantime, however, he needed to see Brooke.

Celynnen was much too busy to attend the Royal Court. Not because she was avoiding it, after Lurien had dared the outrageous and sent her there without her clothes. If he thought it would embarrass her, he was sorely mistaken. She had held her head high, and in the shocked silence of the Court commanded that clothing to be brought to her. And then she had her servants dress her as she stood in the very center of the throne room, before the eyes of all. It had given her an unprecedented opportunity to flaunt her utterly flawless body—and hadn't *that* given the chattering ensemble something to talk about when they recovered their tongues? Some of the comments that had echoed back to her had been extremely admiring. Others hateful and jealous. Both were pleasing. There was no comment from her great-aunt, the queen, of course. Gwenhidw did not grace the Court with her presence unless there was particular business to attend to. Which left all of the gathering's attention to revolve around Celynnen.

No, she had no desire to avoid the Court.

She also wasn't too busy to attend because she was plotting revenge on the Lord of the Wild Hunt (although she *would* even the score between them, he could be certain of that). Right now, her attention was wholly focused on magics, on seeking charms and location spells, anything that might help her find a certain missing grim. She even had servants scour the stone kennel for a few hairs, but the fur proved ineffective. None of her spells turned up any sign of her favorite pet. Which could only mean that the grim had managed to travel much farther than even Lurien suspected. Had the dog managed to cross the Deep Waters to the lands beyond?

What Celynnen needed, then, was a far-reaching spell, something that was effective over extremes of distance. To power such a spell, however, there was only one thing she could use—the bwgan stone she kept in her sleeve. They were exceedingly rare— only one out of ten thousand bwgans would ever grow one. Celynnen had viewed the broad heavy skull of the salamander-like beast that had borne hers. The stone she now held had been embedded in the bone like a third eye, and yet it was undetectable until the pale skin had been peeled back. Who would suspect such an ugly and savage creature of possessing a veritable lodestone of volatile magical energy?

Because of it, her spell could search far beyond the kingdom she would eventually rule. And the one thing that would stand out from all other things in the mortal world would be something she herself had bestowed upon her pet. *Instead of looking for the dog, she would search for his collar.* Because no grim could ever rid himself of the silver torc that bound him to the Fair Ones.

A thousand mortal years ago, she had placed the wide chain-mail band around his black-furred neck with her own hands and sealed it with her own magic. That meant it had a signature of power and therefore *could be followed.* All she needed was a single silver link, one left over from the time that the collar was first forged and crafted. The tiny link was in her personal treasury, somewhere among her vast collection of jewels and ornaments. She'd had her personal servant, the orange-eyed crymbil, searching for it ever since she thought of it.

Finally, the skittish creature had produced what her mistress wanted.

Celynnen held the tiny treasure cupped in her palm, high over the scrying bowl. The ancient silver dish was wider than she could reach her arms around, yet only the depth of a finger. It had been filled with the pure water of Syrthiedig, the lake that held the moon's tears. Her other hand gripped the bwgan stone in the pocket of her sleeve. The fae princess murmured the elemental words, from a language older than mortal men, and let the link fall.

The silver oval tumbled end over end in slow motion—gravity held no sway here—until it sliced cleanly into the water and struck the bottom of the bowl with a loud bell-like chime that should have been impossible for such a tiny thing to produce.

The sound rippled. The water rippled. Vibrations spread outward along the stone floor from the pedestal that supported the bowl, just as swirling shadows spread out from beneath the tiny link and entwined to produce an image. By the time the water was still, its crystal surface gave the fae princess a clear and perfect view of her grim's chain-mail torc.

But it wasn't a dog that wore it. Nor was it Aidan ap Llanfor.

Normally, Celynnen would be consumed with fury. Had she dashed the treasured scrying bowl to the floor, it would not have been the first time. She should have been inconsolable that her plans had not borne the fruit she demanded. But novelty was not only rare in the faery realm; it was its most precious commodity. And so the tywysoges looked upon the unknown human who wore the heavy silver collar as an ornament.

And found him comely.

Perhaps I will pay him a visit . . .

Brooke fed the cats (before anything else of course—Rory wouldn't permit any delay), drank coffee, showered and dressed, drank more coffee, but still felt fuzzy headed. It had been a restless night, filled with tossing and turning and occasionally getting up and pacing her apartment. It wasn't El Guardia this time, but El Código—the Code—that had kept her from sleeping.

To hold the Gift is to protect the balance in all things and to restore harmony. That's the line she'd focused on when she cautioned Aidan about his plans to reclaim a life lost a thousand years ago. His personal harmony might be restored to a large degree, but the balance of many, many lives would be permanently altered, if not destroyed.

There were other lines in the Code, however, and maybe they applied as well. *To hold the Gift is to give hope to the innocent and to uphold the cause of the wronged.* Aidan had been innocent, and he had definitely been wronged. If the tragedy had unfolded yesterday, last week, or last month, Brooke could see trying to encourage his hope of recovering his life. Or helping him achieve his goal. Or at least staying the hell out of his way while *he* attempted to do so. But a millennium had passed—wasn't there some kind of statute of limitations on upholding the cause of the wronged? Because she could see no way of doing so without causing a hell of a lot more wrongs.

And then there was the line of the code she usually liked, the mission statement of her Handcastings business and her life in general: *To hold the Gift is to comfort the mind and spirit, and to heal both heart and body.*

How could Aidan be comforted or healed from what had been done to him? All that pain and anger needed to be lanced and drained like an infected wound. Not only did she not know how, but the subject also had to be willing. In her favor, she'd somehow snatched him from a possibly fatal battle with a faery lord, brought him here, and returned his human body to him—but was that enough to satisfy the Code?

And was it enough to satisfy her? Brooke couldn't escape the fact that she cared. She cared *a lot*, and she couldn't pretend it was just because she felt sorry for the guy, or because he was not just hot but "hawt," as some of her girlfriends would put it. And it wasn't because he had kissed her senseless either. Although that was pretty unforgettable in and of itself, there was more to it than just two bodies responding to some (amazing) stimuli.

No, there had been connection where none should exist at all. She'd never seen this guy in her whole life, yet there had been recognition at some level so deep she couldn't even name it. Then there was the magic thing. She felt it in him every time they came in contact with each other, yet he seemed completely unaware of it. He certainly didn't use it.

None of it made a single lick of sense.

She hoped he was okay. Aidan was out there in an unfamiliar world without a single dollar in his pocket, a piece of ID, or even the jacket that Olivia had loaned him. Had he slept on a park bench? Been mugged on a street corner? Gotten picked up for vagrancy? No, scratch that, she thought. Given his current temper, he was much more likely to be arrested for getting into a fight. She'd even thought about following him last night, making sure he was all right. Considered at least scrying in her mirror to check on him, but common sense prevented her. Aidan was a grown man, an intelligent and independent one. Even in the modern world, he didn't need or want a babysitter. Maybe there were no cars when he was a blacksmith, but if he'd operated as Death's messenger over the past thousand years, he'd certainly seen them. And hopefully knew enough not to walk in front of one . . .

Besides, Aidan was unlikely to welcome her concern, especially after the things she'd just said to him. And if he slept outside? Got cold and hungry? Well, those were just the natural consequences of staying out all night. *Welcome back to mortality.*

All things considered, there was probably a good chance she'd never see Aidan again and wouldn't have to fret about him any further . . . but it was far from being a relief. Dear goddess, she was going to worry about this man for a very long time to come.

Brooke opened the door to her apartment and groaned aloud as she was immediately assaulted by the high-voltage color of her once-calming spell room. She'd deliberately avoided looking up while in her open-ceilinged living quarters, but there was no hiding from the taxicab yellow of the enormous room now. And the morning sun reflecting off the vivid walls did not improve them in the least. Cupping her hands around her eyes like binoculars, she looked straight ahead until she and the cats made it through the oak door that led to the stairwell.

Whew. Feeling like her nerves had just been run through a blender, she gripped the handrail and trudged down the wooden stairs as the cats galloped noisily ahead of her. She definitely didn't have their energy today, but she would order in a breakfast sandwich from the café down the street, and that would help. Olivia would likely stop by for coffee sometime this morning too, and Brooke was hoping George would follow his usual routine—spend three hours at the gym and then take over one of the booths to work on his sketches. She wanted to thank them both again for yesterday. Because of their hard work, today would be a normal day.

Speaking of normal, four appointments were on her calendar, including Mrs. McCardie (and her Chihuahua, Mr. Socks, of course). Brooke would have to remember to keep an eye on Rory, in case he got carried away again and started stalking the little old dog. And there was still a box of tarot decks to be unpacked and added to her display, plus a shipment of new books should be arriving today.

All normal, all good, she told herself. Brooke raised the blind on the glass door of Handcastings, removed the CLOSED FOR REPAIRS sign she'd taped there yesterday, turned the knob of the lock—

And Aidan was there.

FIFTEEN

⌒⋀⋋⋋

Mouthing the words to the song on his MP3 player, George slammed the door of his locker at White Wolf Mixed Martial Arts and snapped the combo lock. He'd worked out for two hours until he felt *the pump*, the blood rushing into his muscles, then he'd gone a few rounds in the octagon with his buddies in the same weight class. He'd won all his bouts, as he usually did, and he was feeling damn good. Maybe he hadn't been able to take down Aidan, but George was still king of the cage here on his own turf. Which just went to prove his personal theory that some kind of magic had been protecting the big guy from the full effects of the Santiago-Callahan treatment.

Still, after his shower, he had waited until no one was in the dressing room before he draped that amazing silver chain mail around his neck and admired his naked body in the big mirror that lined one wall. Holy effin' Conan, the collar looked good. *He* looked good. George struck a few bodybuilding poses and nodded to himself. He had an important match coming up in a couple weeks, and he was going to eschew the usual sponsor's T-shirt as he strode down the walkway to the ring with his team. Nope, he was going to wear this *bling thing* right up into the cage until it was time to touch gloves . . .

Carmelita was parked around the back of the gym, the black-on-black pickup truck cooled by the shade. It was a secure parking lot too, with an attendant—but for some reason, there was no one in the booth.

That was the only explanation for the tall blonde model that was currently leaning on the hood of his truck. Her elbows rested on the hood, her chin in her hands, with long sunlit hair falling in a smooth wave down her backside. Her long, long legs were shown off to their best advantage in a pair of cutoffs and heels. The combination was enough to stop a man's heart in his chest—or speed it up to dangerous levels.

"Excuse me, miss, you're on my truck." Jesus, was that the best he could do? But as gorgeous as she was, he was no idiot. She had to be a hooker. Had to be. *Nobody* dressed like that and struck such a provocative pose on a guy's vehicle unless she was trying to score *something*.

She smiled at him, her teeth dazzling white and perfect. In fact, her flawless skin appeared naturally tanned and healthy, and her whole demeanor was vibrant. This was no meth addict trying to make a few bucks for a hit. But what the hell did she want with him?

"I watched you in the ring just now. You won every time. You're very good."

George didn't know which was more surprising, that she'd been watching him or that he'd missed seeing her. Hell, how did *anyone* miss her? There were some bleachers on the north wall where wives and girlfriends, buddies and rivals, sometimes even kids, hung out, but if this California goddess had been sitting there, surely every man in the place would have been drooling over her. Or maybe not. It was Saturday and the bleachers were usually crowded. George didn't recall even looking in that direction—in fact, most fighters didn't because by the time you entered the ring, you were too busy sizing up your opponent, thinking about your strategy and your moves. *Lose your focus and you lose the fight.*

"Thanks," he said, and couldn't think of a single other thing to say. Especially when she stood up and walked towards him. Most girls in heels that high clicked along in short little steps that were as cute as they were impractical, but this woman glided over the pavement as if she were born wearing those sexy shoes. Her T-shirt was sky blue, like her eyes, and didn't quite meet the low-slung cutoffs. A belly-button piercing boasted a silver loop of beads. Mostly George noticed the deep dip of her neckline and how the fabric stretched tight across her breasts—especially when those heels made her taller than he was. He swallowed, but there was suddenly no spit left in his mouth. At least he managed to drag his gaze up to her face again as she paused in front of him.

"I didn't know if you would talk to me," she said, still dazzling him with that smile. "I just wanted to ask if I could get your autograph."

"Sure," he managed, and miraculously added, "Thanks for asking." His blood was definitely not going to his brain at the moment, and he had to struggle to think. Did he have a pen? A piece of paper. Maybe a program or a brochure from the gym?

He needn't have worried. The woman had come prepared. She handed him a felt-tipped marker and pulled her T-shirt even lower on one side, exposing half of her rounded breast.

Dios.

"Make it to Felicia," she purred, and spelled it for him as he signed her skin. He was grateful his artist's hand didn't fail him, that the script turned out neat and even, and most of all, that he didn't misspell his own damn name.

Felicia seemed delighted with it. "Thank you very much." She leaned over and kissed him on the cheek, then turned and glided away. She looked over her shoulder once and waved. "I might see you if you ever go to the Impulse. I work there."

"Sure." George waved feebly, feeling like he'd taken a flying kick to the head, and watched until she disappeared around the corner of the building. Then he sat in his truck for a long time until he felt steady enough to drive home.

~

For a moment, Aidan wasn't sure Brooke was going to let him in. The look on her face told him plainly that she hadn't expected him. With the way he'd left last night, he couldn't blame her if she thought he'd left for good. Maybe he should—he'd brought her little but trouble so far. But it wasn't in his nature to leave before he'd set things right as well as he could, and perhaps smooth things out between them if it was possible.

"Good morning," she said and, gods be praised, held open the door.

He didn't pass through it, not yet, but moved so his body was holding it open. "You didn't deserve my anger last night, Brooke Halloran. Temper got the best of me. And I hope that's not the reason you didn't sleep well."

"I slept just fine, thanks."

He gave her a knowing look, and she shrugged and rolled her eyes.

"Okay, so I had some things bothering me, and you happened to be most of them."

"I'm sorry for that. I've caused you a lot of trouble—"

"And a lot of worry, mister," she added, folding her arms.

"And a lot of worry. Could we have that over-do you spoke of?"

She put a hand to her forehead then, and to his surprise, began to laugh. "I think we've already had the *over-do* part of it, thank you." Brooke stepped back and motioned him to come inside. "And yes, I think I'm just crazy enough for a do-over."

He followed her into the shop and settled on one of the stools, watching as she opened the blinds on the row of front windows to let in the morning light. One of her cats, a white and tabby mix, ran to the first window immediately, attracted by the buzz of a stunned fly on the sill.

"Jade, no! *Stop that.* Just let me get the damn flyswatter, will you?" Brooke called from the fourth window, but the cat was already crouched and stalking like a little panther. It had the fly in its paw and then in its mouth before her owner could do a thing about it.

Aidan's mouth quirked; the same woman who had fearlessly struck a strange man to defend her friend was distressed over her pet devouring a tiny insect.

"*Yuck.*" Brooke was still scolding Jade. "I totally hate it when you do that. Don't expect me to sit with me for a while—you have *fly germs* now."

The other cats rushed over to see what treasure their friend had, and Brooke came back and grabbed Aidan's elbow. "Come sit over here in this booth. I have clients coming in this morning. I usually phone in an order for coffee and breakfast, but Olivia just texted me and she's going to pick up enough for all three of us." She quickly pointed out the amenities of the place: washroom, bookshelves, and even cat toys. Brooke set a small stack of books on the table, and the message was pretty clear—he was to amuse himself, perhaps amuse the cats, and generally stay out of her way. "Okay?"

"Okay." He slid into the booth, and nearly sighed. His human body was bone tired, his muscles sore, and this padded seat was luxurious compared to the hard surfaces he'd tried unsuccessfully to rest upon during the night. He could see shadows under Brooke's blue-green eyes, though, and wasn't about to mention his own lack of sleep.

He studied the shop, recognizing that it had once been a restaurant but had been cleverly repurposed. The colors were surprisingly appealing. He especially liked the bright turquoise—Brooke's eyes picked up the color readily and claimed it for their own.

While she busied herself, he ventured off to the restroom and cleaned up a little. When he returned, an older lady with fluffy white hair was seated in the large corner booth. She had an extremely large handbag, and a small black and white dog with big eyes and bigger ears poked his head out of it. Strangely, the dog appeared to be wearing some sort of white leather outfit and what resembled a tiny black wig. Brooke sat across from the woman and her odd pet, and spread out a deck of colorful cards. As he slid back into his own booth, he caught Brooke's gaze and she grinned at him.

He grinned back, chose a book from the stack, and opened it as if he were reading. Actually, he was settling in to listen without appearing to listen. She was in her element here, that much was certain. She talked with her customer, Florence McCardie, as if she were a friend, and she very probably was—Brooke cared about people. She'd been right when she told him that she took her calling very seriously. He envied her that, her deep concern for others, the all-consuming purpose that drove her to try to make their lives better even in the smallest ways. She gave of herself freely, generously, like a cool spring in a hillside. She didn't just serve people; she served *life*.

In stark contrast, his only purpose for the past ten centuries had been to serve death—though in fairness, he had never chosen that morbid task. Now that he was a man again, his purpose hadn't changed much. What had been done to Annwyl must be answered, must be paid for, and only blood would do. But once revenge had been exacted, what was his purpose then?

A giggle from Florence brought his attention back to the present. He hadn't gotten a good look at the cards, but they must have been designed for some sort of divination. It fascinated him to hear Brooke discuss the possible meanings and how they might apply to the old woman's life. Brooke was always positive, always encouraging—and from time to time he recognized an underlying pulse of magic in the air around her, like the slight teasing hint of a woman's perfume. It seemed that he hadn't lost all of his fae abilities after all, and he wondered how much of his power remained. Would it stay or fade away to nothing? It might be a very useful tool to have when it came time to fulfill his vow.

Yet again Aidan found himself wondering what he would do once he killed Celynnen. Would his magic be any good to him then? Better still, *could he do any good with it*, the way that Brooke did?

Brooke smiled at him again when, arm in arm, she slowly escorted Florence and her pet to the door and outside to the bus stop just a couple of doors down.

He liked it when she smiled at him—there hadn't been enough of that since he'd come crashing through her roof. It felt good, but perhaps too good. If he wasn't careful, Brooke could unintentionally distract him from his goal. But in all the pacing he'd done last night, he'd come to realize that he was ill prepared to confront the fae princess. He'd also come to the conclusion that proper preparations could take some time. Which brought up yet another reason he'd come back this morning.

He needed Brooke's help.

In order to face down Celynnen, he needed effective weapons. His plan was to use his smithing skills to make sword-sharp blades of iron, small enough to be secreted in his clothing (a trick that Celynnen herself employed), yet weighted and balanced enough to throw if he couldn't get close enough to wield them. She might find them—nay, probably would find them—but she would be expecting him to try to kill her. What she would not expect is that he would also be armed if he was completely naked. He would create long feather-light slivers of iron, like a woman's hairpins, that he could slide just beneath the skin of his forearms, and tinier shards that would fit between the joints of some of his fingers, and allow the tiny cuts to heal over. The scratch of a fingernail would bring the miniscule blades to the surface, where he could use them to deadly effect. Iron was deadly poisonous to the Tylwyth Teg—but where could he obtain it in this time and place? He needed information. He needed materials. And he no doubt needed money—he would have to hire himself out to gain some before he could make the needed preparations. How did one do that in this world?

No doubt Brooke had the answers to all of those things, or she had friends who did. And when he'd succeeded in designing the unique type of weaponry he had in mind, Aidan hoped to persuade Brooke to add her magic to them. His chances of success would be increased if his iron creations could be spelled so that their potency might be amplified, that they might not be taken away from him, and that they might not miss their intended target. Plus, she could heal the little wounds in his arms and hands made by the placement of the tiny weapons so that no scars would be visible.

More than anything, however, he needed to find his way back to the faery realm. All of his preparations were completely useless if he couldn't do that much. The silver torc he'd once worn as a great black dog had disappeared, probably destroyed during his transformation. Otherwise, Aidan might have tried to use it to call on Lurien. *Might*, had they parted on friendlier terms. After all, the last time he'd seen the Lord of the Wild Hunt, Aidan was still a grim and had his long sharp teeth sunk deep into the dark fae's hand. Besides, why would Lurien help him in his quest, when the dark fae had designs on Celynnen of an entirely different nature?

No, it was much more likely that Aidan would have to return to Wales itself, possibly to the mound outside of Aberhonddu, to find one of the ways, the strange doorways that led to and from the kingdom under the Black Mountains. He supposed a way might exist somewhere in Brooke's enormous, sprawling country, although he'd never heard of one. Finding it would be almost impossible, however. He was no longer a grim, no longer a fae creature, and the ways were invisible to most human eyes. *Most.* A few people had the Sight, however—they saw the Fair Ones as clearly as they saw their fellow humans. And those who worked in magic the way he worked in iron? Sometimes they could see the fae as well.

That meant that Brooke Halloran just might be able to find him a way. Once he got to the faery realm, he would take care of the rest himself.

"So, George says he met a new girl at the gym this morning," announced Olivia, as she spread the contents of two bags and a cardboard drink holder in front of Brooke and Aidan. The three of them had taken over the big corner booth. "He asked me to tell you that he can't stop by today. He's going to put some hours in at the studio on the latest *Devina of Hades* issue, so he'll be free tonight to see *Felicia.*"

"Pretty name," said Brooke. "What happened to Cyndi?"

"What happens to any of them? He gets bored, or they do." Olivia drank down half her coffee while fanning herself because the drink was hot, then exhaled heartily. "*Dios*, I needed that this morning. No, no more Cyndi, or Katherine, or Jasmine, or Amber—I could make *such* a list, *m'ija*, but you know what I'm talking about."

"George has had quite a few girlfriends over the years," Brooke whispered to Aidan, by way of explanation. He looked puzzled.

"Why?" he asked.

"That's what I keep saying. Why?" Olivia selected a cruller from the big bag of doughnuts. "No one seems to stay together. Young people just don't take love seriously anymore."

"I do." Aidan's voice was quiet.

"You, sir, are very far from young," said Brooke. "You don't count."

"I am not much older than you."

"Give or take a thousand years!"

"Are you certain we should count that, *m'ija*?" asked Olivia. "After all, he was a dog during all that time."

"I was a *grim*. That's no ordinary dog."

Brooke snorted. "Neither is Mrs. McCardie's Chihuahua. Omigod, did you *see* the outfit she had on Mr. Socks today? He was dressed as *Elvis*." She lapsed into giggles. "Do you have any idea how hard it is to read the tarot while looking at *that*? There was even a tiny little guitar charm hanging from his collar."

"You're kidding me. I would have paid to see that," chuckled Olivia. "But that little dog is the closest thing Florence has to family. A woman has to have someone to fuss over, you know. It keeps her young."

"Now I know why you fuss over me and George," teased Brooke.

"And I have Aidan to fuss over now too. So that'll keep me even younger." Olivia nudged a doughnut his way. "You have *got* to try one of these maple crèmes."

He took Olivia's hand and kissed it, which delighted her. "Thank you for sharing your meal with me," he said. "I was about to ask Brooke how to go about finding work. The mortal world still requires money, and I have need of some. Especially to buy food like this." He hefted his second egg-and-bacon sourdough special.

"You want to get a job?" Brooke exchanged glances with Olivia. "For someone who just became human again, you don't waste any time. But it's going to be a bit of a problem," she said. "You have no ID—no birth certificate, driver's license, credit cards. Most of all, you have no social security number. So basically you don't exist."

Okay, could she have made a poorer choice of words? Brooke had seen that shadow cross Aidan's face before.

"I seem to be very good at *not existing*," he said. He put the food down, his eyes unreadable.

"You know I didn't mean it like that! *Of course* you exist—you just don't happen to be registered in the government's records. And you need that in order to get a job."

"You're saying I cannot take care of myself? I cannot provide for me and mine in this time and place?"

Olivia rolled her eyes and put her hands up in a classic football ref's T. "Time out, you two. It's like listening to George and Lissy," she declared. "*Of course*, Aidan can survive without ID, at least for a while. All he has to do is take on odd jobs for cash."

Brooke was grateful for her friend's intervention—the last thing she wanted was for Aidan to get frustrated enough to walk out again. But she wasn't sure if Olivia's idea could work. "How do you find something like that? I don't see much in the classifieds."

"Word of mouth, *m'ija*. And I have it on good authority that Olivia Santiago-Callahan is desperate to find a big, strong worker to relandscape her backyard."

"Are you making that up?" Brooke mouthed in Olivia's direction.

"No, cross my heart," said the older woman. "*You* try finding a contractor who has the time to spend on little jobs like a broken retaining wall. Landscape the big new airport? Sure thing—that's a nice government contract with nice government wages. But someone like me who just needs her backyard done? Ha! Even if the contractor had the time and the manpower to spare, he couldn't take it on—it wouldn't pay enough to cover his equipment costs and his insurance and all his other business expenses.

"But Aidan, working on his own, could make some money for himself because he has no overhead. And I would finally get my yard done. After that, I have a basement to empty, and the outside of the house needs painting, and the gutters need cleaning . . . My dear Jack left me well looked after, but my children have their own lives now. They do their best—Will and George reroofed the garage last month—but they haven't got the time to do all that needs doing, and I'd rather not have to ask them. Besides," she said, with a wink, "it's much more fun to boss around someone who works for you than your own children, I can tell you that!"

Brooke hated to do it, but she had to ask. "What if Aidan doesn't know how to do some of the things you want done? I mean, you know, *modern building materials* and all that?"

"Then I will ask Will to show him. That much time he could spare. And he would be pleased if I had a handyman close by to call on, someone we could both trust." Olivia looked at Aidan and clasped her hands together as if pleading with him. "So you see, everything would be *perfect*, if only you would agree to work for me. Well, at least until you find something else to do."

Brooke resisted rolling her eyes at her friend's theatrical antics and bit her tongue.

And of course Aidan said yes. What else could he say after a speech like that? They settled that he would begin in two days, after Olivia had had time to get some supplies delivered. And, Brooke suspected, make a very, *very* long list of all the things her new "handyman" could do.

SIXTEEN

A fter her friend left in high spirits, Brooke finished her coffee and rose from the booth. She got a garbage bag and began clearing the table. "Olivia's going to work you to death, you know."

"Work is—"

"*What a man does.* Yes, you told me. Well, you'll feel very manly in no time once she gets hold of you." She handed Aidan a large disinfecting wipe. "You can practice working here, if you like, by cleaning the table for me. And then you can use that dust mop over there to wipe the floor, okay?"

"Okay."

"Don't forget to do under the tables, please." She started unpacking her box of new tarot decks and arranging them on the shelves of her shop. "You know, I've been thinking you're going to need a place to stay for a couple days. Olivia will come up with something, no doubt—if she hasn't already—but until that happens, there's no reason why you couldn't sleep on the long bench by the door right here in my shop. I've napped there before, so I know it's pretty comfortable. There's a pillow and a couple of quilts underneath."

The bench must have once been for diner customers waiting to be seated, or more likely, customers who were just waiting for orders to go. It ran almost the length of the two front windows, about ten feet, and was about three feet wide. Brooke wasn't sure she'd keep it—after all, it used up a helluva lot of space—until she discovered that it opened to reveal an extremely large storage space. It turned out to be perfect for books in particular—it saved her from trying to find them in the storeroom when she had to restock a shelf. So she'd had the big bench upholstered in the same turquoise vinyl as the booths and the stools, and then added a handful of bright vinyl throw pillows in citrus green, fuchsia, and orange. The effect was very pleasing, and the bench was the first thing that people saw as soon as they came in the door. Often as not, all three cats were sleeping on it in the sun.

"That way," she continued, "you'd have access to the washroom down here, plus that kitchen corner in the back." Strange to have to set up such a thing in a former restaurant, but all of the appliances were long gone from the cooking area, leaving only an empty room next to the storeroom. She had divided the space into two areas. One was an office of sorts, with a very large dining table instead of a desk—she liked to spread her papers out when she worked. The remainder was a pleasant little lunch corner, equipped with a microwave and coffee maker, plus a refrigerator. That way, if she was busy, she didn't have to go upstairs to grab something to eat. The cats were down here with her in the shop anyway, so they wouldn't be neglected. And perhaps someday she'd be busy enough to be able to hire staff, and they would need a break area. *I can dream.*

"It looks very comfortable, and I thank you," said Aidan. "But I don't want to be in the way of your business. What about the sofa in the greenhouse? Who uses that?"

"I do. It's my little getaway place, especially when it gets a little cooler towards the fall. Sometimes when I can't sleep, I go up there. Or if I need to think. I put a few strings of tiny lights in there, so it's really pretty. Like a faery land—well, the way I imagined it would be."

"The faery realm *is* beautiful, as one would expect. The Tylwyth Teg, the Fair Ones, are beautiful too, beyond mortal imagining. But underneath, they are coldhearted, and dangerous."

"I didn't know that until you told me. Hell, I didn't know faeries were *real* until I met you—I thought they were just pretty little flying people in storybooks."

"There are many other fae creatures, of every size and shape, that live in the realm as well. And most of them are *not* pretty."

A chill skittered down her spine. Luckily, Aidan had finished what he was doing and was now checking out her selection of tarot cards with interest.

"Are these the type of cards you used with Florence and her dog?"

She couldn't help but laugh. "I didn't do a reading for Mr. Socks, just Flo, but yes, these are the same kind of cards. She comes in every Friday to have me read them for her."

"What do they tell you?"

"All kinds of things, depending on what cards you draw. Where you are in your life's journey. The future. Things to do, things to avoid. Things to be cautious of."

"Can you read them for me?"

Brooke was caught off guard. Maybe she didn't expect Aidan to be interested, but his request surprised her. "I have another client in about thirty minutes. But I could do a short reading for you now if you like, and perhaps a longer one later." She was about to get her standard deck, the one she used for clients only—then something made her change her mind.

"Choose a deck that you like, one that speaks to you, that makes you feel something," she said to Aidan, nodding at the display. "For this, we want to use a new deck that won't have anybody else's energy on it but yours."

"These are your wares. I have no money."

"You have no money, *yet*. We can barter—I give you the cards and do a reading, and you can be manly and move some big boxes in the storeroom for me."

He nodded and reached immediately for a deck near the top of the display and presented it to her. She'd forgotten she had it— the deck was dedicated to Welsh mythology, something she'd chosen from the catalog while thinking of her friend, Morgan Edwards. It had failed to entice a purchaser, however, and had sat on the shelf for over a year.

"Well, I guess that one must have been waiting for you." She led Aidan to the corner booth she favored for this type of work, and sat across from him. "Unwrap the deck."

He struggled with the plastic, but she resisted the urge to help—every instinct she had was screaming that he needed to be the *only one* to touch that deck. Finally, he managed to free the cards, spilling a few onto the table.

"Okay, gather them up and shuffle them around a bit, roll them in your hand like this." She demonstrated with the client deck she used with Flo. "You want the cards to have your energy, and you want to feel familiar with them, and they with you—no, don't look at them, just juggle them around."

He caught on quickly—she hadn't expected such fine motor skills from a blacksmith, but perhaps she was making assumptions. Such work might require far more finesse than she imagined.

"Okay, now draw one card at a time, from anywhere in the deck. Lay them face down on the table like so." She demonstrated again, laying out first a row of three, and a fourth below them. "That's all. Now set the deck to one side and turn over your cards."

The Fool.

Brooke frowned.

The Moon.

Coincidence. That was her mind's knee-jerk reaction. Which

was pretty stupid considering she didn't believe in coincidence—yet right now, she'd gladly embrace the concept with open arms.

The Ten of Pentacles.

She could feel all the blood draining from her face. *This is so not happening. It can't be.* Brooke gripped the table to steady herself as Aidan reached for the last card.

Death.

The next thing she knew, she was being cradled in strong arms, held close to a large male body, with her head tucked neatly between his chin and shoulder. It was steadying, and she took some deep breaths to clear the fog from her head. He smelled really good, she decided, and took a couple of extra deep breaths just for the pure pleasure of it.

Aidan's voice rumbled pleasantly in her ear, even though it was edgy and full of concern for her. "Is my fortune so fearful that even a gwddon must faint?"

"No," she said, and pushed at his chest until she could sit up far enough to look him in the face. "No, of course not. I'm sorry, I guess it was a shock to see that reading again, that's all. Put me down now, and I'll explain."

He didn't return her to her side of the table but instead placed her on his bench and moved in beside her. His big arm rested behind her along the top of the seat back—*obvious, much?* It was perfectly clear that if she so much as hiccupped, he was prepared to grab her. Independent by nature, she normally would have discouraged him. Right now, though, a big part of her was enjoying the notion of being protected. While no longer faint, she still felt *iffy*.

Brooke explained about the card readings she'd been getting before Aidan had arrived. "I can see it now. This reading must have been intended for you all along. Somehow I was picking up on you and your energy before you ever got here."

"What about your own cards? What do they say?" he pointed to the four client cards she had demonstrated with, still lying face-down on her side of the table.

"Oh, never mind those. I wasn't doing a reading for myself. I wasn't doing a reading at all, just showing you. And I never use those cards for myself, only for clients."

"Your *energy*, as you call it, is on those cards, is it not? You use them to read the fortunes of clients, but do you not touch them every single time?"

A little chill shot through her veins, and she suddenly realized she didn't want to look at her own cards. Brooke had done at least a dozen readings for clients in the past week, and nothing odd had come up. It had been business as usual, with the customers choosing combos of major and minor arcana that were uniquely suited to their current circumstances. But she hadn't dared to do a single reading for herself since the one she'd shared with George. *I've just been busy*, she told herself.

Chicken, said the voice in her head.

And damn it, Aidan could tell she was afraid. "Shall I turn them for you?" he asked.

"I can do it myself," she said, remembering a favorite childhood book called *The Little Red Hen*. "And she did," she murmured, repeating the key line of the story as she flipped the cards over as fast as she could before she could change her mind.

The Fool. The Moon. The Ten of Pentacles.

Death.

Brooke didn't feel faint. In fact, the room didn't even get fuzzy, maybe because she just plain *wasn't surprised* anymore. She could feel Aidan's big hand resting on her shoulder, just in case, and she reached up and grasped it with both of hers and leaned against him. Maybe they weren't in a relationship together, but she could use the moral support anyway. The subtle vibration of magic that emanated from him mingled pleasantly with her own power, and that was comforting too.

"Okay, this is where I officially throw up my hands," she said at last. "We need to get Olivia back here."

Lurien preferred to do things himself. His home had not a single servant, as he valued his privacy. He valued his life too—and the innumerable intrigues of the Royal Court made it wiser that he trust no one. The Hunt had been strenuous this night as he fought to train a new horse, a wild fae creature he'd first had to capture with a silver rope. He welcomed the challenge, however. Perhaps that was what he would miss most about his former mount. Bayard had been matchless for speed and strength, but his predatory instincts were better suited to a dragon, and every ride was a fight. The big blue-gray animal had tried to kill Lurien on several occasions, making it more than a little ironic that the Lord of the Hunt had slain him in the end.

Dawn was breaking as he entered his chambers and peeled off his black gloves. One by one, he unfastened his weapons, unbuckling the finely tooled harness of his sword and the holstered throwing knives, slipping the silver bow from his shoulder and the quiver still heavy with silver arrows—there had been no quarry tonight. He enjoyed each tiny sensation of relief as their weight slid from him. He knew no true weariness of body, but he took his pleasures wherever he could find them.

The crumpled golden dress upon the floor reminded him of where he had *not* found the pleasures he'd hoped for. At least, not all of them. The satisfaction he'd gotten from sending the heartless tywysoges to the court without a single stitch of her finery was in itself somewhat pleasing. But not what he'd wanted, not at all.

He kicked the priceless golden fabric into the corner with the toe of his leather boot and set it ablaze with a look. Celynnen had been surprised at how easily he'd overpowered her, how potent his magic was—she relied heavily on the bwgan stone for almost all of her spells. *A grave weakness.* One shared by most of the surviving royals, except the queen herself. Like Gwenhidw, he had studied eons to *earn* his power, and he didn't have to rely on an object to magnify it. That was the thinking of a warrior, of course, and a leader. It had never entered the princess's head that she might someday have her toys taken away from her. She knew it now, of course, thanks to him. The downside was that he'd revealed his own superior ability. Even after she'd exacted revenge on him (or tried) for her naked entrance to the Court, she would forever consider him a threat to her.

What is one more enemy, more or less?

The flame extinguished itself. The finely woven fabric of the dress had been reduced to a scant spoonful of golden ash. A flick of a finger would send the debris to another realm—but Lurien suddenly paused. *There is something in the ash . . .*

A word from him instantly placed every particle of the dress's remains into his cupped hand, where he commanded the ash to separate into its component parts. A miniature vortex rose from his palm as his order was obeyed, and he saw again the tiny fingernail shape that had arrested his attention.

With a shocked curse, he plucked it from the vortex and released the rest of the ash to sift its way to the stone floor. Vitrified now, glasslike from the intense heat of the magical fire, the object was still unmistakable: a reptilian scale.

How had such a thing come to be on Celynnen's dress? Had the hem of her long gown unknowingly swept it up as she walked through the palace gardens? Or had she deliberately placed it in her pocket or her sleeve?

A dozen possibilities came to mind. If she was purposefully in possession of the scale, then most likely, she'd obtained it as an ingredient for a spell. Legend held that drinking a potion made with one of these would render you temporarily impervious to iron. The metal was as poisonous to the Draigddynion as to the other races in the Nine Realms. But unlike the other fae, the dragon men were able to handle the dangerous substance for short periods of time before succumbing to its effects. But why would Celynnen need such a thing? Moreover, how would she get her pretty hands on it? The Draigddynion lived in the damp, deadly forests where bwgans also lived. Lurien himself had hunted those lands and could attest to their extreme dangers.

Had the princess obtained it from someone else? Received it as a gift? Who amongst the Tylwyth Teg would have contact with the reclusive chameleon-like creatures? For none of the Draigddynion had been seen or heard from since the assassination of the king by nine of their kind.

Lurien's hand tightened into a fist around the scale until it cut into his palm. *Only a conspirator would have any connection or commerce with the reptilian fae.* He had to find out who had given the princess such a dubious gift.

But to do that, he had to question Celynnen.

"Why didn't you tell me, *m'ija?*" asked Olivia. "You had all those readings, all saying the same thing, and you did not say a word? I'm in here almost every day!"

"I don't know why. I really was busy, and I wasn't thinking about it when I saw you. I mean, I usually look up my daily reading about six in the morning when I get up and make coffee," said Brooke. "You come by later on in the morning, maybe ten or eleven. In that time, I've been trying to get the store open and look after my first customers and . . ." *And those are all excuses, aren't they? Ah, hell.* "I was afraid."

Olivia shook her head. "There are not many things in this world that make *you* afraid, Brooke Halloran. That should have warned you. Instead, I cannot believe you just kept it to yourself. Why would you try to deal with it alone?"

"I don't know. It was so darn crazy that I didn't want it to be real. Plus, the reading itself wasn't a bad one; the prediction wasn't dire. So even though I was afraid, it could have been just plain pride too—I wanted to be able to figure it out and handle it on my own. I didn't want to run for help at the first sign of a problem."

"Or the *ninth* sign of a problem? To hold the Gift *is not to hold it alone, m'ija. Mi madre* would have had *such* words for you about this. As for me, even as your teacher and your friend, I cannot be angry." Olivia sighed and patted Brooke's hand. "I am sorry for *you* that you did not reveal this sooner. You are the one who has had to bear the stress and the worry over it all alone, and that is punishment enough. Plus, Aidan says you fainted when he drew his cards."

Brooke shot a look at him. His expression was totally unrepentant. "It was a shock, that's all," she said.

The older woman regarded the cards on the table, which hadn't moved since they'd been turned over earlier that day. Brooke had taken care of her next three clients at other booths. "Nine identical readings before Aidan arrived," recounted Olivia, shaking her head. "And this morning, from two completely different decks, we get two readings, for two people, at the same time, and both readings are the same. You two are connected in a way I have never even heard of before."

Aidan frowned. "What do the cards tell you?" he asked Olivia.

"I explained that already," said Brooke.

"I want to know what *our friend* thinks they say. Sometimes two pairs of eyes are better than one, are they not?"

She sighed. It was probably the Fool card that was bothering him—what man wanted to see that? And the Death card often frightened people—no, *scratch that*. Of all the clients she'd ever had, Aidan was probably more comfortable with that card than any of them ever could be. She nodded at Olivia. "He's right. We can't take the chance that I may have missed something."

"The reading came to both of you. I think we have to interpret it for both of you. What it says to one must also be intended for the other." Her friend crossed herself. "*Dios*, I hope I am right in this, but this is one of the few things the Gift has given to me, and it is usually very strong.

"The Fool is an old name for this card, meaning only that he is innocent. I call this card the Traveler, because he is at the start of a journey and does not know what lies ahead of him. It is a good card, a card of new beginnings." She folded her hands and leaned forward. "This card very often means that new love is coming your way, a love that is out of the ordinary."

Aidan narrowed his eyes at Brooke. "You did not say that."

"I didn't think it applied!" defended Brooke. "The card can also mean you're getting a *fresh start*, or it can be literal, and mean you're actually going to *go on a trip*. One of my clients won a vacation cruise after a reading that featured this card."

"And *I* am saying what *I* feel about this reading," reminded Olivia. "And I said exactly what I meant. Also, you must notice that the Traveler does not go alone. The dog at his side stands for faithful friends who will guard and guide him, and I am very glad for that."

She paused and took a deep breath before she continued. "I am glad for that because the second card is the Moon. This is a very frightening card to me. Powerful magic is involved here, dangerous magic, deception, and hidden enemies."

"Um—that's enemies, *plural*?" asked Brooke. "I didn't think I had even *one*. You must mean Aidan's enemies."

Olivia held up her finger. "As I said, this reading is for both of you. You must be on your guard. We all must. I feel we are all involved, every one of us, family and friends alike." She shook her head as if to clear it and continued. "The Moon shows a dimly lit path where ordinary rules won't apply. A different world—"

"The faery realm," Aidan said at once.

"Possibly. You must trust your intuition and reach inside yourself for the courage to move forward." Olivia pointed at the Moon card in Brooke's reading and in Aidan's reading. "These cards were not designed by the same artist. But in both, you see a pair of dogs barking at the moon—once again, you are being guarded. You have friends and you will need them."

Aidan pointed to the Ten of Pentacles. "What about this card?"

"It's a much happier card," said Brooke, glad for the distraction. Everything that Olivia had said about the Moon card had resonated inside her, to the point that she was finally able to put her finger on what had frightened her into saying nothing to anyone about the multiple readings.

Most people were frightened by the Death card, but to a witch, the lunar card was scarier by far. Like the real moon whose strange light leeched the familiar colors of the day into pale, unrecognizable shades, the Moon card almost always meant that something was not as it appeared to be. No clear pathway was visible, and yet above all, the card indicated that a great darkness must be faced. The Moon was an upsetting card before Brooke had met Aidan or learned of his literal experiences with another world and its inhabitants. In light of his vow to confront his enemy, she could now officially declare herself *creeped out*.

"The Ten of Pentacles is a card of great potential," agreed Olivia. "But also great change. It is the end of one cycle and the beginning of another. Sometimes this card signifies great and lasting wealth, but it's not about money at all in this case. Here the reward is in permanent relationships. It could be lasting love, and also strong ties with friends and family."

"That sounds pretty good," said Brooke.

"But," added Olivia. "And it is a very big *but*—you can only have this great reward if you take an equally great risk."

"It sounds like many things in life." Aidan pointed to the card in question. "There are dogs in this picture, too. Why? I see no enemies here."

"In the other cards, the dogs represent the friends that guard and guide you. This card represents a place that is already protected, and permanent. The dogs symbolize loyalty and ties that cannot be broken."

"What about the last card, Olivia?" asked Brooke. "What do you think it means?"

"Death is always the card of change. I am concerned with the card's position—it's at the bottom with the other three above it. That means it influences all three of them."

"That's exactly what George said about it," murmured Brooke.

"In this case, the Death card is in perfect harmony with the Ten of Pentacles—something must end in order for something new to begin . . . But I do not know what."

SEVENTEEN

It was late by the time Olivia left, and Aidan suggested that Brooke close her shop. Usually she would have been open another hour, but she looked worn. The strange events of the day were weighing heavily on her mind.

Brooke searched the back room and came up with some odd little bowls of dry crispy things she called noodles. "These are supposed to be microwaved," she said. "But I need to test something out first." She placed the bowls on the counter and filled each with water, causing the noodles to float on top like corks. Closing her eyes and holding a hand above each bowl, she murmured a few words.

The air suddenly filled with the sharp tang of savory herbs as steam rose from the bowls. Brooke yanked her hands away but bounced on her feet in an odd little dance. "*Yes!*" she shouted. "I'm back!"

Aidan was puzzled. "You haven't left."

She laughed as she used a small towel to carry the hot dishes to the table one at a time. "Maybe I didn't go anywhere, but my magic did. It hasn't worked worth a nickel lately—not since I started getting those weird card readings."

"From the tarot? Olivia was very concerned about the message the cards gave us. And for you, the readings have continued without interruption, so why would your powers suddenly be restored now?"

"Good question." She sat across from him and handed him a fork and spoon. "Olivia and I both noticed a big change in the chi, the vitality and life force that flows through this place, when you arrived. You're the only new factor in the equation, and my magic is working again now that you're here. So maybe it's like Olivia told me: your energy is balancing mine."

Having seen her considerable power at work, Aidan didn't think it was possible for him to balance it in the least, but he wasn't about to argue the point. He wasn't about to complain about the meal either—although he secretly thought the strange salty food was much worse than the bagels he'd eaten yesterday. Brooke was happy—even relieved—and all the more so as she continued to experiment as they ate. A dozen books from the office desk on the other side of the room were levitated, then rearranged midair before resuming their places. Cupboard doors opened and closed, papers whirled about then stacked themselves neatly. She sighed in obvious satisfaction. "I can't begin to tell you how good that feels."

"I'm accustomed to magic in the faery realm—almost every-thing there is accomplished by a word or a gesture. Even as a grim, I required the use of magic to carry out my task." He shook his head. "It's very rare for a mortal to possess so much power, and to control it so well," he said. "Your talent is astounding to me."

"Ha! You wouldn't say that if you'd seen me a week ago. Do you have any idea how many spells and potions I've got on my order shelf, waiting to be prepared and delivered?" she asked, pointing her spoon in his direction. "I can finally get caught up with my work now. So many people are waiting for help. First on my list, though, is going to be a spell of well-being for Rina Carter. She's pregnant with twins, and very anxious about it. She needs to relax and feel some peace."

"That's the difference between you and the fae," said Aidan. "You use your power to help and to serve. They use theirs to amuse themselves—and they care not for the cost, even if harms the innocent."

"That's horrible. That's against everything the Code stands for."

"You abide by a law?"

"A set of laws. Absolutely."

She recited it for him, and he nodded solemnly. "Those are worthy ideals. It's honorable that you regard your powers as a gift and act accordingly. Most of the fae view theirs as a right, without responsibility." He thought of the Lord of the Wild Hunt and wondered if he was an exception. If ever there was a fae with honor, it was Lurien. If there were others, however, Aidan had not met them.

"Thinking of the Code reminds me that I have work to do," she sighed. "Maybe I should work a few spells before I go to bed."

He shook his head. "You've had much to concern you this day, and you will perform your work better if you are rested. The morning will be here soon enough." Aidan encouraged Brooke to go upstairs to her apartment and rest. "I'll be your guard dog down here by the door," he teased. "Instead of biting, I'll be so rude that no one will dare disturb you."

It won a small laugh from her. "Well, then, I'm going to feel very safe."

She led the way back into the shop, and he watched her pull out pillow and quilts from under the bench and arrange them carefully. Brooke was ever concerned about the comfort and well-being of others. Of him. Before he'd fully formed the thought, he had his arms around her. "My *mam* used to say that worry was heavier to carry than stones," he said. "Put the stones down for the night, Brooke."

She hugged him tight, and he was content to hold her for as long as she would let him. He was supposed to be comforting her, but something in him eased as well. Brooke laid her head on his shoulder, and he couldn't help but rest his cheek on her silky hair. He breathed deeply, trying to discern the hints of plants and flowers that enhanced rather than overpowered her own natural scent. It was like trying to pull apart a spring morning.

She sighed. "There it is again."

"What?"

"When I touch you, I can feel power. A lot of it. It's like magic is running through your veins or something."

"Perhaps a leftover from my time as a grim," he said. "I told you that I had powers sufficient to aid me in my task."

"That's what I thought it was at first. But I'm wondering if there's something more to it. Maybe your magic is like mine. It's part of you, something you were born with."

He was about to deny it when a memory stopped him. The blacksmith he'd been apprenticed to had often said he'd never seen a lad so gifted. And it was true that Aidan had never struggled to learn to shape the metal—it was as if the element *wanted* to become what he saw in his mind. Had there been more to his ability than talent alone? "Gofannon is the god of both metalworking and magic. Perhaps it is no accident that magic has found me—it may have claimed me for its own before the metal did."

Perhaps it was no accident that Celynnen had found and claimed him either. He recalled his alarm when the little girl at the bus stop was able to hear Lurien's words. The child's unusual ability had unknowingly brought her to the attention of the Lord of the Wild Hunt. Celynnen had spoken of watching Aidan as a little boy. Had she noticed him, even sensed him at a distance, because of some natural wellspring of magic within him? A flower's nectar attracted a bee. It stood to reason that a human with magic might attract a fae.

"I feel it in you, too," he admitted, and Brooke turned her head to look up at his face. "It's like a pulse beneath my touch, even in the air when we're near each other."

It was here now, throbbing between them, the energies reaching for each other, seeking to entwine. He thought—

And suddenly there was no more thought. Instead, Aidan bent his head and pressed his lips to hers. Some faraway part of him, the civilized part, urged him to be cautious, to go gently, but it was drowned out by the sudden roaring of the emptiness within him. The aching void of a thousand years abruptly reared up and demanded to be filled.

He clamped her to himself with one powerful arm and devoured her mouth. His other hand rubbed her in hard circles from the back of her slender neck to the tops of her thighs, grasping, gripping, kneading. Memorizing her shape by touch and pressing her soft curves into his hard planes. He was starved, and his hunger was a live thing. He wanted, needed, *everything*, all at once. And there was nothing he could do to rein it in.

Nothing, until Brooke responded with wants and needs of her own. Rather than be frightened by him, she reached one hand around his head and knotted her fingers in his hair, holding his commanding mouth in place as her tongue coaxed his into a rhythmic, if forceful, dance.

Meanwhile, her other hand was busy—and so was her magic. He was holding her so tightly against him, she couldn't manipulate her fingers to do more than brush the buttons of his shirt. But as she did so, each sprang open. By the time she unfastened the button of his jeans, he could no longer bear his clothes. Aidan wrenched himself back from her, the separation almost physically painful, and yanked away the entrapping fabric as quickly as possible. She stood perfectly still and put up a hand, as if to keep him at bay.

By Gofannon, he fought to control himself, to hold back the wildness that had overtaken him. If she wanted him to stop, then he must find a way, he *must*. The air in the shop was cool, but he could swear his skin was steaming like a lathered horse. His breath was harsh, as if he'd been running, and his newly freed cock strained towards her.

Brooke spoke a single word—and all of her clothing puddled at her feet. Her sudden lush nakedness was like a hard punch to his belly, driving the breath from his lungs. The glow from the amber streetlights outside filtered through the blinds and softly gilded her rounded curves. She smiled then and took a step towards him, but he had her in his arms before her foot touched the floor.

The hunger of a millennium drove him, and he feasted on her. His mouth was on her throat, her breasts, her navel. With an arm, he swept most of the quilts and the three cats lounging on them from the broad tufted bench. The felines stalked away but he was blind to their indignation. He had eyes only for Brooke as he guided her down with his heavily muscled body. Her arms slid around him and pulled him the rest of the way, and she moaned with deep satisfaction as he lay atop her, skin to skin at last. Yet he couldn't stay still, couldn't linger more than a few breaths. He slid down the length of her, kissing, licking, even biting, until his face was level with her vee. For a moment he laid his face on the soft mound of curls there—then he spread her legs wide, revealing her luscious core. She curved her hips upward, seeking his mouth, and he tasted her greedily even as he reveled in her scent. It was a banquet, and he indulged himself fully, even as she seized handfuls of his hair and pulled his face into her.

The monstrous craving that drove him was far from sated, however. It growled for more, for all. Aidan rose over her until the head of his questing cock found her hot, slick center. The first thrust made him drunk and dizzy at the same time, sending a delicious shiver through him from the crown of his head to the soles of his feet. *More.* He had to have *more.* He pounded fiercely into her as Brooke urged him on. With feral cries, they moved as one, climbing together until the jarring, pulsing release rocked them both—and erupted in a blinding burst of pure magic.

There was nothing to do but cling to each other. The power flowed through them, back and forth, as they lay panting together, blending them into one being, fusing them, encircling them, and shining from them. The darkened shop was brighter than day as the air itself seemed alight. Colors danced and spun, as Aidan and Brooke rode out a storm of purest energy that rattled the jars on the shop shelves.

Finally, the brilliant light softened and faded, and the energies eased and released them.

"What in the seven hells was that?" he whispered. Aidan eased his weight to one side but didn't let go of her.

"I think it's the Universe telling us that we get along pretty well."

Chuckling, he brushed a kiss over her forehead and both eyes, tucked her close to him, and pulled the remaining quilt over them both.

Brooke was soon asleep, but Aidan lay awake for a long time. The broad, padded bench was more comfortable than any bed he'd ever slept in. Bouncer, Jade, and even Rory eventually found their way back to it, too, curling up in purring mounds by his feet—apparently he was forgiven for interrupting their rest so abruptly earlier.

The subdued light that found its way into the shop was soothing to his eyes. Everything about this world was overbright, and there was so much to look at that it wearied the mind. Yet there was much to think about, much that pressed on him. He'd wanted to return to his own time and place—and gods knew, it would be a more peaceful existence. But it would be a lonely one too. Annwyl was dead and gone, and nothing would change that. The Tylwyth Teg had power to call on the dead as temporary puppets, as Lurien had done to swell the numbers of the Wild Hunt. But even the fae's formidable magic could not bring anyone back to true life. What Celynnen had done could not be undone. Ever.

He thought about Annwyl, half wondering if he'd just been unfaithful to her. And he was forced to confront another truth. It had been both a triumph and a blow to remember her after all the centuries that had passed. A triumph after the faery realm had eventually forced him to forget her. A blow when he recalled that *she was dead.*

They had not known each other long or well while she lived, but he had loved her as much as he possibly could have. And he had mourned her with everything he had for as long as he could recall anything about her. Now, however, Annwyl was like a faded painting from a long-ago past, her likeness restored to him, but a likeness only. Somewhere along the way, unbeknownst to him, she'd transformed from living being to cherished memory. He'd done his grieving long ago. All that was left was to give her justice . . .

Brooke stirred in his arms. He kissed her forehead again, and stroked her hip, gratified when she snuggled closer. Here was a woman worthy of love, vibrant and unique, and there was no denying the powerful attraction he had felt for her from the beginning—even after he realized she wasn't Annwyl. She was bold and strong and independent—qualities he wasn't accustomed to in a woman, but he found that he wouldn't change them a bit. There was more to consider, though. Brooke had a business of her own, talents and abilities that she utilized to make a living. Did he have a damn thing in this world to offer her?

And was he going to be long for this world if he returned to the faery realm? Because he would not abandon his vow. Annwyl had not deserved an early death by Celynnen's hand, and he would avenge his betrothed before he undertook to build a life for himself in this time. *If I live.* He wasn't stupid enough to think that confronting the coldhearted tywysoges would be anything but perilous. He had much planning to do, many preparations to make . . .

He shifted slightly, noting that his body was as tired as his mind, perhaps more, and that was new. Although his muscles were strong as ever, still capable of all he asked of them, he had not used them in a very long time. He'd forgotten that they needed rest as much as they needed food.

As a grim, he hadn't truly required sleep but had instead lapsed willingly into a torpor whenever he was not called to attend the mortal world. It was the only way of bearing the endless breadth of days in the faery realm. Many grims were encouraged to follow the Hunt for sport. Those ones lost their inner humanity quickly, delighting in the chase, craving the kill. Other grims tiptoed like great shadows along the outskirts of the colorful, chattering Court. These lost their humanity as well over time, some shedding it willingly for the chance to be near the unearthly beauty of the Tylwyth Teg. They came to adore the Fair Ones and wanted nothing more than to bask in their glittering presence, fawning like the most obedient of pets.

But Aidan had wanted nothing to do with the fae. He'd refused to forget that he was a prisoner, refused to join his captors.

You refused me, too. But not for long, dearest Aidan. Not for long.

Aidan sprang up, his body instinctively crouching over the sleeping Brooke to shield her. Faery laughter filled his head, a thousand tiny crystal bells that chilled rather than delighted. The sound mocked him until it finally faded away to complete silence and a sickening realization.

Celynnen had found him.

A blast of music from her cell phone had Brooke flailing awake and the cats scattering from their snug spots on top of the covers. The loud ringtone had been programmed into her phone by George, of course. It was his *walk-out music*, the pounding beat that accompanied his strutting entry through the auditorium and up into the octagon ring. He'd chosen the song to get him into the right alpha-male headspace before a fight, but the music was also designed to whip up the crowd's enthusiasm. Brooke was not enthused. At present, it was just noise, and it was annoying the hell out of her and she wanted it to stop. Unfortunately, the damn cell phone was somewhere in her pile of clothes on the floor and definitely not within arm's reach.

Oh, for pity's sake! She dragged a pillow over her head to drown out the sound. Finally, the ringtone ceased, replaced by the double beep that signaled a message had been left. Brooke breathed out a sigh of relief, then sighed again as she realized there was no hope of staying where she was—and *where she was* provoked some pretty interesting thoughts. No, now that the cats were awake, Rory was loudly asking for his breakfast. Jade and Bouncer flanked him as if in total agreement. Any hope of sleep had officially left the building. She dressed quickly, ignoring the cell phone that was still uttering periodic beeps from her jeans pocket. Aidan's clothes were gone, and she wondered where he was. But she would get no peace until her furry overlords were fed.

Brooke made her way up the stairs to her apartment and followed her cats to the kitchen, where early morning sun poured through the tall windows like honey. She squinted as she fumbled in the cupboard for the Little Whiskers box and spilled some on the floor as she filled the three stainless-steel dishes. She needed to fill herself with coffee—it was barely 6 a.m. She glanced at the coffee maker, and her tired brain managed to remember that she needed to open a new bag of beans. She opened the door to her pantry—

And the vision overtook her. Without any warning or preamble, or even opening credits, Brooke found herself *on the roof*. The bright morning sun was gone as if it had never existed. Here, night and day had achieved a compromise: full dark was punctuated by chains of streetlights and garish signs bright enough to hurt her eyes. Between the lights loomed the black holes of shadows. The moon and stars had refused to join such an uneasy alliance and had abandoned the sky to the low-hanging clouds and silver rain.

Suddenly naked, she reveled in the summer downpour. The fat silvery drops were warm and soft. They shimmered as they burst upon her skin, as though they not only reflected the city lights but also captured tiny orbs of it. She was painted in light as she walked among her garden plants.

He'd taken the teak futon from the greenhouse and set it up amidst the tall potted fruit trees. The normally green vinyl cushions shone slickly, every color and none at the same time. *Like faery eyes* . . . she knew that without knowing how she knew it.

But her own eyes were admiring Aidan.

He stood with one foot on the arm of the futon, resting an elbow on his knee as if he were a marble statue from ancient Rome. The rain had combed his dark blond hair into darker strings, and his close beard was studded with jewels of water. As she approached, she could see tiny bright riverlets streaming over those heavily muscled shoulders. Some ran down his powerful biceps. Some trickled over the breadth of his chest to be channeled downward into the narrow vee of hair that bisected his taut belly. A single drop of rainwater glinted in his navel; the rest traced a silvery path farther down the darkened line to surround the thick base of his erect cock. There the droplets ran along the underside of the long shaft until they fell like a string of silver beads from the glistening head.

A few droplets that were *not* rainwater tickled down Brooke's inner thighs until they were slick. There was no hesitation in her, and no questions, as she approached Aidan. She was light headed, dizzy with a single thought, and oh-so-thirsty. Cupping him with her hand, she knelt, not in supplication but in triumph. With parted lips, she sipped the rain from his cock, lapping its length with careful tongue in order to catch every glittering drop. She watched Aidan's face as she stroked the water into her mouth with circled fingers, and yet her need was far from quenched. At last she slid her hot mouth over the plumlike head and swallowed it deep. Satisfaction resonated at last: here was what she wanted, this was what she craved.

She exulted in Aidan's groans of pleasure, thrilled at the control that was all hers. His reaction to every nuance of her movements was intoxicating, even as she became aware of something new: a tiny pulse of magic that quickly strengthened into a solid thrum of power. Their energies were in perfect sync, a rare harmony uncovered between them. His strong fingers threaded through the rain-wet ropes of her hair, as if completing a link, a circuit. Sex united them, but magic merged them. Synergy flowed freely—and grew.

Her control was now an illusion. She was spiraling upwards even as Aidan did, both driving him and being drawn to some nameless towering peak. When he bucked and roared to the skies, her own orgasm shuddered and pulsed through her like untamed electricity. In a single blinding moment, sensation and *something more* fused them together, body and soul. That's when the magic erupted—

And the phone rang. *The phone? What the hell?*

Brooke stood alone in her pantry, surrounded by colorful cans and boxes, as the phone rang incessantly in her living room. It was broad daylight. There was no rain here, no nakedness, no sex, and definitely, no swoon-worthy blacksmith. Plus, not so much as a tingle of magic lingered anywhere. The sheen of sweat that made her clothes stick to her skin didn't count.

I hate visions. She really did. Although having *sex* in a vision certainly made it far more interesting—that hadn't happened before. And the orgasm had been real enough, almost as good as the one she'd shared last night with the real Aidan. She could still feel those little inner aftershocks. That made a nice bonus for her body, but her underwear was soaked, her heart was wrung, and her brain was very far from satisfied. What she really wanted was to know what it all meant. Olivia had warned her that visions were difficult to interpret; they were a type of *foresight*, but all too often their significance couldn't be discerned until after the fact.

To Brooke's way of thinking, that made visions pretty much useless.

If the Universe was trying to show her that she and Aidan would be good together, it needn't have bothered. Every instinct Brooke had already told her that—not to mention last night's mind-blowing and magical sex. She knew she had feelings for him, no matter how illogical it was to have those feelings so soon. Her heart had gone ahead and made up its mind to make the leap from attraction to something more, without consulting her.

What that *something more* was, she didn't want to examine just yet. She was very aware that Aidan could bring her far-deeper emotions than she'd ever imagined, feelings that could root themselves in the bedrock of the earth itself . . .

At present, however, Aidan was AWOL. He wasn't in the shop or in her apartment, and she wasn't quite certain how to interpret that. Last night's sex had likely registered on the Richter scale—but it had been a spontaneous thing, completely unplanned (like spontaneous *combustion*). Was he off pacing the city, regretting what they had done? After all, he still had a fiancée in his past, and who could say what stage of grief he'd arrived at? Maybe he wasn't ready to move on.

The thought *hurt*, and it annoyed her because it hurt, and it annoyed her even more that she completely understood how he might be feeling. She sighed heavily. For now, her best bet was to keep herself busy, busy, busy. *Thinking* wasn't her friend right now. Weren't there any errands she could run—like picking up breakfast from across town? Anything to buy her some time to shake off the aftereffects of the daring daylight dream. She couldn't picture looking into Aidan's iron-gray eyes until she could get the word *foresight* out of her head (and stop associating it with *foreplay*, which might take a whole lot longer). And until she could bear the possibility that he didn't share her feelings, at least not yet, and perhaps even never . . .

Wait a minute. It was his damn quest, wasn't it? Aidan was bent on revenge, on making Celynnen pay for murdering Annwyl. And if he survived that, he might still be determined to return to the past. Meanwhile, she still had her responsibilities as a witch. *To hold the Gift is to protect the balance in all things and to restore harmony. To hold the Gift is to comfort the mind and spirit, and to heal both heart and body.*

Dear goddess, who was going to heal *her* heart if Aidan left?

She brushed that thought away fast, even as she scrubbed the corner of her eye with the heel of her hand and tried instead to remember what on earth she'd gone into the pantry to get. The need for coffee brought her the answer, but as she reached for a bag of beans, the landline rang in the living room, making her jump.

"George, what the hell?"

He laughed. "Is that any way to talk to your best friend?"

"It's six o'clock."

"It's seven, *chica*."

She gaped at the clock on the wall. So it was. That meant the vision had taken a slice of actual time. As if it hadn't made things difficult enough . . .

Unaware of her issues, George was still talking. "Look, you got anything on your schedule for the weekend after next?"

Only trying to figure out why she and Aidan had the same powerful and ominous tarot readings. And what on earth the Universe was trying so hard to warn them about. And why she was experiencing visions of hot naked sex, in addition to having her world rocked by the real thing. And how she was falling (or probably had fallen) in love with someone who was likely going to leave her.

She said none of that, however. "Depends, G." Brooke rubbed her eyes and each of her sinuses. "What is this, Wednesday? Thursday?

"Wednesday."

"So the time period in question is a week and a half away. I can't think that far ahead. Hell, I can't *think*, period—I haven't even had coffee yet."

"You don't have to think, *hermanita*. Look, we got those boxes of colored glass in the back of Carmelita, right? And I need some room for luggage because I'm heading to Seattle with Felicia that weekend. So I thought it would make a great road trip if you and Mr. Death Dog drove up to Morgan's place with us. We'll drop the glass off, say hello, and carry on our way. You can catch up with Morgan while your buddy visits Reese to his little Welsh heart's content."

"It's *Rhys*," she corrected. "The way you say it makes him sound like a peanut butter cup."

"Rhys, Reese, whatever. There's more, you know—turns out that Reese built a blacksmith's shop on the farm a few months ago. He's got a couple of guys trying to make swords and stuff. Isn't that what Aidan did for a living?"

"Yeah. Yeah, he did." Excitement woke her up despite the lack of caffeine. *This could be perfect for Aidan.* "You're brilliant, G."

"I know."

Of course he then had to tell her every detail he'd learned about the operation. She'd never remember it all when she told Aidan, but that didn't matter. She'd remember enough.

"I'd have to check with Morgan of course, make sure she's up for company," she said.

"Done and done. Called her last night after Felicia and I made our plans. I mean, we could just drop the glass off ourselves, but I thought you'd like to come along. You'd have to bring your little SUV, though, because I'm not sure when I'd be back to pick you guys up."

She frowned. "Didn't you just meet Felicia at the gym? Like *recently*?" *Like yesterday?*

"Yeah, well, she's something special. Everything clicked, you know?"

Brooke had heard that one before but didn't say so. Being a supportive friend, she expressed as much of the required enthusiasm as she could muster and wished him well. Of course, she also agreed to the weekend excursion—not only did it make as much sense as anything could before coffee; she also owed G *big time* for all the work he'd done to clean up the catastrophic mess in her spell room. If he wanted her to go to Disneyland *in Tokyo* with him this afternoon, she'd do her best to make it happen. And of course he wanted the glass out of his beloved truck—it was above and beyond for the tricked-out Carmelita to be used for such lowly pedestrian purposes as hauling debris, the fact that she was a heavy duty pickup notwithstanding.

Then there was the fact that George, as always, was keen to *get his party started* with his latest girl. It would be interesting to see if the two were even still together by the weekend in question . . .

Brooke hung up, spared a longing glance for her coffee maker, then dragged herself into the shower. When she emerged, she heard footsteps in the stairwell heading for the roof. There was no disguising the racket, as she knew from experience. In the empty echoing shaft with creaking metal stairs, even her small cats sounded like a rampaging herd of elephants. So rather than an invading army, it could only be Aidan—he liked her garden, maybe he had gone up to enjoy the morning there.

Without stopping to say hello to me first? That can't be good.

She finally ground some beans, put on a pot of coffee, got dressed in fresh clothes, and wished like crazy there were at least a *few* more things she had to do before going upstairs. She could sneak out, run those make-believe errands first, couldn't she? But she wasn't a coward, and she believed in grabbing the bull by the horns when necessary. She absolutely refused to be uncomfortable in her own home, and her garden was an important part of that home. Still, she couldn't help but feel that the Universe had a warped sense of humor after giving her that lusty vision. On the roof? Really, *that's* where she had to confront Aidan first thing this morning?

She sighed, poured the coffee, and went upstairs to give Aidan the news about George's road trip.

EIGHTEEN

~⌒⌒~

Brooke passed by her garden, relieved to see the green futon was still safely in the greenhouse—that damn sexy vision was going to be tough to forget—and located Aidan at last. He was sitting at her table and chairs on the far side of the roof. She'd been concerned that she wouldn't know what to say but discovered she needn't have worried.

His eyes were deeply shadowed beneath a furrowed brow.

"You look terrible, like you didn't sleep a wink," she said with real concern, as she handed him a cup. "Didn't you tell me to put the stones down for a while? From your face, I'd say you've been carrying mine as well as yours, plus everyone else's on the block." She could sense some monstrous weight pressing down on him.

"Perhaps I am not accustomed to human sleep yet. It did not visit me, and at dawn I decided to go walking." He had no smile for her and continued to look out over the city rather than at her. Not that she expected a parade or anything, but this was ridiculous considering how good together they'd been last night. Hell, they'd been *spectacular*.

Time for the direct approach.

"Look, is this about the sex last night? Because I really enjoyed it, Aidan, and I'd hate to think you were sitting here regretting it."

His gaze snapped to hers immediately. "No! Not at all. It was—it was indescribable, *cariad*. I never felt anything like it in my life, never imagined anything like it. And you were right about the magic too, but our coming together was powerful long before our magics mixed."

Okay, at least he'd agreed it wasn't ordinary sex. "So what's *cariad* mean? You called me that a couple times in the night." *Dear goddess, don't let him say buddy, pal, or friend, or I'll have to kill him.*

"*Darling one*, of course. *Love*. I think you say *sweetheart* in this time."

She blinked at the unexpected endearment. "If that's so, then why the hell did you disappear this morning? It looked an awful lot like you were avoiding me, and right now you're acting like you're not glad to see me at all."

He was on his feet almost faster than she could track the movement, and he held her tightly to him. "Nay, it isn't so. I am poor company this morning, Brooke, but not because of you. Never because of you." Aidan nuzzled the top of her head and kissed his way down her face to her lips, where he lingered. When he drew back, he shook his head and took a step back, although his big hands continued to rest on her shoulders. "It is as it was last night. I held you and then it wasn't enough. Last night I had to have more. I did not plan what happened, but it would not be denied. If I continue to hold you now, I will want you all over again. I already do."

"Sex is supposed to be spontaneous," she said. "You're human again, with human needs and feelings. And you've been celibate for a thousand years. Don't you think that has something to do with it?"

He snorted. "*Celibate* is when you feel the urge and you deny yourself. Trust me that I felt not the urge while I was a grim. You feel little or nothing in that state—not hunger, not cold or heat, not weariness. And never desire. Only emptiness and anger."

Emptiness and anger. Brooke closed her eyes for a moment. What a horrible way to exist—yet how much of that rage still burned in him? There was something more she had to say too, and she might as well get it over with. "You must still be grieving your fiancée. It has to be hard that I constantly remind you of her."

He shook his head. "Now that I know you better, I don't see Annwyl in you as I did at first. I know you to be very different." Aidan tipped her chin up with his finger then, his gray eyes looking into hers. "What I do see, I find myself wanting a great deal, Brooke Halloran."

Dear goddess, he was attracted to her—as *her.* Then why did he still look so solemn, even unhappy? "Does it make you feel guilty?" she asked gently.

"Some. But once I avenge her death, I will have done all that I can. And that's why I have to leave. I've made my vows to face Celynnen, and that's what I'm bound to do."

"But Celynnen might kill you! In fact, she'll *probably* kill you now that you're human. Annwyl wouldn't have wanted that for you. *I* don't want that for you—what kind of fate is that after a thousand years of captivity? In fact, what kind of *goal* is that, to walk right back into your prison and spit in the warden's eye?"

The imagery won a half smile from him, but his expression was feral rather than cheerful. "I promise I'll do far more than spit at her. And I'm not going there blind—I know the faery realm, I know Celynnen, and I have my plans." He looked away again. "I have to try. Nothing will stop me from doing that. Not even what I might wish for here with you."

Dammit, he *couldn't* leave her! Here was somebody she felt amazingly connected to, and—equally amazing—he had feelings for her too. Why had the Universe brought him crashing into her life when he was determined to run off and get himself—

Before she could finish the thought, the answer was crystal clear in her mind: *So you can help him.*

Brooke nearly smacked herself in the forehead. It seemed utterly simple. The Code clearly said: *To hold the Gift is to strengthen the just . . .*

"You and I are going on a road trip," she announced, folding her arms.

He frowned and shook his head. "*Cariad*, I have to leave."

"No, you don't. Not yet. You want to be as prepared as possible, right?"

"Yes, of course. I have many preparations to make."

"Then it won't hurt to add another one to your list. You need to come and meet Morgan's husband, Rhys. Consider it a fact-finding mission to further your goals. I met the guy last year at the wedding, and a few times since. He was born in Wales. Not only does he speak your language; he seems to know a very great deal about Welsh history and legends, including a lot about the faeries." *And to think I'd once called it mythology.* "You might find out some things you could use to help you succeed in your plans. On top of that, Rhys competes in weaponry competitions in Renaissance fairs across the country, and he teaches swordsmanship and things like that. George just told me that Rhys has built an authentic blacksmith's shop on the farm. I'm pretty sure that I could get you permission to use his forge."

"It appears that you have solved several puzzles for me at once," said Aidan. "Very well. I would like to travel with you to meet with your friends."

"I'm glad that's settled. I have to go open my shop now." She was about to leave her chair, but he put a cautioning hand up.

"I have not told you everything. There is a greater reason why we must part ways for now, and as quickly as possible."

"Why?"

"Celynnen has found me. She used her magic to reach out in the night to mock me."

Brooke was stunned. "Here? Her rotten magic reached into my shop, *my* home? How is that possible?"

"I don't know," he said.

"You told me she was five thousand miles away, under the Black Mountains of Wales in the faery realm, isn't that right? The Hound Lord—"

"Lord of the Wild Hunt," Aidan interjected.

"I don't care what the hell his title is. You said the guy didn't chase you this far. You were in the middle of the goddamn ocean when my spell locked onto you, so he couldn't know your location, you said. Nobody should!" Her voice rose with indignation. "How the hell did she find you, and how did her spell manage to violate *my house*?"

"I told you, I don't know the answer to that. She is very powerful, as are all the Tylwyth Teg, particularly those of the royal family. But as long as I'm here, you are in danger. I must go at once before—"

"Oh, for crap's sake, skip the damn movie cliché!" Brooke looked at her watch. She could close the shop for the morning if she could reschedule a couple of appointments to the afternoon. And then . . . She grabbed the lapel on Aidan's jacket and looked him in the eye. "You told me you've vowed to stand up to Celynnen, right?"

"Aye, that I have. But I will not risk your life as well."

"I think it's way too late for that, mister. Now that she knows where I live, Celynnen isn't likely to leave me alone just because you're not here anymore. In fact, I'm willing to bet she'd try to use me to hurt you or recapture you."

She could see the instant the truth hit him, and he sighed.

"No wonder you're a gwddon. You're very wise."

For all the good it does me. "Maybe, maybe not. What I do have is magic. I have some emergency fortifying to do that I hope will keep Celynnen out of this building, and *I need you to stay right here and help me.*"

He nodded. "My hands are yours to command."

Brooke emptied every big storage jar she had of protective herbs—fennel seed, St. John's wort, marsh marigold, and dried primroses—and mixed them into buckets of coarse sea salt. Aidan took them to the roof and poured a line of the crystalline blend along the entire half wall that formed the perimeter of the roof. She had him sprinkle it around the chimney, and each and every vent up there, plus pour a thin line on the pavement at street level, close to the building. Every possible entry, even where plumbing came into the structure, had to be charmed in some way.

Thank the goddess it's Saturday—defensive magic was particularly effective when performed on this day. And *double thanks* that Brooke had purchased such a ridiculously large quantity of salt. It had been an expensive mistake at first, an accidental tripling of an online order. But if there were no coincidences, then the Universe had watched over her and made sure she had the tools she needed to protect her home. And it gave her some hope that she'd someday find something to do with the overabundance of domestic turkey tail feathers she'd ended up with. She'd ordered three of the large bronze feathers for use in smudging ceremonies. Instead, she now had three dozen *bags* of them in the storeroom.

Brooke placed little piles of black stones—obsidian and hematite—in the corners of the building, grateful that they coincided with the cardinal directions. It would be a lot harder to do if the building was oriented according to a nearby river or a winding street instead of by the compass. She added little fragments of amber to the stones, too.

Next she handed Aidan a bucket of iron nails and a hammer. "Pound a few on the inside of every door frame and every window," she said, adding that the roof's door must be included as well. "Leave just a little bit of each nail sticking out. We'll have to be really, *really* careful that we don't snag ourselves on them, but iron is a protection against otherworldly creatures."

"Aye. It's deathly poison to the fae," he had said.

Good. Brooke wasn't out to kill Celynnen, of course. But she was righteously pissed off that her home and sanctuary had been deliberately violated by such evil intent. She wanted the cold-hearted faery to think twice before trying to insinuate any more of her tainted magic into this building and influence those who were within its walls.

While Aidan busied himself with the nails, Brooke poured salt, herbs, and dried red berries into the depression that had been burnt into her spell room's floor. It was hard to be upset about the scar in the wood when it created such a beautifully symmetrical circle. Her altar was already set up at the heart of it. This time, however, in addition to her own magical tools and her prized stone figure of Hecate with her hound, there were a number of photos printed off the Internet that stood in for real objects not readily available—a smith's hammer, tongs, and bellows, for instance. A yard of real leather, hastily cut from an old coat that had once been part of a costume, formed the tablecloth, a proxy for the protective leather apron that a smith wore during his work. And printed images of Gofannon, the old Celtic god of metalworking, were carefully pinned to the nine candles that Brooke had arranged around Hecate. It felt good, that the deities respected by both Aidan and Brooke were represented. When she'd been online, Brooke had been reassured to find that Gofannon was also the god of magic and weapon makers, although there was one more thing she didn't quite understand: he was also the god of *the fire that transforms*.

She sincerely hoped that was just a blacksmithing term and didn't mean the deity would burn her house down.

Stripping off her clothing, she entered the circle and began to walk slowly deosil—clockwise—around the altar. She lit each candle as she offered up one of the very first spells she had learned from Olivia:

High to low, roof to floor, wall to wall, and door to door;
Basement deep to sky above, fill this home with light and love.

A protection spell was always simple—again, it was the intent with which an incantation was uttered that gave it power. Brooke recited it nine times as she visualized warm amber light surrounding her building, her home. In her mind's eye, the light limned every line, every brick, every timber, every square inch of floors and walls, even the basement and the roof.

As she paced, her circle of salt began to glow. Light in the form of sinuous golden flames rose until they were nearly waist high. They gave off no heat, only a sense of inner warmth and well-being. The candles on the altar were another story. They flared up suddenly into a single column of white light, which expanded to envelope the entire altar as well. Brooke continued her measured pacing just a little closer to the flames of the outer circle as the glowing altar became brighter and brighter. Just as she could no longer look at it, it abruptly winked out as if someone had pinched out the wick of a candle. The flames disappeared from the circle in the same moment. Only silence, the scent of the berries, and a strong feeling of serenity remained. Brooke had spots in front of her eyes though, and it took a few moments for her sight to clear up. When it did, she blinked again, this time in disbelief.

Everything that wasn't metal or stone that had been on, above, or below the altar—*including the altar itself*—was now nothing more than a pile of ash, and a small one at that. Brooke's first thought was for her beautiful table, and all the work she had put into refurbishing the rare cherrywood piece. But then she scolded herself. Sometimes magic required a price, and who knew? Perhaps Gofannon charged a little more than Hecate usually did. Brooke could hardly complain. If her home and all who were in it were safe, it was well worth the little sacrifice.

"Thank you both," she breathed to the gods she had called on as she knelt to rescue her stone figure of Hecate, and brushed the ash from its fine features. Her athame and boline were likewise unharmed. Even the oak floor survived the event. Except for the top layer of varnish being blistered where the altar had once stood, there were no holes, ruts or other impressions.

She left her little statue standing with the boline beside it on the floor and used her athame to "cut" a door in the circle so she could leave without disturbing the magical energy. Once out, she sprinkled salt over the spot where she had crossed over to seal it and went to get dressed as quickly as possible. The CLOSED sign was just going to have to stay on the front door of Handcastings a little longer—there was more work to be done today, she'd decided.

They would have to go over to Olivia's house and repeat the entire process.

To hold the Gift is to guard the helpless and to remove power from the cruel. Brooke wasn't about to allow her friend and mentor to be endangered because Aidan was working there. Nor was she about to let Aidan be taken by Celynnen if she could help it. Because if intent was the most important factor in magic, then Brooke had the key ingredient: *You can't have him, you bitch.*

NINETEEN

～刀Ω～

Olivia's large home was beautiful, and apparently very old for houses in this time and place. She said it was Victorian in style. Aidan admired the grand height of it—two and a half ornate stories of wood and brick with a steeply pitched roof.

With only George living with her, there were empty bedrooms upstairs, and Olivia encouraged Aidan and Brooke to stay in one for the time being.

"The faery found Aidan at Handcastings before all the protections were in place, and that is where she'll be looking for him again," said Olivia. "All the work you did will prevent her from knowing if he's in there or not—and even if she suspects he's not, she won't know where to look next."

"And we've just fortified your protections too," said Brooke. "So chances are good she won't see Aidan, right?"

"Not even if she scries for him—and that's likely how she found him before."

Aidan alone objected. "I do not like this idea. It's not right to place everyone in danger because of me."

Olivia simply patted his arm. "If evil must be opposed, then we are stronger together, *m'ijo*. Besides, to hold the Gift *is not to hold it alone*."

"I don't have the Gift. Not the way you mean."

She eyed him speculatively. "I'm not so sure about that, but it doesn't matter. We're sticking together."

"But it puts you and George at risk . . ."

"I am at the shop almost every day and so is George. We are already in danger." Olivia was not going to take no for an answer, and she shooed the pair to the door. "Get your cats and your things, Brooke, plus the spells you need to put together for your orders. You can close the shop and work here this week.

"And as for you," she said to Aidan, "don't forget I've hired you to perform miracles with my yard. If you're staying here, I know you'll never be late for work!"

A smart man knew when to admit defeat. Olivia was a force of nature, and Aidan wasn't going to win, especially when Brooke had sided with her. Besides, he couldn't disagree with one aspect of her reasoning—it would be easier to work on the property if he was staying here, and the more work he did, the faster he could earn the means to buy iron. He might even be able to purchase some before they traveled to Brooke's friends' home. She had indeed won him permission to use their forge, and he was looking forward to trying out his weapon designs.

The sooner he did that, the sooner he could deal with Celynnen once and for all.

Olivia's house was even grander inside than it looked from the outside. The dimensions of the bedroom Aidan shared with Brooke amazed him every time he was in it. His entire shop could have fit into the space, living quarters and all. Although Deykin the Magistrate had had a much larger house than this one, the bedchambers weren't of such impressive size, nor did they boast such large windows.

The bed was enormous, too. And soft. Whatever it was padded with, it was even and smooth. There was no tossing and turning to find a comfortable spot in which to lie or to avoid a lump. Although if the luxurious bed had been made of wooden planks covered with straw, it would have made little difference to him, not when he could make love with Brooke every night. It truly seemed that his heart had found its home, as the bond between them grew. They both laughed that their only difficulty lay in being quiet enough so that their friends could not hear their nightly activities.

No, the only things that kept Aidan from sleeping like a lord were his own dreams. Dreams of Celynnen finding a chink in the magical protections that surrounded both this house and Brooke's building. Dreams of the fae princess harming his friends and his lover, perhaps callously murdering them with a word, as she had done with Annwyl, or torturing them horribly while he watched. Dreams of facing the coldhearted tywysoges, and of failing in his attempt to avenge Annwyl by slaying Celynnen.

Most of all, he dreamed that he would fail to protect Brooke and his friends.

Aidan had planned his vengeance carefully, but he had yet to create his weapons. Until he stood over a forge again, they were still just designs in his mind. And he had no hope of leading the ruthless fae away from those he loved and cared for—he had to admit that the stand-together-and-fight approach that Olivia had advocated was the only possible option. But if Celynnen were to find him here, what would they do? Would the defenses hold?

He borrowed an unused hunting knife from George (apparently a gift from a relative who didn't know the young man very well). Made of steel, a stronger, purer form of iron that was new and fascinating to Aidan, he fastened its sheath to his belt and carried the knife with him constantly. It took a while to persuade Brooke to spell it for him, however. She believed in doing no harm, yet she finally conceded that, in dire circumstances, it was best if the knife were charmed to find its mark. He had her charm a bag of iron nails as well and then loaded his pockets with them. Although he quickly discovered they made sitting very uncomfortable if he wasn't careful, he felt better having as much iron on his person as possible. The weapons were not formidable, by any means, but he would not be caught defenseless either.

Meanwhile, he was glad to have work to do, to keep body and mind busy, else the waiting would have driven him wild. While the house was grand, the half-acre backyard was not—and once he'd seen that, he could understand Olivia's utter frustration with it. Though George kept what little grass there was cut regularly (Aidan would have preferred to keep sheep or goats), the rest was a sprawling, overgrown forest. Rock retaining walls had fallen apart over time, stone pathways were heaved up and lost to encroaching trees and shrubs, and if there had once been an orderly garden, there was only an impenetrable riot of half-wild flowers now.

Armed with garden tools, many of which were surprisingly similar in shape and style to what he'd grown up with, Aidan spent his day taming the enormous yard. He enjoyed the work, although he still missed his forge. His right hand itched to hold his smith's hammer again; his left hand craved the clutch of his long-handled tongs. The heat of the fire, the bell-like clanging as he struck the metal—he missed it all.

Yet even as a smith, he'd cultivated a plot of carrots, cabbage, onions, and peas in the field behind the forge. In his time, everyone planted what little they could in order to have enough food for winter and to vary an otherwise plain diet. Pleasure gardens had been a luxury for the wealthy—and something they hired workers for. Annwyl's father had a flower garden in his courtyard that boasted many roses, a gift he had created for his wife. Here, however, it seemed that almost every home now had such things.

As Aidan labored outside, Brooke worked on her business in Olivia's spell room off the kitchen, catching up on all the charms she had orders for. Olivia herself was seldom at home during the day. She instructed Aidan to help himself to whatever was in the fridge for his lunch, though. He chose simple things, familiar things: meats and cheeses, bread and butter. But it was a source of unending novelty to him to eat such foods icy cold. He was certain that his *mam* would have disapproved on the basis that it would upset his bodily humors, although no such thing occurred.

At night, he'd meet again with Brooke and Olivia over a late supper to discuss the day's progress. Olivia often talked them into visiting with her until George finally came home. If he came home at all.

"He spends all his time with this Felicia," said his mother. "Perhaps he is finally settling down. It's about time."

"You'll know if he actually brings her home to meet you," laughed Brooke.

"I would faint from amazement, *m'ija*—he's never done that. Not once have I met one of my son's many girlfriends, unless I bumped into him at a mall or a restaurant with one or two on his arm."

"Two?"

"*M'ija*, as a mother I have learned not to ask questions I do not want the answers to."

Their nightly entertainment—a thing called TV—was a complete puzzle to Aidan at first. He'd seen the invention of course, as a grim, but had never stopped to watch what passed across the smooth black surface. Gradually, he began to understand. Human beings had not changed so much over the centuries—TV was simply the modern equivalent of sitting around the fire and telling stories.

He liked the feeling of home and family he felt here. The company was good. He held Olivia in great affection, and George, while not home very much, was still slowly becoming a friend. Even the cats, Bouncer, Jade, and Rory, had attached themselves to Aidan. They played in the garden around him as he worked (and often as not, getting in the way). At night, at least two sat in his lap, and often Rory would climb on his shoulder and purr into his ear.

And as for Brooke—she hadn't needed one bit of magic to transform his heart. The wrath and rage within him had eased. He was still righteously angry at the horrors that Celynnen had wrought, and he would kill her without a second thought—but the volatile fury had yielded to control. Most of all, the gnawing emptiness that had marked his time as a grim was abundantly filled in by Brooke's loving nature. With her, he felt whole again.

Still, all the loving tenderness in the world could not bring him a peaceful sleep. He was wakeful, refining the designs of his weapons in his mind, planning how best he might confront his enemy. Considering all the things that might go wrong, and the terrible price that not only he but also those who stood with him would pay. And when weariness finally overcame him, he was tormented by nightmares. Over a week went by like that, until Olivia put her hand on his at breakfast one morning.

"You look exhausted, Aidan," she said. "You're working miracles in that yard, but are you working too hard?"

He was about to protest that he was fine, but there was no deflecting those knowing eyes of hers. Like Brooke, he suspected she would see the truth—or a lie—immediately. "The task is satisfying to me; it's not as difficult as smithing so I am far from overworked. No, it is my mind that is weary. There is much that weighs upon it, and many questions without answers."

"Perhaps I can help you with that, *m'ijo*. Come with me."

She led him through the small door off the pantry. It appeared as simply another closet, but instead, it led to a sizable room with a high ceiling. One wall was completely covered with shelves, all groaning with many books and objects like the ones in Brooke's shop, but Aidan's attention was riveted on an enormous shallow bowl on a tall oak table in the exact center of the room. The bowl was old and rather plain, but his practiced eye told him it was pure silver and not plated. Olivia produced a matching silver pitcher and filled the bowl with a scant inch of water. Carefully, she set the pitcher on the floor and then took both of Aidan's hands.

"Do you trust me?"

He nodded. "I have the *curitas* to prove it."

"Good. Look into the water, and when I tell you to, put your hand in it and grasp whatever you see."

"But it's empty . . ."

Olivia shook her head. "It only looks that way. As I told Brooke, I have few skills with magic, but the ones I have are very strong. I can read the cards. And I can *scry*."

"What does that mean?"

"To scry is to view the future or the past, sometimes even the present. Most of all, it used to see *truth*. Look into the water, Aidan ap Llanfor."

He bent his head and did as she instructed, staring into the water, looking *through* the water and noticing only some minute scratches in the silver on the bottom of the bowl. Olivia recited something in Spanish, a solemn poem, an incantation. Her voice was so soft that he couldn't catch all of the words, so simply did his best to focus on the task he'd been given: he looked into the water. He saw nothing there but found himself wondering at the broad span of silver that held the water: it was so light and thin. It had to be cast, something that wasn't done until after his time. He could not imagine shaping such a large sheet on his anvil. No matter how careful he was, surely it would tear beneath the hammer long before it became so—

"¡*Mira el agua!*" Look in the water!

He looked but the bowl was gone. Instead, he was staring into the water barrel from his forge. The water was steaming and his long-handled tongs were sticking out of it. He didn't think; he didn't need to think. He quickly grasped the tongs, and as he did so, an image appeared in the water.

A man in black leathers on a dark horse rode before a storm. His hair was wild to the wind and he held a whip of lightning that sizzled and cracked. A horde followed him, the Wild Hunt in all its power. But the rider wasn't Lurien. This man was fair and bore features very like his own . . .

Aidan shoved himself away from the barrel.

"Well done," said Olivia, and he was suddenly back in the room with her. His hand was empty, and his arm was wet to the elbow, shirt and all. The tongs, the barrel, all were gone, however. Only the bowl of water remained with its scant inch of water still in it. And the older woman who was looking at him approvingly.

"What was it?" he asked. "What did I just do?"

"You drew your future from the water. Oh, not all of it," she assured him. "No one can do that. You saw a part of your future, a symbol of something that will create balance for you."

"Did you see it too? What did it mean?"

She shook her head. "I did not see what you did. It's the feel of the magic that allows me to judge that this reading belonged to the future. I don't know what it means for you. But you definitely have magic in you, to be able to draw it to you so strongly."

Aidan felt different—like himself, but somehow *more*. A strange feeling, not necessarily comfortable, rather like a bucket overfilled. "I did not know I had any magic of my own until I met Brooke. At first I thought it was only the remains from my time in the faery realm, but it seems that is not the case." He forced himself to smile. What had appeared to him in the water was not Olivia's fault—she'd only been trying to help. "I wonder if Gofannon had something to do with it. He is the god of both metal and magic, and I was pledged to him at an early age."

"Perhaps so. I just hope this has given you another tool to aid you in your struggle with the faery princess, and perhaps as you wrestle with yourself as well."

Aidan thanked her and left. Olivia couldn't know that what he had just seen only troubled him further and had given him many more questions than he had before. He well remembered his conversation with Lurien outside the home of Maeve Lowri Jones, when the Lord of the Wild Hunt had proposed that Aidan take his place for a time. How could such a thing have anything to do with restoring balance?

George was on top of the effin' world. He had three uninterrupted days in Seattle with his new woman to look forward to. More important, three *nights*. Maybe even four if he could talk Felicia into it.

The drive to Morgan's place in Spokane Valley was a nice bonus, though. He'd get to see his old schoolmate and her new man for an hour, show off Felicia to one and all, and then drive off to the big city for some serious fun. In, out, and *gone*.

But what was even better, he didn't need to feel guilty that Brooke was alone. Yeah, yeah, yeah, it wasn't usual for men and women to truly be *just pals*, but she was his best friend in the entire world, and it bothered him that she'd had no one in her life for a while now. She was always so caring and kind to people, and she deserved the best, she really did. Mind you, a thousand-year-old death-dog-turned-human wasn't quite the companion he'd have chosen for her, but Aidan was clearly one of those straight-arrow types, all about honor and vows and hard work. And it sure didn't hurt that he was good looking, artistically speaking. George could picture the dude as a barbarian hero in one of his comic books, and he had already considered getting him to pose for some sketches. After all, even Devina of Hades could use a man in her life occasionally.

Sure, Brooke had had previous boyfriends. All three of them (he didn't count the one she'd gone to the senior prom with, since they'd broken up a week later). Each had lasted a couple of years—the last one, almost four. But then, she was more the serious relationship type, not like him at all. George was perfectly happy with the casual dating scene and even *he* didn't know how many girls he'd gone out with since high school. Keeping it light had always worked for him, so why change? He worked intensely on his art, he worked hard in the ring, and he made a good living from both. The rest was all fun.

But his mother had been on his case lately about settling down. When he'd finally shown his face at home this morning, she surprised him by not taking him to task about being out all night. Instead, she suggested he bring Felicia by the house to meet her, maybe invite her over to dinner. What was up with that? He laughed aloud as he polished the headlights on Carmelita. *Mom, you should know better by now. I only love you and my truck.*

But who knew? Perhaps he'd have some feelings for Felicia by the end of the weekend. Because unlike any of his other girlfriends, when he was with her, he didn't think of much else. Not even his next art project or his upcoming match in the octagon. There was Felicia, and pretty much *only* Felicia. Wasn't that what love was supposed to be like? George wasn't sure it was possible to feel the sting of Cupid's effin' arrow in a single day, but he was dead certain he'd never had a relationship quite like this one.

And he'd never, ever, had sex like this in his life. *Dios,* he'd never *imagined* sex like this, and he thought his imagination was pretty damn good. He hadn't slept a minute all night. The woman was a total *goddess* in more than just looks.

He sighed as he felt the tingle in his groin anew. *Damn.* Looking for distraction as well as what he liked to call *vehicular perfection*, George knelt on the pavement and scrubbed dirt off the rim of a tire. It wouldn't last, of course—his dear Carmelita was going to get even dirtier driving on a country road to Morgan's place, but it would be worth it. Not just for him, but hopefully for his best friend.

George had proposed introducing Aidan to Morgan's husband, Rhys. And Brooke had heartily agreed. Since both men were Welsh, it was a no-brainer that they'd have plenty in common—even if Aidan was accustomed to a much older Wales. And Rhys had a forge set up and Aidan was a blacksmith, so hey, perfect fit, right? Brooke's goal was to help Aidan, but what George really wanted was to help Brooke. Hopefully a little time alone together during the drive up and back (not to mention being exposed to all those super sweet *love vibes* that a newly married couple like Rhys and Morgan would naturally exude) would strengthen what had already developed between Brooke and Aidan.

Because even though he'd been majorly preoccupied with Felicia, George couldn't forget seeing Brooke and Aidan lip-locked in the middle of what looked like effin' Armageddon. The scene seemed to be permanently inked onto his brain, and he found himself sketching it again and again with various couples from his comic books—and *Dios* help him if Brooke ever recognized the image in a future *Devina of Hades*. The image wasn't compelling or unforgettable because Aidan was pretty much butt naked and Brooke nearly so. It was something about that totally amazing kiss . . . Like some wild affirmation, maybe even a homecoming, *at-last-I've-found-you* kind of thing. Hell, it was like the goddamn *movies*. Which made some sense from Aidan's point of view, since he had thought Brooke was his long-lost woman at the time. But Brooke had poured herself into that kiss too. She didn't know Aidan—nobody knew the guy at that point—but she sure as hell had recognized *something*.

Meanwhile, it had been pretty cool to have Brooke and Aidan staying at his mom's house. She was obviously enjoying their company. Maybe it reminded her of when all of her kids were at home. And it certainly took the pressure off *him*—he worried about her being alone, and that's why he volunteered to live there, and yet he wasn't a stay-at-home kind of guy.

All that crap about fairies had been a surprise though. George had come home one night to find a thick layer of salt and marigold petals on his bedroom windowsill. At first he'd wondered if his mother had discovered the damned house was haunted after all. He'd warned her about that when he begged her not to buy the big old thing (although his main concern had actually been the heating bills, not ghosts). But nope, his mom had cited *fairy problems* of all things, and Brooke and Aidan had moved in the same day. The women had busied themselves with spells and charms to protect the house ever since. Aidan, thankfully, had spent his time doing something much more useful—taming that jungle of a yard. George had been afraid that daunting chore would fall to him.

Fairy problems, *Dios*. He shook his head. *Tough to imagine a cute little fairy being dangerous.*

George sat back on his heels to study the tire rim for any more offending grunge, and a thrill zinged through him like electricity as he heard the sultry stride of Felicia's high heels on the pavement. He remained where he was, perfectly still until her long legs brushed his back and her fingertips played with his cropped mohawk.

"Hey, lover, are you ready to rumble?" She laughed as she said it. It was a unique sound, sort of like a cascade of little bells or something, and he'd heard it often in the middle of last night's passion. In an instant he was on his feet, clutching her amazing ass as he kissed her hard.

"You know it," he murmured.

"Then how about a little romp before we go?"

Hell yeah. It was going to be the best damn weekend of his life.

TWENTY

⌒⫘⌒

Celynnen had not been at Court since the day he'd sent her there without her fine clothes.

While it was possible that she'd experienced a certain amount of humiliation and might avoid the place for a time, Lurien found it difficult to believe that she would stay away this long. It was also exceedingly strange that she had made no attempt to visit some sort of revenge upon him. Perhaps she had, and he was simply unaware of it yet. More likely, the spoiled tywysoges was merely biding her time, waiting for precisely the right moment in order to gain maximum effect. She adored playing games, and plotting revenge for real or imagined slights was one of her favorite pastimes.

No matter. He did not fear her in the least. But the discovery of the Draigddynion scale in her clothing made it imperative that he find her and get some answers to his questions. Yet try as he might, he could not locate her in any of the Nine Realms—at least not by ordinary means. Neither could he draw too much attention to the fact that he was looking for her, in case he alerted whoever had given Celynnen that ill-starred scale.

He already knew she wasn't in her chambers, but her servant, the orange-eyed crymbil, was always there. Lurien watched as the stubby-winged creature in baggy robes labored to scrub the glittering mosaic floor. A mote of dust hadn't fallen in the realm in years (and if it had, a simple word of magic would eliminate it instantly), but Celynnen enjoyed giving impossible commands. It allowed her the opportunity to reward and punish—and from the look of the welts on its wings, the unfortunate crymbil—a female, as males could not fly—had been punished a great deal recently.

Lurien tried to soften his voice. "What is your name?" he asked gently, wincing as the creature jolted and cowered.

"N-Nyx."

"Where is your mistress, Nyx?"

"I cannot say. I-I am very sorry."

A crymbil couldn't lie, but she was unlikely to offer the truth if she'd been instructed otherwise. Lurien considered carefully. "Nyx, I see plainly that you are not being treated well here. The queen would not want this for you. In her name, I have the authority to free you if you wish. Tell me where your mistress is."

Her orange eyes widened, and for a moment, hope made her face almost beautiful. Then the light faded and she bowed low to the floor, shaking like a poplar leaf in a storm. "I cannot tell you. I cannot say."

"Why? What will Celynnen do to you?"

"My children . . ."

Lurien was sickened. The Tylwyth Teg had once been honorable and just in their dealings with both fae and mortal. *Are we nothing but bullies now?*

"Give me your hand, Nyx." He held out his to receive it. Trembling, she finally reached up and placed her long-fingered hand in his palm. It was clear she was expecting to be punished, and she was baffled as he carefully helped her to her feet. Still clasping her hand, he murmured an incantation. Immediately, a thin silver band became visible around the crymbil's slender neck, and he shook his head. Like too many in the Court, Celynnen liked to use collars and slave rings and anything else that reminded the wearer that they were not only beneath her but *owned* by her. He touched the ring with his finger and it shattered like glass, its shards tumbling to the floor. Automatically the crymbil made a move as if to catch them, but Lurien's grip on her hand kept her from doing so.

"You are not in the service of Celynnen anymore," he said. "I know you cannot tell me where she is, Nyx, and I will not pressure you further. Go get your children and return to your lands." He released her then. As an afterthought, he handed her a silver token. "This is my seal. Show it to anyone who questions what you are doing; use it to acquire anything you need for your journey. It should give you safe passage—I will know at once if anyone troubles you in any way. I will deal with Celynnen myself."

Nyx put both of her hands over her face and wept copiously as she stammered her thanks.

"Thank me by going as quickly as you can," Lurien whispered. He watched as she ran from the room, then left it himself at a more thoughtful pace.

The poor crymbil hadn't told him where the princess was, and yet she'd given him the answer. The tywysoges liked to torment her servants? Then she'd be certain to be searching for the one that got away, the one she'd never had the chance to enjoy in the way she had planned.

Lurien didn't need to look for Celynnen at all. He needed to find Aidan ap Llanfor.

Dios, he was over an hour late. Brooke would have words to say to him about that—although George could count on her to save them until they were alone.

He pulled up to the curb in front of the Handcastings shop and looked over at Felicia. She beamed at him, then made a little kissy moue in his direction. He couldn't get around his truck fast enough to open the door for her, and she stepped out like a queen alighting from a carriage. Holding hands, they crossed the treed boulevard and sidewalk . . .

Until Felicia yanked her hand away and took a couple of fast steps backward.

"What is it? What's wrong?"

"There's something here . . . I'm . . . well, I think I must be allergic to something, George. Can't you smell it?"

George sniffed the air and caught nothing but the usual pleasant scent that emanated from Handcastings. "I guess maybe there's some dried flowers and herbs in here. Is it bothering you?"

"The doctor says it's a mild allergy. I'm a little afraid it might trigger a headache if I go in there; you know how those things can be. I never go inside flower shops either. Why don't I just wait in the truck while you get your friends?"

"Sure thing, if you think that would be better. I want you to feel good for our trip." Kissing her long and deep, he whispered, "So I can make you feel even better later." He waggled his brows, which won him a little peal of that delightful chiming laugh, and then he helped her back in the truck. "I'll just be a minute."

George jogged to the shop and pushed open the old oak-framed door. He immediately scratched his upper arm on something, just where the sleeve of his T-shirt ended. *A goddamn nail,* of all things, protruded slightly from the doorframe. As he tried to remember when his last tetanus shot had been, he was glad that he hadn't tried to talk Felicia into coming inside. What if she'd hurt herself? "Hey, Brooke!" he yelled out. "You got a hammer or something? You got something here that needs fixing."

"We're in the back room, G," she called.

He followed her voice to the former kitchen that she'd turned into an office. Aidan was holding open a small leather bag as Brooke spooned in herbs from an assortment of jars. Last, she dropped several tiny stones into the bag and softly recited a spell, one he'd heard his mom use over him when he was little and going away to summer camp. *A spell of protection.* He waited respectfully until she was finished before speaking.

"Hey guys, I'm really sorry I'm so late," he said. "I just got behind, that's all. I should have set our meet-up time for later."

"No problem, G. It worked out well in fact. It gave us more time to put some final touches on our magical defenses," said Brooke. "Last night I thought of a few more precautions we could take." She drew the little bag shut, then threaded it onto a long leather thong.

"Is that what the sachet's for?"

"It's not a sachet. It's a medicine bag. And I have a couple more for you and Felicia if you want them. I already charmed my SUV—I can spell Carmelita too if you like."

George held up both hands in front of him. "No juju around Carmelita, thanks. She has her own special magic. And I don't want to bring up charms and spells and all that shit in front of Felicia. I grew up with it, but what if she thinks it's weird? Or downright crazy? No way am I risking my weekend in Seattle, *hermanita.*"

Aidan stooped a little so Brooke could hang the bag around his neck. He picked it up and examined it, then tucked it beneath his shirt out of sight. He thanked her, and she turned her full attention to George. "Are you sure, G? I know you're probably not on the fae's radar anyway, but better safe than sorry."

For about three seconds, he considered it—he really did. While he didn't practice magic himself, between his mother and grandmother he'd seen plenty of woo-woo stuff his whole life and knew it to be real. But the thought of offering the little leather pouch to the goddess in his truck just seemed wrong. Felicia should have diamonds laid at her feet, not rocks in a bag. "Naw, we're good, thanks."

"Well, then, Aidan and I are ready to go when you are," said Brooke. She shouldered a bright yellow tote bag the size of Rhode Island. "Where *is* your new girlfriend?"

"She wanted to wait in the truck. I thought the four of us could have breakfast together, but I've kind of blown it now that I've made us all late. I told Morgan we'd be there by noon, so she's expecting us for lunch."

"That'll work. We can save the visiting till we get there. Let me at least say hi to Felicia, though, since we're taking separate vehicles."

George led the way outside and briefly introduced Aidan and Brooke. Though she didn't offer her hand, Felicia beamed at them, and even from the interior of the black-on-black truck, she seemed to glow with all the vitality of a beach volleyball champion. He was so effin' proud to be seen with her that he almost puffed out his chest. Maybe he did, just a little.

"I've heard so much about you," she said to his friends with enthusiasm. "George talks about you all the time." Felicia assured them both that she was looking forward to getting to know them.

That was pretty far from a sexual comment, but *damn*, he found himself looking forward to getting to know some parts of *her* again. They'd only just engaged in some pretty wild sex, yet his jeans instantly got tight all over again. *I'll never even last till we get to Morgan's at this rate.*

Everyone finished making nice, and then his friends headed off to Brooke's little white SUV that was parked down the street. Strangely, George was glad they were gone. It felt like an honest-to-god *relief* to be alone with his gorgeous goddess again. He couldn't recall *any* girl ever making him feel like that before—his friends had always come first.

"I told you you'd like them," he said to Felicia. "Brooke's been my best friend since grade school. Kind of like another sister, you know? Aidan's only been on the scene recently, but he seems like a stand-up kind of guy."

"They make such a cute couple," she said sweetly. "I hope we see more of them."

"As soon as we get to Morgan's place, we can all hang out for a while."

For a fragment of a second he thought he saw a green flash in her eyes, like a feral cat's eyes in the dark when you shone a flashlight on it. Just as quickly, though, it was gone.

Weird, George thought, but he chalked it up to the sun reflecting off the hood of the truck. It was promising to be a bright and clear day weather-wise.

A great start to a memorable weekend.

Celynnen rearranged herself on the passenger seat. Riding in the truck was fascinating, although being this close to so much iron was disconcerting. The iron was in its purer form of steel, making it particularly toxic to fae beings, and though she touched nothing made from metal, her skin tingled from the proximity of it. Any sensation, even unpleasant, possessed great novelty. Nevertheless, she would like a rest from its intensity for a short time.

She would also like more sex from her newest human toy before she tired of him. George Santiago-Callahan not only had much stamina but also was quite a bit more fun than many of her previous conquests. He didn't know what she was, of course, but he was powerfully attracted to the appearance she'd assumed; other than that glamor, she didn't have to use magic to draw him to her. That was a highly enjoyable part of the game, the luring and the enticement, the utter and complete deception. Later would come the best part of all—

The reveal.

Celynnen had just received a stunning revelation of her own. Aidan ap Llanfor was no longer a dog. Small wonder she'd had little success in searching for him. Of course, it had to be the fault of the silver collar; the chain-link torc had inexplicably come loose from his neck, affecting his return to mortal form. Fortunately, George Santiago-Callahan had succumbed to the siren call of the beautiful fae artifact—and had unwittingly led her directly to her true quarry.

Her quarry was blissfully unaware of who she was of course. Aidan ap Llanfor had not been able to see past or sense her disguise. Of course, neither he nor the woman he was with had looked upon the mask of extraordinary human perfection she displayed so radiantly to George. No, no, she'd shown them a far more ordinary face and form, one less likely to draw suspicion.

She was very good at playing games.

Aidan ap Llanfor had paid little attention to Felicia at all, just enough to greet her politely as he stood back on the sidewalk. His companion, Brooke Halloran, was friendly enough, but she was a puzzle. Celynnen had sensed at once that she possessed a deep wellspring of magic within her, highly unusual for a human. While it was almost impossible that she'd been the cause of the silver collar's failure, the little mortal was most definitely responsible for the protective warding that now surrounded the building. That it was able to repel even a member of the royal family was astonishing—and quite annoying.

But the woman wasn't inside her bespelled building now, and neither was Aidan ap Llanfor. Celynnen could feel that they were both wearing charms, of a type she hadn't encountered before, but she doubted the protective magic was potent enough to keep her from doing as she pleased. The most delightful part, however, was trying to choose what it was that pleased her most. How should she advance the game? Much could depend on what the woman meant to Aidan ap Llanfor. It was unlikely the witch was more than a simple acquaintance to him. He who had spurned the advances of a flawless tywysoges, a princess of the Fair Ones, surely could not prefer the company of a mere mortal. Although he had placed an unexpected amount of value on a lost love—

Ah.

That was why Brooke Halloran looked so familiar. She bore more than a passing resemblance to the much-mourned Annwyl. Perhaps there was more between her and the blacksmith than first appeared. Celynnen smiled with the sudden abundance of delicious possibilities. The game had just become much more interesting. Was there a way in which Aidan ap Llanfor might finally surrender to her? Of course she could threaten his little witch to win his cooperation, but where was the fun in that? He'd give in, no doubt, but she still wouldn't have what she really wanted: Aidan ap Llanfor as a *willing lover*. She needed a strategy that would put his strong arms around her and his pulsing cock inside her *because he found her irresistibly beautiful*, because he worshipped her perfection as George Santiago-Callahan did. As if he'd sensed she was thinking about him, her newest pet looked over at her and grinned. He was very handsome for a human. For now, perhaps she would simply go along with him to the city of Seattle that he spoke so glowingly of. Why shouldn't she have just a little more fun and enjoy what other novelties he could show her? There would be time enough later to pursue her agenda with the blacksmith. Right now, her agenda called for more sex with George Santiago-Callahan.

Immediately.

It wasn't difficult to persuade George to elude his friends, who were following on the highway somewhere behind them, and drive onto a side road. As she left it to him to search out a suitable stand of trees in which to sequester themselves, she amused herself with thoughts of all the things she might do with Aidan ap Llanfor when she finally got him into her bed.

TWENTY-ONE

～⋙～

Morgan's veterinary practice was in Spokane Valley, but she owned a farm several miles north of the city. It was a long daily commute to her clinic and back, but every time Brooke saw the countryside surrounding her friend's home, she understood why Morgan lived there. She loved the dry grassy hills dotted with clusters of long-needled pines. Denser stands of trees surrounded farmyards and homes or gathered along riverbanks. There were vast orchards too, where apple trees appeared to march in tidy rows up and down the rises.

Aidan had been silent through most of the drive, appearing to be deep in thought. She knew he was tired. Perhaps he would sleep better at the farm? Brooke tried again at conversation. "I guess this landscape is a lot different from Wales."

He nodded. "The land here is wide and open; the fields very large. Cymru is greener, though."

"Kumree?"

"Very close. *Cymru*," he corrected. "The name of Wales to the Welsh in these times."

"Do you miss it?"

"You ask hard questions, *cariad*." He favored her with the first smile she'd seen in a couple of hours. "I've seen the country change and grow over ten centuries. What I remember from when I lived as a man there, that's what I miss. Family and friends and neighbors—I miss them most, much more than the place. I do miss my forge. I like to be working with metal, making things with my hands. But the country itself—Wales, now? It's not mine anymore, not the place and not the people."

A man outside of time. Where had she heard that saying before? Perhaps a movie or something . . .

A series of crab-apple trees lined a mile of rail fence along the gravel road they were traveling, and Brooke knew they'd reached their destination. She turned her SUV into the long winding laneway of the Celtic Renaissance Training Center. Flanked by freshly planted catalpa trees, the large green sign on Morgan's farm was brand new and cleverly framed in welded iron horseshoes.

Brooke sighed inwardly as she drew up to the house, however. There was no sign of George and Felicia—how had she managed to overtake the speedy Carmelita? Unless they stopped for a break . . . She realized with exasperation what the couple had probably stopped to do. *For pity's sake, G. Couldn't you wait till you had a room?* As if the Universe were chiding her, she suddenly recalled her vision of hot, wet sex in the rain with Aidan. It played in her head in vivid detail, and she could feel twin spots of heat glow high on her cheekbones. Heat was glowing between her legs too . . .

Thankfully, Morgan and Rhys came out to greet them, followed by their enormous mastiff, Fred, and she was distracted from her X-rated thoughts for the moment. Brooke ran to hug them all, and she noted that while Rhys and Aidan were close to the same height, Aidan was built differently, more powerfully, across the shoulders and chest. Probably from his years of hammering metal as a smith. Whatever the reason, she had to take a moment just to admire his masculine form—and the heat returned full force.

Meanwhile, the tall and handsome object of her oversexed mind greeted her friends pleasantly enough, paying particular attention to rubbing the ears of the big brindle dog. Then something curious happened—the moment Aidan clasped hands with Rhys, Brooke's ears popped as if the air pressure had abruptly changed. There was, well, some kind of *hiccup* in reality, as if a few seconds of time had abruptly speeded up, then stopped. The two big men stared at each other in disbelief, then both began talking at once. Actually *talking* was too mild a term. It was more like a verbal avalanche of what Brooke could only assume was high-speed Welsh. Morgan stood close beside her, and she saw that her friend was as baffled as she was. "What is it? What's wrong?"

Morgan shook her head. "He's been teaching me the language, but they're going too fast. I'm only picking up a few odd words here and there."

Eventually, Rhys stepped back and put his big arm around his wife and a reassuring hand on Brooke's shoulder. "Not a thing is wrong, only strange beyond wondering. He's a grim—or was one."

Brooke goggled. "How the hell did you know that?"

"Because I've been one myself."

Morgan served lunch on the porch as Rhys told his story and how the spell that bound him had eventually been broken. Brooke was utterly astounded by it all. Her friend, Morgan, had never said a single word about Rhys's true origins—but then, how could she?

Of greater concern was that the Fair Ones, as Rhys called them, had been increasingly active on this side of the waters, despite their kingdom being located under the Black Mountains of Wales. How long had this been going on, Brooke wondered.

To hold the Gift is to protect the balance in all things and to restore harmony . . . How much harmony had been disrupted already by faeries meddling in the affairs of human beings? The problem was so much bigger than Aidan alone. She needed to learn all that she could and discuss the situation with her mentor and friend, Olivia.

Neither Morgan nor Rhys seemed offended when George and Felicia were still *missing in action* at the end of the meal. "It's no big surprise. Really, I've never seen that guy with the same girl twice," said Morgan. "In fact, at our wedding, he didn't even leave with the same girl he came with! It's just *typical George* to be crazy in infatuation with a new woman. By next week, he'll have moved on to somebody new."

"I thought he'd be over that by now. You know, mature or something," said Brooke.

"Yeah, me too." Morgan shook her head. "Growing up takes longer for some than others, I guess, but George is a really great guy and I love him to bits. Late bloomer maybe?"

Rhys and Aidan had headed off to the newly built forge the moment lunch was finished. Brooke wondered what kind of conversation they were having. Both were from Wales but from completely different time periods. Aidan had been born a thousand years ago. And Rhys? Two thousand. One a medieval smith, and the other a Celtic warrior. They might as well be from different countries after all. All they truly had in common was imprisonment at the hands of the fae.

At least they seem to be getting along . . .

With the big brindle mastiff at her heels, Morgan showed Brooke some of the horses they'd acquired since the last time she'd visited. A big dapple-gray mare hung her enormous head over the corral's fence to greet them. "Of course, you remember Lucy, here. She's our original. Rhys adores her, and she's his personal mount in any and all events. Fred and Lucy have become close friends too—they play together."

"The dog and the horse?" As if in answer, Fred touched noses with the big mare, his tail wagging. She snorted and blew grass all over him, which made Morgan laugh.

"Eeewww!" said Brooke. "Your brindle dog is green now!"

Morgan chuckled. "As a vet I can testify that there's always a lot of *eeewww* around animals, but they're worth it. He'll shake it off or jump in one of the ponds. Anyway, horses like company and they tend to pick their friends. Dogs too. These two hit it off as soon as they met. Kind of like love at first sight."

Brooke thought of Aidan. Had that happened to her? Did that explain the depth of feelings she had for him when she'd barely even met him? Not realizing her friend wasn't paying attention, Morgan continued talking. Brooke tuned back in in time to hear—

"And those black ones over in the far pasture are purebred Friesians, and we have some Andalusians and Percherons as well."

"You're raising all these big horses for Renaissance fairs?"

"And training them too. That's the most important part. Medieval sporting events have become very popular, and yes, people buy trained horses to use in tournaments."

"So, are you talking about jousting? Knights in armor and all that?"

"Absolutely. It's a real spectacle, and it requires a skilled horse as well as a skilled rider. The weapons aspect has really taken off as well. Rhys is a gifted warrior—hell, he grew up with a sword in his hand—so now he teaches classes here. Broadsword, archery—you name it. That's one of the reasons we have the forge. Two of our friends work in metal. They're wonderful craftsmen and they're re-creating swords from various time periods—or at least that's their goal. Although their work is beautiful, they haven't produced a blade that Rhys approves of yet. I have to keep reminding him that it's pretty much a lost art."

Brooke couldn't help but wonder if making weaponry was one of Aidan's skills. If so, his work could be in demand, and he could find a niche for himself in the modern world, without having to leave the old one completely behind. That was exactly what Rhys appeared to have done. As they walked, Morgan pointed out the innumerable horseshoes and iron nails that decorated everything from the rooflines of each building to the top of every fence post that surrounded the two-hundred-acre farm. "Some of these were mounted by Rhys for protection against the fae before the Wild Hunt came. Since then, we put up more all the time. If you look closely, there are little copper wires and bells and all sorts of strange little gizmos attached to a lot of them. My favorite is a horseshoe out by the machine shed, which has a silver fork and spoon dangling from it. It looks like some strange art form, but actually, it's a kind of magic. All of the iron you see has had protective charms added to it by our friend, Ranyon. He's an *ellyl* from the faery realm, and kind of a refugee."

"An ellyl? What's that? I didn't even know that faeries were real until Aidan showed up."

"The term *faery* takes in a lot of different creatures. Ranyon is a little guy between two and three feet tall, all covered in brown leaves. He's got the brightest blue eyes, and a great sense of humor. The Tylwyth Teg destroyed his clan and enslaved him—that is, until Rhys got hold of him."

The strange name was familiar. Aidan had said that Celynnen was of Tylwyth Teg. "Is this Ranyon here on the farm?"

Morgan shook her head. "I really wish you could meet him but he lives with our friend, Leo, and the two of them are in Toronto right now at a Blue Jays game."

"A *faery* wanted to go to a ball game?"

"Not just any baseball game. Ranyon's crazy for the Jays. And he loves Leo too—they've been good for each other." Morgan ran her finger around an exceptionally large horseshoe wrapped in copper wire and tiny bells. "Except for Ranyon, Queen Gwenhidw declared our farm off limits to the fae, but even though she's my friend and I trust her, Rhys and I don't take chances. There are too many factions working against her, and they don't care what she decrees."

"Hold it right there. The queen herself is your *friend*?"

"I'm still not used to it myself," laughed Morgan. "But yes, it's true. She was best friends with some ancestor of mine, I guess, and we happened to hit it off when I visited Wales. Plus Nainie—my grandma—gave me some kind of mojo, to be able to see and know a few things, so the fae can't hide from me very easily. It made a real difference the night of the battle here." She laughed again and put her hands on her hips. "But it's nothing compared to what *you* can do, lady! I thought you ran some sort of cute little New Age shop, and now I find out that you're a powerful practicing witch! I mean, *holy crap*, that is *so* awesome!"

"Do you remember when we had to write that paragraph for grad about what we thought our futures would bring?" asked Brooke.

Morgan snorted. "I planned to be a veterinarian, and that certainly worked out fine. But the rest of my life? Or Rhys? Never saw it coming. You too, huh? How serious are you and Aidan?"

Brooke's smile faded. "I guess loved him the first time I saw him. I'm crazy about him. But Aidan's a good man, and an honorable one—"

"He's not married is he?"

"Oh, *hell* no, not married. It's not that. A thousand years ago, a fae princess killed his fiancée. He's made a solemn vow to avenge her before he moves on with his life. With our life together." She swallowed hard. "I'm just hoping he lives through it so we *have* a life together."

Morgan put an arm around her shoulders. "Believe me, I know the type. My husband would cut off his own arm before he'd break a promise or a vow. It's admirable and scary at the same time. But it's how things were done in the past." She paused for a long moment. "Does this particular faery know where Aidan is? Or you?"

Brooke nodded. "As a matter of fact, yes. She found Aidan at my shop in the middle of the night a little over a week and a half ago. I guess she sent him a creepy message. I was in bed with him at the time, so if she was scrying, then I assume she saw me too. We moved out of the building immediately though, and we set up all kinds of magical protections in the house we're staying in, and—"

Morgan looked around and motioned Brooke to a bench. "Look," she said. "I don't want to scare you, but I have to scare you—understand? If a faery has your number, they'll never stop hunting you. It won't matter where you go on this planet, they'll find you sooner or later. You're going to have to be on your guard constantly." She smiled weakly. "It's become a lifestyle for us."

"But it's wrong for them to interfere in mortal lives."

"They don't care about that. They want what they want, Brooke. And they live practically forever, so they've got all the time in the world to spend on getting it."

They want what they want. George had said some people were just like that, and she'd certainly had more than a few potential customers that fit the mold. "Then what do we do? What *can* we do? I don't want to live my life in fear."

"Maybe Aidan's doing it. Maybe killing this Celynnen is more than a matter of revenge for him. He might be doing the only thing that will protect you and everyone you love."

"I have a hard time with that. It seems wrong to do harm."

"Yeah, I hear you," Morgan sighed. "I'm a veterinarian, and that makes me a healer first. Speaking of which, maybe you could give me some advice on my four-legged patients. Right now I have a pudgy spoiled lizard named Petrie that has a skin infection, and I just can't seem to find anything that will treat it effectively." They resumed their walk as they discussed herbs and charms that Morgan might try. Brooke offered to go to the clinic the next day and see what she could do for the little lizard with her magic. As they rounded the corner of the barn, however, a loud argument reached their ears. It was coming from the direction of the forge.

Oh crap, thought Brooke, hurrying after Morgan to see what was going on. *And I thought things were going well.*

～

"You're a damned *twpsyn*," Rhys shouted. "Only a fool would think you could just walk into the realm and make one of *them* do as you please. By all the gods, you'll be a grim again in a heartbeat, if they don't feed you to a hungry bwgan a piece at a time just for the fun of it."

"They fear iron. It is their weakness."

"They don't fear it from a distance, and you'll never get close enough to them to use it."

"'Tis Celynnen I'm after. And, aye, she'll let me near enough all right. She wants me to bed her. It's what she's wanted from the damnable beginning." And because of it, he would get very, very close if he appeared willing to finally give her what she wanted.

"And how will you secrete an iron weapon on you then? Up your arse?"

Aidan shook his head. "'Twill not be the kind of weapon she expects. I'll have a dagger for show, and she'll take it from me, thinking she's disarmed me. But I have another idea, and I believe it will work." The slim iron blades would be small, but just one would be more than sufficient if he used it well. A wound made with iron would not close, not without considerable magic from a healer. If he was alone with Celynnen, he would have to ensure that he aimed for something vital. *Like her flawless white throat . . .*

Rhys took a deep breath as though calming himself. "I understand revenge more than most. I have hungered for it more than most," he said. His voice had lowered, yet it felt far more intense than when he had been shouting. "The Romans made war upon my people, burned my village, killed my family. And when they were done with that, they made me fight for my life in the ring, over and over again. They were cruel and I hated them. But they were men, human, each of them mortal like me. When the Tylwyth Teg took me, I found I hated them far more than the Romans. Because their hearts were ice. Their cruelty was worse because of their apathy. I was but a toy to them at best, an insect in a jar.

"'Twas Morgan made the difference. Because of her kindness, I escaped the Fair Ones. *And I escaped the craving for revenge as well.* The love I have here with this woman is worth far more than the satisfaction of standing over a thousand dead fae."

"Aye, I'm wanting a life with Brooke too," declared Aidan. "But I'll be true to my vow to avenge Annwyl's murder. I must settle the past before I build the future."

"Then you really are a twpsyn," said Rhys. "Because you have no future if you go after a fae, especially one of the Royal Family. And Brooke will have no future either, because once you're dead, the tywysoges will come after her and everyone connected to her."

"Do you think I don't know that?" growled Aidan. "All you're giving me are more reasons to kill Celynnen. We'll have no peace until she's gone."

"There is no peace to be had in this time. The faery realm is in chaos right now, everyone vying for power and conspiracies springing up everywhere. The queen is honorable enough, and powerful beyond words, but even she can't control all of her subjects. She can't control her own family, or Celynnen would not be keeping so many *pets*."

"I'll not be spending my life in hiding, behind walls of horseshoes and charms, like you are here. You're living in fear, man."

"If we were that fearful, we wouldn't have chosen to stay here, to make our stand here. The entire Wild Hunt has ridden through this very farm, so the Tylwyth Teg know exactly where we are," said Rhys, bristling. "We're living with *an abundance of caution* because some things are worth fearing, and that's reality."

"Some things are worth fighting for, and that's reality too," declared Aidan.

Rhys's voice dropped to a dangerous tone. "Don't speak to me of what's worth fighting for. I've seen far more battle than you have."

"You didn't take on the whole Roman army at once. You picked them off, here and there. You chose your fights and you harried the Romans at every turn. They feared you. You were not called the Bringer of Death for nothing."

Rhys appeared stunned. "How would you know? I didn't tell you all of that."

"Did you think you would not be remembered? In my time, the stories were still being told of you. As a boy I pretended to *be* you, with a wooden sword my *tad* made for me."

"The Romans were not immortal. And neither are we, not now. Taking on even one faery would be suicide—or worse."

"Evil must be opposed," declared Aidan.

"Among humans, yes. But the Fair Ones are a law unto themselves. They do not think of things as we do."

"It matters not what they think," said Aidan, and threw down the hammer he was holding. "You said the fae are making their mischief here on the mortal plane, in this time and place. We cannot allow them to do so unchallenged."

"Perhaps you *should* spend another thousand years as a grim— you didn't learn a damn thing about the fae while you were there the first time." That was as far as he got before Aidan's great fist blindsided him.

⁓

Brooke looked on in horror as the two men grappled and rolled on the ground outside the forge, throwing punches and elbows, and straining to gain the advantage. Morgan was more philosophical.

"They're pretty evenly matched," she said. "I'm in favor of letting them work it out their own way. In fact, let's you and I go put the dishes in the dishwasher and have some coffee and dessert. I have a chocolate cheesecake in the fridge that needs to be tasted to be believed."

Brooke looked back only a couple of times on the way to the house. "You're not worried?" she finally asked.

"When the guys are practicing for the Ren fair events, there's always a lot of excess testosterone in the air. A guy's temper can get pretty hot, especially if he's just gotten knocked on his ass in a joust. So, hey, I don't even pay attention much anymore. If someone's bleeding, I'll take a look at it. Otherwise, it's their problem."

They could hear the sounds of struggle, the curses, and the shouting subside by the time they neared the house. "See? Better already," said Morgan. She glanced over at a paddock and stopped. "Hey!" she suddenly yelled, and jogged over to the gate. "Cygnus, what are you doing in there?"

Brooke looked up just as a big white draft horse raised his

enormous head. Morgan looked tiny next to him, but she scolded him as if he were an errant puppy. She tugged at his halter, and Brooke expected her efforts to be as effective as pulling on an ocean liner's mooring ropes. Incredibly, however, Cygnus allowed himself to be led, following Morgan easily and amiably.

He was even bigger close up. "Holy cow, Morgan, he's . . . he's . . ." She had no words as the great white beast loomed over her, regarding her with intelligent brown eyes that were both calm and full of mischief. His head alone probably weighed as much as she did.

"I named him Cygnus, Latin for *swan*, because of his color," explained Morgan. "He's young, so he's not full grown yet, but he's going to be our herd sire." She patted his wide neck with her free hand. He snorted and stomped the ground with one of his dinner-plate-sized hooves, then bent his head to nose Fred. The mastiff wagged his tail. "And Cygnus sure seems to want the job. He keeps jumping into that paddock and cozying up to a couple of mares we have in there, whether we want him to or not." Just then, a black-on-black pickup entered the farm's laneway.

"Finally," said Brooke. "It's about time George—"

Without warning, a thousand chimes, clangings, and rattles sounded at once, as though a hurricane had just blown through a hardware store. Cygnus flattened his ears, but to his credit, the steady beast stayed where he was, with Morgan clinging to his halter. Despite the tumult, the air was still as death, and the hair on the back of Brooke's neck stood up. From the corners of her eyes, she could see that every strange addition to every mounted horseshoe in the vicinity was behaving as if it were alive. Coils of copper wire waved wildly. Bells shook themselves. Keys and gears and all sorts of metallic paraphernalia moved of their own volition, vibrating, scratching, banging against one another or the horseshoes they were tied to.

A magical alarm system had just been tripped.

Fred growled low in his throat and his hackles were raised all along his brindled back. Yet he wasn't reacting to the noise. Brooke looked to Morgan for explanation, surprised to see how much her friend had paled. "What is it? Tell me what's wrong."

"One of the Fair Ones just crossed the property line."

As the pickup neared the house, the cacophony died away, allowing the sound of pounding feet to be heard. Brooke turned to see the men arrive. Rhys's mouth was a thin-set line, and he had an authentic *sword* in his hand. Held vertically, point down, the blade was hidden as Rhys quickly stood just behind Morgan. In a well-practiced move, Brooke saw him slip her friend a dagger, which she turned neatly in her palm so it was pointed towards her elbow and concealed by her arm. Apparently, they'd been through this drill many times before. Even more surprising, Rhys spoke a word to Cygnus as Morgan released his halter. The creature stood rock steady as if his great feet were glued to the spot.

Aidan placed a solid hand on Brooke's shoulder as he stood close behind her and spoke in her ear. "Rhys says one of the fae is here. The charms are a warning."

"Do you have a sword too?" she asked quietly.

"Aye. And my knife, and a fistful of iron filings and nails. Be ready to get behind me, *cariad.*"

The truck rolled to a stop, and George came bouncing out, grinning. "Hey guys, I made it! I meant to be here a whole lot sooner, but Felicia was tired so we stopped to rest for a bit."

Brooke resisted the impulse to roll her eyes. *Some rest.* "You missed a great lunch," she said instead. She noticed that the monstrous dog by Morgan's side wasn't looking at George at all. His entire attention was on the passenger side of the truck—and his lips had pulled back from his formidable teeth. *No,* she thought. *It can't be. No, no, no, no, no.*

"I want you to meet my girlfriend," continued George, as he

jogged around the front of the truck to open the door for her. He brought the blushing, beaming Felicia around to the front of the truck like a footman presenting a queen, despite the fact that her T-shirt was on inside out and her hair was mussed. "Morgan, Rhys, I want you to meet—"

"Celynnen of the House of Thorn of the Tylwyth Teg," she said, drawing herself up to her full height and dropping her glamor to reveal her true form. Her ethereal beauty burst out like the sun from behind a cloud, and George stood with his mouth open in apparent shock. Brooke was stunned too—she had never imagined the existence of such a glorious being. Celynnen seemed lit from within, her luminous white hair cascading over a gown that was the exact blue of a cold autumn sky, its hem and sleeves dusted with vivid golden leaves that seemed alive. Her iridescent eyes were her most arresting feature, however, so beautiful that it hurt to look at them, yet Brooke could not look away. The faery princess smiled then, a perfect smile, a radiant smile, one that could delight children and break hearts and awaken yearnings from solid rock. But there was no feeling behind it. No warmth passed into those incredible eyes, and that was what finally snapped Brooke out of her fascinated state.

"Oh, and did I mention, *heir apparent to the throne of the Nine Realms*," the fae continued. Without missing a beat, she reached into the back of George's T-shirt and seized a wide silver torc that looked to be made of chain mail. George made no move to pull away; he was still staring at her with wide-eyed disbelief.

"Recognize your collar, Aidan ap Llanfor?" she asked, and blew him a delicate kiss.

In less than the blink of an eye, Aidan grabbed Brooke and moved them both to one side in the same motion, as if the kiss had been a live round of ammunition. Perhaps it was. Brooke felt a tingle of magic pass by them.

"Now, now, it's no fun for me if you move," chided the faery. "You were never very good at games, Aidan. In fact, come to think of it, you weren't very much fun at all. You could take a lesson from my darling George Santiago-Callahan. Isn't that a grand name for an ordinary mortal? It rolls off the tongue just like honey." Still retaining her grip on him, she looked at George and stroked his face with her free hand as if bestowing a loving caress. He didn't resist in the least. "You and I have had a lovely time together, now, haven't we?" He was barely able to nod. Apparently satisfied, she returned her attention to the little group, and Morgan's dog began to bark at her.

Immediately, Brooke thought of the Moon, one of the tarot cards that she and Aidan had both drawn. The dogs on the card barked at the moon as if it were something evil to be kept at bay. The card had frightened Olivia, and Brooke felt fear now as she saw Olivia's words embodied in the faery princess. *Powerful magic is involved here, dangerous magic, deception, and hidden enemies.*

All of them had their weapons out now, Brooke noticed, except for her. She had no dagger or sword, not even so much as an iron nail to throw. All she had was her magic—and what spell could she use that would be effective in such a situation? Her focus had always been on defense, and she hoped the medicine bags that she and Aidan were wearing were of some help, although they seemed pitiful indeed against such a magnificent being who was clearly not from the mortal plane. "Reach inside yourself for courage," Olivia had said.

Courage Brooke had, but nothing else that she could see. Despite all her studies, her practices, her strict observation of the Code, and her respect shown to the deities who ruled the elements, Brooke Halloran felt completely helpless. She might be a powerful witch on her own turf, but *here* she was clearly out of her league. She had no idea how to protect George.

Or anyone else.

TWENTY-TWO

"You left before the game was over, Aidan," chided Celynnen. "You left before I was finished with you. That was rude. So now I'm making up a brand new game."

George was a full-grown man who had won many bouts in the mixed martial arts ring, yet the tall faery lifted him by the back of the neck until his toes barely touched the ground and shook him like a rat being shaken by a terrier. And as if her sudden show of sheer strength wasn't scary enough, her angelic face changed dramatically. Its cold and feral ferocity belonged more to a master predator than a goddess of unearthly beauty.

But she's not a goddess at all, thought Brooke. She's a creature masquerading as one. And she's going to hurt George. *To hold the Gift is to guard the helpless and to remove power from the cruel.* Brooke knew she had to do something. The Ten of Pentacles had been in that tarot reading as well: a great risk was necessary, and it was up to her.

When all else fails, return to the basics. Intent was the key to magic, plus anything that could help her focus that intention. So what *was* her intention? What she really wanted to do was give Celynnen a helluva black eye, but that seemed a little vague. Somehow she had to create enough of a diversion for George to get away—the fact that the powerful faery was quite likely to kill her for her interference notwithstanding. There was no getting around the fact that once in a very rare while, so rarely that it was almost never mentioned, the Death card actually meant what it said.

A black eye . . . In one of his first bouts, when his career had barely begun, G had come out of the ring unconscious with a pair of shiners. He'd laughed about it later, of course, even though the purple swelling around his eyes seemed to take forever to go away. *That guy's punch was like being kicked by a mule.* Out of the periphery of her vision, Brooke studied the big white horse that towered over Rhys and Morgan, and she imagined several of the enormous beasts kicking Celynnen full in the face—and instantly, Brooke knew what her intent was going to be.

"George and I are going to have that delightful *weekend getaway* in Seattle, just as he planned for us," continued Celynnen, beaming her perfect smile and obviously enjoying herself. "Then I'm going to treat *him* to a little trip to the faery realm. He won't be coming back, of course. Unless . . ." She looked squarely at Aidan.

"Seven days, Aidan ap Llanfor. You have one mortal week to surrender yourself to me *as a willing lover*, or George will wear your collar in your place as a grim. That is, after I finish playing with him." Hanging limply in Celynnen's grip like a puppet, G was helpless to resist. His friends were helpless too, unless . . . Tears stung Brooke's eyes as she fought to plan a way to beat back the monster that held her dearest friend.

Without warning, Celynnen flung George forward onto the ground as if he'd been nothing more than a crumpled tissue. He lay unmoving, clutching the silver chain mail with both hands as if the torc had tightened around his throat. His eyes had rolled back in his head so only the whites could be seen. "Of course you know what a grim looks like, don't you, dear Aidan? But for the benefit of your new friends, here's a little preview."

George began to writhe on the ground, gasping and choking as his eyes bulged. His fighter's muscles contorted horribly, and bones began to shift beneath his tanned skin. Brooke was grateful that Aidan had placed his tall, powerful body in front of her. Not only did it shield her from Celynnen's direct view; it prevented Brooke from seeing more of what was happening to G—and right now, she needed every bit of her concentration to be of any help to him. Quickly, Brooke slipped out of her sandals and stood on the ground in bare feet. Reciting a spell in her mind, she summoned every ounce of magic she could muster from within herself, even as she knew it was far from enough. The farm itself should have been a veritable hotspot, a deep reservoir of the earth's power, but the power was largely blocked from countless wardings against faery magics. Nevertheless, she drew what she could through the ground and into her body through the soles of her feet. She held her hands over her ears to block George's moans as he made his slow and painful transformation. Tears fell free as she half closed her eyes, acting as if she couldn't bear the sight—which wasn't far from the truth.

In reality, however, Brooke was looking *everywhere*, making note of every iron horseshoe within her field of view. There were dozens upon dozens of them, all of a size fit for mighty warhorses like Cygnus. But she still needed more power, dammit, or her plan would never work. Where could she possibly find more?

As if he'd heard her, Aidan brandished his sword in front of him to keep the faery's attention even as he slid his free arm behind his back, his hand reaching for hers. "Take it," he breathed. "Take whatever magic I have, even if it means my life. Understand, *cariad? She must be stopped.*"

What he had was considerable. Brooke grasped his big strong hand, and fought to stand still as a torrent of magic simply flowed into her from Aidan's fingers. It blended seamlessly with her own and that of the earth, and suddenly her vision came back to her full force. Not the rain-soaked sexual heat, but something else, the underlying revelation she had missed. Sex had united them, certainly, but it was merely the physical expression of something much bigger. It was the magic that truly merged them, as they were merging now. Synergy flowed freely, blending body and soul into something greater and grander and more potent than she could have imagined. Brooke drew the power as if it were the string of a bow, drew it back to its farthest point . . .

And let it fly.

With a sound like a thunderclap, every iron horseshoe within a hundred yards instantly tore loose from its moorings and slammed into Celynnen. The impact was horrific. Blue blood spattered in every direction as fae flesh tore and bone shattered. The wounded faery sank to her knees, keening in pain and terrible rage, her flawless features ravaged beyond recognition.

Brooke didn't know if the Tylwyth Teg could die, but Aidan was taking no chances. He ran at the downed creature with upraised sword, and Rhys was barely two strides behind him.

Without any warning, both of them were knocked backwards as if they'd struck an invisible wall. A tall man, in sable leathers and long black hair, suddenly appeared beside the fallen Celynnen. His eyes were dark and dangerous, but it was the sheer power that radiated from him that made Brooke's heart sink to her shoeless feet. He was obviously fae, and that probably meant they were all dead. Brooke had spent every last molecule of magic she had, making it impossible for her to even light a candle, never mind deflect whatever this being was about to do to them.

Strangely, the dark fae paid no attention to any of the humans. Instead, he regarded the horribly wounded Celynnen, who was kneeling crookedly with her ruined face in her broken hands and listing to one side. Her keening had given way to strange rasping sounds, as if she were having trouble breathing.

"I seem to have caught you at a bad time, *princess*," he said. His voice was hard and businesslike, as if her ghastly condition mattered not at all. "But this is more important than your latest game."

"There is nothing more important than the game, Lurien," she wheezed, and blue blood ran between her fingers. "And no one has ever played it as well as I do."

"There was a Draigddynion scale found in your dress. How came you by it?"

Incredibly, the princess began to laugh. Hideous and hissing, bereft of the musical lilt it had once had, there was no mirth in her laughter. Slowly, painfully, she removed her hands and gazed up at all of them with a mocking nightmare smile of broken teeth, the torn lips smeared lopsidedly over her unrecognizable face. "You foolish lackey," she jeered at the man who had questioned her. "How came you by the scar on your chest?"

She laughed madly then, clawing at the wounded skin on her face, tearing it away in jagged strips to reveal scaled reptilian features beneath it. Only one eye was still open, but it was no longer the beautiful iridescent eye of a fae princess. It was green like a cat's, with an elliptical pupil. A dragon's eye.

Lurien appeared horrified. "What have you done with Celynnen?" he demanded.

The creature cackled louder then. "I *am* Celynnen, you ridiculous excuse for a hunter," she wheezed. "You knew my mother, Drysi. A full-blooded tywysoges, in direct line for the throne—but Gwenhidw and Arthfael were never going to leave it. Drysi allowed herself to be bedded by the king of the Draigddynion, who promised to put the crown on her head.

"He was far more clever than that, of course. He had her killed, so that I, the true daughter of both realms, would rule the entire kingdom as its rightful queen."

"You were the ninth assassin," he breathed. "Murderer of the king. But you leapt into the chasm . . ."

"So you thought, just as I thought I had killed you. *Surprise.*" She coughed and dark-blue blood coated her chin. "I gained a ledge below just as I had practiced, and reentered the palace as Celynnen, tywysoges and heir apparent to the throne. Fair and beautiful and perfect. Known by all and suspected by none. Your search was pointless."

"So is your quest for the throne." Lurien drew his sword in a flash of obsidian, but he was too late. The creature that had been Celynnen screamed shrilly as smoke suddenly began pouring from every wound, from every orifice. A flash of orange light enveloped her, illuminated her hideous features for a brief second—

And she was gone. The fae used the tip of his black sword to stir a pile of white ash that lingered on the ground, his face unreadable save for a slight glint of moisture at the corner of one eye. "Indeed, Celynnen," he said quietly. "I never played the game as well as you. But then, we were never playing the same game, were we?"

For the first time he looked over at the humans who watched him, and Brooke was holding her breath. He lifted a hand, but instead of destroying them all with a snap of his fingers, the silver collar around George's neck shattered into a thousand pieces. Every one of those pieces, plus the mound of pale white ashes vanished.

The tall dark fae strode forward and knelt to press a hand to George's forehead, as if feeling for a fever. Brooke was frantic. *Don't kill him. Don't kill him, dear goddess—I have no magic left!* But the fae did not appear to harm him. Instead, he passed his hand over the length of G's contorted and mutated body. As he did so, the form relaxed into its proper shape, like it was made of soft clay. George lay unmoving, however. Was he dead? Brooke launched herself towards him—but Aidan caught her and held her fast. "It will be all right, *cariad*," he whispered to her.

As the fae rose and approached them, Aidan surprised Brooke by tossing his sword to one side. "I have no quarrel with you, Lurien, Lord of the Wild Hunt."

"Nor I with you, Aidan ap Llanfor, though you gifted me with a fine scar. Celynnen helped to murder King Arthfael. That truth may never have come to light without human intervention." His black eyes looked down at Brooke, as if considering. "You have much power for a mortal."

"No," she replied solemnly. "I have much responsibility."

Her answer seemed to surprise him. "Well said, good lady. I wish that more of my people understood that. I would not be here if they did." Lurien paused and looked around at each of them in turn. Rhys still had his sword at the ready, but finally he stepped back and drove the point into the ground at his feet. Morgan slipped beneath his shoulder. All four of them waited.

"What I say, I say in the name of her royal highness, Queen Gwenhidw of the Nine Realms," said the fae. "I do not have to tell you that the kingdom is in disarray. Its effects are spilling into your world as we speak."

"People are dying," accused Rhys.

"Mine as well," Lurien replied, and Brooke sensed an undertone of pain behind the sharpness. "There was a time when the fae helped to keep the balance in your world as well as ours."

"Maeve told me that," said Aidan. "Generosity and unselfishness were rewarded, she said. They punished the greedy and the mean spirited."

Morgan shook her head. "I'm sure not seeing it. There's an awful lot of greed and meanness out there. If anything, it's getting worse."

"That is because there is no balance in the faery kingdom, and unless the queen succeeds in bringing peace to the realms, both fae and humans will suffer alike." Lurien seemed to take a deep breath. "She will not be able to do it alone. I am empowered by Queen Gwenhidw to ask for the aid of mortals with integrity and honor. For your help."

Brooke was astonished. "The fae are overwhelmingly powerful. How could we possibly be of use to you?"

"Do not underestimate the influence of the lives you lead. You help to balance the world simply by being who you are," said Lurien. "The queen needs allies on the mortal plane, particularly here. Many of the faery kingdoms of the earth have already established themselves in these younger lands. And when our king lived, he had the foresight to draw out a section of yet unclaimed territory and negotiate with other fae tribes in order to claim it. It's rightly called Tir Hardd."

"Beautiful land," Aidan murmured.

"And the queen wishes to announce it as a new kingdom for her people, a colony if you wish. It is her belief that we have outgrown our traditional home."

"How can that be?" asked Rhys. "The fae realm is so much bigger than what lies above it."

Brooke remembered that strange phenomenon from old fairy tales she'd read as a child. It had been remarked on by poets and storytellers throughout the ages that the faery lands beneath the ground outshone the mortal country overhead in both glory and sheer size.

"The earth magic that binds everything together is finite. There are too many of the Tylwyth Teg drawing on the magic beneath the Black Mountains of Wales, wresting every bit of power from it they can for position and false strength," explained Lurien. "We have need of new horizons. It is the queen's hope that spreading out will help to quell some of the unrest among us. It would have been done a long time ago, had we not been too busy fighting among ourselves."

"Wait a minute," said Brooke. "You're telling me that the fae are going to live *here*? In this country? Right under our feet?"

"They're already here," said Morgan. "Aren't they, Lurien? You said the king negotiated with other fae tribes."

"The ones who already lived here, yes. Vast settlements from many places in Europe have been on this side of the waters for a very long time. As for my people, few have made the journey except for a small group of Tylwyth Teg who invaded the land without the queen's approval. Most of them are fugitives from our justice, but they have not mended their ways. Even now, they are spreading ever-increasing malice and mischief in the human world. By officially announcing Tir Hardd as one of her territories, the queen will have control of it. The Wild Hunt will be empowered to guard it, and our laws will be in force to govern it. More of our people—better ones, I hope—will make their home here."

"So the plan is to take power away from the rogue fae who are already here," said Brooke. "Almost like taming the Wild West by turning it all into states and diluting the criminal element with law-abiding colonists."

Lurien gave her a grim smile. "It may remain the Wild West for quite a while before it's tamed. But yes, something like that."

"You're not here to ask our permission," said Rhys. "Why bother telling us?"

"I do not require permission. The endless realms below are not under mortal rule. But I do need someone to lead the Wild Hunt in this new territory for a short while. Until I can ferret out the conspiracies that threaten the realm, there is no one left to me in my world that I dare trust with the task." He looked pointedly at Rhys and Morgan. "Some of you know what happens when the Hunt is not led by the just and the honorable."

"How long?" Aidan asked suddenly, and Brooke turned to stare at him.

"I will return you to your world in six mortal months from this moment. You have my word upon it. And any protection I can give."

Brooke put a hand on Aidan's face and turned it towards her. "What the hell are you doing?" she whispered fiercely. "Are you honestly thinking of saying yes?"

"I vowed to kill Celynnen, to put an end to her evil, thinking all would be well if she were gone. Rhys made me realize there are many more like her, and they will be happy to cause as much suffering here as possible. For endless years I thought only of revenge, but I see now that I was shortsighted. You told me about the Code you follow, the good you try to do, and it made me think. There are three or four lines from it about guarding and balance, are there not?"

With a lump in her throat, she recited:

To hold the Gift is to guard the helpless and to remove power
   from the cruel.
To hold the Gift is to strengthen the just and to turn greed
   upon itself.
To hold the Gift is to protect the balance in all things and to
   restore harmony.

"That's the very thing. I see you working to make a difference in the world, to improve it for others, and I admire you for it. I didn't know what I could do that might help, but I saw something in Olivia's silver bowl that gave me the answer. I didn't understand it at the time, but I think I do now. It's about helping to restore balance. For all of us." He leaned down and kissed her then, long and deep. "I need to do this, *cariad*. I love you. And I will come back to you."

She shot a look at Lurien. "Unharmed?" she asked.

The fae nodded. "I will do all within my power to keep him safe. On my honor and my life, good lady. The queen has vowed her protection as well." He touched his brow and vanished.

Rhys cleared his throat suddenly. "You're going to need a good horse, Aidan." He led Cygnus over. Aidan clasped the man's hand and took the halter from him. The big white horse bumped him with his nose as if pleased with the arrangement.

Brooke wasn't liking the arrangement much herself, although she was glad for Rhys's gift. She looked up into Aidan's gray eyes. Dear goddess, could she let him go? Yet how could she not, knowing what she did? "Okay, then," she said with difficulty. "Okay. You help to straighten out the faery world, and I'll keep working away at balancing this one. But—"

He kissed her again—and disappeared, along with the great white horse. Startled, she stood there with her suddenly empty arms.

"But I'll miss you."

TWENTY-THREE

~~~

As the coffee maker brewed, Brooke filled the cat dishes with Mighty Bites. Bouncer and Jade paused, sniffing it suspiciously, then tucked in as if they'd been eating it all their lives. Rory seemed positively offended, sitting back on his haunches and swatting the air over his dish as if the smell offended him. Then looked at her as if to say, "Nice joke. Now where's the real chow?"

"I'm sorry, buddy, the grocery store was out of your favorite yesterday. I'll have to try that new pet store on the other side of town, but I can't do it till later."

He wrinkled his black nose and stalked away, taking up a perch on the couch with his back to her.

Brooke sighed as she filled her cup with coffee and dressed it with cream. At least she'd slept through the night again. Her sleep patterns were almost back to normal now that the nightmares had finally ceased. Olivia had helped her a great deal with spells and potions and a charmed dream catcher—not to mention a listening ear and a wide shoulder—but Brooke had been haunted for the first few months by what she'd done to Celynnen.

"You had no choice, *m'ija*," her friend and mentor had reassured her, countless times. "That horrible faery would have killed my George. Perhaps even killed all of you. The Code calls for you

289

to protect the helpless and remove power from the cruel. That is what you did."

The Code had never said a damn word about having to use violent means. Brooke had decked Aidan once, but that was a far cry from effectively causing the death of a living being. Celynnen was very far from human, and she was as deadly as she was beautiful. Yet Brooke had been jarred awake for weeks by the thunderclap of sound as all those horseshoes obeyed her own command and slammed into the faery princess, maiming her horribly and revealing her true nature beneath the glorious facade. Would she have died of her wounds? Brooke wasn't sure. Morgan explained that Celynnen's fate had been the same as the other assassins of the king—their discovery had apparently triggered a spell that incinerated them from the inside out. It was a brutal but effective safeguard. Anyone captured would not live to be questioned, and the identity of the other conspirators would remain a secret. Although Lurien was certain to pay a visit to the king of the Draigddynion . . .

George had awakened in his proper human form. He was stiff and sore for days, although he didn't remember he'd nearly turned into a grim. He did remember Felicia's unveiling, however, and he'd been almost as shell shocked as Brooke over the past few months. At first he didn't date at all, but finally he met a woman, Shelby Yellowknife, who practiced mixed martial arts in the ring just as he did. They'd been inseparable for nearly three months now. *A record*, thought Brooke, and smiled a little. George had done something else that made her smile. Yesterday he'd come over with a new comic book—correction, *graphic novel*—which was nothing unusual in and of itself.

"Remember that time I wouldn't show you my sketch pad, *hermanita*?"

"Um, vaguely. I think you slammed it shut, but I thought you were just kidding around."

He shook his head. "I had the preliminary sketches for *this* in it. I've been working on it for a long time, trying to get it just right." He placed the freshly published booklet in her hands.

Brooke had expected the latest issue of *Devina of Hades*. Instead, her mouth fell open as she realized that the kick-ass heroine on the front cover had chin-length black hair marked by a single lock of white the width of a finger. The character even had Brooke's white eyebrow and turquoise eyes. And damned if she didn't have tiger-sized versions of Bouncer, Jade, and Rory at her side.

"It's a brand new series, *Bryanna Whitelock*. She's a witch who fights evil," he said. "I modeled her after you."

Brooke shook her head in disbelief, and laughed, "But G, my boobs aren't *nearly* as big as hers."

George only shrugged. "Hey, ya gotta sell comics. Besides, you could always get implants, and then you could come to all the Comic-Cons and I could introduce you as the real-life heroine behind the story."

"Whoa, that is *so* not happening, bro."

"Padded bra?"

"*No.*"

"Well it was worth a shot." He kissed her forehead. "You'll just have to be my secret superhero then." G left to meet up with Shelby for a road trip to Oregon to *meet her parents*, an announcement that stunned Brooke even more than the comic book had.

Her own love life was sadly lacking, but that was understandable with Aidan gone. In retrospect, he'd left her life as abruptly as he'd entered it. The Lord of the Wild Hunt had promised to return him to her, and even Morgan and Rhys said that Lurien's word was good, but some nights when she was alone in her bed, she doubted. She'd hoped that Aidan would be able to call or write or whatever the hell fae did when they wanted to get in touch with someone, but there was nothing. Not even scrying brought her any sign of him. Olivia told her that this was because few things originating in the mortal realm could reach into the fae realm. Sometimes scrying would work, but sometimes it wouldn't. *Figures that it wouldn't.* It didn't stop her from trying again every few days, and it certainly didn't make her worry any less about the man she loved.

Damn it, she should have asked more questions before letting him go.

The only good thing that had come out of this separation so far was the fact that she now knew she loved Aidan and her feelings were rock solid. Real. Committed, even. She could admit that a tiny part of her had thought those feelings might fade—after all, she hadn't known Aidan for two solid weeks before he disappeared! It could have been infatuation, attraction, just a fleeting whirlwind romance—

Except for the fact that her heart felt like it was missing from her chest. Her magic worked just fine, but after the intensity of the power they'd shared as a couple, it felt as weak as water.

Last week, Morgan was able to bring Brooke some news from the queen. Aidan was doing great work with the Hunt that Lurien had organized to guard the peace on this side of the waters. Because of it, the Lord of the Wild Hunt had been able to discover the names of more conspirators and bring them to justice. Even Cygnus was doing well, proving a far more reliable mount than the wild and often vicious faery horses. All good, all *very* good, and she was glad enough for the news, but Morgan's update didn't answer any of Brooke's real questions. Not the nagging insecurities that seemed so silly in the daylight but all too real in the middle of the night in her empty bed. Was there a chance Aidan hadn't contacted her because she was a painful reminder of his lost Annwyl? He'd volunteered immediately to go to the fae realm, as if he couldn't wait to leave Brooke behind, and she hadn't heard from him since. Over the months, she'd affirmed her feelings were real. Had he discovered his were not? The biggest question of all, then, was, *how did she get over him?* Was it even possible to get over someone like that? Because she was dead certain there was no one like him anywhere on the planet. Although she supposed another grim could always fall through her roof . . .

Which reminded her, this afternoon she had to go see the glazier who was going to rebuild her skylight. Olivia, bless her, was going to mind the shop for her while she was gone.

Brooke poured another coffee, then picked up her new phone and ran her finger over the screen until she got to her tarot app. Her readings were simple now, and thankfully, nothing had ever repeated itself. She called up her daily four-card spread.

Nothing really stood out about the first three cards—it was like drawing threes and fours in a game of poker. Pedestrian cards, everyday affairs; their usefulness was all in how you chose to look at them.

The final card, however, the one that influenced the meaning of the previous cards, was the Two of Cups. No matter what deck was used, the card always depicted a man and a woman trading goblets. But this deck was one of her favorites, the artwork particularly beautiful. In the sky above the couple were cosmic symbols and glowing energies of brilliant red and gold. For her clients, it might mean a new relationship, full of passion, or it might mean a healing. For a witch, however, it meant balance in all things had been achieved.

Balance is good. Especially after she'd once worried that the balance of ten centuries might be turned on its head. And now, she was missing Aidan again. *Crap.*

She jumped up from the table to get her day started. Because so far, the only cure for those feelings was distraction. *Lots and lots of distraction.*

~

It was closing time when she returned from her appointment with the glazier. She pushed open the door to her shop with an apology on her lips. "I'm sorry, Olivia, I didn't know it was going to take three whole hours. I just thought I had to pick out a picture and some glass."

Her friend emerged from behind the counter and hugged her. "No worries, *m'ija*. You should see the cash register—I've had lots of sales while you've been gone."

"Are you using a spell you haven't told me about?" asked Brooke. "Because you always seem to sell an awful lot when I'm gone."

"I simply help your customers to find what they're looking for." Olivia blinked innocently, and Brooke knew she'd never reveal anything more.

"Well, thank you again for watching the shop. With the loan I just took out to rebuild the skylight, I don't dare close it for a minute if I don't have to."

"You know I don't mind a bit. I enjoy being here, but I'm going to go home now because Lissy's coming by. She has a few days off from her teaching job, and she says she wants to spend them with her dear old *madre*."

Brooke pretended to look exasperated. "There's that word, *old*, again—I keep telling you it doesn't apply to you at all." They hugged again, laughing. "Tell Lissy I'll drop by and see her tomorrow night, if that's okay with you."

"Of course it is!" Olivia said. "Then *two* of my darling daughters will be at home." She gathered up her purse and her bag to leave but paused in the doorway for a moment. "I fed your cats for you. The little things were absolutely *starving*. And we got a call asking for fresh-cut yarrow. I don't remember if you have any left in your garden or not, but I took the number down and told them you'd call them in the morning." She waved, and the shop bell rang as the door closed behind her.

Starving? Really? Brooke shook her head. Those conniving cats had Olivia wrapped around their sneaky little paws. She locked the store and went up to her apartment, but there were no purring felines to greet her when she came in. In fact, not one of the three cats moved from their sprawled position on the couch, although Rory did blink once in blissful satisfaction. They probably *couldn't* move, since a formerly new box of Little Whiskers now sat half empty on the table.

Sighing, she decided to leave the comatose crew behind and head up to the roof to check the plot of yarrow. It was late in the season, and she wasn't sure she had much that was worth cutting. She didn't bother with a flashlight; the darkness was no hindrance to her. The moon was beginning to rise in a clear sky, plus the big red and gold sign for Mel's Gas and Grocery would be coming on in a little while. Despite being down the block, it provided plenty of pleasant glowing light, so she should be able to examine her plants without any trouble.

Besides, she enjoyed being on the roof. Despite the missing skylight—which was *finally* going to be replaced—the place was still a sanctuary to her. With the starry sky above her, it was a perfect place to regroup and rethink, and sometimes gain a little peace. She might even stretch out in the greenhouse for the night.

The door to the roof had barely closed behind her when she saw it: the green futon in the middle of the garden. Her heart banged against the cage of her chest, hard, and she lost the fight to keep a lid on the hope that geysered up inside her.

Aidan.

He approached her from the direction of the evening star, slowly but purposefully, and she held both her ground and her breath. He was dressed in black on black, which made his gray eyes seem all the more intense. His riding leathers and tall boots were tailored perfectly to his muscled frame, sleek and powerful. The moment stretched out, agonizingly long, until he stood before her, scant inches away. Immediately, she felt tiny currents of energy flow freely between them and wondered if he sensed it as well. She didn't care about that though, not right now. All she wanted was to throw her arms around his neck, but she couldn't do that either, not yet. Not until she knew how things stood.

"You've been gone a long time," she managed to say, pleased that her voice didn't shake, although her knees threatened to. "I didn't think I was going to see you again."

"I promised you I'd come back, *cariad*. Did I not tell you I loved you?" He took a seat on the futon and put an inviting arm out to her. She sat beneath his shoulder, and it was the closest thing to bliss she'd known in a very long time. It felt safe and good and right, like she belonged there—but after six months without so much as a faery postcard, she damn well deserved some convincing.

"I didn't hear a word from you. Not a word. How was I to know you hadn't forgotten me? Or changed your mind about us?"

"I know my own mind, Brooke Halloran. And I knew it before I left you." He cupped her face with his enormous hand, the same strong hand that wielded hammers and swords, now made gentle as if stroking a kitten. "There isn't a wonder in the faery realm that holds a candle to you, that could entice me to stay a minute longer. Although Lurien surely tried to convince me to stay on."

"He did not!" If the Lord of the Wild Hunt was present, she would *so* have words to say to him.

"Aye, he did. Offered me gold and silver, enough to live like ten lords all my days. But I knew what I wanted, and he sent me back here as he promised. Cygnus was returned to his home with Rhys and Morgan too—although I hope Lurien remembered to remove the glamor that made the good beast look like a fierce faery horse. I don't know that they would appreciate the tusks and the horns." He took her hand in both of his and kissed it slowly, softly. His mouth was hot and she jumped as a trail of sparks seemed to shoot through her bloodstream, a mad mix of magic and sexual desire. "I am so sorry I could not get a message to you. Cygnus was not the only one in disguise. I was spelled to appear to be Lurien and was watched at all times by his enemies. I understand better why he needed my help. If I had tried to contact you, bridged the two worlds, it would have been noticed at once and aroused suspicion. It may have endangered you as well, and that I would not do."

"I guess that's a pretty good explanation. But it was still damn hard not to hear from you."

His mouth was on hers, and her arms wound around his neck as he pressed her tight against him. The kiss was long and sweet, but with an edge to it that expressed the sudden release from their fears for each other. She felt like she would never get enough, yet she was forced to come up for air at last. Her brain kicked in and she sat back a little.

"So, what is it that *you* want, *cariad*?" His face gave nothing away, but she could sense that maybe she'd managed to rattle him a bit. Was it so wrong to enjoy that just a little?

Brooke knew her own mind too, and she knew exactly what she wanted. "All," she said. "I have to have it all, or we have nothing."

He nodded. "Aye, you deserve all, and nothing less. What is it that troubles you?"

"I need you to tell me that it's me, really me, that you love. I had two weeks with you and six months without you. I've had plenty of time to come up with questions. Is it Brooke you love, or am I a stand-in for a ghost? I keep remembering your face when you first saw me. Can you ever look at me and not see Annwyl?"

That big hand tilted her face to his, and his voice was firm. "I stopped seeing her the minute you knocked me on my arse. And I've wanted you ever since."

He kissed her again, his big hand cradling her face, Energies swirled through her system like an impending storm, hungry for the lightning to come.

"I wanted you then. Now. Always." He punctuated the words with kisses to her brow, her eyes, her cheek. "You already possess all of me, *cariad*. Is it enough?"

"It's plenty," Brooke laughed and let go then; her worries, her concerns, her fears, just *let them all go*. She gave herself to this moment and this man.

She met him kiss for kiss now, a brush of lips, a tease of the tongue. The deliciously gentle scrape of his close-trimmed beard on her face made her eager to feel it against other parts of her body. But not yet. She drew him from the couch and her magic slowly unraveled the leather laces and intricate fastenings of his vest and shirt. She planned to enjoy every second of this. Her lips pressed each square inch of that powerful chest as she exposed it. Finally she pushed the black leather from his muscled shoulders, momentarily capturing his strong arms. He was hers to taste, to touch. The moon glinted in the blond hair across his chest and she nuzzled it, savoring the scent of him, memorizing it anew. Her fingers circled lightly through the fine dusting of hair that curled around his nipples, and a fine trail of magic followed, sensitizing them. She breathed on them, watching them contract and stand out. An experimental flick of the tongue on one delighted her when the nipple seemed to strain toward her for more. She lavished attention on them both then, sucking them as Aidan's strong, certain hands slowly, painstakingly unfastened her silk blouse. It was like a dance. Kiss and touch, then angle to allow this button to be undone, that sleeve to be drawn away, only to kiss and touch again.

Her breasts ached when he freed them, a delicious pain. The cool night air barely cooled them before they were cupped in Aidan's heated hands, to be fondled and softly squeezed as he sought the nipples with his mouth. Currents of energy pulsed beneath his lips, as if he were caressing her magic as well as her body. He drew her back towards the couch and sat down, standing her in his legs so he could sample her breasts at his leisure. Brooke wound her fingers into his long hair and held his face to her, exulting at each hard pull of his mouth that was instantly soothed by a swirl of his tongue. Each time he sucked on a nipple, it was as if a tiny inner wire were strummed, one that ran from breast to core, and the vibrations were getting stronger.

From the waist up, she was naked. From the waist down, her jeans were getting wetter by the minute.

Finally, she straddled his knees and slid down Aidan's leather-clad thighs to press her breasts against his hard chest, skin to glorious skin, heat to heat. And magic to magic. She shivered deliciously as her nipples tickled against the fine dusting of hair on Aidan's body, and his energy tantalized them.

Lifting her face to be kissed again, she worked her mouth down his throat, lapping at the little dip at the base of it, before moving on. She wriggled downwards so she could plant soft, open-mouthed kisses in a more or less straight line, down the center of that broad, powerful chest, over muscles made hard by the hammering of iron, following the vee of hair that pointed south like a compass. The magic followed her trail of kisses like flowing water.

Aidan's clothes had been faery crafted, and his leather jeans hugged his strong thighs. Brooke spoke a word and the clever fastenings undid themselves until his cock sprang free. It was firm and thick in her hands, hot velvet against her cheek as she rubbed her face along its length. Aidan stood and shucked his tall riding boots off, allowing her to peel the leather leggings away from his skin until he was fully naked under the night sky. *At last*, she thought, as she pressed her moist lips to his luscious tip, planning to reenact the vision she had once experienced.

He groaned in pleasure but pulled away from her. "I had a dream of a moment just like this, *cariad*, and in this very spot. But I have other plans for you tonight."

Startled, she looked up at him with his member still hot in her hand. "Wait a minute. I dreamed about doing this—in fact, I had a vision of it, couch and all. You had the same dream?"

"Aye, it would seem I did. And it nearly felled me at the knees, so strong it was. Where do you think I gained the idea of pulling this great stuffed chair out of the greenhouse? I wanted the stars to witness me making love to you, *cariad*."

Later she would wonder at the depth of connection that allowed them to share such an erotic vision. For now, she allowed him to guide her however he liked. He returned to sit upon the couch and coaxed her to stand in front of him, where he kissed and lapped at her navel while he undid her jeans. He drew the fabric from her slowly, kissing her belly and hips as he went, turning her so he could kiss and nip at the cheeks of her ass, drawing her jeans down and down until finally she could step free of them. A rush of energy shot through her the moment she was triumphantly naked, and it felt like tiny shooting stars burned in her blood. He ran his great hands down her naked body, tracing her curves, from shoulders to knees, throat to belly, breasts to hips. "By Gofannon, you're a fair and glorious sight, Brooke Halloran," he breathed as he guided her to stand before him again—but this time she straddled his knees. He kissed both her hands and set them on his powerful shoulders, then slid one of his own hands between her legs as he looked up at her face. A rush of moisture met him, and he laughed and licked it from his fingers before he began to explore her. Gradually, he worked his knees apart until she was spread wide for him, vibrating and wet beneath his touch. Magic flowed from the tips of his clever fingers. Strong and sure, they circled her clit and slid inside her, then crooked *just so* on their way back out, and slicked around her clit again . . . repeating endlessly. Every now and then he'd suck one of her nipples in his heated mouth, sending a string of electricity throughout her already-sensitive system until she dug her nails into his shoulders. Tension grew in her magic as well, her entire system vibrating like an overtaxed engine about to explode. It was too much, all too much, but she couldn't pull back: his other hand was on her ass, clutching it and pulling her towards him, trapping her so she couldn't escape his questing fingers.

The intensity overwhelmed her until she could barely stay on her feet. He plunged his fingers deeper then, and then suddenly splayed them as if he were trying to touch every hidden part of her. The result was devastating. Her breath hitched hard as she bucked against his hand. He brought his knees together and settled her on his muscled thighs then, holding her around the waist to support her even as she clutched his muscled arms. Deep inside her, the aftershocks of the orgasm pulsed and so did the wellspring of power, a heartbeat of magic that shook her.

A moment later Aidan leaned forward and breathed into her ear, "Again, *cariad*. Again."

What? The orgasm had left her stunned and breathless, but the moment she lifted her head, he was kissing her deeply and guiding her arms around his neck. In the next moment, he was lifting her—standing straight up from the couch, with her ass cupped neatly in his big hands and her legs wrapped around him. He held her high for a long moment, her face above his, foreheads pressed together, both laughing. They kissed, tongues seeking, as

Aidan slid her soft, curved body a scant inch at a time down his hard and powerful chest. Lower, lower, in painstaking slowness, until the head of his thick shaft barely touched the still-pulsing vee of her legs—and a burst of magic arrowed through her, tipping her into another orgasm just as his cock drove into her hot wet core. Gloriously impaled, she arched her back and rode out the tremors that shook her, the magic that shuddered through her, as Aidan's powerful arms held her securely.

Brooke relaxed at last, draped bonelessly over Aidan with her face on his broad shoulder, yet incredibly, her entire being was still vibrating. She could feel the energy like an electrical current connecting every part of her from the top of her head to the tips of her toes. She could feel it in him too. Just as she wondered if maybe they should take a break or something, let the magic power down, Aidan began to rock his hips.

She gasped for breath as sensations overtook her faster than her brain could process them. She was caged loosely but securely in his iron-muscled arms, and her body moved against his with each and every thrust, responsive to every minute vibration. The magic pulsed hard and fast too, like a deafening heartbeat. Sensations piled up on each other until she was certain she would start screaming and never stop. And then she was screaming, and she didn't want anything to stop, no, *no, don't, don't stop, don't stop* . . . Aidan had begun kneading her ass every time he thrust into her, her nipples were rubbing his chest, and her clit had found itself a little piece of heaven between the base of his cock and his pubic bone.

And through it all, their magics merged and blended into something greater, higher, brighter. *Stronger.*

"Come with me," he managed to say. "Come with me. Be with me. Now. Always."

"Hell, yeah," she gasped. Their shared magics erupted skyward as they shattered. Magic steamed from their bodies in the cool night air, escaped from every pore. Its bright energies entwined around them, tendrils of red and gold light that fused them together, bound them into one. It dazzled them both as they sank down, spent and exultant.

They missed the couch but were happy to lay in a contented heap of arms and legs on the cool hard slate of the rooftop. And they laughed helplessly when the Mel's Gas and Grocery sign came on a few moments later. Its usually glaring light was almost too pale to be seen. The shining power of their shared magic had already painted the night sky with red and gold.

ACKNOWLEDGMENTS

It's not easy being married to a writer—there are long days and longer nights with your spouse all but physically attached to the computer, meals missed, a house that often looks like it's been ransacked, a shortage of time for fun, and sometimes special events missed during deadlines. There just aren't enough words with which to thank my husband, Ron, for picking up the slack, for being patient, and for being loving no matter what. You rock, sweetheart.

I'd like to express my appreciation to my editor, Maria Gomez, and to the entire author team at Montlake. I couldn't wish for a more enthusiastic and forward-thinking group to work with!

An extra special thanks to Melody Guy, for her eagle eye and great suggestions. You helped me take this particular project to the next level after I managed to write myself into a corner!

Hugs and thanks to my beta reading team, Samantha Craig and Ron Silvester. You've been a huge part of my writing journey, and I'd be lost without you both.

Thanks as always to my intrepid agent, Stephany Evans of FinePrint Literary Management. You haven't had to talk me off a ledge for a while, but I knew you were always there just in case.

Last but never least: A very loving thanks goes out to my four-legged friend and faithful executive secretary, Fiona the Pug. You left unexpectedly and far too soon, but I'm certain you're reading this as I type.

ABOUT THE AUTHOR

Ron Silvester, 2011

Dani Harper is a former newspaper editor whose passion for all things supernatural led her to a second career writing paranormal fiction. A longtime resident of the Canadian north and southeastern Alaska, she recently ventured south with her husband, Ron, to rural Washington to be closer to their grown children. Dani is the author of *Storm Warrior* (the Grim Series) and *First Bite* (Dark Wolf), for Montlake Romance. She is also the author of *Changeling Moon*, *Changeling Dream*, and *Changeling Dawn*. For full details, visit her website at www.daniharper.com.